NOT READY FOR
MOM JEANS

Also by Maureen Lipinski

A Bump in the Road: From Happy Hour to Baby Shower

NOT READY FOR MOM JEANS

· ·

MAUREEN LIPINSKI

Thomas Dunne Books
St. Martin's Griffin 🐎 New York

This is a work of fiction. All of the characters, organizations, and events portrayed in this novel are either products of the author's imagination or are used fictitiously.

THOMAS DUNNE BOOKS.
An imprint of St. Martin's Press.

NOT READY FOR MOM JEANS. Copyright © 2010 by Maureen Lipinski. All rights reserved. Printed in the United States of America. For information, address St. Martin's Press, 175 Fifth Avenue, New York, N.Y. 10010.

www.thomasdunnebooks.com
www.stmartins.com

Library of Congress Cataloging-in-Publication Data Furnished upon Request.

ISBN 978-0-312-53728-9

First Edition: June 2010

10 9 8 7 6 5 4 3 2 1

For my mother

Acknowledgments

. . . .

Where to begin?

To my agent, Holly Root: Thank you for always using exclamation points in your e-mails and for making me laugh, no matter what news you deliver. Your editorial eye and chill demeanor are the perfect combination. You are a slave driver, in the best possible way.

To everyone at Thomas Dunne Books and St. Martin's: Katie Gilligan, thank you for being so real and down-to-earth, your suggestions and edits for this book were spot-on and invaluable; Katy Hershberger, you are sent from the heavens above by the PR gods; and copyeditor Barbara Wild, thank you for your keen hawk-eye.

I did this for the first book, so one more time: Thank you to all of my friends, especially my college roommates Barrie, Carrie, Sheryl, and Pam. Yes, a fair amount of our hilarious nights made it into this book, too. Seriously, drinks on me, if only because I need some new material.

Thank you to everyone who supported my first book and helped make my "debut" year the best of my life, especially Lisa Ackeret, Jillian Cantor (whose daily e-mails keep me sane), Kristin Celing, Stephanie Elliot, Jill Williams Krause of Baby Rabies, Jen Lancaster, Lesley Livingston, Tracy Madison, Lisa Patton, and Amy Sprenger. You guys rule.

To the whole extended Leurck family: Thank you for your unending support. Each of you enriches my life in a different way. My life is better with all of you in it. Once again, I'm so lucky to have in-laws that are nothing like Clare's!

A huge amount of gratitude for my family: Mom, Dad, Patrick, Mary Claire, and Chris. Thank you for always believing in me and for never rolling your eyes when I ask you to babysit. I love you guys!

Kevin, thank you for being my rock through the crazy roller-coaster that is publishing and for always reminding me of the cost of not pursuing my dreams. You are my everything.

And to my big baby boy, Ryan. Thank you for giving all of this meaning. You always make me laugh and keep me grounded, especially when you throw a tantrum in a public place, such as a bookstore during a signing. I pray that you always stay hilarious, independent, and free-spirited.

Hush, little Sara, don't you scream,

Aren't we supposed to be on the same team?

It's after midnight and Mama's gotta sleep,

Would you like a new pretty Jeep?

Your cries give Mama a hunch

That she'll get into the office sometime around lunch.

Please let's not make this a fight,

You're just going to have to sleep through the night.

Because Mama's gotta go back to her job

And your screams are making her head throb.

Mama would really love it if you could learn

To only cry when it's your dad's turn.

Monday, March 10

. . . .

4:00 A.M.

I am so incredibly screwed.

In four hours I'm supposed to shower, apply makeup, and put on pants that have an actual zipper on the front and aren't a cotton-Lycra blend. I'm supposed to leap out of bed, get ready, and appear at work as though I'm the same woman who left a mere ten weeks ago.

Sara was also supposed to start sleeping through the night at eight weeks, or so said all of those worthless infant books.

Yet here I am, awake. Feeding my two-month-old daughter while blankly staring at an infomercial of Erik Estrada peddling vacation property in Arkansas. And wondering how in the hell I'm supposed to do this working mom stuff.

It finally happened. The sand ran out of the hourglass.

My maternity leave is over.

The panic began three weeks ago, when I realized I was due back at work soon and Sara still only slept in two-hour stretches. My panic took me to the bookstore, where I bought every book remotely referencing "sleeping through the night." Jake and I devoured them in one sitting. We excitedly read the "real stories" about infants who slept for six hours after being swaddled and rocked to sleep. Or the infants who slept through the night after being allowed to fuss for a mere fifteen minutes. We were *sure* Sara would be another success story. We'd give her a tiny crown and a sash that read, "Miss Grand Supreme Super Sleeping Through the Night Champion."

But, as most parents know, everything we tried had the opposite effect.

Swaddling: So difficult and frustrating that Jake and I argued over the optimal snugness. Not to mention the second we'd tuck her in, her limbs would shoot out like water cannons and we'd have to start all over again.

Rocking: Helped her to fall asleep, but only if the motion continued. So I'd be stuck in that damn chair for hours, contemplating the theory of quantum physics, the meaning of the show *Lost,* and other topics that seem really intriguing around 3:00 A.M.

And the minutes of fussing followed by hours of sleeping? Sure, worked like a charm. She'd scream her head off for forty-five minutes and then sleep for twenty before waking up and repeating the cycle.

Thanks, *Sleeping like a Baby: Healthy Strategies for a Good Night's Sleep,* the $22.95 I spent on you was so worth it.

I would've been better off spending $22.95 on a nice big bottle of Jim Beam. Washed down with a couple of the narcotic painkillers left over from her delivery.

In Dante's *Inferno,* the sinners were given horrible punishments based on their earthly sins. I'm starting to believe that this is my punishment for sleeping until noon pre-baby as a snake pit sounds pretty good about now. Maybe I could take a quick nap before being bitten to death.

Since none of the "miracle sleep cures" worked, Jake and I gave up and resigned ourselves to getting up every two hours to feed her. Then, a week ago, something magical happened: Sara slept for five hours.

In a row. Consecutively.

Jake and I nearly died.

Her sleep continued to improve slowly until yesterday, when Sara pulled out her picket sign and chanted, "Hey hey, ho ho! This sleeping stuff has got to go."

Good-bye, sleep.

Hello, Erik Estrada. And hello to my first day back at work.

9:00 A.M.

Sara finally went to sleep sometime around dawn. Of course she only fell asleep after I woke Jake up and he took over. I roused him by violently shaking him and hissing, "She won't sleep. Get up. Get up now. Get up before I throw myself out the window."

"I'm so sorry . . . didn't even wake up . . . totally unfair to you . . . your first day . . . so sorry . . . I suck," he mumbled as he stumbled out of bed.

"Just take her," I said as I handed Sara to him.

"I'm the worst husband ever," he muttered before he nearly headbutted the door and spilled out into the hallway. I collapsed into bed and slept dreamlessly for an hour and a half until my alarm went off.

"Are you going to be OK?" Jake asked me as I stood in front of my closet. He held Sara against his chest as she made little gurgling noises. He was dressed in a pair of khaki pants and a blue polo shirt—perfect for his job in IT sales: professional but not too stuffy. I joke that he always forgets his pocket protector until he reminds me that nerds will rule the world someday. I want to be one of the Chosen Saved Ones, so I don't jest anymore.

I gave him a pitiful look and sighed. "I think so." I plucked a seemingly huge pair of black pants off my shelf. The waistband seemed sized for Miss Piggy after a Twinkie binge.

Jake stepped forward and put his right arm around me and pulled me close. "Everything will be fine. You'll have a great day. It's just hard now."

I nodded into his T-shirt as I tried to remember all of the reasons why I love my job. Yet with my infant daughter cooing in my ear, I only wanted to remain by her side. The cocoon of my husband and daughter thinly surrounded me, and I wanted its delicate strands to never break apart.

Sara started squirming and we released each other. "Time's up," Jake said, and smiled. "C'mon, Miss Chunk, let's get you ready for your big day," he whispered into her ear. He leaned over and kissed the top of my head before leaving the bedroom.

Thank god for Jake. He's the only way I'll be able to get through this. I'll just lean against him and hopefully he can support both of us, like the stake that holds up a tomato plant. Firmly planted in the dirt next to me, he will remind me of all the reasons why this decision was made so long ago.

During my maternity leave, I didn't really allow myself to wrestle with the psychological ramifications of going back to work. It was simply something I planned on doing because I loved my job and we needed the money. No sense in getting emotional about it.

I swallowed hard as I put on my Miss Piggy pants and held my breath as I zipped them up. I cast a rueful glance at my pre-pregnancy pants, tucked high into a corner of my closet. They taunted me with their low waistbands and slim stitching: *Don'tcha wish your Miss Piggy pants were hot like us? Don'tcha?*

I burst into tears as I pulled the Lycra up around my hips.

"What's wrong?" Jake said with alarm as he ran into the bathroom.

"Still fat. I'm still fat," I said as I grabbed more than a handful of butt chunk. I didn't dare look over my shoulder at the Sara weight still lounging around my midsection.

Jake's eyes softened and he walked over to me. He gently removed my hand from my ass and put it around his waist. "You look great. You're the only person who thinks you look fat."

"Whatever. I am," I grumbled as I gave him a quick squeeze. I gulped hard and thinly smiled. "I'll just stand next to Mule Face at the office and feel like Miss America."

"There you go. Just do that." Jake nodded, proud of himself as though he'd specially placed Mule Face / Annie in my office for this reason.

After two hours of prep, Sara and I were physically ready for the first day of day care.

"I love you. Things will be great," Jake said as we stood in the parking lot of our apartment building. I nodded and he leaned in and kissed one of Sara's tiny hands. "And you, I don't want any reports of sneaking out or games of spin the bottle at day care, OK?"

I managed a rueful smile at his joke.

"You're going to be great. I know it; you'll fall right back into the routine," Jake said. He reached into his messenger bag and pulled out a brown paper bag. "Now this," he said with a laugh, "is for your first day back to work. Big day, you know."

"What?" I said as I pulled the bag from his hands. I peeked inside and saw an apple, some Wheat Thins freely floating around the bag, and a crudely made sandwich. "You made me lunch? I'm not starting kindergarten." I laughed.

"An apple, some crackers, and a jelly sandwich. We're out of peanut butter. Need some quarters for the vending machine so you can get a drink?" His eyes twinkled as his eyebrows rose. He pretended to search his pockets for change.

"You're a nerd," I said as I gave him a tap on the arm. I started to move away when he pulled me toward him, which made it awkward since my arm was nearly ripping out of its socket thanks to the World's Heaviest Car Seat and Child Ever in my left hand.

"It'll be great," he said as he kissed me on the forehead.

I smiled and looked down at Sara. "Your dad is weird."

I loaded Sara into the car and the clouds soon returned as I drove away. Each second of the drive increased my anxiety by a thousandfold, so by the time I was a block away I nearly pulled a U-turn into oncoming traffic and headed home. Every rotation of my tires echoed thoughts in my head like: *I can't do this. She's too little. I'm not only a horrible person, I'm a horrible* mother. *Who leaves a two-month-old with strangers? Oh, wait, I know—an abusive mother who values her material goods and her job over her child. Do I even like my job enough to leave my fragile, defenseless infant with people I've never met and who probably are secret baby snatchers who will sell her on the underground adoption market?*

I pulled into the parking lot of the day-care center and wept. Many times during my leave, I would shoot invisible daggers at Jake while he blissfully slept in bed next to me, oblivious to the Clare versus Infant battle raging outside. Yet, in that moment, I just wanted to drive home with Sara, put her back in her cradle swing, throw on my sweatpants, and turn on *Oprah*.

I mean, how will they know that 11:00 A.M.–12:00 P.M. is Afternoon Dance Party, when we twirl around and listen to Sara's favorite song, "I'm Too Sexy" by Right Said Fred? How will they know that stories about Champagne Wayne, our alky neighbor, are what make her laugh the most? Who will be there to pretend to be a monster and gnaw on her chubby toes?

Who will whisper that they're in this together, that they're on the same team, that napping is the greatest thing ever when she won't go to sleep?

I started the car back up and then remembered one teeny-tiny detail: *money.*

It helps to have money for things like electricity, food, clothing, and diapers. And no job equals Clare and Jake living on the bench outside

our apartment building. Which I'm sure would be fabulous accommoda-
tions in the summer, but seeing as how it's March, I don't think that's an
option for us.

So, I lugged the car seat out of the car, dried my tears on a burp cloth,
and brought my two-month-old daughter to day-care.

I cried as I drove to work.

10:00 A.M.

My eyes are burning out of their sockets. Not because of tears over Sara,
although I've spent the past hour obsessively watching the webcam on
our day-care center's Web site, making sure she's not being handed over
for a stack of hundreds to some random couple, but because of Mule
Face's outfit today. She's donned a fabulously tacky eggplant polyester
pantsuit, no doubt purchased from her favorite store, Dressbarn. The material hugs every roll and contour of her enormous butt and the jacket
button looks like a person dangling off the edge of a cliff, hanging on for
dear life.

Side note: What genius came up with the idea to name a women's
clothing store Dressbarn? Besides Mule Face, most women I know would
rather not shop at a place that has any connation to obese farm animals.
They should just go ahead and call it Fat Girl Fashions 4 U. Although I
guess I should be slightly more introspective and forgiving, since I'll
probably have to shop in the Big Girl section now, thanks to the extra
twenty pounds still lounging around my midsection. Thankfully, Jake is
either an Academy Award–winning caliber actor or he really hasn't noticed my new muffin top.

When my muffin top and I walked through the door of Signature
Events, Mule Face, as expected, acted like I had been gone for several
millennia. I had left my job as an event planner at Chicago's most prestigious firm only three months ago, yet my coworker Mule Face / Annie
couldn't resist an opportunity to capitalize on my discomfort.

"OH. MY. GOD. Everyone, look who's here!" She smiled wide, giving
me a great shot of the raspberry doughnut she'd just shoved into her
mouth. Raspberry seeds were stuck in between the abnormally large ve-
neers that had inspired her moniker. She quickly surveyed me up and

down. "You look great! You probably only have what, twenty-five pounds or so to lose?"

I sighed wearily at her. "More like twenty, but thanks, Annie."

"We-ell. Don't be surprised if you don't take it off. I read somewhere that women keep on an average of ten pounds per child. Just be prepared!" She wagged her finger at me, her corkscrew-curled hair bouncing around her hot pink lips.

"Thanks. Will do. I'm not worried." I started to walk toward my office, praying she'd stop eye-raping me with her too-tight pantsuit.

"So, aren't you going to ask me how the Parkview Hospital fundraiser went?" Mule Face asked me as she followed me down the hallway. The Parkview Hospital fundraiser was my client's event, and it nearly killed me to turn the reins over to Mule Face when I went on leave.

"OK. How did it go?" I stopped walking and faced her.

"Fantastic! They said they were so impressed with how it was handled this year and it was much more organized than in previous years." She smiled sweetly at me.

I bristled. "I'm glad it went well. I was sorry I had to miss the event this year."

"Get in here, MOM!" Christina's voice bellowed from her office.

I turned around the corner and appeared at my boss's office.

"You look fabulous. Can't even tell you're probably getting five hours of sleep a night." Christina stood up from behind her desk and I noticed she had on a pair of Christian Louboutin pumps I would prostitute Jake to buy.

"Thanks. Last night it was more like three hours, but who's counting other than the exhausted girl inside of me who is still wondering what 'sleeping through the night' means." I exhaled loudly and smiled slightly.

"Well, I know you have a mile-high pile on your desk, so I'll let you get to it," Christina said as her phone rang. She walked back to her desk, her high heels sinking into the carpet. "Just try not to fall asleep during the day," she said as she reached for her trilling phone.

"Sounds like a plan," I said, and walked over to my office. It was so strange walking in there again for the first time since having Sara. The last time I left here, I was just a really pregnant, swollen lady. Now I'm walking back into it as a mom.

I sat down at my desk and looked at all of the neat piles of files stacked on top of one another and remembered how I carefully arranged them the day before I left. I looked at the Post-it note on my computer that read, "Call florist for Shepard wedding," and a strange pang ripped through my stomach. I felt like Ebenezer Scrooge traveling with the Ghost of Christmas Past, only it was Clare Finnegan and the Ghost of the Super Pregnant Woman.

It's like I went away on an extended vacation, only I came back a different person. It wasn't like I just took a margarita-soaked sabbatical and played Pictionary for a few weeks. No, I'd spent the last two months in Parental Boot Camp. With activities like "See how many nights in a row you can go without sleep before you think your cat is your husband" and "Time how quickly you can eat a meal one-handed before cramping and/or choking."

As I opened my planner, three blank months straddling the pages with scribbled dates, a tiny part of me started to feel better. I'm good at my job and I love it. It's wonderfully fulfilling to pull off a huge event and hear complimentary feedback from a client. Not to mention, I've worked hard for all of this, for every success.

Letting the tiny glimmer of acceptance soak into my bones, my body relaxed into my desk chair. Until I heard Christina's voice.

"Don't forget we have that meeting with the Leukemia Foundation's staff about their golf outing at eleven. They're having the event in September at the Chicago Club," Christina yelled through the wall between our offices after she hung up the phone.

I completely forgot about that meeting. What the hell was I thinking to schedule a meeting the day I got back from maternity leave? Not just any meeting, a meeting with a new client where I have to pitch new ideas and appear as though I've had more than a few hours of loosely arranged, jumbled sleep.

If this new client wants to judge my efficiency, they should come over to my apartment around three in the morning. I can successfully make a bottle, pee, soothe Sara's screams, turn on the television, and shove a bottle into her mouth within four minutes. But I doubt any of those things qualify.

I opened up my e-mail and shook my head a little, still trying to clear the morning cobwebs. I had 257 e-mails. I paused for a minute, hand frozen on my mouse, before I quickly closed my Outlook. I pulled a framed picture of Sara out of my bag and set it on my desk next to my computer. I sighed and opened my e-mails back up.

I was so engrossed in reading about the latest office mandates and debates on which kind of copy paper to purchase thanks to everyone repeatedly hitting Reply All to every freaking e-mail, I jumped when my phone rang.

"Clare Finnegan," I said, my voice still not quite in Office Mode.

"So, how's it going?" My mom.

"Sucks, but what can I do? Leaving her this morning was tough." My Working Mom Determination wavered a little at the sound of my mom's voice.

"I know, it gets better though." My mom's voice was soft.

"When?" I said as I stared at Sara's picture.

"Just give it a few days. Remember, you guys were all in day care and you turned out fine." I could hear her clicking on her laptop in the background. Always working and multitasking, my mom's the Vice President of Development for Indux Software.

I snorted. "Is that really what you think?"

"What?" The clicking stopped.

"That your children are normal. I mean, I turned out OK and Mark can be fine on the days when he's not acting like a post-college moron with his drunk friends, but Sam? Sorry. She doesn't fall on the spectrum of normal on *any* day."

My mom sighed, "Yeah, I know, but she's eighteen, cut her a break."

"Please. I can't discuss Sam and why you think I should brush it off when she asks me if my stretch marks have faded or if I fit into any of my Seven jeans and, if not, could she please have them." I tapped my pen against my desk like a drumstick, accentuating my point to, well, nobody.

"All right, all right. Forget it. But I promise, it does get easier"—she paused—"just as soon as you realize you only really need a few hours of sleep and lots of caffeine to function."

"Mom, I'm not you. I can't survive on four hours of sleep, nor do I want to. I have no desire to be Superwoman." My mother was the quintessential 1980s working mom: shoulder pads, blouses with weird necktie bows, socks and running shoes over her panty hose while she walked into the office. Her favorite movie, to this day, is *Baby Boom*—wherein Diane Keaton struggles with managing her demanding corporate job with a child.

It's no wonder my mother bought me Working Woman Barbie when I was eight—the only Barbie I was allowed to own. All I know is that I didn't understand why Barbie's office skirt reversed into a minidress and her briefcase morphed into a handbag for "after work." Looking back, maybe she really was a "working girl" after all.

"You know, the women of my generation felt like we had to be Superwoman so we could have a family and a career." My mom's voice was proud and stiff as though she was teaching me a valuable lesson.

"Yes, I know. And my mother-in-law, who is a whole one year older than you, tells me how the women of 'her generation' considered their families to be their careers and is horrified I'm going back to work," I said, and laughed.

"Yeah, well, Marianne and I grew up on two different planets. Listen, I have to jump on a conference call here in a few minutes, but I just wanted to make sure you were OK."

"I'm about as OK as you could expect today." I put my chin in my hand and sighed loudly.

"Well, I'm sure Jake is being supportive," my mom said.

"Of course he is—he's almost like a mutant that way. He said all the right things this morning and even packed me this sad little lunch. Listen, I have to go. Talk to you later, Mom," I said, and hung up the phone.

"OH MY GOD, THAT IS SO CUTE. A MOM TALKING TO HER MOM ON HER FIRST DAY BACK AT WORK. DID SHE HAVE A HARD TIME LOSING PREGNANCY WEIGHT, TOO?" Mule Face screeched from outside my door as she walked by and picked a wedgie.

Realizing I only had a few minutes before the new client meeting, I scrambled to the bathroom to check my sure-to-be-haggard appearance. I stared in the mirror, not recognizing the homeless woman looking back at me. I ran out of concealer over the weekend and forgot to buy more, so this morning I tried to cover my bluish black under-eye circles with mere translucent powder. I also put highlighter on my brows and cheekbones, desperately hoping to distract from the whole wife-with-an-abusive-husband look.

It was to no avail. I just looked tired, sick, and sorely misguided with shiny brow bones and cheeks. I sighed and washed off the highlighter and tried to convince myself that my appearance probably wouldn't matter to the Leukemia Foundation staff.

As I smoothed my hands down my Miss Piggy black wool crepe pants, I looked down toward my feet.

That's when I noticed I was wearing two different shoes. Not just two different shoes, two *completely* different shoes. Different colors, different heel heights. One black pointy-toed mary jane, approximately two inches high, and one gray crisscross peep-toed pump, approximately three inches high.

Thanks to extreme sleep deprivation, motherhood has officially made me resemble a homeless person. Who is blind. With very poor taste.

I wearily smoothed my frizzed-out hair over my shoulders and walked back to my office. I heard Mule Face leading the foundation staff into the conference room, so I grabbed a pen and paper and met Christina in the hallway.

"My kid really needs to start sleeping through the night," I whispered to her.

"What?" she said. I noticed her makeup looked perfect. Not to mention she appeared to be wearing matching shoes.

"Look." I pointed down and she snorted.

"Nice. Sure to make a good impression on the new clients." She sympathetically patted me on the back.

We walked into the room. There were three foundation staff in the room, all resembling slightly dorky suburban moms, and one man, the chair of the golf outing. He was young . . . hot . . . familiar . . .

Holy. Shit. Why today? Why now?

Seriously, God, what did I do? Was I a serial killer in a previous life? Did I abuse little children and defenseless animals? Or am I just your court jester, existing only to provide comic relief?

Greg Thompson. My ex-boyfriend from college. The guy I dated for two years before Jake. The guy who dumped my ass in the middle of a fraternity party. The guy who broke my heart, because I really thought I would marry him. Until one day until he met someone else. It crushed me and nearly killed my fragile twenty-year-old confidence, as I had to undo all of the dreams of us together in the future.

And now, after eight years, here he was—standing in front of me. And I in front of him, wearing two mismatched shoes, twenty extra pounds behind my flabby, stretched-out skin covered by black Miss Piggy pants.

"Clare, wow. What are you doing here?" Greg said, his eyes crinkling up at the corners.

I felt my morning bagel start to rumba in my stomach. "Um, I, uh, wow," I said brilliantly. "Hi!" I finally said as I felt my skin flush.

Everyone looked at me, eyes narrowed. We all stood in silence for a minute.

"I work here," I finally said. Brilliant once again. Step right up, ladies and gentlemen, and the Genius Clare Finnegan will wow you with her amazing IQ and eloquent verbal skills.

"How do you guys know each other?" Mule Face asked, keenly aware of my discomfort.

"We went to college together," Greg said quickly.

True, technically. But it would've been nice if he said: *Clare and I dated in college for the best two years of my life until I made the biggest mistake of my life and broke up with her. I've been pining for her ever since, but alas, I heard she got married and now I spend every night of my life dreaming of her. I am also celibate now, since she was so good in bed, no woman could ever compare.*

"Wow, that's amazing," Christina said, and quickly moved over to the foundation staff and began shaking their hands and handing out her business card.

Greg and I just stood inches from one another, radio silence between us. I noticed his gaze moving down toward my shoes and I quickly threw myself in a chair. Except it was a rolling conference chair and it kind of slid out from under me, so I almost toppled out of it. Not exactly a graceful move.

"Er," I said as my throat closed. I felt my face begin to grow hot as I adjusted the chair. I took a deep breath as I tried to regain my professionalism and composure.

Mule Face's head snapped back and forth like a rubber band. "So," she said coyly, "you two were friends in college?"

"Something like that," I said, and smiled. My lips quivered a bit and my breathing was erratic, but I tried to appear collected. Because, twenty pounds, hideous Big Girl pants, and two hours of sleep be damned, I'm not twenty anymore.

"What a coincidence. And you haven't talked since?" She pursed her hot pink lips together and tapped her cheek with a Lee Press-On nail.

"Not really," Greg said. Now it was his turn to look uncomfortable.

Besides, for all he knows I'm living some fabulous life in the city, eating at hip restaurants every night and attending movie premieres.

"Well, I'm sure you two have *lots* to catch up on. Greg, you really should be congratulating Clare right now." Her eyes narrowed as she got ready to lower the boom.

"Doesn't she look fantastic for just having a *baby*?" Mule Face said.

I silently wished in that moment that either (a) the world would open up, revealing a secret society living at the Earth's core where Jake and I could take up residence, or (b) sulphuric acid would rain down upon the conference room, requiring immediate evacuation.

At the very least, I wished Mule Face would spontaneously combust and flail around the room before disintegrating into a pile of ashes at my feet.

"Really? Congratulations! Boy or girl?" Despite seeming gracious, Greg cleared his throat nervously.

"Girl. Sara," I said briskly as I organized my papers in front of me. I looked over at Christina and she widened her eyes a little, silently asking me to end the reunion already and start the meeting. Mule Face waddled out and everyone sat down to begin. Yet as soon as I turned my attention to the foundation staff, I became keenly aware of one of the women intensely staring at me. I figured she was wondering if I was an escaped mental patient impersonating an event planner (due to the fact that I failed the whole "wear matching shoes" fashion rule and "sit down in chairs without wobbling" motor skills test) until she finally clapped her hands together and said, *"That's* how I know you!"

I blankly stared at her, wondering if she was another ex from college I'd forgotten about.

"You're Clare, right? From *Am I Making Myself Clare?* The blog?" Heads snapped in my direction as Christina rolled her eyes.

"Yep, that's me," I said quickly.

"I love, love, love your blog. I read it every day. I just loved your last entry about your theory on a global conspiracy between battery companies and infant swings, thus why no infant swings have electrical cords."

I kept a smile frozen to my face. I saw Greg shift in his chair and look confused. I turned to him. "I have a blog on the Internet." As I said it, I realized that sentence was probably, um, unnecessary.

"Sounds like it," he said.

"It's not just any blog, it's like one of the most popular on the Internet. All of my friends read it." She tucked her hair behind her ears and nodded her head. She turned to Greg. "It was even featured in *The Daily Tribune* and now she's going write some columns for the newspaper!"

"Impressive," he said, lacing his fingers together.

"So, the outing is going to be at the golf club on September thirtieth?" Christina gave me a pointed look.

"Yes, the golf club. September thirtieth," I repeated, and opened my notebook. I was thankful the conversation had turned away from my personal life to my professional.

He looks exactly the same, I thought to myself.

I saw one of the foundation staff members write "Golf Outing" at the top of her page, like a fifth grader doing a history report.

Exactly the same as when I met him freshman year in college.

Exactly the same as move-in day at school, when we met in the quad outside our dorm.

Exactly the same as the day he told me he loved me.

And exactly the same as the day he dumped my ass.

Too bad he can't say the same for me right now.

"So, we're lucky to have Greg as the Chair this year," my blog fan said. She beamed at Greg and he smiled at her.

He always did have that effect on women.

"We roped him into this since we consider his family some of the foundation's closest friends and family," my fan said.

Read: they have a ton of money.

"Yeah," Greg said, and adjusted himself in his chair. "I really don't know much about planning an event like this at all. So, I'll be relying on y'all a lot," Greg said, and looked around the room at each of us.

I smiled at him, bristling at his use of "y'all." I mean, *c'mon*. We live in Chicago. He's from Illinois. Using random southern slang does not equal charm.

Christina and the foundation staff did most of the talking in the meeting. As it ended, we all stood up and Greg and I awkwardly shook hands.

"Well, I guess we'll be seeing a lot more of each other," Greg said.

"Absolutely. We'll ensure the event is a success," I replied as I made unflinching eye contact.

"Give Jake my best," he said as he walked out the door.

"Will do," I said. Right, I'm sure Jake will be just thrilled to hear I'm going to be working with Greg. Jake doesn't harbor any anger or feelings of ill will toward Greg, since we broke up long before I met him, but I'm sure it'll make him a little uncomfortable.

"So, details please." Christina stood in front of my office, blocking the doorway, after Greg and the staff left.

I sighed. "Not a whole lot to tell. College. Two years. He dumped me for some anorexic-looking chick in the middle of a party. Public humiliation followed by heartbreak. Then I met Jake. End of story."

Christina nodded. "I'm sure you will be a total professional, as you are with all your clients."

"Thank you. I will be," I said firmly. At least Mule Face isn't working on the project. She'd just spend hours pumping Greg for information and filling him in on every stupid thing I've ever done, like the time two years ago that I broke the crown on my front tooth trying to open a package of M&Ms.

I settled back down into my office chair, picked up my phone, and dialed Julie, my best friend. I knew if anyone could appreciate the drama of the situation, it would be her. Thankfully, she didn't have a nursing shift today and picked up her phone on the first ring.

"What's goin' on?" she answered.

"Julie, you're going to die when I tell you who my newest client is," I said.

"Never say 'die' to a nurse. Do you know how many times I hear people say that when they're admitted into the ER? It has little to no dramatic effect on me," Julie said. I could hear her favorite show, *General Hospital,* on in the background.

"Greg, you know, *Greg,* is the chair of this golf outing that I've been assigned," I whispered into the phone.

"Greg as in GREG GREG?" Her voice rose about fifty octaves.

"Yep," I said, and sighed, happy I got a reaction out of her.

"So, let me get this straight. You have to work with Greg, as in your asshole ex-boyfriend who deserves to have his balls cut off and fed to his dog, on a golf outing?"

"Apparently, yes. He's my new client."

"I'm sure you were great, though. You probably look fabulous."

"Something like that," I said. I put my head down on my desk as I thought of my two mismatched shoes.

"Are you going to tell Jake?" Julie said.

"Of course. It's not like he has anything to worry about."

"Why is he the chair of a golf outing anyway?" Julie asked.

"He got roped into it or something. I don't really know," I said as I lifted my head up and noticed a streak of baby puke on my Miss Piggy black pants. Note to self: hire stylist when rich enough.

"Just don't go drinking too many Natural Lights and then call him Dildohead again like you did junior year when you saw him out with his new girlfriend, OK?" Julie said, and laughed.

"I'll try." I ran my fingers through my frizzed hair.

God, I'm exhausted.

"This is why I never dated anyone seriously in college—too many opportunities for humiliation later in life," Julie said.

"Thanks. But dated? Would you even call it that?" I said, and laughed.

"Funny. Listen, I gotta go. I'll see you Saturday."

I hung up the phone and sat silently for a moment, giving myself a mental pep talk on how I handled the meeting with Greg. I was pretty sure I kept my head straight and came off as professional and capable. I felt brave enough to pull my compact out of my purse and open it up.

Gah!

My appearance was not what I had hoped. I looked like I should be at a soup kitchen, standing in line and begging for an extra piece of bread.

Note to self: hire makeup artist when rich enough.

I got home later, ready to regale Jake with my tale of the Ex Who Won't Die, but he and Sara were passed out on the couch, asleep, with an episode of *Mystery Science Theater 3000* on softly in the background. My heart vibrated a little at the sight of the two of them, peacefully snoring away together. A frozen pizza, still in its box, was sitting on the coffee table, as though he meant to have dinner ready but sat down for "a few minutes" to rest. It was fine; I wasn't really hungry anyway.

I gently picked Sara up off Jake's chest and pressed her to me. She sighed as I carefully folded down onto the love seat and kicked off my two different shoes. I smelled the top of her soft curls, closed my eyes, and whispered, "We survived."

Sara tried to lift her tiny head and look around, but I put my hand on her and rubbed her back. She relaxed and I snuggled down against her, amazed again at how such a tiny little being could flip my emotional switch so drastically.

"What? Sorry! What time is it?" Jake said as he bolted up and looked around, confused. He looked at his watch and then at the pizza box on the coffee table. "Oh. Sorry," he said as he frowned. "I meant to have food ready for when you got home." He shrugged.

I smiled. "It's OK. I had a late lunch." I patted Sara's back as I closed my eyes.

"How was your day? Better than you thought?" Jake said hopefully.

"Mmmmhmmm," I murmured. I didn't want to think about any-thing but never leaving the couch.

"Can I get you anything?" I think I heard him say before the exhaustion set in. Within seconds, I was fast asleep, dreaming of a world where ex-boyfriends are rounded up and made to live on a desert island together and contemplate their romantic errors. Or at least, I'm not forced to take them on as new clients. But if I am, I can be twenty pounds thinner and wearing matching shoes with my Big Girl pants burning in effigy all around me.

I feel like I'm in a Jackie Collins novel. Or at least a bad Lifetime movie of the week. Like *She Didn't Want to Work with Him While Wearing Miss Piggy Pants: The Clare Finnegan Story.*

Tuesday, March 11
. . . .

My second day back at work. Only slightly fewer tears.

I told Jake this morning about working with Greg. True to male form, Jake downplayed and shrugged his shoulders a lot.

Apparently, Julie and I are the only people who think this is a big deal. But I guess it's better than him getting all possessive on me like those boyfriends in after-school specials. And if this were a made-for-TV movie, he would've thrown me down a flight of stairs, I would've had to prostitute myself to support my gambling addiction, and my sorority sisters would've killed me in a hazing incident gone horribly wrong.

Or wait. I might be mentally combining a few.

Jake and I played the hot potato game again with Sara as we got ready this morning, which worked until I started freaking out about my flatiron going on strike. I was calmly (read: waving my hands around like an air traffic controller, flatiron and all) explaining to Jake why this is a problem when a deep belly laugh came from the tiny infant on the bed. I froze, hands in air, and looked at Sara. I waved my hands around again. Her face lit up, she flashed a gummy smile and cackled again.

"Get the video camera!" I shrieked to Jake as I bounced up and down like a mental patient.

"Woo-hoo!" Jake said as he jumped in the air in front of Sara. Her giggles turned into deep belly laughs.

"Keep doing it! She loves it!" I yelled, video camera in hand. "You think Daddy's funny, huh? Do a cartwheel!" I commanded.

Jake stopped moving. "A what?" he said, looking confused. Sara started to cry.

"A cartwheel. You know—gymnastics stuff! She'll love it," I said impatiently. "She's crying! Hurry up!"

Jake looked at Sara and shrugged his shoulders and started jumping up and down again. Cartwheel or not, Sara laughed like the first time I saw Jake try to sing karaoke. After ten minutes, we were both late for work and desperately wishing it was Saturday so we could spend the day waving random objects around to see what falls into the Things Sara Finds Awesome category.

Clare breaks flatiron; hilarity ensues.

The familiar white-hot pit of regret gnawed at my stomach on my way to day care. The actual dropping off part was only slightly less traumatic than yesterday, as I was pretty sure from my detective work yesterday that Sara wasn't going to be sold into infant slavery. I kissed her and whispered into her tiny, soft ear, "I'd much rather spend the day with you."

Although it was a little easier today, the exhaustion still all-consumed me, culminating in nearly spelling my name wrong in an e-mail this morning. My brain was swirling with visions of eight hours of sleep and mismatched shoes when an Outlook reminder popped up. *Lunch with Reese.*

Shit!

I completely forgot. The prevalence of Things Clare Forgot Due to Baby-Having was quickly becoming old.

I grabbed my purse, threw myself in my car, and sped over to the Belvidere Bistro. Thankfully, she wasn't there yet, so I sat down and waited. As she walked in, four men jumped up to hold the door open for her. She smiled gratefully, her blond hair matted to her sweaty face and her blouse wrinkled, with a screaming Grace resting on her hip. Or what's left of her nine-months-pregnant hip.

"Sorry, sorry, sorry. We're in the midst of a three-year-old temper tantrum," she said as she leaned forward and kissed my cheek.

"No problem. I'm sure it's a serious tragedy whatever it is," I said, and tried to touch Grace's arm, but she jerked away and buried her face and snotted into Reese's beautiful silk shirt.

"They ran out of grape lollipops at the shoe store—a real crisis." She pulled her hair off her neck and tried to fan her face. "I'm dying. It's like I'm burning from the inside out. I forgot what it was like to be fat and pregnant."

"Fortunately, I remember it quite well and those memories will serve as fabulous birth control anytime I might even consider another kid. And you're not even close to fat." I surveyed her tiny frame.

"You'll so have more, don't even say that."

"Honey, this one wasn't even planned. I'm still trying to wrap my brain around the idea that I'm old enough to have a kid, let alone think about another one." Grace started screaming again. I looked at Reese. "Exactly."

"Did you see how many people ran to hold open the door for me when I walked in?" she said.

"I did." I nodded.

"Well, in about a month, people will let the door hit me in the face before they'll hold it open." Reese pushed her hair off her face again.

"What do you mean?"

"I mean, people are anxious to help pregnant ladies. But a woman with a stroller and a screaming kid? She can fend for herself. I'm surprised you haven't found that out yet." She tapped me on the shoulder sympathetically.

"Probably because I never go out in public anymore." I smiled at her.

After we sat down, Reese gave Grace some crayons as I stared at her enormous engagement ring and diamond-encrusted wedding band. "So, how's everything going?"

She looked at me and cast her eyes quickly to her menu. "Oh, you know."

"Reese, no, I really don't. How's everything at home?"

"Same. I hear their salads are really good." She still wouldn't look up.

"Screw the salad, how's Matt?" My eyes bored into her skull, willing her to raise her head. Matt and Reese were married a few years back in a beautiful wedding, complete with champagne bar and glorious center-pieces. None of us knew at the time that their wedding would be the highlight of their marriage, rather than the start. Because perfect china and an oyster bar at a reception does not a good, faithful husband make.

She put her menu down, took a sip of water, and shrugged. "Like I said, same."

"So he's still sleeping in the guest room?"

"Yep." She slowly twirled the glass around on the table.

"And you guys barely speak to each other?" I leaned forward as my voice became a whisper.

"Yep." She shrugged and exhaled.

"Have you guys talked any more about a . . ." I almost said the D word but trailed off when I saw Grace watching me intently.

"Yep. Do you want to order an appetizer?" Reese picked up her menu again.

I sighed and nodded. Getting through a Reese Block is more improbable than being released from a mail-order music club contract.

Halfway through lunch, though, she put her fork down and dabbed at her mouth with a napkin.

"I need to ask you for a favor."

"Name it. You know you can ask me for anything," I said.

"Sure about that?" Her finger absentmindedly twirled her engagement ring around.

"Pretty sure." I smiled.

"Be my labor coach. I'm delivering at Chicago Memorial." Her words fell around me like bricks.

"Wha?" I shook my head violently.

"Be with me in the delivery room when I have the baby." Her blue eyes widened and she folded her arms across her huge stomach.

"Why? I mean, really?" I cleared my throat.

"Because I need someone there to support me and . . ." She stopped and we locked eyes. I knew she wanted me there because she couldn't count on her asshole husband to emotionally support her. Bastard.

"Of course. I'm honored you asked." I tried to appear excited, but the prospect of being present during labor and delivery was *not* something

I'd put on my "Top 10 Things to Do This Year." If Reese wants me to have more kids, asking me to watch another birth isn't the best motivation.

"I know it doesn't thrill you, but I need you there." Her jaw set into a determined stance, but her eyes were soft.

"Don't worry. I'll be there for you the entire way. I don't know how much help I'll be, but you can count on me for whatever." I silently added, *And Matt better not piss me off or else I'll find a fun place for one of those internal fetal monitors.*

"God, twenty-nine and two kids. Can you believe it?" Reese shook her head and laughed thinly.

"No. Twenty-eight and *one* kid is freaky enough for me, thanks. Speaking of which, can you believe my new client?" I shook my head and widened my eyes. I had e-mailed Reese right after I got off the phone with Julie, not wanting to recount the story with Grace screaming in the background.

"I know. That's crazy! Well, I'm sure it will be fine, though. He's a nice enough guy," Reese said as she handed Grace an orange crayon. I watched as Grace furiously scribbled on her children's menu.

"Yeah, it's just a little weird."

Reese didn't say anything else, even though I desperately wanted to analyze the situation from fifty different viewpoints. But I didn't want to let on the true extent of my fixation and bewilderment, so I just asked her some more questions about my duties as labor coach.

As I drove back to my office after lunch, I alternated between inventing various medical instruments I could use in my Karate Match of Emotional Pain against Matt and horrific, bloody scenes of labor and delivery. The problem was that when I was pregnant with Sara, Jake banned me from watching any TV show about delivering babies, since invariably I would end up in tears, convinced that my child, too, would be born with a lobster claw for a hand or something. After I had Sara, the ban lifted and I wound up DVRing every episode, fascinated. So now I'm extremely well versed on every single complication that can arise when a baby is born. Should make for a fun-filled time in the delivery room.

I announced to Jake my very important title of Best and Most Awesome Labor and Delivery Coach Ever when I got home from work.

"Are you going to spout off the statistics of how many women die in childbirth each year to her like you do to me constantly?" he asked while changing Sara's diaper.

"Jake, I only tell you those facts to make you realize how lucky you are I didn't die while giving birth to our child." I walked over to the changing table.

"Yeah, OK. I get it. But you didn't. Your delivery was easy, just like I knew it would be." He picked Sara up and patted her diapered butt a few times.

I reached for her and held her close, smelling the top of her soft head and kissing her chubby, Michelin Man arms. "It was uneventful, but I'd hardly call it easy."

Jake leaned over and kissed her head and placed his hand on her back. "Relatively speaking, it was easy."

"You have no idea. If men were the ones who had babies, they'd be on bed rest for all nine months, you would all gain like two hundred pounds while pregnant because all you'd do would be lay around, maternity leave would be like five years paid, and you'd invent a way to give birth painlessly and easily during halftime of a football game."

He put his arm around my shoulders. "Probably." He pulled me toward his broad chest, which smelled like a combination of fabric softener and pine. I rested my head against him, Sara in my arms. I let both of us lean against him, supporting us as he held both of our weight.

Our quiet family moment didn't last long, as the phone rang, cutting through any contemplation. I picked it up and checked the caller ID. I held the phone out to him. "It's your mother."

"I'm busy. I need to throw this out." He waved the dirty diaper around in the air and walked two feet away to the garbage can.

"I hate you," I sighed, and answered the phone. "Hi, Marianne."

"Oh, hello, dear. I thought I'd get Jake. I figured you'd still be at work since you're such a career girl and all. How nice you're home to spend time with your family for a while."

I gritted my teeth. "Yes, it's just wonderful."

"How's my Sara adjusting to being taken to a day-care center?"

"She's doing great." I pantomimed shooting myself in the head to Jake. He laughed and took Sara from my arms.

"I saw a report on the news the other day about this day-care worker who beat an infant to death because he wouldn't stop fussing. It made me sick to my stomach, thinking about my precious granddaughter with god-knows-who. . . ." She choked up and sobbed a little.

"Sara's at the best day care in the city. Trust me, I'll show you the monthly bill."

"Oh, I'm sure, dear. You know what I always say, though, there's no substitute for a mother's love."

I contemplated which extremely sharp object I wanted to stick in my eye.

Steak knife? Nah. I'd ruin my new set.

Stiletto heel? Just got the pair polished.

Sewing needle? Still in the package.

Corkscrew? Too important to risk.

"Do you want to talk to Jake?" I said.

"Sure, hon. Oh, before you go, I wanted to tell you that Natalie and Doug set a date for Ash Leigh's first birthday party. It's going to be June twenty-second. I'm sure it's going to be great, since Natalie stays home and has so much time to plan the party."

"I'm sure we don't have any plans, since it's like three months away, but I'll mark our calendar. Here's Jake." I thrust the phone toward my husband.

"OK . . . Sure . . . Yeah . . . OK . . . Love you, too. . . . Bye" was all he said.

"Did you know that recently a day-care worker killed an infant?" I asked him when he hung up.

"Did you know that my mother wants me to talk to you about staying home?" he said as he put the phone back in the cradle.

"Did you know Natalie is throwing Ash Leigh the best birthday ever since she has time and stays home?" I said, and rolled my eyes.

"Did you know that I have no idea why my brother married her?" Jake asked with a laugh.

"Did you know that Natalie makes me want to physically abuse my-self?" I pantomimed slitting my wrists.

Jake walked over and patted me on the head. "Yes, I did know that," he answered.

Friday, March 21
. . . .

It's Friday! I've almost made it through my second official week as a working mom. To celebrate, I'm making chicken divan for dinner. I found the recipe while searching on the Food Network's Web site last night. The chicken, coupled with some wine after Sara goes to bed, should be fabulous.

Having a glass of wine is one of the huge benefits to not nursing Sara anymore. I gave it a valiant effort for two months, and then she decided that eating every hour rocked. Oh, and she would take forty-five minutes to eat. What those worthless baby books don't tell you is that the time between nursing sessions begins when you start feeding your kid. So, it would be 2:00 P.M., she'd eat until 2:45 P.M. and then want to eat around 3:00 P.M. again. Fifteen minutes barely gave me time to pee or check my e-mail. After much tears and frustration, and despite a serious case of guilt and remorse, I remembered that bottle-feeding isn't the devil, and we haven't looked back since. Besides, I feared Mule Face walking in on me while I was pumping at the office. No doubt with a camera.

So yes, I will be having a glass of wine tonight.

12:00 A.M.
Tonight was horrific. Much worse than the Time Our Cat Butterscotch Accidentally Got Locked in Our Car Overnight with My Bridesmaid Dress for Reese's Wedding—the reigning Worst Night Ever.

After work, I picked up Sara from day-care. The second she saw me, she gave me one of her huge, toothless smiles that make my insides melt. I scooped her up and kissed her about fifty times on her soft hair and whisked her outside and into the car. She cooed happily the entire way to the grocery store. I had briefly contemplated getting the groceries before I picked her up, but I couldn't wait to see her.

Besides, she usually behaves in stores and I was just popping in the store for a wee moment. Except I forgot that I am a huge idiot who is very, very stupid and wrong.

She smiled at me from her car seat the entire way from the parking lot until the second we walked into the store.

"We're just going to pop in for a quick moment and then we'll be on our way!" I said cheerfully as I wheeled her through the doors. I deftly maneuvered the cart around an old lady studying coupons. *I'm so good at this taking my kid out in public stuff,* I thought smugly.

Yet, as I got about ten feet into the store, dark clouds began to gather and Sara's brow furrowed. I knew the heavens were about to open up and punish us all.

"It's OK! Like I said, just a quick lil' minute!" I said loudly, hoping my three-month-old daughter would suddenly become familiar with the English language.

Except her face instantly turned beet red and she opened her tiny mouth. A wail of epic proportions emanated from her head.

"No panicking," I muttered to myself. I didn't worry because I knew all the tricks. A little jiggle here, a little bounce there, and she'd be fine, right? Oh, so, so wrong.

I jiggled her, which only made her more angry. "Shhhhh," I awkwardly hissed at her as people began to stare. I stood in the produce aisle and began to sweat. Finally, I unstrapped her from her car seat and cradled her. When that didn't work either, I reached into the diaper bag for her bottle. Panic washed over me as I groped around desperately.

Nothing.

I'd forgotten the bottle at the day-care center.

"Jesus," I muttered as Sara turned purple. People around me began to whisper to each other. I felt a bead of sweat run down my back as I contemplated running out of the store. But I was determined to make my celebratory dinner, so I blazed over to the baby supply aisle, grabbed a pack of ready-made formula and a package of bottles. I ripped them open, made a bottle, and shoved it into Sara's mouth. I was then able to shop a little, albeit awkwardly, trying to push the cart, feed her, and grab ingredients all at the same time.

After five minutes, the bottle became futile as well and she started screaming again. This time I was ready to screw the dinner and leave, but now I had to pay for the formula and bottles I'd already opened. So, like a total idiot, I waited in line, screaming child and all. A woman next to me on her cell phone glared at me as I stood next to her.

"... I know, so rude ... What? ... What? ... I'm sorry, I can't hear you. There's a baby next to me ... I know ... She's not even trying to make it be quiet."

I immediately felt my face flush as anger bubbled up inside me. I caught her eye and said, *"What?"* The cell-phone woman rolled her eyes and looked away.

I got in line behind the old woman with the coupons and prayed she was one of those Super Fast and Efficient old people and not like my grandmother, who takes ten minutes to remember her debit card's PIN.

"OK, good," I said as I saw the clerk speedily move through the order. Then, sudden death appeared. The woman pulled out a checkbook. (I seriously didn't think anyone paid for anything with checks anymore. I thought they were obsolete, like laser discs or something.) Ten minutes later, it was our turn.

Items purchased: formula, baby bottle, almonds, and paper towels.

Needless to say, I arrived home, still red-faced and sweaty and burning inside from humiliation and anger, plopped Sara's car seat in front of Jake, and announced, "We're having goddamned pizza for dinner." He took one look at the frizzed-out hair, beet red face, and sweat marks ringing my armpits, silently nodded, and grabbed the phone book.

"I can go back out and get ... ," Jake started to offer when I shook my head violently.

"No. Stay. We're all in for the night. Going outside is bad," I said ominously.

"But I really don't mind. I can make something for dinner," Jake said. He leaned forward and pulled Sara out of her car seat. "Shhhh," he whispered as he patted her on the back.

"We're safe in here," I said solemnly. "Outside, bad. Inside, good." I nodded, my proclamation handed down.

The worst part about everything is I didn't get to buy any wine, so we have to drink the Merlot that Natalie bought us for Christmas. It doesn't taste *exactly* like a dead animal but pretty close. But it's better than nothing.

Not to mention, Jake and I have Adult Time planned for tonight, and I would prefer that he drinks a few glasses of wine before getting a good look at what these Miss Piggy pants are a-hidin'. We've had a handful of Adult Moments since Sara was born, and all I have to say is thank god our bedroom has bulbs that are about 15 watts.

Sunday, March 23
. . . .

I woke up yesterday with a headache thanks to the no-doubt poisons in the Merlot from the Roadkill Vineyards, but ignored it since last evening required full strength. I was invited a while back to participate in something called Local Bloggerpalooza at a bar called the Wine Seller. Apparently, a bunch of Chicago bloggers were supposed to read blog entries. Or something like that. I didn't know, I just figured I'd show up with a few printed entries and toast the crowd. I spent yesterday trying to calm my nerves, but publicly reading my writing is so much more frightening and panic-inducing than just blogging.

My blog, *Am I Making Myself Clare,* was mildly successful, as I mainly wrote about going out in the city and getting drunk at happy hours. Until last year, when an article about my site ran in the national paper *The Daily Tribune* and I suddenly had twenty thousand hits a day. Then, because my life is Just. That. Funny, I unexpectedly got pregnant immediately after, thanks to an unkind mixture of antibiotics and my punk-ass birth control pills. My pregnancy led to lots of sweet comments, a serious increase in stalkers, and many, many links to pregnant lady porno Web sites.

I invited Julie to join me, for both emotional and possible physical support, should the wine drinking be vigorous. Jake offered to join us, but I was due for a girls' night in the city with Julie. So, he booked a poker night and my parents offered to babysit.

Jake and I started preparing for the space shuttle launch a.k.a. getting out the door and Sara over to my parents about three hours ahead of time. Traveling with Sara is what I would imagine it's like when Mariah Carey goes on vacation, except our bags are filled with diapers instead of Fendi purses. We arrived at my parents' reasonably on time. I heard Sam screaming as I opened the front door.

"... MAKE FUN OF ME! MO-OM, I LOOK HIDEOUS! THIS IS THE WORST THING THAT COULD'VE POSSIBLY EVER HAPPENED TO ME! MY LIFE IS RUINED!" Her voice bounced across the walls of the house.

Jake and I stood in the foyer, not sure whether it was safe to proceed or not. I heard a door slam upstairs.

"It really doesn't look that bad. Sweetie, come out and let me take another look." I heard my mom use her most gentle, Sam-specific voice.

"MOM! I'M HUMILIATED! JUST LEAVE ME ALONE!"

Jake cowered and covered his ears.

"Sam, please, it'll be—"

My mom's efforts were cruelly rebuffed. "GET OUT! GET OUT! GET OUT! GET OUT!" Sam's voice sounded like a tortured squirrel.

"OK, I'll leave you alone." My mom appeared at the top of the stairs, her brow furrowed. "Hi, I didn't even hear you guys come in."

"What's going on?" I asked, and tried to hide a smile.

"Your sister's highlights didn't turn out the way she wanted. I think they look fine, but she's obviously not happy." My mom threw her hands up and rolled her eyes and walked down the stairs. She bent down and looked at Sara, "Hey, beautiful. Come to Grandma." She unbuckled Sara from her car seat and picked her up.

"Where's Dad?" I smiled as my mom cuddled Sara.

"Working. One of his patients was admitted into the hospital." She kissed Sara's cheek and squeezed her.

"Welcome to hell," a voice from around the corner said. Mark appeared, two beers in hand. He reached out and handed one to Jake.

"Hey! What are you doing here?" I said to my younger brother.

"Just stopping in to raid the kitchen and do some laundry." Mark took a long swig of his beer.

"Looks like you need it." I gazed pointedly at his stained T-shirt.

"Gotta look good for the ladies. Big plans tonight, Sis?" He leaned against the stairs and burped.

"Nice. I'm going out with Julie." His face broke out into a smile and he raised his eyebrows. "And no, we're not meeting up with you."

"Why are you so against Mark and Julie hanging out?" my mom asked.

"Because I deal with enough drama in my life just trying to go to Target with Sara. The last thing I need is my brother and my best friend screwing each other and then screwing each other over," I hissed, and narrowed my eyes at my brother.

"No shit. Bad idea, my friend," Jake said. He clapped Mark on the back and took a long drink of his beer.

"What's a bad idea?" Sam appeared at the top of the stairs. Apparently, her grieving period had ended.

"Julie and Mark. Hey, how are you?" I surveyed her hair. She was right, it wasn't attractive. I imagined she'd asked for a Jessica Simpson baby blond, but it turned out more like Pamela Anderson after about fifty hours in the sun.

"Hel-lo, didn't you hear? My hair is effing messed up. My life is basically ruined. God!" She collapsed on the stairs and leaned against the railing, her white hair falling around her face.

"I don't think it looks bad at all. I think it looks really cute!" I nodded my head, smiled, and tried to look sincere.

"Oh, great, it really must be one hundred percent awful if you think it's cute. You probably think Mom Haircuts are in style now," my sister wailed from underneath a curtain of strawlike hair. "Why can't you be like my friend Kristen's sister? She's awesome and works for as a buyer for Jimmy Choo."

"She's so pleasant," I said to my mom.

"Sam, your sister is still very cool and hip, even though she's a mom," my mom called up the stairs.

"OK, fiberglass mascara," Sam said to me, her mascara-crusted eyes narrowing.

"What?" I said, and leaned forward.

"Fiberglass mascara. What is?" she repeated slowly, as though she was talking to a developmentally handicapped person.

"I have no idea," I finally said after a few moments. "Mascara with fiberglass in it?"

"See?" Sam said pointedly to my mom. She stomped up the stairs. Seconds later, I heard "Crazy Game of Poker" blasting from her room.

"O.A.R. I know that one!" I yelled up the stairs.

"Don't even try. Communication with Sam is futile. Much like communication with houseplants," Mark said. "I got it!" he exclaimed, and raised his arms. "SAM! I FINALLY FIGURED OUT WHO YOU LOOK LIKE. REMEMBER BRITNEY SPEARS WHEN SHE HAD THOSE PLASTIC EXTENSIONS AFTER SHE SHAVED HER HEAD?" he yelled up the stairs.

"THIS WHOLE FAMILY IS SERIOUSLY RETARDED!" Sam screamed from her room.

"Mark!" My mom elbowed him in the ribs.

"Ow. What? She does." He rubbed his side.

"Sam, you know I don't like that word!" my mom called up to Sam, and what sounded like a shoe hit her closed door.

"As much as I hate to leave this family party, Jake and I have to run," I said.

"OK, don't worry about anything. Miss Sara and I are going to have a great time together. Jake, you'll be back to pick her up later?" My mom turned to Jake as she kissed Sara's head.

"Yep, see you around midnight," he said as she turned toward the door.

"Sounds good. And Clare, good luck with the reading. Try to behave." She narrowed her eyes at me.

"Thanks. But Mom, it's Julie. That's kind of unlikely." I shrugged.

"Right," she said.

"Have Julie call me for phone sex when she's wasted! Ow, what? Mom, I'm just kidding," Mark yelled as I closed the door.

Not a chance in hell.

I parked my car on Julie's street a good three hours later, still shaking with anger. Although I'm sure that man didn't necessarily mean to have a tire blowout in the center lane of the expressway, it does not mean I didn't want to roll down my window and spit on his car as I drove past. (Much like when my car crapped out in the middle of rush hour and someone threw a McDonald's Big Mac at me while I was lifting the hood of my smoking car. Eye for an eye, no?)

I stood in the entryway to Julie's apartment building, freezing in the chilly spring air, and pressed the intercom. "I'm here," I called into the speaker. The wind whipped through the glass alcove as I waited.

Nothing.

I checked my watch. Right on time. I pressed the button again.

This time, "UN-ING FU-ING LA—" was all that came out of the intercom.

I pressed the button again. "Julie? I'm here! I'm freezing!"

The intercom crackled to life again, deleting every other syllable.

"Late? Did you say you're running late?" My voice rose as I pressed the button again, startling a smoker huddled against the apartment building wall.

"LAAAAAA" came across the speaker.

I checked my watch again. I pulled out my cell phone and called Julie.

"Just go. I'll meet you there. Goddamned flatiron not worth a goddamn . . . ," she muttered into the phone.

I shoved my cell phone back and into my purse and stepped out onto the sidewalk to hail a cab. The wind whipped against my face and surely took my makeup off in one clean slice. I pictured a mask of foundation, eyeliner, eye shadow, blush, and lip gloss sailing down Diversey Avenue.

I threw myself into a cab, which was when my anxiety started to climb. Blogging is one thing, reading my writing aloud is another.

If I wanted to experience this much stress, I should just go to IKEA on a Saturday morning. Much like last year, when Jake and I nearly got decapitated by a college student looking for Box 2 of 3 to build a FLOG-ERSHAM media cabinet.

I arrived at the Wine Seller a few minutes early. I'd never been to this particular bar, but I fell in love with it as I walked through the heavy oak doors and into the warmth. Dark wood paneling covered every inch of space, with bookshelves piled high to the ceiling. People lounging around, drinking glasses of wine and reading the newspaper. It seemed like a perfect spot to hide out from the cold and whisper gossip.

Yet I didn't really know what to do as I stood in the doorway, nearly expecting to see a sign reading, "CLARE FINNEGAN. WALK OVER TO THE BAR. GET A DRINK. ASK FOR JANE. SHE WILL HELP YOU," like in one of those James Bond movies.

When Jane e-mailed me a few weeks ago, she said she had invited a few local bloggers to read some of their entries at what she called Local Bloggerpalooza. I skimmed over it until I got to the "free drinks" part. With the astronomical cost of day care, "free" means a lot these days.

I walked over to the bar anyway. I figured a little liquid courage couldn't hurt. I sat down at a bar stool and reached for the wine list as a voice said behind me, "Are you Clare?"

I turned around and saw a slight woman with tightly cropped gray hair and cool black glasses.

I nodded and smiled. "That's me."

"I'm Jane. Thanks so much for coming today. We should have a pretty good turnout," Jane said, and thrust her hands into the pockets of her jeans.

I resisted the urge to look around the room at the, oh, ten people in the bar.

Including waitstaff.

Whatever. It's a few free drinks. Besides, aren't there supposed to be other bloggers here, too? It's not like they can blame the low attendance all on—

"We had another blogger scheduled. Do you know Mike from *Lakeshore Jive*?" Jane said.

I nodded my head enthusiastically. "I've never met him, but his blog is hilarious. He's going to be here, too?"

Wow. It'll be great to meet him. Fellow Internet stalker magnet, I thought.

Jane shook her head. "No. He was supposed to come but canceled at the last minute. So, it's just you."

I stared at her, waiting for my brain to translate the linguistics. I think my brain flashed into the Blue Screen of Computer Meltdown Death.

Jane saw the look on my face. "Don't worry! It'll be a piece of cake. I'll just introduce you over there." She pointed to a small stage with a microphone and bar stool. "And you can read a couple of entries and take some questions, OK?"

My head snapped back and forth between the microphone and her.

Like, uh, This. So. Was. Not. The. Deal.

"I don't think—," I started to say when a flash of red hair caught my eye.

Julie. She'll definitely save me.

"Hey!" I waved to her.

"I'm so fucking sorry. My shitty flatiron shorted out on me," Julie yelled across the bar, startling the seven people quietly sipping drinks. She pulled off her coat as she walked toward me, and again, the seven people seemed rattled, since all of them were dressed in cold-weather-appropriate gear, like turtlenecks, sweaters, and scarves. With very little cleavage.

Meanwhile, Julie was dressed in a tight long-sleeved black dress with fishnet tights and knee-high boots. With very much cleavage.

By self-admission, her trailer park roots run deep.

"What's going on?" Julie said as she walked over to me, red hair tangled around her shoulders. "Hey, I'm Julie," she said to Jane.

Jane seemed slightly disturbed. "Oh, hello." She looked at me. "Julie as in Julie from your blog?"

I nodded and picked up the wine list again.

"Good to meet you! You look"—Jane stopped and looked Julie up and down—"great."

"Thanks, so do you," Julie said sweetly.

Recognizing the calm before the proverbial Julie Shitstorm, I thrust the wine list in front of her.

"Order," I said. I turned to Jane. "So what time am I supposed to do this thing?" I said as I waved around to the empty tables.

Jane looked at her watch. "Right now. But get a glass of wine first." She looked around the empty bar and back to me. "We've got time."

Right.

After Jane walked off to test the microphone, Julie sat down next to me. "What? Did she not like my outfit or something?" She leaned forward and her massive boobs rested on the bar.

"Forget her. Listen. There was supposed to be other bloggers here, but it's just me! I can't go up there and read some lame entries to like four people." I leaned forward and gripped her arm.

"Relax, drama queen. Just have a few free drinks, get up there and read your shit, and then we'll bail." Julie rolled her eyes. She glanced around the room. "Let's go to a normal bar next."

I smiled. "Normal like how?"

"Normal like I can dance on the tables and no one will give a shit. Bars should be loud, with drunks puking their guts out, not quiet and studious," Julie said, and signaled to the bartender. "Two glasses of Pinot Noir."

"What if they boo me offstage?" I mused as the bartender set two glasses of wine down in front of us.

"There's like two people here. You probably won't even be able to hear it. Speaking of which, *why* are there only two people here?" Julie whipped her head around, nearly smacking me across the face with her bright red hair extensions.

I shrugged as I watched Jane get ready to introduce me, to send me out as a sheep amongst the wolves. "No idea," I said to Julie as I shuffled the papers with my printed-out blog posts in my hand.

Maybe I could just go up there and read from the newspaper. People might want to hear the news, right?

"No, really. You have so many readers. How many hits you up to these days?" she asked as she pulled a tube of lip gloss out of her purse.

I shrugged. "Same as always. About twenty thousand, I think."

Julie shook her head and laughed.

"What?" I asked.

"Nothing. No offense or anything, but it's still just weird that so many people read your blog." She squinted across the dark bar at a guy wearing a black turtleneck and gray skinny jeans.

"No kidding. I started it because I had that lowly assistant job and answering the phones didn't exactly entertain me all day long. I thought it would be hilarious to write about my obnoxious coworkers and new martini recipes." I fidgeted with the silver bracelet on my arm, pinching it on my forearm until it left an indentation.

"And, for whatever reason, people started reading and now thousands of them read about your life." She grabbed her wineglass and downed the liquid in a quick gulp.

"If you would've told me in college that I'd have thousands of people reading stories about my kid's diaper rashes and my husband's hate for the cable company . . ." I stopped and shrugged. "Guess there's still a lot of bored people at work." I picked up my drink.

Yet I brought the wineglass just a wee bit too fast to my lips, and it clinked against my front teeth.

Which, of course, led me to jerk my head back.

Which, of course, led the red wine to splash down the front of my shirt.

Which led my Dignity to leave the bar and go down the street for a smoke break.

"Thanks for coming, everyone. We have a special guest in the house tonight. Her name is Clare Finnegan, of the popular blog *Am I Making Myself Clare,* and she's here to read a few of her entries tonight. So please give her a warm welcome," Jane said from the stage.

I remained frozen on my bar stool, still holding the wineglass, red wine soaking into my shirt and pants.

"Go," Julie said, and took the wineglass out of my hand. She gave me a little shove forward on the shoulder. "Now."

My hand still in the air, I said, "But I—"

She shook her head. "Go up there. Read. It'll give me something to do while I'm stuck in this shithole."

I slowly got up, walked toward the microphone, and stepped onstage, red wine stain and all. I felt all of the people in the bar freeze as they watched the stained, freaked-out girl walk toward the stage. I stood up and was nearly blinded by the spotlight. I leaned into the microphone and glanced over at Julie, who waved her hand at me.

"Uh, hi, everyone. I'm Clare. I have a blog. On the Internet. Of which I am going to read you some materials publicly," I said.

Yeah, so that's pretty much how that went.

Jane, despite being very gracious and insisting that I wasn't The Worst Person to Ever Speak in Public *Ever,* didn't seem too excited when I offered to come back anytime.

I figured I'd tortured everyone enough, and Julie and I walked down the street to another bar.

"That one guy, with the balding head, kind of laughed at one point," Julie offered as we settled into a booth at a sports bar.

"Thanks, but don't even try to make me feel better. Let's just pretend it never happened, OK?" I muttered as I took off my coat. I glanced down at the red wine stain still covering my shirt and pants. "Can't wait for the comments on my blog."

"Do I look like I've gained weight?" Julie asked me later as we sipped on a couple of beers.

"No," I lied. "You look great."

"Thanks for being a liar, but my love handles aren't looking so hot these days. Ah, well, what am I going to do? My love affair with food isn't ending anytime soon." She sighed as she adjusted her boobs and fiddled with her silver earrings.

"And it shouldn't. You've never had a problem finding a guy and besides, you always look hot," I said as I took a swig of my drink.

"You're the one who looks hot, and you're the one who had a child living inside of you." She pointedly looked me up and down and rolled her eyes.

"I wish. My body is still all messed up—spare tire, stretch marks, and varicose veins, not to mention flabby boobs. It's like pregnancy is nature's birth control—you end up so hideous no one wants to have sex with you until desperation sets in. Look at my pants!" I shrieked as I pointed to my jeans. "These are four sizes bigger than normal. And they're ugly, since I refuse to buy cute fat pants. It's so depressing!"

"Oh, please, you look great," she insisted.

"You should see these black pants I had to wear the other day. I call them Miss Pig—," I started to say.

"I'm sorry, I hate to interrupt, but are you Clare, from the Internet?" A cute blond girl with enormous brown eyes stood at our table.

Oh no! The witch hunt has begun already! They're probably going to show me a petition titled "Clare Should Never Leave Her House Again."

Or maybe I can just say, *Clare? Who's Clare? My name is Jenipher.* Or something.

"Yep, she is. She's like a famous Internet Rock Star," Julie said proudly before I could catch her eye.

The blond girl signaled to a brunette at the bar and nodded her head. "I'm Beth. My friends and I all love your blog. It saves me from killing myself at work every day," she said as she turned back to our booth.

"Thanks," I said, wondering if they'd yet heard I wouldn't soon be teaching Public Speaking 101.

"We came to hear you speak tonight, the event you talked about on your blog, but the address you posted was for the grocery store down the street," Beth said as her brunette friend joined her.

Suddenly I realized just how handy typos can be. Huzzah!

"Oh no!" I said as I clapped my hand on the table. "So *that's* why no one was there!" I turned toward Julie, who shook her head.

"Fucking unbelievable," Julie muttered.

"You didn't miss much," I said to Beth and her friend. I gestured toward the red wine stain. "Seriously."

Despite feeling guilty about the address typo, I praised the heavens for my Get Out of Jail Free Thanks to Poor Proofreading Skills card.

"Sit," Julie said, and waved her hand around the booth.

"No thanks, we're just about to leave. This is Heidi," Beth said. She pointed to her brunette friend.

"I loved your recent entry on who you would cast in a remake of *St. Elmo's Fire.* Colin Farrell in the Rob Lowe role would be perfect," Heidi said.

"I think so, too," Julie chimed in.

"And I love the entries about your cat Butterscotch. Is he still gay?" Heidi asked.

"I think so. He's obsessed with the new season of *Project Runway.* He purrs every time it's on," I said, and shrugged. Last year, my cat declared his sexuality when he became obsessed with frilly pink Barbie clothes and anything with sequins or faux fur. As much as we've tried otherwise, he also prefers his hot pink collar with "Princess" spelled out in rhinestones.

"Do you guys want a tequila shot?" Beth asked.

"No, that's—," I started to say.

"Love one, thanks!" Julie interrupted, and Beth signaled to the bartender, who began pouring the amber-colored liquid of death into shot glasses.

After Beth and Heidi left to go to another bar, Julie pursed her lips and folded her hands on the table. "So, did I tell you I think I'm finally ready to have a boyfriend?"

I paused, my drink frozen in midair. "What?"

She nodded. "Yep. I think I want a boyfriend." She said it as though a guy would magically appear next to her if she sounded firm enough.

"You?" It came out way harsher than I thought. "I mean—"

She waved her arm around. "I know what you meant. And yes. Me. But just a boyfriend though, those kid things sound like a lot of work."

"Er, great." I took a sip of my drink and set it down. "Anyone in particular?"

"Mark." She saw my head start to vehemently shake. "Calm down. I was kidding. No, there's no one in particular. I'll keep you posted if there is."

"Well, here's to hot men," I said, and lifted my drink in the air as a passing guy flashed me a thumbs-up.

"Not you. You're not hot," Julie muttered at Thumbs-Up Guy. We clinked glasses and set the barware down. "So, are you ready to leave?"

"Sure, where are we going?" I grabbed my purse and straightened my wine-stained clothes.

"There's a drag show down the street. One of my coworkers told me it's hysterical." She stood up, adjusted her outfit, and fluffed her hair. "Move," she ordered a group of college students drinking Miller Lite in front of us.

I laughed and shook my head. "Sounds great."

And it was, although after a while all of the drag queens all ran together in a mix of platform heels, eyeliner, and glittery hairspray. At the end, Julie got onstage and sang a rendition of "Hot Child, Summer in the City" while I clapped along and cheered from the audience.

At four in the morning I posted this on my blog: *Yeahiosyu!!!!!*

When I finally got the courage this morning to open my eyes in Julie's apartment, I looked over at Julie on the couch, sleeping in her skirt, boots, and a T-shirt, and poked her. "Are you dead?" I whispered, my voice sounding like an eighty-year-old woman.

"I hope so," she croaked.

"Why did we stay out so late? More important, why did I think I could party like I used to?" I moaned and threw my blanket over my head, which only caused immediate feelings of suffocation, so I flung it off and panted.

"No shit, Mom," Julie mumbled.

"This is why I don't go out anymore. So I can be in bed by eight and wake up not feeling like a corpse," I moaned.

"Sounds thrilling. You guys get the Early Bird Special at Denny's, too?" Julie croaked.

I rolled over and saw my wallet lying next to me on the floor. "I didn't order anything off the Home Shopping Network, did I?" I whispered to Julie, terrified. I've been known to decide I need hideous jewelry and animal-print lampshades after a couple glasses of wine. This is why I will never move to Las Vegas—twenty-four-hour stores with nothing but sequins and faux fur. Apparently, I have the taste of a mobster's girlfriend when drinking. Or my cat.

"I don't think so, but I guess you'll just have to wait two weeks and see if any packages arrive."

"Jake will kill me if I ordered something after a few drinks again." I threw my hands up and covered my face.

"Yeah, what was it you ordered after that one New Year's Eve when you did all those car bombs?" Julie laughed.

"A zebra-print sheet set complete with matching duvet," I mumbled into my fingers.

Despite my raging headache, I couldn't throw myself in my car fast enough to race home to see Sara. I walked in the door, immediately scooped her up out of her cradle swing, and kissed every inch of her head. She looked up at me and narrowed her eyes as if to say, *Dude, you stink. What the hell did you do last night, Mom?* Jake actually did say something of the sort.

Later, I logged onto my blog to read my drunken posting. I cringed at the incoherent words and braced myself as I scrolled down to read the comments. Most were supportive, offering hangover remedies, but jen2485 posted: *Clare, u r a drunk. How can u drink when you have a baby? What if u were drunk and dropped your precious Sara? U r a bad parent.*

Thanks. Just what I needed to see. I was cheered by wifey1025, though, who asked if I wanted her to come over and take care of me during my hangover (and no doubt tie me up and throw me in the trunk of her car). Wifey1025 is by far my favorite Internet stalker. She's always quick with the wit and creative with her kidnapping methods.

Tuesday, March 25
. . . .

Despite the lingering aftereffects of Saturday night, I made sure my shoes matched this morning and my Miss Piggy pants were free of baby vomit. I had a meeting with Greg and wanted to present myself as the professional and pulled-together woman I usually project, rather than how I looked last time: Clare Finnegan—*Blind Date* contestant.

I didn't even get the chance to turn on my computer before Mule Face appeared at my door this morning. She stood there silently, tapping her foot and shaking her head.

"What?" I finally asked after ignoring her didn't make her go the fuck away.

"Someone had a good time on Saturday night," she said, and smiled.

"Oh yeah. I had fun." I didn't look up at her while pretending to organize blank paper on my desk.

"You know, your posts have really gone downhill lately." She stepped into my office and sat down.

I stared at my phone and tried to will it to ring.

"Two days ago you posted an entry about how you don't like Precious Moments figurines. I mean, who DOESN'T love Precious Moments? You really missed the mark with that one. Then, you posted about some drag queens. You know what you should really write about?"

I opened my file cabinet and began randomly picking up folders.

"You should really write about the show *Touched by an Angel*. You could start a mass Internet campaign for the show to come back on the air!"

I bent down and scratched my ankle.

She sat and stared at me for a minute and finally got the hint and stood up when I didn't make eye contact. "Just an idea!" she said. She turned to leave and stopped. "Oh, I almost forgot! Here!" She dropped a mail-order cosmetics catalog on my desk. "We have some great new stretch mark cream, if you're interested."

"Still not interested," I said, and pushed it back to her.

"The commission would really help me buy this litter box furniture for my cat. You see, it looks like a regular houseplant, but it is really a litter box." Mule Face pushed the catalog back toward me a bit, nearly knocking over my penholder.

"I repeat: Not. Interested." I remained very still and stared at her, like we were in a gunslinging duel. I learned this was the best way to deal with door-to-door salesmen, telemarketers, and Mule Face pushing her mail-order cosmetics line. I should know, she's been at it for two years and I've remained victorious. (Good thing she's not with me after I have a few drinks, because I would *so* buy the rhinestone-encrusted blush compact.)

She caved first. "Cranky, cranky!" she said in a singsong voice as she left.

Around noon, Greg arrived for our meeting. I smoothed my hair back and took a deep breath before I walked into the conference room.

"Hey there," I said warmly as I clutched my leather portfolio to my chest.

"Hi, how are you?" Greg said, and stood up.

"I'm good." I stuck out my hand.

Greg looked confused for a moment at the gesture but returned the handshake. "Good."

I nodded and offered him a chair.

We sat down and I opened my folder. "So, I've been looking over the event specifics and everything looks pretty straightforward. We'll be handling the invitations, registration, golf shirts, printed golf balls, foursome groupings, the lunch, and running everything on the day of. Right?" I looked up at him.

"If you say so. Listen, I just got roped into this and I really have no idea what I'm doing."

"Well, don't worry about that. I've done a few golf outings and I can assure you, it'll be great." I smiled, thrilled my composure had remained intact. So far. I looked back down at my notepad. "So, I've been working with the graphic designer on a few invitation mock-ups. What do you think?" I slid three pieces of paper toward him.

He held my gaze for a few extra seconds before looking down at the paper. "I think this one will work," he said, and pointed to one of the designs.

"Great, I'll get that moving."

"So, how's your family?" Greg asked.

"Same as usual." I smiled at him and began to let my guard down a fraction of an inch. "Sam's a teenager—What?" I stopped as he started shaking his head.

"Nothing. Just last time I saw her, she was . . . well, not a teenager." He laughed.

"Trust me, she's all teen now." I smiled and nodded my head. "My parents are doing well and Mark's living in the city, doing the bachelor thing." I shrugged a little. Greg was never this interested in my family. I'm surprised he remembered that I had an actual family and was not just raised by wolves in the forest. With him, it was all career first, family second. Children, bad; living with five-thousand-dollar couches and city lofts, good. In fact, it was shocking to me when Jake actually wanted to meet my parents when we were dating and still always suggests that we hang out with my family. A mutant, he is.

"Did Mark tell you I saw him at a bar about a year ago?" Greg said as he laced his fingers together on the dark oak table.

"Yeah, I think so." I tried to look nonchalant but remembered Mark said Greg was with some stunning six-foot brunette.

"I think I was with my ex at the time," he said.

"Oh, huh." I tapped my pen against the table. "How's your family?" I asked nonchalantly as I fiddled with my wedding band.

"Great. Mom and Dad are doing wonderful." He smiled and folded his arms across his chest. His white oxford shirt crinkled at the elbows.

"Huh. Well, anyway, let's meet again in two weeks. Sound good?"

"Works for me. " He sighed and stood up

"Yeah." I led him to the door. "Well, call me if you have any questions," I said, and stuck out my hand.

"Good to see you, Clare," he said, and shook my hand with both of his.

I made it all the way to my office before I exhaled. As I sat down at my desk, relief washed over me because I felt like I had pulled it off; I kept my composure, wore matching clothes, and conducted myself professionally, as though I didn't still harbor an urge to drive to Sara's day-care, snatch her up, and head for Mexico. I appeared like a successful working mom—to my ex-boyfriend, nonetheless.

Yet as I allowed myself to acknowledge some pride, a small part of me screamed, *Fraud! Liar!*

Thursday, March 27

. . . .

I was at my desk, in the middle of drafting a deadlines calendar for Greg's golf outing, when my phone rang, jolting me out of my musings about the invitation print run.

"Clare Finnegan."

"Clare, oh good, I'm so glad I got you!" Reese.

"Why? What's going on?"

"I need you to meet me at the hospital."

"Are you in labor?" I clutched the edge of my desk. It was too early; Reese wasn't due to give birth for a few more weeks.

"I think so. Meet me over there as soon as you can," she said, and hung up.

I jumped up and stood still for a minute, paralyzed. I wasn't sure what to do, so I stared at an invoice for the golf outing for a minute. Then a voice inside my head yelled, *Get moving, asshole. Reese is about to have this baby while you stare at the price of golf balls.* I immediately raced around my office and collected my purse and coat and threw myself into the car. I narrowly avoided four accidents on the way to the hospital and finally arrived at the maternity wing, red-faced and panting.

"Where's Reese?" I yelled to a nurse.

"What?"

"REESE! You know, blond lady. Tiny. Pregnant."

The nurse stared at me.

"Hel-lo? Do you understand? REESE!"

More stares.

I was about to start screaming when I heard a voice behind me.

"Clare, I'm right here. Leave that poor woman alone."

I whirled around and saw Reese, looking excited but nervous and in obvious pain.

"Oh my God! Are you OK? What do you need me to do? Where's Grace? Where's Matt? Are you in pain? Where's the doctor?" I knew I sounded like I was under the influence of an amphetamine, but it was as if my brain had no control over my mouth. (Not the first time.)

"Clare, I'm fine. Grace is with my mom, Matt's on his way from work. The hospital lost my preregistration paperwork, so I need you to take my insurance card downstairs and register me so I can be admitted." She held out a card in her hand as she winced in pain.

"I can do that. Are you sure it's OK if I leave you?" I asked her.

"I'm fine. Matt should be here any minute." Reese waved me toward the door.

"Sure?" I stood there, unsure of whether to go east or west.

"CLARE!" I hadn't heard Reese raise her voice in years.

"Sorry! I'm on it!" I raced to the elevator and down to Registration. When I got there, I discovered an enormous line of people, many of whom looked as though they had been waiting since about, oh, 1986. After tapping my foot impatiently and silently cursing every person in front of me, I made it to the front of the line.

"I need to register my friend. She's having a baby upstairs." I waved my hands wildly around my midsection.

"We need her to come down here and sign consent forms." The woman didn't even look up at me.

"She's in labor, she can't. She told me to sign them."

"Uh-huh," the woman said, and examined her long, decal-covered nails.

"Uh-huh so we're OK, then?" I leaned toward the exit.

"No. Let me see her insurance card." I forked over the card. "It says here her deductible is five hundred dollars. We take check or credit card."

"What? No. She hasn't been treated yet. She's just being admitted." I shook my head as though I hadn't heard the woman correctly.

The woman stared at me as though I had told her aliens were upstairs administering colonics and would she like one?

"She just got here," I repeated, my eyes wide.

Nothing.

"She just needs to be admitted." I stared at my registration nemesis.

"Her co-pay is one hundred dollars. Do you have a credit card?" Registration woman spoke her words slowly, like she was trying to help me understand English.

"No, you're not listening." I slapped the card back down on the table.

"We take debit cards, too," decal lady said.

That. Was. It.

"Are you enjoying your first visit on Earth?" I said.

I knew it was rude, but it worked. She gave me an evil look, slid Reese's card back to me, and waved me off.

"Your friend is admitted." She made a big deal of rolling her eyes at her coworker. I really wanted to engage her in a verbal altercation but didn't really want to have my eyeballs scratched out by fingernails decorated with stickers. I flew back upstairs and found Reese in one of the labor rooms. She had changed into a hospital gown and was lying in bed watching *Oprah*.

"OK, I think everything is fine except this bitch downstairs—" I waved my arms around until Reese put her finger to her lips.

"Shhhh!" she said, and intently watched the television.

"What?" I sat obediently down next to her.

"Shhh!" she said again. I sat silently and watched as Oprah talked to the designer Nate Berkus about what lighting to use in small spaces. After he finished, Reese turned to me. "OK, sorry. I just really wanted to see that."

I guess women really are more laid-back with their second pregnancy.

"Uh, OK. Is there anything that you need?" I asked, and tried not to stare at the stirrups.

"Yes, call Matt again. I keep getting his voice mail. He should be here by now."

I picked up the phone and dialed Matt's number, but it went straight to voice mail again.

"Sorry, voice mail again. I'm sure he's on his way," I said as I snapped my phone shut. I said a silent prayer to God that Matt truly was on his way, not porking his secretary in a seedy motel or something.

"Uh-huh," Reese muttered, and stared at the fetal monitor.

"How's everything going in here?" a voice said from the doorway. Dr. Clarke.

"Hey, going well. Boring as usual," Reese said. She fanned her face and I stood up to hand her a rubber band.

"Hi, Dr. Clarke," I said.

"Clare, hi! I didn't expect to see you here. The last time I saw you in one of these rooms, you were giving birth yourself." She smiled and patted me on the back.

"Yes. I'm glad it's not me in the bed this time."

"Oh, come on now, it wasn't so bad." Dr. Clarke smiled and I got a really strange flashback of her yelling, "PUSH!" a few short months ago.

"Easy for you to say. Sorry." I turned to Reese.

"Reese, you're at four centimeters, so I anticipate it'll be a few hours before you deliver. We'll give you an epidural in a little bit. But for now, I'm going to go ahead and break your water to get you moving along." She wheeled a cart full of Scary Medical Things over to the bedside.

"Sounds good," Reese said.

I wasn't sure what to do, but I walked over to Reese's other side and grabbed her hand. I stared at a picture of a little boy playing with a sailboat as Dr. Clarke did her magic down there. I wondered how the hospital picks out their artwork. Do they go to a gallery and pick stuff out or is there like a general "Ugly Yet Adequate Paintings for Hotel and Hospital Rooms" package they can order off the Internet? And who is the artist who does those paintings? Is he/she proud to have his/her artwork in hospitals or is it the equivalent to a rock band having their music played in elevators?

"Got it! OK, fluid looks clear. Now we wait," Dr. Clarke said, and snapped off her gloves.

"Clear fluid is good. That means there's no meconium in the fluid. Meconium is baby poop, which an unborn child can aspirate if it is expelled in the uterus. The baby might express meconium if it is stressed, and thus tinged fluid is a sign the baby is experiencing some kind of stressor," I told Reese.

She stared at me. "Still watching *Maternity Ward* on the Discovery Health Channel?"

"Uh, yeah. Sorry."

"Couldn't have said it better myself, Clare," Dr. Clarke said as she walked out of the room.

"Call Matt again," Reese said as she aimlessly channel-surfed.

"OK." I picked up my phone. Voice mail again. "I'm sure he's about to walk in the door."

"Who's about to walk in the door?" Julie appeared in the doorway, dressed in her scrubs.

"Hey, Julie!" Reese perked up. "Matt, he's still not here."

Julie ever so slightly glanced at me out of the corner of her eye. Matt isn't exactly her favorite person, starting with his cheating in college and culminating when he hit on her in a bar a few months ago.

"So, how are you feeling?" she said.

"Fine. Bored. Nothing exciting is happening yet." Reese shrugged.

"That's good. Just don't be one of those pregnant women in labor who scream and flip out." Julie shuddered.

"I'll do my best," Reese said.

"I witnessed one delivery when I was training, it was this hippie woman who was doing it naturally without drugs. She was fully naked the whole time and her husband kept saying, 'Push it out your butt, honey,' while she was pushing." Julie started squatting and grabbing onto the IV pole, a perfect imitation.

"Ugh. That couldn't have been fun to watch," I said.

"Not really, considering the woman was close to four hundred pounds." Julie shrugged.

"Take my mind off this labor stuff. Tell me what's new in the land of singledom," Reese said.

My head snapped back and forth between the two of them, thrilled. It still hasn't quite sunk in that they're friends again after a year-and-a-half-long feud that began at my bachelorette party and involved lots of verbal venomous barbs and near death threats. It ended when they each wanted to throw me a baby shower and I forced them to do one together. After much arguing over favors—tiny bottles of liquor versus chocolates—they found a common ground: me.

And now they're as close as they were in college. My mediation skills must be off the hook; the Middle East should definitely give me a call.

"I'm ready for a boyfriend," Julie announced as she stopped using the IV pole as a faux birthing device. She spread her arms wide.

"Really? Anyone in particular or just generally?" Reese said as she winced and shifted in bed.

"Generally. Although I hear Greg is single these days," Julie said, and tapped a finger against her cheek.

"Funny," I said to her.

"What's the big deal? So she has to work with him? They broke up a million years ago and she's happily married. We're all adults, right?" Reese said, her voice with a slight edge. She looked at me. "Right?"

I nodded mutely.

Yeah, who cares? It's not awkward or anything, right? I totally have it together. I'm not still fat, exhausted all of the time, and a mere shell of my formerly fabulous self, right? Right?

"Whatever you say." Julie rolled her eyes. "Forget about Greg. Back to me and my sex life. The Internet is going to do all the work," Julie said.

"Online dating?" I said, my mouth open slightly.

Julie nodded and crossed her arms in front of her enormous chest. "Yep."

"Internet dating? Isn't that kind of unsafe?" Reese said.

"Get with it, O ye of little technology. Internet dating is socially acceptable now," Julie said to her. She pointedly turned to me and raised her eyebrows.

"She's right. It is," I said to Reese.

"*And* I'll even help Clare out. I'll let her recap my dates on her blog," Julie said.

"Really? Are you sure?" I said, already thinking of the fabulously hilarious possibilities.

"Yep. I mean, no offense or anything, but your blog could use some material these days other than babies and diapers and bottles." Julie patted me on the back sympathetically.

"Gee, thanks." I brushed her hand off my back and smiled.

"Well, OK. If you say it's safe. But just use protection or else you'll be the one in this bed next year," Reese said.

"I will. But seriously. What is it with you two? Don't you guys know that condoms were invented for a reason? Having a child shoot out of my crotch is *not* on the agenda, thank you very much." Julie shuddered, as though she could shake off any kid cooties like a dog shaking off water.

"Only you would say something like that to a woman in labor," I retorted as Reese laughed.

"No problem. Listen, guys, my shift is about to start, but I'll be back to check on you during my break." She blew us a kiss and waved her hand Miss America style before walking out, her scrubs swishing.

"Do you think he got into an accident or something?" Reese wondered out loud.

"I'm sure he's fine. There's probably traffic or something. Don't worry, he'll be here. How are you, in any pain?"

"Nothing too bad yet, just tightening." She picked up a *People* magazine and leafed through it without reading anything.

We sat around for another hour, alternately looking at magazines and flipping through the channels. "Hey look! Here's the channel with the educational videos on how to care for your new baby. It has important tips like, 'Don't leave your baby in the tub by itself. Babies can drown,'" I said as I clapped my hands together.

"Gee, really? You're kidding! You mean I can't just drop my kid in a swimming pool and expect it to swim?" Reese said as she stopped on a story about Justin Timberlake.

"Nope! Apparently, some women believe that babies can breathe underwater since they spend nine months in utero in amniotic fluid. I'm not kidding. It actually covers this."

"Some people are so—" She was interrupted by a loud alarm sounding from the fetal monitor. Each number was jumping all over the place. "What's going on?" She looked at me.

"I don't know. Let me get the nurse." I stood up but didn't take more than three steps when Dr. Clarke and a nurse came rushing in.

"Flip over on your side," Dr. Clarke ordered Reese. The tone in her voice iced my blood.

Reese turned over and the nurse said, "It's still not going up."

"Flip over to your other side." Reese obliged again and I could see the rising panic in her eyes.

"Reese, we're going to put an internal monitor onto the baby's head. The monitor is showing the baby's heart rate is dropping and we don't know if it is because the baby's in distress or the monitor is just goofy."

Reese silently nodded and turned over on her back. I gripped her hand and whispered in her ear that it would be OK. I closed my eyes and prayed for Matt to walk in the door, but when I opened them the only person who walked by the door was an orderly.

The room was silent as Dr. Clarke put the monitor in.

"There! It's on."

We all stared at the fetal monitor, willing the heart rate to go up. The heart rate dropped from 150 to 50, then it went back up again to 150, then it dropped to 70.

"C'mon, c'mon," Dr. Clarke muttered.

Finally, the monitor registered.

The baby's heart rate was 45.

"We're going to a C-section!" Dr. Clarke yelled to the nurse. Immediately they began unplugging cords and monitors.

"Reese, it's going to be OK. The baby's going to be fine," I said, my voice shaking. I tried to be positive, but Dr. Clarke and the nurse's reactions made my stomach drop.

"Where the hell are the other nurses? We need help in here! What are they doing, sitting on their asses?" Dr. Clarke barked at the nurse. Two other nurses appeared. They started to wheel Reese out of the room and down the hallway.

"You can come in after we have her numbed up," the nurse yelled to me over her shoulder.

Reese burst into tears as they wheeled her down the hallway. "Call Matt!" she shrieked.

My hands shaking, I snapped open my phone and dialed Matt one more time. Voice mail again. This time, I left a message: "Listen, asshole. Get your fucking piece of shit ass to the hospital right now. Your wife is having an emergency C-section, you prick!"

Do I regret it? Yes and no.

I had stood in the hallway for what felt like an eternity, waiting to be given scrubs, when a nurse appeared. "Are you with Reese?"

"Yes," I said.

"Baby boy. Six pounds, two ounces. Born two minutes ago."

"What?"

"He was just born. We didn't have time for a spinal to kick in, so we had to put her totally out. She's in Recovery and you can see her in a minute."

"What? You mean she already had the baby?"

"Yep," she said, and walked away.

I stood there by myself for a few moments until another nurse appeared and led me into Recovery and over to Reese.

"Oh my God! How are you?" I said, and threw my arms around her.

"In pain. My stomach hurts. What happened?" she slurred.

"You have a baby boy!" I said to her.

"What?" Her head flopped over to the right and she closed her eyes.

"A boy!" I said again, and shook her arm a little.

"Oh. Should I get a tattoo?" she mumbled.

"A tattoo?" I looked at the recovery room nurse, who shrugged.

"Over my C-section scar. I'm gonna get a tattoo of butterflies." She smiled and nodded her head.

"Um, sure." I patted her hand and shrugged at the nurse.

"What did I have again?" Reese mumbled. A tiny stream of drool fell down onto her white-and-blue-dotted hospital gown.

"A boy!" I shrieked.

"Oh. Good." She fell asleep.

"Why don't you let her get some rest, she's pretty out of it from the morphine," the recovery room nurse said as she checked the IV fluid.

"OK," I said, and kissed the top of Reese's head.

"Do you want to see the baby?" the nurse asked.

"Of course!" I said, and followed her out the door.

She led me into the nursery and over to one of those plastic bins, where Reese's beautiful pink, squirmy, wriggly baby boy lay, looking very surprised and not quite sure what had happened. I picked him up and held him against my cheek, amazed at how different he felt from Sara. I couldn't believe how much smaller he was. I felt a twinge in my stomach as I realized how big Sara was getting and, for a second, wished I could zap her back to when she was that little. A huge part of me wanted to book it straight out of that hospital and run home to scoop up my own little wriggly child.

The nurses finally pried him out of my hands, insisting he needed to go through some tests, and I went back to Reese.

Whoa. Reese has two kids. Jake and I are just two people with a kid. But Reese? She has a family.

When did we all get old enough to have children? Let alone multiple children?

"He's beautiful!" I whispered to her.

"Grocery shopping," she replied, her eyes closed.

Just then, Matt appeared, looking disheveled in his suit.

"Oh my God, is she OK?" he said as he raced over to her bed. His tie was askew and his shirt was rumpled.

"She's fine. Sorry you couldn't be here," I said tightly. I crossed my arms over my chest and took a quick step backward.

"Yeah, sorry. I got hung up at work." His eyes briefly met mine before shifting away quickly.

"Sure you did." I curtly nodded and rubbed my forehead.

"Is the baby OK?" he asked as he looked around the room.

"He's fine," I said flatly.

"It's a boy? Oh, wow. That's amazing." Matt's voice carried so little inflection, it was as though I just told him that the Cubs won this afternoon.

"Listen, I'm going to go call her mom and then go home. I'll be back later, OK?" I started toward the recovery room exit.

"Oh, right. Hey, do you think you could stay with her in the hospital tonight? I have a meeting I can't miss," Matt said nonchalantly.

I stared at him, hoping to convey my feelings of I-Wish-You-Would-Burn-in-Hell-and-Get-Your-Right-Arm-Painfully-Cut-Off-by-a-Rusty-Saw.

He just stared back.

"I'm not going to let her be alone," I said. My eyes grew wide.

"Great. Thanks, you're the best, Clare."

So, here I am. At the hospital. Attempting to sleep in one of those chairs that semi-fold out into a very narrow twin bed while wondering how many ads I'd have to place on my blog to earn enough money to hire a hit man for Matt and buy Reese a new husband.

Friday, March 28

. . . .

Ugh.

I'm dead from last night. I think I slept maybe an hour. I took the day off work, but I have Sara home with me.

Today reminds me of the days right after Sara was born and Jake and I operated in this half-awake, half-asleep state that allowed us to perform basic biological functions such as eat and pee but rendered us useless for much else. Not surprisingly, that is also the time when I found myself watching a lot of *Full House* reruns on television while feeding Sara. Anything else would've been futile, as my brain could not comprehend anything above Danny Tanner's cleaning obsessions and Uncle Jesse's mullet. I would definitely watch one today, yet I'm pretty sure I hit every episode by the second week of maternity leave.

Witnessing Reese's train wreck of a marriage only fueled my desire to see Jake and Sara. I immediately threw my arms around Jake when he walked in the door from work this afternoon. Well, my one arm, since I had Sara resting on my hip.

"Hey," he said. "Still tired from last night?" He leaned forward and kissed Sara on the cheek.

"Oh lord, don't ask," I said, and tried to disengage Sara's fingers from my earring. "What do you feel like doing tonight?"

"Don't you have to work on your column this weekend?"

Crap. I forgot.

My first column for *The Daily Tribune* is due on Monday. They ran a story about my blog last year and apparently it got a great response, so they offered me a guest columnist spot. For which I was thrilled, but now I actually have to produce something worth publishing in a newspaper. One that people read, not just one of those crappy free newspapers in the stand next to the auto magazines at Blockbuster. I'm supposed to write about being a new mom, which I think is hilarious, since a couple of months of having a child have left me with zero infinite wisdom or kernels of truth to pass along except for (1) Suck it up. It will get better. If you are lucky. (2) Start happy hour around noon. A few bottles of wine can make anything better. (3) Looking at your butt in the mirror will have dire consequences. Such as your retinas burning off.

"Uh, yeah. Thanks for reminding me. What should I write about?" I asked, and followed him into the bedroom.

"How about why people should order off the Home Shopping Network when they're drunk?" he said, and pointed to the open box on the floor.

"Whatever. Those scarves are cute."

"We don't need matching His and Hers scarves."

"Er, yeah," I said, and discreetly shoved the box of matching gloves under the bed with my foot. "Sara, what do you think I should write about?" I turned to her and asked. She smiled, cooed, and farted loudly. "I'll take that into consideration." I turned to Jake. "Let's go out and grab dinner while she's in a good mood. I can work on my column after she goes to bed."

We got ready and lightly packed Sara's diaper bag (meaning no less than four bottles, twelve diapers, two packs of wipes, two pacifiers, a jingly thing that she likes to look at, three burp cloths, gas drops, and a changing pad) and drove to Adobo Grill for dinner.

Jake and I glanced at each other before we walked in the restaurant, silently communicating our prayers for a quick, calm, peaceful dinner without any infant meltdowns.

Futile prayers, indeed. Sara took our request into consideration, weighed her options carefully, and chose option B: scream head off the second Jake and I order drinks, turn bright red so other diners believe we are choking her and/or injuring her in some way, stiffen up like a board so the only way to hold her is on our laps, with her standing, doing afore-mentioned screaming, resulting in profuse sweating, embarrassment, and general pissed-off mood inside the restaurant.

Before Jake and I had Sara, we vowed we would take Sara out in pub-lic as much as possible. We figured it would be so easy—just put her in the car seat, give her a paci, and Mommy and Daddy can drink margari-tas, right?

Wrong again. We have become more like a highly trained SWAT team or on-call firefighters, ready at a moment's notice to jump into action if she starts crying. Not exactly a relaxing evening out with our child.

As I carried her outside after our Meal O' Shriek, I sadly noted all of the couples taking their time over glasses of wine, sharing appetizers, and generally enjoying themselves. I really wanted to hold Sara up in front of the couple who appeared to be on a date and remind them to use protec-tion, but Jake wouldn't let me.

When people said having a baby would change me, I figured they were right. I just didn't expect that I could never go out to dinner again. I guess I should've enjoyed all those alcohol-soaked dinners in my twen-ties, because now it seems I'm going to be spending quite a large quantity of time indoors watching *Jeopardy!* and eating TV dinners.

The second I was ready to ship Sara off to Bali, she stopped scream-ing. The minute we walked inside, Sara quieted and smiled. She rested her head against my chest and relaxed. As she sighed and wrapped her teeny fingers around a strand of my hair, I whispered, "It's a good thing you're so cute. You just bought yourself more time."

It's amazing. She can take me to the brink of desperation, the edge of the cliff, and offer a little sigh or grin in return. And suddenly it's OK. And I thought Sam had manipulation down pat.

After the Adobo Grill scream-a-thon, there was no way I was ready to write a column for the *Tribune,* so I posted more pictures of Sara on my blog.

"Hey, Jake," I called from inside our bedroom. "Guess what? Wifey1025 just commented that she thinks Sara looks like a Gerber baby model. In fact, she knows someone at Gerber and would love to submit Sara's picture if I could just meet her in the parking lot of Discount Cigarettes 4U at three A.M. tomorrow."

Jake appeared at the doorjamb and leaned against it. "Just make sure to pack your Mace and collapsible billy club."

"Funny," I said as I closed the laptop and stretched my arms over my head. I noticed he was still standing in the doorjamb, smiling. "What?" I said as I retracted my arms.

"Well, I was going to tell you at dinner, but Sara made things too crazy." He walked over to the bed and sat down next to me.

"What?" I said, my voice raised.

I hate surprises. But maybe it's something good, like he won the lottery or something. Yeah, right, that kind of stuff doesn't happen to us. He probably got laid off and I'll have to—

"Clare, relax. It's nothing bad," he said, and laughed. His eyes sparkled a bit. He reached over and took my hand. "My boss called me into his office for a meeting with the VP today."

My ears started ringing. *I knew it. We're screwed. Maybe Princess can get a job.*

"A promotion, Clare. They're giving me a new senior title and a big bump in base salary plus guaranteed bonuses." Jake's hand grew tighter on mine as I allowed his words to settle in the space around me. I stared at him, eyes wide. "Clare?" he said after a few silent moments.

A smile crept across my face, crinkling my eyes and flushing my cheeks. "Really?"

"Yes, really," he said.

I threw myself toward his body and hugged him tight. "That's so amazing! Holy crap! I'm so proud of you!" All of my words ran together as I squeezed him.

Yes! I knew things would get better soon! Maybe we can get a house now!

"Maybe you can stay home now," Jake said into my ear.

I quickly released him and leaned back. "What?" I said as my brow furrowed.

Jake looked down at the bed quickly. "Stay home. With Sara. It's what you want, right?"

"What? When did I say that?" I said, and scooted away from him a bit. "I've never said that." And I hadn't. Truth was, going back to work was always just simply a given, financial need or not.

"You . . . well . . . I guess . . . never." Jake fumbled over his words, confusion twisting his features.

I nodded my head. "Working is hard, but you know how much I like my job and how hard I've worked to get to where I'm at." I shrugged my shoulders and twisted my hands in my lap. "And besides, if I stopped working, we couldn't ever move or take the next step in our lives. It would be like one step forward, two huge steps back."

Jake's arm extended forward as he grabbed my hand again. "We still could move. I think we could still swing it financially. Especially if we weren't paying for day care anymore."

"Even still, I've always planned on being a working mom, so that's what I'm going to do. Like I said, it's hard, but I'm sure it'll get easier." As I said the words, they sounded more like a prayer, a hope, rather than a real belief. I shook my head slightly, as if to clear any opposing thoughts.

"OK, if that's what you want. It's just an option that you'll have if you want. I just want you to be happy," Jake said. He pulled me toward him, against his chest. I hugged him again and tried to ignore the disappointment I thought I saw flash across his face.

Saturday, March 29

. . . .

3:00 P.M.

I have spent most of today saying things like, "I *love* being able to run errands on my lunch hour!" and, "Remember how excited I was to land my
first job in event planning?" Jake is looking at me like I've gone clinically
insane. Truth is, I'm not sure if my proclamations are more for his benefit
or mine.

Naturally, my *Tribune* article is still not done. It didn't help that Jake
and I disappeared into a black hole this afternoon, i.e., Costco.

Ordinarily, I would be too smart to even set foot inside Costco on a
weekend, but my recent lack of sleep has rendered me malleable to nearly
any suggestion, so I agreed. Not to mention, I thought it was a fabulous
procrastination avenue and a wonderful distraction from any Serious
Thinking.

If this is any indication of how it went, my blog entry today was titled: "This Day Needs to Come to Life So I Can Painfully Kill It."

After I pumped Sara up in the car with so much formula Jake and I
could've used her as an inflatable raft in case of a sudden flash flood, we
set forth to the giant windowless building that houses things like five
hundred empanadas in one box. As we walked through the parking lot, I
snickered at the people around me trying to fit things like boxes of seven
thousand Cheese Nips into their trunks until Jake reminded me that the
last time we came here I bought a box of Pringles so large we had to strap
it to the roof of our car.

We walked in the door and I futilely tried to distract Jake from the
huge televisions displayed as we walked in the door.

"I think the diapers are over here." I pointed to the left.

"Just one second," he said, and wandered over to the electronic section.

I sighed and leaned my head forward, resting it on Sara's car seat.

"Your daddy is going to drive me nuts here, isn't he?" I asked her.

She grinned at me and said, "A-Gee," which I took to mean *You can
bet your ass, Mom.*

After ten minutes, I steered the extra-large cart over to Jake.

"We have one of these giant TVs, remember? It makes me nauseous every time I watch it, since our place really isn't big enough for a sixty-inch screen."

Silence as he ignored me and continued to stare at the whopping electronic.

"You know, we should probably get a new television. Thanks to my promotion and all." Jake walked forward and pretended to pet the large black thing. I have no idea what it was, possibly some kind of speaker.

"Jake?" He still didn't move. "JAKE. I DON'T HAVE THE STRENGTH TO ARGUE WITH YOU ABOUT WHY WE DON'T NEED THIS. WE DON'T NEED EYEGLASSES, AN ENGAGEMENT RING, T-SHIRTS, OR RANDOM WEIRD BOOKS OR ANY OF THE OTHER CRAP THEY SELL HERE. CAN WE PLEASE JUST BUY DIAPERS? AND MAYBE SOME VALIUM?"

That did it.

"OK, sorry. I just wanted to see what deals they had. Costco kicks ass."

We made it another ten feet before my husband wandered off again. A Siren, a.k.a. the free-sample-dispenser lady, enticed him to crash his boat into the rocky cliffs by waving around some spring rolls, and I knew I'd lost him. I watched as he jockeyed for position, trying to get a sample amidst all the people who stand in front of the displays for hours on end, jamming free food into their mouths.

He handed me a small cup. "Try it."

He extended his arm, like Eve giving Adam the forbidden fruit. I gave in and tried the spring roll.

"So good!" I proclaimed, and 750 frozen spring rolls entered our cart.

Another five feet and Jake said, "Hey, look! Taquitos!"

This time, I resisted temptation. "Jake, fifteen hundred taquitos would slowly colonize in the freezer, become self-aware, and hypnotize Butterscotch into believing Zoltan is coming down from the cosmos to save him, so he should throw himself out the window to join the spaceship. And they will force me to get really, really fat," I said. The free-sample lady shot me an evil grin as she turned to peddle her wares to a different customer.

"Fine." Jake's shoulders slumped as he pushed the cart away.

As we turned down the aisle with twenty-three thousand Band-Aids in one box, an elderly woman with a very large, silver beehive cooed "How cute! She's adorable!" as she pointed at Sara.

Jake and I smiled at each other, beaming at our supermodel-like daughter.

"Thanks," I said to the elderly woman as I leaned down to pat my daughter.

Sara grinned at her and kicked out her fat, luscious legs.

"What a sweetheart! You look just like your daddy!" the elderly woman said as she patted Jake on his arm.

Jake smiled broadly as she left.

"What?" I said to him as I eyed a seventy-four-ounce bottle of shampoo.

"Nothing. She said I'm cute," he said.

I shook my head. "No, she didn't. She said Sara's cute."

"Yeah, but she said Sara looks just like me. So, that means I'm cute." Jake smiled again, proud of his fabulously attractive appearance.

"What about me? I'm not cute?" I said as I stopped the enormous shopping cart and looked at Jake.

Jake looked thoughtful. "Yeah, you're cute, too. But apparently I'm adorable."

I rolled my eyes and pushed the cart forward.

"Aren't you happy you married someone so adorable? I mean, so your kids could be so cute?" Jake continued.

"You're not going to be adorable in like five seconds after I punch you in the face." I looked over at him and smiled.

"Maybe you'd be more adorable if you didn't threaten me all of the time," Jake said as I steered the cart down the diaper aisle.

"Your dad's nuts," I whispered to Sara. I leaned forward to kiss her and whispered, "You *are* pretty much the cutest child ever to have lived."

Jake reached up and grabbed a huge package of diapers that Sara will no doubt outgrow before it runs out. We'll have to use them in other ways, like for dishrags or possibly materials for an art-mural for above our fireplace.

"You know, if we bought in bulk, we could really save money on our groceries," Jake said.

"Yes, in theory. But we'd spend two hundred and fifty dollars today and how fast do you think it would take us to get sick of only eating Kashi freezer meals, hash browns, and pumpkin pie? We'd still end up at Subway while twenty frozen pizzas languished in our freezer," I said.

Sara cooed in agreement.

As we walked past the alcohol section, Jake wandered off again to check out the wine selection. I put my head down on the front of the cart and wondered if I could sleep just for five minutes. Or maybe I could go to the car and sleep while Jake checked out. Kind of like the afternoons at work when I'd go and sleep in my car at lunch because I was hungover from the night before.

I wearily lifted my head as a crazy woman behind me clipped the backs of my heels with her enormous shopping cart. A huge display of beer caught my eye to my right. Cases of beer, all on sale.

A case of beer. Like in college, when my roommates and I would buy the cheapest beer possible and split it. Before there were important questions to answer like Am I a Bad Mother for Choosing to Work Even Though I Don't Have to Anymore?

"Petite Sirah for eleven ninety-nine!" Jake's voice brought me back to reality. He stood in front of me, holding three bottles of wine. I nodded and exhaled loudly. We steered the cart toward the checkout and waited amongst the chaos.

I longingly looked back at the wine section, remembering the days when Jake and I would stay up until the wee morning hours, not caring how much wine we drank, comforted by the knowledge that we could sleep in as late as we wanted the next day.

"Is Julie's birthday coming up?" Jake said as he pointed to cigarettes sold in groups of ten cartons.

"Ha-ha, very funny," I said. I eyed the couple next to me, who were clearly having a marital meltdown. It was also obviously their first trip to Costco. The husband kept muttering, "But *why* do we need four bottles of ketchup? It's just us two!" as the wife hissed, "It's supposed to save money or something. I don't know, either. But this is how it works."

Jake and I stood in line for twenty minutes, patiently waiting with our items, behind people with giant grocery carts filled to the brim to check out. Then we waited for them to bag their own groceries. Then we waited behind them as the Costco Nazis checked their receipts to make sure they weren't stealing anything. Then we waited for Sara to stop screaming before we left the parking lot.

Total time spent in Costco: two hours.

Total money spent in Costco: $42.95

Items purchased: diapers, spring rolls, and wine. So, if on the way home we are stranded in a snowstorm, we can at least change Sara's diaper three hundred times and consume approximately 57,890 calories.

All in all, quite the productive afternoon.

5:00 P.M.

I still haven't started my column. I asked Jake if he thought I could write eight hundred words on the amazing rate of speed at which Sara's Freddy Krueger–like nails grow and he stared at me for a few seconds before turning back to some football game.

"Well?" I said.

"Sorry, were you serious about that?" he said.

"Jake, you have to help me. I can't think of anything to write that people will want to read." I stood next to him, hands on my hips.

"You write about things like that every day on your blog. And what, something like twenty thousand people read it every day, right?" His eyes were still firmly fixed on the television.

"Yeah, but this is different. It's like important stuff. In February, during my haze of sleep deprivation, I did an entire blog entry about how I pissed I was that Paul Giamatti's character in *Sideways* never got a book deal. I don't think that would be good enough for a regional newspaper." I put my hands over my face and peeked at Jake through my fingers. It had no effect.

"Was that the night we watched *Sideways* and drank like fifty different kinds of wine?" He leaned forward toward the television.

"Yeah, I think so. Anyway, do you have any ideas?"

"Yes! Touchdown!" He leapt in the air, scaring Sara, and she started to wail.

"Very helpful, thanks," I said, and took Sara from his arms and walked toward our bedroom.

"Sorry," he called down the hallway.

Maybe I should write my column on husbands who don't help their wives brainstorm.

10:00 P.M.

I did not work on my column tonight. I instead, in a sort of reverse nesting after the fact, decided to start to baby-proof the entire apartment. I covered electrical sockets, hid all the R-rated movies, and marked the liquor bottles.

Although my column remains unwritten, Jake and I are now prepared for when Sara starts crawling and walking, becomes interested in sex, and starts drinking. Hopefully not all at the same time.

Sunday, March 30

. . . .

8:57 P.M.

My column is written!

After hours spent staring at a blank computer screen, I decided to exploit my own struggles for the sake of material, even though I basically do that every day on my blog. I briefly considered writing about my choice to continue working, now that it's actually a decision rather than a necessity, but I didn't have the emotional fortitude or enough introspection yet to deal with that giant boondoggle of a topic.

Instead, I literally chose to exploit *me*. Namely, my expansive hips and Dumpster-size ass. I wrote about the dreaded post-baby weight or, more accurately, ice-cream-and-Twinkies-every-day-for-nine-months weight. Here's an excerpt:

> From the moment the pee stick turned pink, I knew I would be forever changed in so many ways. It didn't help that my daughter was a surprise and my husband and I were at the stage where we were much more

likely to splurge on a Nintendo Wii than a box of diapers. I didn't know much about having a baby, and I certainly wasn't prepared for how it would change me physically. Sure, I expected sleepless nights and fewer adult dinners, but I honestly didn't fathom wearing stretchy black pants, dubbed Miss Piggy pants, on my first day back to work after maternity leave. No, the weight didn't just "fall off" like so many of those celebrities proclaim. Liars!

It doesn't help that my closet is full of pre-baby low-rise jeans and skinny pants, all of which appear small enough to fit my three-month-old daughter. Even if I never fit into my Seven jeans with the four-inch zipper again, I pray that I never have to resort to wearing high-waisted Mom Jeans with a twelve-inch crotch and elasticized waistband. I'm prepared to concede my tops and leggings forever, but I will never be ready for Mom Jeans.

Monday, March 31

· ·

The verdict on my article is in: it doesn't blow.

My editor called me this morning and congratulated me on a great first column and said, with a few minor changes, the copy was almost perfect. I'm going to be an official, real-live published writer by week's end.

Even though so many people read my blog, it's strange to think people will read my column in an actual newspaper—not just one of those free ones next to apartment guides and stripper advertisements. I'm also slightly regretting that my first widely published article details the size and shape of my love handles, but that milk already be spilled. I mean, I write about personal details all the time on my blog, but that's kind of . . . my space. (Not to be confused with MySpace, landing strip for teenagers and socially stunted adults.) A newspaper is a professional gig and a whole new level of "out there."

I'm going back to the hospital tonight to see Reese. She's doing OK, all things considered. Her mom's been staying with her at the hospital, since Matt's been so busy "working."

I'm going to sneak in a margarita for her—the only thing she requested I bring. I think her words exactly were, "Flowers are always nice, but they don't contain tequila."

10:00 P.M.

I just got home from visiting Reese in the hospital. Thank God Matt wasn't there. I'm too exhausted to make fake-nice conversation with Husband of the Year.

After work, I picked up Sara from day-care and went to the grocery store to buy margarita mix to bring Reese. I figured I'd just get one of those premixed bottles with the tequila already in it, but the only kind they had was the kind that requires adding alcohol. And they didn't sell tequila. So, being the super-klassy-with-a-capital-K mom that I am, I lugged my baby into the liquor store to buy a bottle of tequila.

"Can I help you?" a salesclerk said, eyeing Sara.

"Yeah, where's your tequila?" I said, and shifted Sara's car seat to my other hand while thinking, *Would it be possible for car seat manufacturers to make a heavier car seat? I mean, I really enjoy lugging around thirty pounds of plastic and baby, but I think I'm starting to develop some kind of serious rotator cuff injury.*

"Aisle six," the clerk said.

So, I made my way to aisle six, maneuvering between the woman talking to herself in front of the bourbon and the teenager nervously standing in front of the beer, trying to pick out which beer would make him seem of age. "Heineken," I whispered to him as I breezed past. I finally located the tequila, but all they had were huge jugs of tequila.

So I found the clerk again. "Excuse me, do you have any other bottles of tequila?"

"What are you looking for?"

"I need something smaller."

"Smaller?"

"Yeah, something that will fit in this." I pointed to my diaper bag.

He looked quizzically at me, no doubt calculating how fast he could grab the phone and dial Child Protective Services.

"I'm going to the hospital and I need something to fit inside my diaper bag." That explanation didn't seem to make the look of *you are the worst mother ever and possibly a raging alcoholic* disappear from his face.

"We have pints of tequila behind the register," he finally said, shaking his head.

"It's not for me. It's for my friend," I tried to explain.

"Honey, that's what I tell myself every time I come here," the woman who had been talking to herself in front of the bourbon said behind me. "Nothing wrong with a cocktail after work. Or a whole bottle."

"I know, I mean, no, it's really not—never mind." I turned and headed toward the register.

"The cigarettes are up there, too," the clerk called out to me, and snickered.

Reese thought my baby / liquor store incident was quite funny.

"Oh God, don't make me laugh." She winced and gestured to her abdomen. She lay back in her bed, her baby-blond hair fanned out around her head. God, it's disgusting. Even in the hospital after a C-section and doped up on narcotics, Reese looked beautiful. After I had Sara, I think some of the nurses thought I was receiving charity care. One of the nurses even kept mentioning, "You know, you're free to use the shower," despite the fact I showered twice a day.

"Oh, sorry. How are you feeling?"

"Better." She reached for her hospital tray and picked up a giant pink plastic pitcher of water.

"So where's the little guy?" Sara started to fuss, so I let her suck on my car keys.

"Clare!" Reese shrieked, nearly spitting out her water.

"What? It's fine." I shrugged but quickly grabbed the keys out of Sara's mouth. "So where's the little chunk?"

"He's in the nursery for the infant hearing screening. Brendan, by the way." Reese smiled.

"What a cool name. Brendan is definitely a hot guy name. He'll be a hit with the girl babies."

"He only needs to be a hit with one." She pointed to Sara, who was transfixed by the ceiling tiles.

"Right, should we start planning their wedding now or wait until their first birthdays?"

"Eh, give it at least a month or two."

"Hey, you've got a great view." I walked toward her room's window to try to get a better look at the garden below. But instead of gazing out the window angelically, I did something very, very Clare. I didn't realize the window was a double pane and bounced my head off the first pane of glass. "Shit!" I said, and rubbed my head.

"Ow, ow, ow! I told you not to make me laugh!" Reese patted her abdomen again.

"I'm fine." I rubbed my head and looked at Sara, who smiled widely, as though to say, *You're such a dumbass, Mom, but it certainly is entertaining.*

"Sorry, this time it wasn't intentional. I'm like an accidental Patch Adams. Maybe I should go down to the pediatric ward and cheer up some sick kids."

"Just as long as you don't say, 'Shit,' next time."

I noticed a copy of *Goodnight Moon* next to her bed. "Another copy?" I said as I picked it up.

"Yep, now we have one for every room in the house. People just love to give that book. But that's OK, it is pretty darn good."

"I should write a version for new moms called *Good-bye Life,*" I said.

"What, like 'Good-bye showers, good-bye skinny jeans'?"

"Good-bye pretty hair, good-bye social life everywhere."

"Oh, come on, it's not that bad," she said, and smiled.

"I know." I laughed.

"I know. How's the new daddy handling everything?"

"He's doing well. We're both just so exhausted all of the time and there's basically no alone time, since I usually collapse ten minutes after Sara goes to bed. I vaguely remember sex. I think it made me pregnant or something. I don't know, I don't really remember." I shrugged as I picked at my cuticles. A voice in my head whispered, *Maybe you and Jake would have sex more if you weren't working full-time. You wouldn't be as tired, right?*

"I remember those exhausted, random fights over what brand of baby wipes to buy." Reese's voice interrupted the stay-at-home-mom devil on my shoulder.

"Oh yeah, big-time. Last week, I became unreasonably furious because he wouldn't listen to me about how to properly adjust the straps on the Baby Bjorn. I threatened to call Customer Service so they could properly teach him. Then he accused me of buying cheap diapers but splurging on expensive shampoo and we wound up not speaking for an hour." I folded my hands in my lap, still irritated that Baby Bjorn's customer service took Matt's side.

"Ah, yes, the important things in life. Matt and I don't even fight anymore, it's like it's not worth—" She stopped herself and her eyelids blinked rapidly for a moment until she shook her head. "Let's see what's on television, shall we?"

I hung out with her for a while and mixed us a couple margaritas while we watched a rerun of *Grey's Anatomy* until Sara decided she'd had enough of the hospital, margaritas, Reese, me, and behaving in general, so I hugged Reese and we left. I'm so proud I was able to stifle any questions about Matt. Another fifteen minutes, though, and the dam in my mouth might've exploded and I might've blurted out, *WHY AREN'T YOU DRAWING UP DIVORCE PAPERS RIGHT NOW?*

This must be a sign of maturity: a growing ability to not to blurt out inappropriate questions.

Next up: how to wear white without spilling anything on myself.

Friday, April 11
· ·

"We be pimp chillin' in Sara's hot tub. Me an' my peeps won't you bring four of your friends," I sang to the melody of Chingy's "Holidae Inn" to Sara as I gave her a bath.

"What are you singing to our infant daughter?" Jake called from the next room.

"Just some Chingy," I said. "You love Chingy, don't you? You love it because you have no idea what he's saying, do you?" I cooed to Sara, and she looked very serious.

"Ahgoo," she replied.

"Do you know you're singing a song to our daughter that starts with the words 'bomb ass pussy'?" He walked into the kitchen and placed his hands on the counter and looked at me with his eyebrows raised.

"No, it doesn't," I said quickly, and turned away from him.

"Yeah, it does. Maybe you could just go all the way and get her some gold teeth."

"Jake, I figure we have a small window where we can say whatever we want without her going to preschool and telling her teacher that her mommy called another driver a douche bag, so I'm trying to get all the 'Fuck Shit Fuck Motherfucker Assholes' out now. In two years we'll be forced to watch *High School Musical* and *Hannah Montana* over and over." I lifted Sara out of her bath and wrapped a hooded towel around her.

"Good point. Rap away. Maybe we can let her hang out with Julie's dad. I'm sure she could pick up some great new words." Jake reached out and took her from my arms. Sara peered at him beneath her hooded robe, looking like a midget wizard.

"Whatever. I'd rather she hung out with Julie's dad in his trailer than with your friend Bill-Until-Two-Months-Ago-I-Still-Lived-with-My-Parents."

"You look like Obi-Wan Kenobi," he whispered to her as he brought her over to the changing table. "Hey, what time are we dropping her off at your parents' house tomorrow?" he asked.

"For what?" I crinkled my eyes and squinted at him.

"The wedding, remember?" he said in an exasperated tone.

I stared blankly at him, as though he just spoke in Finnish. No comprendo.

"Carrie and Patrick's wedding." Carrie, Jake's only normal relative, is definitely getting married in two weeks. I know this because I've been alternately dreading and looking forward to her wedding. Because Carrie and her friends are awesome, yet my mother-in-law and sister-in-law are not.

"That's not tomorrow." I shook my head firmly.

"Yes, it is." He nodded and took a step toward me.

"No, it's not. It's next week."

Why can't men ever get a date right?

"Tomorrow."

"Jake," I said, exasperated, "I'll show you, it's right here on the . . ." I walked over to the fridge and pulled off the Save the Date magnet. "Shit," I whispered. My brain is so overloaded with details for the golf outing, topics for my column, and grocery lists that it's like a leak sprang and information keeps seeping out.

"Told you," he called from the next room. "Sara, don't throw a baby kegger at your grandparents' house tomorrow. I don't want to hear about any kegs of formula or you sneaking out to the baba bar, OK?" he said to her.

I walked around the corner. "What the hell am I going to wear?"

He shrugged, his stained San Francisco IT conference 2005 T-shirt bunching around the neck. I hate that shirt, as it is probably the geekiest shirt ever created. It has a drawing of a laptop computer holding a drink and says, " 'Puter Party."

I wish I were kidding about this.

"Nothing fits yet. Shit! Do you think I could get away with my Miss Piggy pants?" My voice squeaked out in a decibel six levels too high.

He stared at me as he adjusted his T-shirt sleeves.

"I guess not. I'm so screwed." I flew to my closet and pulled out every dress I owned and yanked off my clothes. I found most of the dresses would require a serious amount of Crisco, a shoehorn, and possible removal of some internal organs to wear, thanks to the ten pounds of Sara still sitting on my midsection. With the aid of some Spanx, though, I was able to squeeze into a basic black tank dress I bought after gaining the Freshman Fifteen in college, which I reasoned I could accessorize with sparkly earrings.

Unfortunately, the dress had a small cigarette burn toward the bottom of the hemline from when Julie dropped her cigarette on me after hearing another keg was tapped. It's practically unnoticeable to most people. Except my mother-in-law is not most people. She will definitely notice it, comment on it, and probably point it out to others. I just hope she wears her hideous fuchsia 1987 prom dress. Because I don't mind being insulted by someone who is dressed like Rainbow Brite.

Saturday, April 2

. . . .

I knew it would be a torturous evening when Jake and I arrived at the church a few minutes late, due to the fact that getting out the door with Sara is about as simple as a shuttle launch. We were so late that we wound up walking in with the bride. The bridesmaids had already gone down the aisle, so the entire church was standing up and staring at the back of the church, expecting Carrie and her dad to walk down the aisle. Instead, Jake and I slunk in, red-faced and disheveled. Thankfully, Carrie is the only normal person in Jake's family and she laughed as she saw us come in.

Marianne did not and as soon as we sat down leaned over and hissed, "You've ruined the wedding. It's so embarrassing when my own son can't even show up on time," while Natalie smugly smiled and patted Ash Leigh on her lap.

"I can't believe they brought their baby," I whispered to Jake, and poked him in the ribs. He nodded and shrugged.

I couldn't reach the bar fast enough after we got to the reception. Jake and I had just taken long swigs of our ice-cold beers from frosty mugs when Marianne appeared.

"Hello, you two. I see you didn't waste any time ordering alcohol." She wagged her finger in front of us.

I took another long swig of my beer and eyed her shocking-pink taffeta dress with ruffles jutting out at odd angles, making it resemble a pseudo–Judy Jetson skirt.

"You look lovely, Marianne," I said sweetly.

"Thanks." She surveyed me up and down. "Still a few pounds to lose?"

My face burned as I quickly adjusted my Spanx. My dress was a little too tight and I suddenly wished for my Miss Piggy pants. Or my old ass.

"Clare looks great, Mom," Jake said quickly.

Marianne tittered. "Of course she does, I was just teasing." She craned her neck around the room. "Did you see Ash Leigh with Natalie? Isn't she getting so big?"

I held back from saying, *Who? Natalie or Ash Leigh?* and said, "Yep. It's so great that Natalie and Doug brought her. I'm so glad she didn't cry during the ceremony." I signaled to the bartender for another drink.

"You know Natalie's relationship with her own mother isn't so strong, so Frank and I are really the only babysitters she has. She won't allow anyone but family to watch her precious baby. Isn't she such a good mom?"

Her mother must be a genius. Must find way to make my relationship with Jake's family "not so strong," I thought as I drummed my fingers against the bar and waited for another drink.

"Oh, there they are! Natalie! Over here." Marianne waved them over. Natalie and Doug walked over, Ash Leigh in tow.

"How's it going?" Doug said, and shook Jake's hand and kissed me on the cheek.

"Great. Even better with a couple of nice cold beers," Jake said.

"Sign me up for that," Doug said, and waved to the bartender.

"Hi, Natalie, you look wonderful," I said to her.

"Thanks, Clare. So do you." She stared at the burn mark on the bottom of my dress.

Jake and Doug wandered off to go pillage the appetizer buffet while I was stuck in In-law Hell.

"Hey there, Ash Leigh, you look like a little princess." I leaned forward and stroked Ash Leigh's hand and her face contorted and she screamed and buried her face in Natalie's shoulder.

"Nice going, Clare," Natalie said.

"When did you pierce her ears?" I said.

"Just last week."

"I love little girls with pierced ears, don't you?" Marianne chimed in.

"Definitely," I said.

"Thanks for coming, everyone!" Carrie appeared next to us. "Can you believe I'm married?"

"Congratulations! You look stunning!" I said as I drooled over her gorgeous ivory silk ball gown.

"Thanks. Oh, beer, that sounds awesome. I'll take one!" I handed her a beer and she took a long swig of it. "So how are you guys?"

"We're doing very well. I just love being a mom to my sweet little girl," Natalie said.

"God, she's getting so big, Natalie!"

Again, I had to fight the urge not to chime in, *Just like her mom!* I'm not one to throw stones, seeing as how losing the baby weight hasn't been the easiest thing in the world, but Natalie falls squarely in the "morbidly obese" range.

I'd say anywhere from 250 to 300 pounds.

On a day when gravity isn't so strong.

"And how nice that you brought her," Carrie said, her mouth twitching.

"I just don't trust anyone to watch her other than family. I just couldn't imagine leaving her with total strangers. Sorry," Natalie said, turning to me.

"What?" I said, totally distracted after having spotted an ice sculpture with chilled cosmopolitan running through it.

"Did you hear that Clare and Jake use day-care?" Marianne asked Carrie. Except she mouthed the word "day-care" as though it was too terrible to vocalize.

Carrie knew that was her signal to get the hell out rather than be stuck in the middle of another one of Marianne's passive-aggressive tirades. "Gotta run! Lots of people to see!" She leaned forward and whispered in my ear, "Just drink heavily," before she left.

At least Jake has one splendid relative.

"But Clare, now that Jake got his promotion, aren't you able to stay home?" Marianne said, sticking her finger a little further into the wound.

I smiled at her and slightly shook my head. "I like my job. It's hard to work full-time, but I really love it."

Marianne's eyes flashed before her face relaxed. "But wouldn't you love to spend every day with Sara?"

Yes, my brain said automatically. I wanted to tell Marianne that working is like being ripped into two clean halves every day. I wanted to say that there's no easy, black-and-white answer like "yes" or "no." But then the dinner bell rang and the conversation was over.

At dinner, halfway through the goat cheese and endive salad, Doug turned to me. "So, Clare, I read your essay in *The Daily Tribune*. Cheers to the writer in the family." He lifted his vodka tonic and took a sip.

"Thanks," I said.

"Mom, did you read Clare's column?" Jake asked Marianne.

"Oh no, dear, did it run yet?" Marianne looked confused.

"Yes, just this last week," I said.

"Hmm," Marianne said, and furrowed her brows. Well, as much as she could furrow them thanks to Dr. Ashiel and her Joan Rivers amazing brow lift. "You know who is a very good writer? Nicholas Sparks. So romantic. Maybe you could write like him," Marianne said.

"I'm sure her writing is just fine," Jake's dad, Frank, interjected gruffly, silencing the table.

"Clare, do you still have one of those log things?" Natalie said as she dabbed at Ash Leigh's mouth.

"Do you mean blog?" I said. I watched with great satisfaction as Ash Leigh clocked Natalie right across the face.

Kids. It's like they instinctually know who deserves a punch in the face and can completely get away with doing so.

"Whatever, the thing on the Internet or something." She waved her arm around dismissively, like this thing called the Internet was one of those newfangled technology whozywhatzits that the kids nowadays were a-talkin' about.

"Yes, I still have my blog." I braced myself for the inevitable response.

"You know thousands of people read it every day, right, Mom?" Jake said.

"Oh yes, I'm sure. But I don't really ever have time to use the computer. I'm just so busy with going out to lunch with my friends and my housekeeping. That's nice that other people read it," Marianne said as she waved to someone across the room.

I zoned out after Natalie complimented Jake on "helping" me take care of Sara. As though he had a choice and should be lauded for his sacrifices and for giving me a "break." Instead of responding, I focused on remembering all the lyrics to R.E.M.'s "It's the End of the World As We

Know It (and I Feel Fine)." As soon as dinner ended, I grabbed Jake's arm and towed him over to the bar.

"Your mother and Natalie are killing me," I said.

"I know. I'm sorry she's driving you nuts. We'll just hang out here, near the bar." Jake put twenty dollars into the tip jar on the bar and nodded at the bartender, then leaned forward and kissed me.

"Can I get a shot of you two?" The wedding photographer appeared next to us.

We obliged and turned toward the camera and smiled.

"OK, great. Look right here," he said, and positioned his camera. "OK, OK, great, ready? Smile!" he said, and dropped his camera down to the level of his crotch and took the picture. "Good one," he said, and walked away before either of us could react.

"Did we just get our picture taken from a guy's crotch?" Jake asked, looking confused.

"I think so," I said. We watched the photographer move around the room, doing the same thing to other guests, leaving them befuddled as he left.

"What if that's really not the photographer but just some sick guy who wants people to look at his crotch?" I said.

"Like if he didn't even have film in the camera?" Jake said.

"Hey, did you guys get your picture by some guy's penis?" Doug said from behind us.

"Yes! What do you think the deal is with that?" I said.

"Either some pervert or it's a new style technique in photography," Doug said.

"Whatever the reason, it necessitates a glass of wine," Jake said, and signaled the bartender again.

I reached into my purse to grab my lip gloss and felt photographs. I pulled them out.

"Jake, did you want to show these pictures of Sara to your great-aunt before you get too impaired? She's been asking to see them forever." I waved the photographs around and gestured toward Aunt Ellen's table.

"Oh yeah, good idea," he said, and put down his drink.

I grabbed a bottle of water off the bar and we walked over to Great-aunt Ellen, who was delighted to see new pictures of baby Sara. Until she came upon a picture of Jake holding Sara in the Baby Bjorn.

"Oh no! You don't put her in one of those, do you?" Aunt Ellen looked alarmed.

"The Baby Bjorn? They're totally safe, Aunt Ellen," Jake said. "She won't fall out."

"Fall out? I'm not talking about her falling out. Those things can hurt a little baby's . . ." She trailed off and nodded at me, like I was supposed to know what the hell she was talking about.

"Hurt what?" I couldn't resist asking.

"You know, this area," she whispered, and motioned to her lap.

"Oh no, that's . . . fine. That . . . isn't hurt at all," Jake said.

"No! It does hurt them! She might not be able to have children! And little boys—did you know those can push their penis back inside their body?"

That did it. I was in the middle of taking a sip of water and I nearly spit it out.

"Sorry, sorry," I said, choking.

"Promise me you won't use that ever again! Don't you want to be a grandmother someday?" crazy Aunt Ellen asked me.

"For sure, I promise!" I said enthusiastically, nodding my head. "I think your aunt is off her meds again," I whispered to Jake as we walked back to the bar. Aunt Ellen was also off her meds at our wedding, when she asked if Jake and I had met while dancing in the circus.

An hour later, when Marianne suggested we hold a family vote as to who was cuter—Ash Leigh or Sara?—I signaled to Jake and we left.

In summary, I did not kill anyone or, more important, myself yesterday.

That's all I can really ask for when I am forced to spend time with my in-laws.

Monday, April 14

We had dinner tonight at my parents' house since we missed Sunday night dinner due to my pounding headache caused by thousands of pints of ale and Marianne's nasally voice.

Dinner was not what I would call awesome.

It started off business as usual as we arrived. My mom was in the kitchen, simultaneously stirring beef stew, typing an Excel spreadsheet on her laptop, and watching the news while my dad sorted through the mail.

"Hey, you two! Come on in, dinner's almost ready," my mom said, and gestured for us to sit down.

"There's my beautiful granddaughter!" my dad said, and rushed over to Sara, still in her car seat.

"Be careful, Dad, she's been a beast today," I said.

"She probably just missed her grandparents," he said, and jiggled her little foot as my mom walked over, too.

Sara took one look at them and started wailing.

"She's probably thinking, 'Oh no, not these two again.'" My mom laughed.

"She should be so lucky," Jake said.

"Where's the siblings?" I asked.

"Mark's watching some game on TV and Sam's upstairs on her phone. She had a really rough weekend, so give her a break," my mom said.

"What happened?"

"From what I can tell, something about her best friend going out with some guy she liked. Anyway, she was sick all day yesterday and stayed home from school today."

Jake and I exchanged knowing looks.

"Sick or hungover?" I asked.

"She's not—I don't—hungover, probably," my mom sighed.

"Who's hungover?" Sam asked as she walked into the kitchen. She had eyeliner smudged around her bloodshot eyes and her face was pasty white.

Oh yeah, definitely a hangover.

"You," I said.

Sam rolled her eyes and flicked her long, straight hair, with hundreds of dollars' worth of products in it, over her shoulder and put her hand on her hip. "Whatevs. Why are you so annoying?"

"Not sure," Jake responded evenly.

"No, seriously. You think you're so cool, but you're not." Sam threw her arms over her head and her shirt lifted. I could see she had a belly button ring with a bejeweled dragonfly dangling from it.

"Did you hear that, Jake, we ain't cool!" I laughed as I brought my hand to my cheek.

"Dorks," she muttered. She leaned forward and peered at Sara. After a moment, Sam turned to my mom and asked, "Why's her head so big?"

I reminded myself strangling my sister in my parents' kitchen with her iPod earphones would probably not make for a relaxing dinner. Jake rolled his eyes and went into the family room.

"Her head's fine, Sam," I heard my mom say as she picked Sara up.

Sam shrugged and shuffled out of the room.

"I'm going to go find Mark," I said, and jogged out of the room. I found him sprawled out on the couch in the dark watching a baseball game.

"Cubs winning?" I asked as I kicked him a little on the couch.

"No, losing. As usual. What's new?" he said in the darkness.

"Nothing besides plotting new ways to kill our sister." I sat down next to him.

"Always good family fun," he said. "Hey, I wanted to ask you something?"

"Why are you such a leech who practically lives at Mom and Dad's when you have your own apartment in the city?" I said quickly.

"No. I already know the answer to that one and it involves the fact that my apartment doesn't have toilet paper or food. I wanted to ask you: what's a good restaurant in the city?" he asked.

"For what occasion?" I asked him as I stood up and flicked on the light.

"Ow, not cool," he said, and squinted his eyes. "To take a, um, friend."

"Like a date?" I said, and stood over him.

"No, not a date. Like a friend who is just cool," he muttered.

"Right, sure. Do you love her? Do you want to marry her?" I clapped my hands together.

"Forget it, this is why I never tell you anything," he said, and turned his eyes back to the television.

"OK, OK. Um, take her to Nacional 27. Good music, good food, and even better drinks." I nodded.

"Thanks. Was that so hard?" He stared at the television, ignoring me.

"So, who is she?" I punched him on the arm.

"Just someone I went to college with." Mark grabbed the remote and turned the volume up.

"Do I know—"

"Dinner's ready!" my mom called from the kitchen.

"Just don't talk with your mouth full," I said to him, and punched him on the arm again as he stood up off the couch.

"She's out," Jake said as I walked into the kitchen. I looked down at Sara, angelically asleep in her car seat.

We all sat down for dinner.

"This stew is great," Jake said as he shoveled the beef into his mouth.

"Hmmm . . . mmmhhmmm," Mark said.

"What was that?" my mom asked.

"What? I'm trying not to talk with my mouth full," he said, and smiled at me.

"Thank god, it's only taken twenty-three years," my dad said, and passed me the bread. "Sam, bread?"

"What? Oh no." She didn't even look up from her US Weekly, totally engrossed in a story about Suri Cruise.

"Sam, could you put down the magazine and talk to your family during dinner?" my mom said.

Sam didn't respond.

"Sam?" She tried again.

"SAM!" This time I yelled.

"Jeez, relax. This whole family is so effing psycho. Mark and Clare do,

like, whatever and I'm the one who gets ripped on." She threw her magazine down on the floor, narrowly missing Sara, and crossed her arms.

"Get over it," my mom said to her. "Clare," she said, turning to me, "I
never got a chance to congratulate you on your essay. We all loved it."

Sam perked up. "Yeah," she said enthusiastically.

I almost asked if she was kidding. A warm feeling came over me like,
*She likes me! She likes my writing! She thinks I'm a cool big sister! She wants to
hang out and be best friends!*

"I was wondering, since you're a writer or something, if you will write
my college entrance essays?" she said.

And . . . back to reality.

"What?"

"My. Essays. College. You. Write. Do. Understand. English. You?" Sam's
eyes widened and she stared at me.

Jake started laughing and he and Mark high-fived each other, like
they always do whenever Sam says something particularly obnoxious.

Before I had a chance to respond, my mom put her hands out.

"Enough. We're done."

"Really? It was just starting to get funny, Mom," Mark said.

"Ew, what's wrong with you? Why do you have to be so—," Sam
started.

"YOUR MOM SAID, 'ENOUGH'!" my dad yelled.

We all jumped a little and knew we'd gone too far if we'd pissed my
dad off. He was mild-mannered; the only time I'd ever seen him truly
blow up was when Mark was in high school and he and his friends chopped
down our neighbors' tree while they were on vacation to use the wood to
build a bonfire.

We all sat silently, admonished.

"Guys, listen. We have to talk to you about something." The catch in
my mom's voice made all of our heads snap up in unison and look at her.
She looked at my dad and continued. "It's really no big deal. I don't want
anyone to worry, or to freak out."

I knew right then I wasn't prepared for whatever was going to come
out of her mouth next. I just sat frozen, my heart pounding.

"I went to the doctor a few weeks ago and they found a lump in my right breast," she continued.

The ears began ringing and I prayed she would stop and say, *Just kidding! Let's have dessert!*

"I had a biopsy done and it came back malignant."

She stopped and took a deep breath and my dad squeezed her hand. We all just continued staring at her.

"Malignant is . . . ?" Mark asked.

"Malignant is bad. Malignant means"—she took another breath—"cancer."

There are very few words in the English language that inspire instant dread, instant nausea. "Cancer" is definitely at the top of the list.

I looked at Jake, who looked like he'd turned to stone. Sam was quietly examining her nails and Mark was turning red.

"This is bullshit!" Mark exploded, and slammed his fist against the table, causing all of us to jump. "You're totally healthy. How the fuck does something like this happen?" He jumped up and paced around the table.

Sara woke up and started wailing. I mutely went over to her and picked her up, feeling as though my insides were hollowed out.

"Mark, I'm going to be fine. We caught it early. Fine, I'm going to be fine," my mom repeated.

I wordlessly handed Sara to Jake. I didn't know what to say. I didn't know what questions to ask. I felt like I should react, but I didn't know how. So I just sat in my chair and stared at the patterns on the wood floor.

I saw mascara-stained tracks across Sam's face. I stood up and walked around the table. I tried to put my arm around her, but she jerked away.

"I'm fine. I'm just worried," she said, and wiped her face.

My mom explained that even though they caught it early, the doctors still wanted her to go through radiation and chemo as a precaution. Radiation and chemo mean real-life sick stuff. They mean she really has cancer. They mean sickness, losing her hair, exhaustion . . .

I don't understand why this is happening. My mom has always been there for every one of us. She's been a great person her whole life; she's been a healthy person. She used to run fucking marathons in college. This feels like one big joke, like I'm expecting God to jump out from behind the bushes and say, *Gotcha! Man, you should've seen the looks on your faces! Oh, and here is a million dollars for your troubles.*

Life is supposed to get better every year, not worse.

And Sara.

What would Sara do without her grandmother?

What would I do without my mother?

I need more time with her.

Oh God.

I can't even begin to think like that.

She's going to be fine. She's going to be great.

Everything's going to be fine.

She's going to get through this with flying colors and we'll all have a big party. Maybe she and my dad can even take a trip or something to celebrate.

So, yeah. She's going to beat it.

Fuck you, cancer.

Tuesday, April 15

I went to work this morning, kept my head down, and slunk into my office. I couldn't deal with anyone, least of all Mule Face. She has an uncanny ability to sense when something's wrong, and the last thing I wanted was for her to twist the knife in my heart any deeper by asking asinine questions. Thankfully, though, as I turned on my computer I heard Christina mention to Abby, the receptionist, that Mule Face was out for a few days due to a severe allergic reaction to one of the facial creams she peddled from her mail-order catalogs. Normally, that news would make me smirk, but all I felt was relief.

It's hard to feel much of anything, though.

Jake stayed up late with me last night, saying and doing all the right things, but my body still feels completely hollowed out.

I sat at my desk for ten minutes this morning before I felt compelled to *do* something, so I went to my trusty friend Google, who helped me when I first discovered I was pregnant, and started looking up as much information as I could find about breast cancer. I skimmed a few articles until I caught sight of Scary Things like survival and remission rates, so I quickly closed the Internet. I sat at my desk and stared at my penholder for a while, wondering if the workers in the pen factory who made my black pen knew anyone who had cancer. Even just that word: "cancer." They need to come up with a new way to describe it, something that sounds hopeful, like "Kinda Serious but Your Mom Will Be Fine" disease.

As I kicked around the covers last night in bed, one sentence ran through my head like a neon marquee: I need more time with her.

With my mom. With my daughter.

And I was brought right back to the same question, the same dilemma. If my family is the most important thing in the world, if my world can crumble so quickly due to my mom's illness, what am I doing here at work?

Don't I owe it to Sara, to myself, to at least consider the option of spending our days together?

I was so engrossed in my mental battle, I completely forgot about my meeting with Greg this afternoon at the golf club until I caught sight of the meeting reminder on my calendar. So I jumped into my car and flew over to the club as fast as was humanly possible. I found him inside, waiting, looking bemused.

"Sorry, I'm so sorry! Traffic!" I panted.

"Sure there was." He smiled knowingly at me. "You forget we dated. I think the only thing you were ever on time for was a beer pong contest."

Uncomfortable that he referenced my, um, less-than-professional days, I said, "Uh, yeah. Sure." I quickly regained my composure. "Let's go meet with the club's golf pro, shall we?"

"Sounds good," Greg said, and we walked over to the pro shop.

"Len Kasper, please," I said to the clerk, a teenaged boy who looked incredibly bored.

"Sure," he mumbled, and trudged his body over to an office, clearly very put out from having to stop texting on his phone. "Some people are here," he announced.

Len appeared outside his office. "Clare Finnegan?" he asked.

"That's me," I said, and shook his hand.

"And Greg. How's everything going, Mr. Thompson?"

I smiled at his formal greeting. Len looked quizzically at me.

"Sorry, it's just . . . nothing," I stammered.

"I address all of our club members formally," Len said stiffly. "Let's go into my office."

"Yes! Let's!" I said just a bit too enthusiastically.

We sat down in Len's office and I quickly became aware he was much more comfortable speaking to a male.

"So, we're going to have a shotgun start, right?" I asked Len, glancing at my notes.

"Yes, shotgun start at eleven A.M.," Len said to Greg.

"And you know we're giving prizes out to the winning foursomes for things like best score, longest drive, and closest to the pin, right?"

"Yes, I have it all here." Len smiled at Greg.

"And everything is set up for the golfers' lunch and dinner, right?"

"The menu is complete, Mr. Thompson."

It started to become a game.

"Len, if you could just review this list here of the foursomes." I stuck the paper in front of him. "Look here at the handicaps for the golfers." I pointed to the third column. "Does everything look copacetic?"

"Sure does." He lifted his head and craned his head to nod at Greg.

I pretty much gave up at that point.

A few minutes later, we all stood up and Len shook Greg's hand and said, "You've really got everything covered, Mr. Thompson, this is going to be a great event because of you."

Greg didn't say a word the entire meeting. I think he grunted once.

"So, are you hungry?" Greg asked as we walked back toward the lobby of the club.

"I'm good, thanks," I said quickly. I was still exhausted from last night. I think I got about an hour of sleep in between crying hysterically, and obsessively searching on the Internet for rah-rah breast cancer survival stories. Not to mention all the questions popping up in my brain like in that Whac-a-Mole game.

Should I really consider staying home? Would I be happier if—

"Are you sure? The food here is great. My treat." He smiled at me.

"I'm not really hungry, but thanks," I said, and pointedly fished around in my purse for the keys.

"We should probably eat, though, we need to make sure the quality of the food is still up to snuff for the event."

He had me on a technicality. It was a good idea to do a tasting before the event.

"OK, fine. But I can't stay long." I sighed. I prayed the dark circles under my eyes would magically disappear. Much like my memories of last night.

"Great," he said, and pointed toward the dining room.

I was determined to keep the conversation strictly professional, but before I even had a chance to order a Diet Coke, he started with the personal questions.

"So, tell me what Jake's up to these days."

"Um, IT sales," I said, and delicately sipped my water.

"Sounds like it. And you guys are doing well?" Greg brushed an invisible piece of lint off the tablecloth and looked at me earnestly.

"Great! Better than ever! We're fantastic!" I felt like Pollyanna on uppers, but I hoped if I seemed *really, really* excited he'd lay off.

"Good to hear. How're Julie and Reese?"

"They're doing well," I said quickly. I mentally sat on the words: *Why do you care? You never seemed thrilled about my friends anyway.*

"That's great. Tell them I said hello," he said.

"Sure." I nodded and thought about Julie's response. Which would include several four-letter words and a few obscene hand gestures. "So, how's everything with your friends?" I avoided mentioning his friends by name, as though they were so insignificant and unimportant, I couldn't be bothered with remembering each one personally.

Greg nodded. "Great." He smiled, flashing his white teeth. "Couple are married, couple are single. I was just in Ethan's wedding." He laced his fingers together on the tablecloth as I nodded.

"Great, great!" I smiled, even though the ticker running across my brain said, *Who the hell would marry Ethan? That guy is the biggest asshole on the planet.*

"Yeah, he's pretty happy. Just bought a place out in the suburbs. On the North Shore. Right on Lake Michigan."

I kept the smile pasted on my face, willing my features to show no discernible dismay. But seriously? North Shore? Right on the lake? There had to be more zeros attached to that sale price than chips in my nail polish.

"His wife is great. She used to work in advertising but now volunteers and things like that." Greg shrugged.

"Sounds fabulous!" I said brightly.

I was suddenly and furiously aware of the great divide. The chasm between Those Who Can Buy Million-Dollar Houses at Thirty and the rest of us. And just how firmly I belonged in the second group.

Working mom. Long hours. Never enough time, quiet moments, sleep. No volunteering.

But it doesn't have to be like that, whispered the voice on my shoulder.

"How's work?" I said before my thoughts began to appear across my face.

"Business is good. Sales are up. Even though the market's not doing so well, my investments are." He said it nonchalantly, like he wasn't just in *Crain's Chicago Business* 30 under 30 last month thanks to the success of his law firm.

I nodded, like, *Yeah. Totally. I totally have investments, too. I definitely don't have ANY credit card debt, car payments, student loans, or anything like that. Just investments. Good ones.*

"Still living in the city?" I said instead.

"Of course. I can't imagine living in the suburbs, can you?" He laughed.

"Um, yeah. Jake and I moved out of the city a couple of years ago."

"Oh, well, sure, it makes sense. Of course." He shifted uncomfortably.

"We like it." I shrugged.

"Do you have a minivan, too?" Greg teased, and flashed his white teeth.

"No! But what's so wrong with minivans? I mean, the extra space would be nice and there's a lot of room for my groceries and—" I stopped when I saw the teasing look in his eye. "Yeah, yeah," I said, and smiled. "So what if I'm domesticated now?"

"There's something I never thought you'd be."

"What?" I said, and stared at him.

"Nothing. You just always talked in college about how you never wanted to have kids or live in the suburbs." He crossed his arms across his chest and smiled at me.

He had me there. "I know, but . . ." I trailed off. "Things change. People change. Plans change," I finished. Suddenly uncomfortable again, I said, "We really should order. I have to get back to the office."

I opened my menu and pretended to study it. But his words rang true in my head. *I never wanted this.* Well, at least at one point in my life I didn't. I planned on living in the city ("suburbs are for people who can't make it in the city"), remaining childless ("kids are for people who don't like to sleep in"), and having lots of disposable income ("beach house in South Carolina").

In ten years, it was as though my life wholly shifted from white to black, without stopping to hang out in the gray for a while.

Not to mention, at one point I thought that I would spend my white life with Greg—expansive condo in the city, the best restaurants, country club memberships, important friends with clout. I don't care about most of those things anymore, but I do wonder how I got from point A to Z seemingly all at once.

Maybe it was Jake. After I met Jake, everything changed. He muddled my black and white into gray. Having children didn't seem like a burden; it seemed like a possibility. Of course, I thought we would have Sara much, much later in life.

As I closed my menu, Greg asked, "So how's your family doing?"

"Fi—," I started to say when life punched me in the stomach. A jolt of emotion ran through my blood. I cleared my throat and opened my menu back up again. "Fine," I said into the dessert list.

"You OK?" I felt Greg lean in closer.

Keep it together, Clare. There's no getting emotional in business.

"Yeah, they're great," I said. I said it as though it was three days ago, as though I truly believed it. "Yours?" I dragged my eyes upward and met his gaze.

"They're good. Been back to school at all recently?" Greg's voice brought me back to reality.

I shook my head. "Nope. Life's been kind of crazy. I'd love to go back soon and check out some of the bars."

"Yeah, although you'd only be allowed in two of them." Greg leaned forward slightly and his eyes sparkled.

"Oh, whatever! I was kicked out of a bar one time in college and it was completely justified. You can't just cut in line for the bathroom at a bar." I smiled at him and tucked my hair behind my ears.

"Right." He nodded and smirked.

"Whatever." I rolled my eyes and laughed, grateful to think about something other than my mom for even a few moments.

I survived the rest of the lunch by keeping the dialogue out of my court. I took advantage of silences by asking, "How's that been?" and, "What's that like?" to anything he mentioned. By the end of lunch, I felt exhausted, like I'd just conducted an intense interview.

As we left the restaurant and walked to the door, he said, "It's been great catching up, Clare. Maybe we can do this again sometime soon."

"Well, with all of the golf outing tasks, we'll be seeing a lot of each other," I said lightly.

"Looking forward to it," he said, and signaled to the valet to bring his Mercedes to the front.

"Same here! It was great to catch up!" I chirped. I waved quickly to him and hightailed it over to my car.

Friday, April 25
. . . .

"Just tell him you're so exhausted all of the time due to having hot married sex every night," Julie said as she uncorked a bottle of wine.

"Jules, he's a client. I actually have to be a professional around him. I'm not going to make inappropriate comments and risk losing the account. Besides, it's really not like that. We're just friends."

"Ha! He's just this 'friend' who you haven't seen in years and who completely screwed you over?" She poured the Cabernet into two wine-glasses. "Here," she said, and extended her arm, "drink up."

I took a long sip of the deep, velvety liquid and enjoyed the slightly bitter aftertaste.

"Ohhh," I sighed. "I've needed this."

"I know, hon," she said sympathetically. "Julie knows what you need," she said, and downed half her glass.

"I'm so exhausted. No, scratch that. I'm sick of using that word. What comes after exhausted?" I leaned forward and rested my head against the cool kitchen countertop.

"Forget about Greg. Not worth the discussion," Julie said as she took another sip of wine.

I weakly lifted my head off the countertop and looked at her through strands of hair. "I know. It's not that, it's . . ." My eyes filled with tears and I quickly put my head down again and closed my eyes.

"Hey! None of that! Look at me." Julie tapped me on the head lightly.

I obligingly lifted my head again and stood up straight.

She wagged her finger at me. "She's going to beat it, right?"

I nodded slowly. I could barely get out the words when I told Julie about my mom the other day.

"Then, don't waste your tears. She's going to be great," Julie said firmly.

I took a deep breath and exhaled. "Let's talk about something other than cancer or exes. What movie did you bring?"

"Well, I knew a good comedy was in order, so *The 40 Year Old Virgin*."

"Perfect. Sara's down for the night, so we should be good." We grabbed our wineglasses and walked into the family room. I flopped down on the couch and tucked my legs underneath me as Julie walked over to the television, DVD case in hand.

"Where's Jake?" she asked as she fiddled with the DVD player.

"Out with Bill-Until-Two-Months-Ago-I-Still-Lived-with-My-Parents." I took another sip of wine and smiled.

"Oooh, that guy is such a winner. Is he still toking up every day at four twenty like he did when we were in college?" Julie rubbed her hands together like she was starting a fire.

"As far as I know. I'm sure he doesn't let his job at the sporting goods store interfere with his marijuana habit." I pulled a blanket down off the back of the couch and tucked it around me.

"How does he help customers if he's high all the time?" she asked as she sat down next to me.

"Not customers. Climbers," I said.

"What?" She leaned forward a bit.

"Climbers. He runs the rock-climbing wall." I pulled the blanket up around my shoulders and laughed.

"You're fucking kidding me! He supervises rock climbers while he's high? What does he say? 'Du-ude, hurry up and get down here. It's my break and I really need some Cheetos.'"

"Or, 'Just like, sign this release and shit saying you won't sue us if I drop you or something.'" I laughed.

"Exactly." Julie shook her head. "At least he finally moved out of his parents' house."

"Um, yeah, only because his parents freaking bought him a place because they were so desperate for him to move out. Ew, I can't believe you made out with him in college." I crinkled my nose.

"Yeah, well, you had some winners yourself. How about the guy who you made out with freshman year who had hair plugs?" she said, and took a long sip of wine.

"He didn't have hair plugs! It just looked like that," I defended him, despite the mental picture of tufts of hair plugged into a scalp, much like one of those plastic baby dolls.

"Sweetie, he could've been on the Hair Club for Men commercial." Julie pursed her lips.

"Whatever. Speaking of which, how's the online dating coming?" I said quickly to change the subject. I didn't want her to remind me how I cried when hair plug guy didn't ask me out.

"Ugh. Not so good. First date was a disaster." She leaned her head against the back of the couch and closed her eyes.

"Julie! You didn't tell me you went on a date already!" I said, and tossed a pillow in her direction.

"Hey, watch the wine! I'm telling you now," she said smugly, and took a sip of her wine.

"So spill," I said.

"You're going to love this." She paused and took a sip of wine. She leaned forward and set her already empty wineglass down on the coffee table in front of her.

"Stop stalling! Tell!" I demanded.

"Relax. So, OK. This guy seemed normal enough from his online profile, right? Well, he comes to pick me up and he brings me flowers, which is kind of lame but was fine. But then, he smiles real wide at me as I take the flowers and I notice . . ." She paused and leaned forward.

"What? Noticed what?" I shrieked at her.

"He had no back teeth!" She sat back and crossed her arms in front of her chest.

"NO!" I covered my mouth with my hands.

"Yes! So, yeah, no back teeth. But I felt really bad because he said he already got show tickets for us, so I figured I'd just go see the show and then ditch him after."

"What show? *Wicked*? *Jersey Boys*?" I asked as I hugged a pillow to my stomach.

"You wish," she said, and cocked her head to the side. "Try rodeo."

"What? Like with horses and stuff?" I tilted my head to the side and thought, *Maybe he's a cowboy?*

"Yeah. A fucking horse rodeo. I didn't even know they had any around here. Oh, and get this—we got a behind-the-scenes tour because his brother was one of the rodeo clowns! And the rodeo, let me just tell you that while I make no attempt to hide my white-trash roots, this was like a *Deliverance* convention."

"Oh my God!" My hand flew up to my mouth and I started laughing uncontrollably.

"But wait, there's more!" she shrieked.

" 'But wait, there's more!' You sound like one of those people on infomercials who . . ." I trailed off when I saw her Look of Death.

"This rodeo was like way out in butt-fuck land, so he's driving me back to my apartment and we have to go through all these country roads and crap. And the entire time I'm convinced he's either going to molest me, kill me, or sell me into white slavery. He didn't do any of that, but he did pull off the road and ask if we could make out underneath the stars."

"What? Like on the roof of his car or something?" I shrieked, and clapped my hands. Julie's stories always thrill me in a way that no movie, TV show, or book ever could.

She shrugged. "Who the hell knows? I told him the only stars he'd be seeing were the ones after I punched him in the face if he didn't keep driving." She threw her hands up in the air. "So yeah, not a good one."

"Wow," I said. We sat silently for a moment before I cleared my throat and said, "Can I—"

"Yeah, go ahead and blog about it," she finished for me.

"Cool. That's going to be an awesome one."

This. This is why I have to be Julie's friend for the rest of my life. Even if she burns my house down, kidnaps my daughter, and sleeps with my husband, I have to be her friend. Because her life will provide an infinite amount of writing material for as long as we both shall live.

We turned on the movie and settled in on the couch with a big fluffy comforter and our wine.

Halfway through the movie, the baby monitor crackled and horrid screams began to emit from it.

"Shit," I muttered. "Pause it," I said to Julie.

I walked into Sara's room and picked her up.

"What's the matter, baby girl?" I cooed to her. "Are you jealous we're drinking wine?" She continued to scream and started batting at her ears. "What's wrong?" I looked at her as though I expected her to say, *Well, Mom, thanks for asking. I don't really like this new brand of diapers you started using and my room is a touch on the warm side.*

I thought she might be hungry, so I brought her out into the living room and tried to give her a bottle, which only made her make these horrid sucking noises and then scream harder.

Julie, at first, tried to help. "What's the matter? Do you just want some wine, too?" she said to Sara, and held her glass out. When it did not seem, in fact, that Sara wanted any wine, Julie asked, "Do you want to hear about the rodeo?" Sara turned purple in response. Julie turned to me. "I've got nothing," she said, and shrugged her shoulders.

I tried to rock Sara. I tried to walk around. I tried to give her a pacifier. Basically, I did everything short of buying her a pony and giving her a credit card.

After an hour, Julie said, "Uh, Clare, I hate to leave, but . . ."

"Get out. Seriously, go. You shouldn't have to listen to this. I might just put her in her crib and let her fuss anyway."

"Sure?" Julie said, even though she already had put her shoes on.

"Absolutely." I watched Julie walk out the door and close it behind her. I realized I didn't have a chance to talk her about my latest mental wrestling match, i.e., Clare versus Working, but I figured it was for the best. I've always been so adamant about going back to work that she might suspect me an imposter and start asking secret questions, like my bank's Web site when I forget my log-in: *What's your mother's father's third cousin's middle name?*

It's probably best to allow myself to distill my emotions without any additional input. I mentioned to Jake last night that I might want to consider the option of staying at home. I said the sentence with enough qualifiers that he knew better than to push a discussion. He just kissed me and told me he'd support whatever I decided. Which was great, but sometimes I wish someone would just tell me what to do.

Or, at least, why my daughter won't stop crying.

I turned back to Sara, still screaming in her swing. "What's wrong? Tell me."

She considered it but decided screaming her head off was more the way to go.

But as she cried, I caught a glimpse of something in her mouth. I stopped the swing and bent down. The mouth-gaping-open screams made it easy to examine her. Her bottom gum was swollen. I stuck my finger in her mouth and peered at her gum. I could see a faint white pellet like object beneath the skin.

Fark.

She's teething.

DUM, DUM, DUM, DUM, DUM . . .

I called Jake and told him we needed to start ordering wine by the case rather than just the bottle, as excessive amounts of alcohol are really the only aid we have. I heard Bill-Until-Two-Months-Ago-I-Still-Lived-with-My-Parents laughing and playing Super Mario Brothers in the background and told Jake to get his ass home and help me. I had little tolerance for potheads playing Nintendo when I was trying to endure what I have now dubbed The Great Tooth Debacle.

Nice timing, teething. Way to roundhouse kick me when I'm down.

Wednesday, April 30

Roundhouse kicks to the noggin continue.

Very, very little sleep.

Jake and I have been surviving on very, very little sleep.

Today, I opened my lunch at my desk, expecting to find my yummy left-over spaghetti Bolognese from last night, and found a bottle of baby lotion.

That's it.

Just a bottle.

Placed inside a paper bag.

Last night, I was trying to give Sara her bath and pack my lunch for today at the same time, amidst all of the I Hate the World and My Teeth screaming. My spaghetti Bolognese is probably sitting inside Sara's baby tub in our laundry room right now.

I think the sleep deprivation has finally won.

I'm so drained I kind of wish I would break my arm or something and have to be admitted to the hospital—where I'd get to sleep in a bed, be brought my meals, and get to watch television. Yes, I have now reached the point where I am so miserable that breaking body parts sounds like a vacation.

And each day like this that stacks upon the previous one, I start think that staying home would be an attractive option. But I'm afraid to make such a huge decision when so many other things are happening, and without proper sleep. I don't want to give in just because of a few bad days or sleepless nights. Because if there's one thing that I've learned so far, it's that the grass might be greener, but there's probably dog crap hiding in there somewhere.

But this time, it's not Sara's evil teeth or family health concerns that are causing the sleep deprivation, it is also due to a lovely gift from my aunt Kristen.

My aunt Kristen is a wonderful woman, who loves Sara dearly. So much so that she always buys her presents. Lavish, expensive, generous presents. Sometimes she doesn't even give them to us in person, sometimes they just show up on our doorstep, like gifts from Santa.

Well, Monday I came home from work and found a huge box on our doorstep. Excitedly I tore open the box and found inside one of those music activity centers. It's this thing Sara's supposed to play with that makes a bunch of noise. It's for when she's a little older, so I stored it in the back of our closet.

At four in the morning, the thing awakened us out of a deep, coma-like sleep by beeping, whistling, and playing a song that has now seared itself into my very cerebral cortex. Jake stumbled around in the dark and finally located the stupid thing and turned it off.

Just as he lay back down in bed, *Do Do Do Dee Da Doo Dee Dee dee!*

This time, it was my turn. I yanked on the light switch and he groaned and threw the covers over his head. I ripped open the closet door, and just as soon as I picked the godforsaken thing up it stopped.

An hour later, it went off again.

Satan himself was punishing us. It's a sign of the End of Days, I swear.

Last night, after it went off for the second time, Jake put it in the hallway of our building. We figured any thieves were welcome to it. We slept great until around 3:00 A.M., when our alky neighbor Champagne Wayne came home and drunkenly tripped over the thing and passed out on top of it. We woke up to Butterscotch howling at the front door; we knew it had to be serious if it made our cat leave his pink feather boa bed.

We walked out in the hallway and found Champagne Wayne, signature purple leisure suit and all, sprawled out in front of our doorway with the stupid music going off. Apparently, he also broke whatever internal off switch the thing had and now it just plays continuously. We quickly threw the thing down the garbage chute and prayed it would find some other family to torture.

Reese said, "Just wait until you start to get toys that require batteries. Of course, the gift-giver didn't buy batteries and do you think your three-year-old wants to wait until tomorrow to play with her new toy? So, you end up going out in a blizzard, desperately searching for eight D batteries. It's always people who don't have kids that buy that stuff, too." I immediately thought back to what I bought Grace for her second birthday: a Disney karaoke machine requiring something like sixteen batteries, and realized it was not Satan punishing us but rather God, with his infinite humor and ass-biting Karma.

"And wait until you get things like Bratz dolls," Reese continued. "That's when it really gets scary. Or when Sara wants to wear makeup and dress in low-rise jeans at two."

"God, our toys used to be so much more harmless, right? My favorite toy when I was little was my Barbie Bubbling Spa, the hot tub for Barbie." I twisted the phone cord of my office phone around my index finger.

"Who *didn't* have that?" She laughed.

"It was also educational. It taught me patience, since my mom never let me play with it because it required full use of the entire bathroom, like three gallons of water, and fifteen towels to clean up all the excess that spilled out."

"Or how about Operation? That was a good one," Reese said.

"See? That taught self-soothing skills. Playing that game nearly caused me an anxiety attack every time I played it. I still hear that shrill buzzing noise sometimes in my nightmares."

"No kidding!" She paused, then continued, "So, how's your mom?" Her tone was light.

"She's great, it's the rest of us who are falling apart. But we'll know more soon! I'm sure everything will be fine!" I tried to gather my strength and inject my words with a shred of cheer, but my efforts fell flat and sizzled around me like bacon grease.

"You know I'm here anytime you need me," Reese said quietly.

"I know." I nodded into the phone.

"I'll keep praying, but you're right, she's going to be fine."

"Thanks," I said.

After I hung up with Reese, I called my mom under the guise of getting her opinion on kid toys that make noise.

She said, "You guys are getting off easy so far. You loved this puzzle which made car noises. Except it didn't have any batteries. It was powered by an internal nuclear power cell and would go off anytime anyone opened or closed a door in the house. Eventually, your father took it outside and banged it on the ground over and over. It didn't work, though. It kept going off. It basically won."

"So, just Karma again, huh?" I said.

"Sounds like it. Sorry!" she said.

"So . . . how's everything?" I asked.

"Doctor's appointment on Friday," she said evenly. "We'll know more then. I'll figure out my radiation and chemo schedule and all those kinds of things."

"OK," I said. I didn't really know what else to say.

"Clare?"

"Yeah, Mom?"

"Remember what I said, everything's going to be fine."

My eyes welled up. "Shouldn't I be the one saying that to you?" I said with a laugh.

"You never really stop being a mom. Even when your kids grow up. You'll see," she said.

Part of me wants to post something about it on my blog, but a larger part doesn't. Most of my readers are so supportive and I'd love to hear stories from others who have gone through the same thing. But the 1 percent of people who read my blog seemingly just to find things to blast me about, people like jen2485, it's like they don't deserve to know. So, I'm not going to say anything for now.

Besides, I really don't want wifey1025 showing up on my front doorstep wearing a pink shirt, pink breast cancer pin, and, undoubtedly, with pink handcuffs to use to restrain me while she breaks my kneecaps, à la Kathy Bates in *Misery*.

Not to mention my readers have more than enough material to discuss, since I just posted about Julie's blind date. Now there's a heated debate happening over rodeos: Cultural Expression or Hillbilly Tradition?

Monday, May 5

. . . .

The Gods are appeased.

Sara's tooth finally broke through and the non-stop screaming has ended.

Jake is still quite cranky from the lack of sleep. Case in point: today I got home from work and found him mumbling expletives at the television.

"Motherfucking cable . . . no concept of good movies . . . who writes this shit . . ."

"Why are you muttering at the television?" I said as I dropped the diaper bag and put Sara in her Bumbo Seat on the floor. I sat down in front of her. "How's my best girl?" I asked her.

"Because of the stupid descriptions on the guide."

"Oh," I said, totally uninterested. Let's just say this wasn't Jake's first rant about our cable company. It's become like a hobby to him. Bored? Rage about how expensive our wireless Internet is. Nothing to do? Flip out about the occasional digitizing of the TV picture.

"Why do these idiots think they have the right to judge what's a good movie and what's not?" He banged the remote down on the end table.

"OK, I give," I said, and sighed.

"Look!" He pressed the info button on the remote and I read the description of the movie *Road House.* Something about Patrick Swayze as a bouncer.

"Yeah, so?" I said.

"Didn't you read it? It calls the movie 'laughable' and 'poorly acted.' *Road House* is a great movie."

"OK," I said slowly. I turned to Sara and whispered, "Your daddy is nuts." She giggled. Her laughter made a tiny crack of sunshine in the rain cloud that had been following me around the past few weeks. I hugged her to me, trying to absorb some of her happiness, as Jake continued his tirade.

"I mean, who even writes this stuff? Like, is there some little old man who watches all of these movies to provide a description of them? And why does he think he's qualified to comment on the quality of the shows and movies?" Jake snatched the remote again. "Look! It says *Legally Blonde* is a 'heartwarming comedy.' I think my IQ dropped out fifty points when you made me watch it."

"So, uh, what do you want for dinner?" I said in a desperate attempt to divert the truck before it fell of the cliff and I was forced to hear another retelling of The Time Our Cable Company Charged Us for HBO Even Though We Don't Have HBO.

"I don't know. I'm too pissed to think about it. Whatever you want," he said, and slumped back against the couch.

I stood there, silently holding Sara, staring at him. He looked up at me and his expression changed. "Jesus, I'm being an ass. Sorry. I'm just . . ."

"Tired, I know. Me, too," I said to him quietly as I carried Sara into her room.

"Let this be a lesson to you," I said to Sara as I changed her diaper later. "For some reason, all men feel cheated by their cable companies. Don't try to argue or reason with them. Just intercept the bill each month and pay it yourself. Trust me, this will save you countless headaches. There was one time in college when Reese's husband Matt—the asshole I keep telling you about—went to the cable company office and played the receptionist a PowerPoint presentation on why he felt they were price-gouging." I started laughing as I thought about him coming back to my apartment, looking defeated when he left with a five-dollar credit and a brand-new premium channel package.

It felt good to laugh. It seemed like it had been years. It made me forget about the thoughts lingering in my head, thoughts I've tried so many times to ignore. Thoughts that whisper questions about what the hell I'm doing and why I'm doing it when I don't have to.

Sara didn't seem to care. She gazed at a picture on the wall.

"You'll learn," I whispered to her.

Tuesday, May 13

. . . .

"Then, my rash started oozing pus everywhere. My doctor said it was the worst reaction he's ever seen. So, they gave me a different cream and it finally cleared up. Can you believe it?"

I listened from a safe distance in my office to Mule Face recount her allergic reaction to one of the mail-order face creams she peddles. The same face cream that she tried to sell me sixty ounces of this morning. And suggested I mention in my blog.

Not too bright, that one.

"Clare Finnegan," I said distractedly as I answered my phone.

"Hey! Are you busy?" my mom's voice said.

"Not really. Just listening to one of Mule—Annie's stories."

"Might not want to call her Mule Face while in the office. Bad idea. Anyway," my mom continued, "your dad and I just met with my oncologist."

As she said it, my heart started to pound again, but my denial muttered in my head, *Oncologist. Why does she need an oncologist? Only sick people need them. Oh, right. . . .*

"And?" I squeaked out as I stared at a tiny gnat landing on my desk.

"I'm having surgery in three weeks to remove the lump. A lumpectomy. Then, I start chemo right after that and then radiation."

I slumped down a little in my chair.

"Oh," I said quietly.

"It's the standard course of treatment. He also said that everything is, for the most part, precautionary, since it hasn't spread to my lymph nodes, and he expects a great outcome."

"That's great, Mom," I said meekly.

I wanted to be positive, I wanted to congratulate her, I wanted to be strong. But I didn't know how. I wanted my mom to tell me everything is going to be OK. Even though *she* is the "everything."

"So, listen. Your father and I had an idea. I'm going to be out of commission for a while, obviously, so . . . what are you guys doing this weekend?"

"Um, laundry, scrubbing the microwave, lint-rolling the couch, and looking on the Internet to see if our neighbors are sex predators."

As I said it, my inner voice shouted, *YOU ARE A LOSER. LO-SER. DID YOU HEAR ME? GET A LIFE, YOU DORK. HAVING A CHILD HAS TURNED YOU INTO YOUR MOTHER-IN-LAW.*

"Oh, exciting. Do you think you could tear yourselves away for a trip to Lake Kilgore?"

"You guys want to go to Lake Kilgore this weekend?" I asked.

"Sure, why not? I'd like to get everyone together before I start feeling yucky. That is, if you guys can tear yourselves away from your exciting plans," she said.

"I don't know, it would be pretty difficult . . . I guess we can come," I said, and laughed.

". . . shots of steroids in my fanny . . ." Mule Face's voice wafted into my office.

"So, this weekend, let's do it," I said loudly, in an attempt to speak over Mule Face's story.

"OK, great. Your dad and I were thinking about renting the old cottage from Mrs. Sweet."

"You mean the one we used to rent when we were little?"

"Wouldn't it be cool?" my mom asked.

"I guess so. Do you think Mrs. Sweet updated the place? I remember it being somewhat rustic, to put it nicely."

"Eh, who cares? It'll be fun."

I immediately pictured Sam's brain exploding when she sees that we have to share one bathroom.

"Fun? Yes, it will be," I said.

Friday, May 16

. . . .

"Is it Route 4 or Route 173?" Jake asked as he clutched the steering wheel.

"Uh, I don't know," I said, and Jake's head snapped like a rubber band toward me. "Route 4," I said quickly, and prayed I was right and we wouldn't end up in Iowa instead of Wisconsin. "I forgot how pretty the drive is up here," I said lightly.

"I have no idea how pretty anything is right now. My head is pounding and none of these jerks will let me change lanes," he said. "Thank God," he said as he successfully wedged our car in between two others on the parking lot that was the highway.

Apparently, every other person in the Chicagoland area decided to drive up to Lake Kilgore this weekend.

Goody.

Also, Sara decided that today would be a good day to let us know *exactly* how much she hates cars, her car seat, her new shiny Whoozit toy, and me.

She didn't stop screaming the entire way up to the lake.

At some point after we passed mile marker 83, I got out of the car (on the highway, which should give an indication of how awesome the traffic was) and plopped into the backseat. I tried to shove everything from a bottle to a pacifier into her mouth, but to no avail. She wasn't having any of it. So Jake and I drove with our screaming child in the back for the next two hours before we finally arrived in the town of Lake Kilgore.

"Why are there so many bikers here?" Jake asked as he surveyed the motorcycles zooming by our car.

"I don't know. I don't remember it being a biker town. It doesn't look that bad," I said as I eyed the swarms of leather and bandannas. "Maybe there's some kind of bike rally or something."

(For the sake of accuracy and proper reporting, it was more like, "MAYBE THERE'S . . . SHHH, SARA . . . DON'T YOU WANT YOUR PACI? . . . ARE YOU HUNGRY? . . . SOME KIND OF . . . WHAT'S WRONG, BABY GIRL? . . . BIKE RALLY . . . PLEASE STOP CRYING . . . THIS WEEKEND.")

"What road are we supposed to turn on?"

"Um . . . Bloomfield Road," I said as I checked the directions.

Jake peered at every street sign as he drove ten miles an hour, which did not make the bikers very happy, so they whizzed by us and occasionally gave us the finger.

I rolled down my window, stuck out my hand, and yelled, "RIGHT BACK AT YA!"

"Nice," Jake said.

"Three hours in a car with a screaming baby and I've turned into Gary Busey," I muttered.

"Bloomfield Road!" Jake said triumphantly. At least, that's what I think he said. All I could really make out was "B . . . eld . . . oad!" since I was still deaf from Sara's screams, which resembled the sounds of a lamb being butchered.

He turned the car down a gravel road, peppered with beautiful lake homes.

"Oh! Look!" I said as I caught a glimpse of the shimmering lake. "We're going to have *such* a good weekend," I said to Sara, who responded by turning a new shade of purple.

I opened the window a little more and stuck my face out. "The houses look like little gingerbread houses!"

"3789 . . . where are you?" Jake muttered.

I got excited when he slowed down in front of a huge, palatial beach cottage. "Is this it? I don't remember it being so big! It's amazing."

"3758, no, that's not it. Here it is! 3789. It's . . ." He trailed off.

Not exactly what I would call a resort home. One level. White peeling paint. Plastic flamingos dotting the front yard.

"Why is that woman with purple hair waving at us?" Jake asked, and pointed to a woman standing on the front porch.

"Oh God. That's Mrs. Sweet. I can't believe she looks the same as she did twenty years ago."

Jake pulled the car up the long driveway and parked. "I'll stay here with Sara, why don't you go talk to the owner," he said as he stretched his arms over his head.

"Good idea," I said as I leapt out of the car, away from my screaming child.

"Hi, Mrs. Sweet," I said as I walked toward her. Her expression changed to one of confusion.

"Who are you?" she said, and furrowed her penciled-in eyebrow.

"Clare Finnegan," I said as I surveyed her false eyelashes.

"Who?"

"Clare. Finnegan. My parents rented this place this weekend. They're coming up in an hour or two."

"Oh. I don't know any Finnegans." The poor woman looked totally confused.

Then, I remembered.

"Flannagan," I said, and her face lit up.

"Oh yes! Flannagan! Come right in," she said, and waved me into the cottage. Even though my dad's family rented the place every year for like twenty years or something, Mrs. Sweet still thought we were "the Flannagans."

"Probably looks the same as you remember it! I kept all of the original furniture," she said proudly.

It was not something to be proud of.

The first thing that hit me was the smell of mildew and old, musty furniture. Clearly, cleaning or Scotchgarding the furniture hadn't been done in, oh, a hundred years or so. The next thing I noticed was a six-foot-tall statue of a knight in a suit of armor in the kitchen.

"That's Charles," Mrs. Sweet said, and jerked her thumb in the knight's direction.

"Um, great. And the bedrooms?" I said as I walked toward the back of the cottage.

"Three bedrooms just back there."

I peeked my head into the master suite. Well, OK, "master suite." Towels tacked over cracked windowpanes and a king-sized bed with mattress hard enough to crack vertebrae.

"I redecorated that second bedroom," Mrs. Sweet called as I peeked my head into a bedroom decorated with a wolf theme. A giant mural of a wolf killing what appeared to be a rabbit hung on the wall and the twin bed was adorned with sheets depicting wolf slumber.

I stifled a laugh and peeked my head into what would be Jake's, Sara's, and my bedroom. It looked somewhat normal, until I caught sight of the bed.

"Where's the mattress?" I said to Mrs. Sweet as I pointed to the bed, which only had a metal frame and a full-sized box spring.

"Oh, my last renter burned it down while smoking in bed. Good thing I was able to save the box spring," she said, and smiled at me, pumpkin orange lipstick on her teeth.

"Good thing," I said, and tried to decide how to break the news to Jake we would be sleeping on metal coils all weekend.

"Oh, and you probably have one of those cell phones, right?" Mrs. Sweet asked.

"Yes."

"Good. There's no phone line here. Never has been." Mrs. Sweet adjusted her purple hair a bit.

"Oh, right, I forgot."

I stifled a laugh as I remembered how, in the days before cell phones, phone calls for us would go to Mrs. Sweet's house. She would stand on the front doorstep of her house, located next door, and ring a cowbell and shout, "FLANNAGANS! YOU HAVE A PHONE CALL!" loud enough to awaken the dead three states over.

"How old's your little one?" she asked.

"Four months," I said.

"Oh, well, there's a swing set in the backyard." She pointed out the window.

I leaned forward and peered out of the dusty glass. I saw a swing set, oh, 98 or 99 percent covered in rust, with a very dangerous thorn bush planted right behind the swings.

Since Sara isn't up-to-date on her tetanus shots and I do not wish to spend my weekend picking thorns out of her skull, I think we'll pass on the swing set.

After Mrs. Sweet left, Jake and I started to unpack all of the crap we brought. Sara, thankfully, had worn herself out and passed out in her car seat. As Jake and I were unloading the travel swing we bought specially for this weekend, seeing as how Sara turns into Captain Howdy from *The Exorcist* whenever she doesn't have access to a swing, we heard my parents' car pull up the driveway.

I smiled and waved my hand. "Hello all!"

Sam was the first to get out of the car.

"What. The. Hell." She yanked off her sunglasses. "Is. This?" she said, and surveyed the cottage.

"Our beautiful vacation cottage for the weekend!" I said, and smiled widely.

Oh, this is going to be good. So, so good, I thought.

I might even forgive her for asking me if I'm allowed to wear two-piece bathing suits now that I have a kid. (For the record: I'm terrified to try on my bikini. I'm afraid no fabric would be visible, for all of the stretched-out white skin would encompass it like a volcano swallowing a tiny pebble.)

"No. Hell no. This place is disgusting," she said, and wrinkled her nose.

"It'll be great," my dad said, and placed his hand on her shoulder.

"Are you serious—" She started to shriek when my dad squeezed her shoulder. "OW! What? Fine," she grumbled as he gave her a *shut the hell up now* look. She snapped open her cell phone and started dialing.

"Aw, it looks just the same, doesn't it?" my mom said.

"Sure," I lied.

"You'll see it's *exactly* the same," Jake chimed from the trunk of our car.

"Yeah. . . . Yeah. . . . For sure. . . . He is so weird. . . . Can you say freak?" Sam droned into her phone as she wandered inside.

Jake and I grinned at each other and he held his hand up in the air and started to count down.

Five . . . four . . . three . . . two . . .

That's all it took.

"MO-OM," Sam shrieked from inside.

"Jackpot!" Jake yelled as he pumped his arms into the air.

My dad glared at both of us as he walked in the door.

"Sam, I told you not to complain this . . ." His voice disappeared as he walked in.

"So, Mom. Feel good to get away?" I said as I put my arm around her shoulder.

"Yep." She nodded firmly, but her voice was soft.

"When's Mark coming up?" I asked as we walked toward the cottage.

"He's coming up for the day tomorrow. He has to work tonight. One of his Asian Web sites is going live, so he'll be working until late," she said.

The three of us walked inside together.

"Dad, I refuse to sleep in a room that has wolves all over. Who effing decorated this place? I—" Sam stopped as we walked in the door.

"Like your room?" Jake asked her with a grin.

"At least you have a mattress," I quickly added.

"What are you talking about?" my mom asked.

"Nothing," I said with a smirk.

"Wait a freaking second," Sam said as her eyes tore from one corner of the room to another. "Where the eff is the television?"

"Oh yeah, didn't I tell you? There isn't one," I said sweetly.

Sam's eyes widened. She opened her mouth. Jake, my dad, and I all glowered at her. She closed her mouth and narrowed her eyes and stomped into the Wolf Room, slamming the door.

"WAAAAAA!" Sara wailed as she woke up.

"Thanks, Sam! You rule!" I called through the closed door as I picked up Sara.

"I hate you! I want to punt all of you!" she called back.

"Punt us? Like a football?" my dad said, confused.

"Apparently." Jake shrugged.

"Hike! Hike!" I called through the door to the Wolf Room.

After we unpacked, we went out to dinner. My mom wanted to go back to a restaurant my parents used to take us to when we were little, the Red Caboose.

I used to call it The Funnest Restaurant Ever, since it had about twenty different video games, three or four pool tables, and one of those bowling games with a hockey puck. It was the most happening place in Lake Kilgore.

The five and a half of us walked in and the first things we noticed were (1) it was completely empty, except for three drunks at the bar, and (2) the video games had all been replaced by slot machines.

We stood next to the front door, huddled together, until my mom stepped forward.

"Let's sit here," she said, and pointed to an empty table.

We all silently stared at her.

"This looks good," she said, and we realized she was serious about wanting to eat here.

"Oh! Sure! C'mon, kids!" my dad said, and gestured for us to sit down.

Sam rolled her eyes so hard I was sure one of her retinas detached.

We all took our seats. Well, Sam perched on her chair, afraid to touch anything, while Jake and I tried to figure out the best place to put Sara's car seat. We didn't really want to set it down on the cigarette butt–covered floor, but the chairs were folding chairs that we were afraid would collapse and trap her. We decided to roll the dice and set her down on one of the vinyl chairs.

"WOO-HOO!" one of the drunks yelled from the bar. "That one HU-URT!" he yelled.

"Do you see what they're doing?" Jake asked.

I craned my neck toward the scarred bar. "I have no idea."

"The woman is plucking that guy's beard hairs out with tweezers while they watch NASCAR."

"OK, should we order?" I said quickly.

As we opened our menu, the door opened again and a crowd of guys walked in. I didn't really look at any of them until I heard, "Clare?"

I looked up.

Greg.

I swear, I heard the music from *The Twilight Zone* in the background.

I stared at him, openmouthed, as my family snapped their heads back and forth.

"Uh, Greg! What are you—" I stood up and took a step closer to him. Immediately I regretted it, because I wasn't sure if I should act professionally and shake his hand, punch him in the arm like he was my buddy, or just look like a dork and give him a lame wave. I settled for the lame wave.

I hate, hate, *hate* seeing clients, even ones I know personally, out in public. It forces me to become some strange hybrid of Working Clare and Normal Clare. It's kind of like the time I saw Mrs. Edison, my seventh-grade teacher, buying a bra in a department store. I wasn't sure whether or not to say hi or turn in my math homework.

Greg hooked his thumbs into his cargo shorts as the group of guys all gathered around the bar and ordered pitchers of beer. "Just up here for the weekend with some friends from work."

"Right! That sounds like perfection!"

O-kay. Apparently, being really, really uncomfortable makes me say words like "perfection."

I think I even gave one of those little "attaboy" arm swings.

"Yeah, it should be fun. Golfing, hanging out, you know." He shrugged his shoulders and gazed behind me.

"Oh! Right!" I turned around and faced my family. "You remember my parents and Sam. Oh! And Jake! Can't forget about him! Oh! And my daughsara." I tried to say "daughter" and "Sara" at the same time. I felt my face burning as I made exaggerated hand gestures.

"Nice to see you guys again." He nodded at everyone. "And Jake"—he stepped forward and stuck his hand out—"good to see you."

Jake leaned forward and shook Greg's hand. "Yep. Same here."

Greg gave a quick glance down at Sara's car seat and nodded before turning back to me.

My forehead was starting to grow damp and I could feel my hair sticking to the back of my neck.

"Well, I should get back to—" Greg pointed to his group of friends in the back.

"Yes! Yes! Good to see you! I'm sure I'll see you soon!" I sputtered to him. I turned back to our table and sat down casually.

I felt my entire family and Jake looking at me. "Weird!" I said, and bent down and fussed with Sara's T-shirt.

"Why the eff is he here?" Sam asked loudly.

"Shhh!" I hissed at her. "He's a client, remember? Anyway, I think his parents have a house up here."

"Or maybe he's just following Clare," Jake said, and smiled.

"Funny," I whispered to him.

Throughout dinner, I heard snippets of conversation from Greg and his friends. They were talking about the usual—sports, work, and drinking. Halfway through our meal, they got up to leave and Greg gave a quick wave as he walked out the door.

As I watched them walk down the street, presumably to head to another bar, Sara started fussing. I picked her up and she barfed a little on my shirt. As though my reality needed to get just a bit more clear.

While Greg was going out and leisurely drinking and playing pool with his friends, I was changing diapers and cleaning baby puke off her shirt.

With Sara beginning to fuss, Jake and I knew our time was limited, so we shoved our burgers down our throats and rushed out the door.

We figured, *No worries! We bought a travel swing, right? Just a quick session in the swing back at the house and she'll be out like a light for the night.*

Once again, our assumptions prove us to be total idiots.

For some reason, Sara *hates* the travel swing. She doesn't just dislike it or it's not her style or something, she absolutely, 100 percent, despises the thing with every nuclei in her little body. Whenever we set her down in it, before we can even press the on button, her face contorts and she wails. I don't know if she doesn't like the fabric, thinks the attached mobile looks tacky, or generally just feels like driving us insane. Whatever the reason, she refuses to spend any time in it, which also meant she refused to allow us to put her down for more than a micro-second. It also means she's so pissed we even *attempted* to place her in the swing, she won't sleep. At all. For more than fifteen minutes. It's like she's on strike, with a miniature picket sign, chanting, *Sleep? Hell no! That travel swing has got to go!*

Which is why it is now 3:30 A.M. and I am awake, staring at the hideous orange flower patterns on the couch, rocking her. I'm sure Greg and his friends are still up, grilling pizzas and having one more drink.

Is there something wrong with me because I'm sort of jealous?

Because as I sit here, rocking my screaming daughter who has declared war on Fisher-Price and her parents, I feel like I'm being punished.

Saturday, May 17
. . . .

"You look like shit," Sam declared to me as she stumbled out of her bedroom this morning, her blond hair tangled around her shoulders.

"Thanks. Sara was up all night."

"Whatever," Sam said as she walked into the bathroom.

"Everyone ready to do some boating today?" my dad said cheerfully as he walked into the living room.

Jake and I grunted in response.

"Oh, come on. It'll be fun!" my dad said, clearly not having a clue Jake and I got about fifteen minutes of sleep between the two of us.

"It's not that. We got, like, zero sleep last night," I said.

My dad looked pointedly at Sara, snoozing away in her stroller.

"She's only sleeping because I took her for a walk at six this morning," I retorted.

"Oh no, were you guys up all night?" my mom said, looking worried as she poured a cup of coffee.

"We're great," Jake said quickly. "Never been better! Can't wait to rent a boat today!"

So, here's how the rest of the afternoon went:

Rent boat.

Listen to Sam whine about how the boat we got "isn't cool" and people are going to "totally laugh" when they see her riding around in it with "us losers."

Watch as Jake silences Sam by whispering something threatening into her ear.

Park boat in the middle of the lake and drink beer.

Loudly proclaim, "This is the life!" as Sara happily sleeps and we gaze at all of the lakefront mansions.

Duck when we see Greg's huge Cobalt speedboat whiz by.

Pretend I was just looking for something in bag.

Laugh hysterically when Sam finds a leech on her toe after swimming.

Duck when Sam throws her pink bedazzled Sidekick at my head.

Smile and tear up when my mom says, "This means so much to me that we can all get away this weekend."

Outstretch arms as I (in my head) lightly float (more like stumble) across the crab apple–covered lawn to greet Mark . . . and some girl he's brought.

"Hi! Hey! What's going on?" I say to Mark as I eye the brunette checking her lipstick in the car before she gets out.

"Hey, Sis," he says as he gives me a hug.

"Who's that?" I whisper as I poke my index finger toward the car. He smiled broadly at me. "Is that Nacional 27 girl?" I asked.

Nacional 27 girl stepped out of the car and smiled warmly at me. "Hi, I'm Casey," she said.

"Hi! Nice to meet you! I'm Clare, Mark's awesome older sister." I waved.

"Nice to meet you, too. Is that a Blue Moon in your hand? That's my favorite beer!"

I gave Mark a look that said, *OK, she can probably stay.*

"Yep!"

"Oh, and I love your sundress! Where did you get it?"

This time, I gave Mark a *she's staying even if you're not* look.

The three of us walked toward the cottage and I could see the growing alarm in Mark's eyes. I silently snickered to myself. This wasn't exactly a place I'd bring a date to impress her.

We walked inside and my family wasn't very impressive, either.

Jake was walking around the cottage holding a wailing Sara, muttering, "Fucking travel swing. Die, Fisher-Price."

My dad was passed out on the couch in his bathing suit, snoring.

My mom was e-mailing on her laptop.

And Sam was in the shower, loudly (and horribly) singing along to Fergie's "Big Girls Don't Cry."

"Hey, everyone! Meet Casey!" I announced over the wail of ". . . LIKE A CHILD MISSES THEIR BLANKET . . ." as we walked in the door.

Casey was pretty cool and took everything in stride. She handed a bouquet of flowers to my mom and said, "I'm so sorry."

Nice touch, I mouthed to Mark.

Casey did everything right. She complimented Jake on his parenting skills. She held Sara and didn't mind when she screamed her head off. She asked my dad insightful questions about the state of health care and what it's like to be a physician. She even won Sam over by gushing over her Prada beach bag.

We all pretty much fell in love with her.

The girl could do no wrong.

After we went to dinner, we all came back to the cottage and Mark and Casey left to go back home. As we waved them off, my mom said, "Sweet girl."

"Yeah, I know. That's what worries me. Anyone that dates Mark has to be insane. She must have a flaw somewhere. Maybe she's secretly a transvestite or something," I said as I waved.

Sunday, May 18

After Mark and Casey left yesterday, I walked out onto the deck overlooking the lake. Happy to escape the cacophony of sounds inside, I took a deep breath and tasted the lake air. I squinted my eyes and pictured Mark, Sam, and me running around on the pier as little kids, splashing each other, our Snoopy fishing poles dangling into the lake.

"Hey." Sam appeared next to me.

"Hi," I said.

We sat silently for a minute and listened to the lake lap against the rocks. I could faintly hear Jake tell my parents a story about the time in college when Bill bent his car door backward, like in the movie *Tommy Boy*.

"Remember when we used to sit out here and listen to the song 'Stand by Me'?"

She smiled. "Totally."

"We used to love the lyric about the moon being the only light we can see. Or something like that."

"Yeah, yeah," she said, and twisted a strand of her hair around her finger.

"Mom's going to be OK, you know that, right?" I tried to sound confident.

"Duh," she said softly.

I opened my mouth to say something else but quickly closed it. My sister and I sat in silence, hearing the bullfrogs across the lake croak in unison.

"Nice to spend time with Mom." Sam mumbled so quietly I had to lean toward her to hear.

"It is," I said, and nodded my head.

"I feel like we never got to take long weekends like this with Mom. Growing up, I mean," Sam said as she twisted a silver and gold ring around her index finger.

Because Mom was always working, I silently finished.

"I know. It's nice," I said, and smiled at my sister.

But she worked because she loved her job; it made her happy, the working-mom devil on my right shoulder said into my ear.

Before Sam and I could say anything more, she heard her phone beep from inside and ran in to check her text messages. I lingered on the deck for a few more moments before going inside. I looked up at the stars and wished they would answer all of my questions in a finite manner. But all I could discern was the Big Dipper.

Jake and I stayed up late talking with my parents. And by "stayed up late talking" I mean "drank beer and played Monopoly."

There's nothing like my dad drunkenly yelling, "Two hundred dollars! Passing Go is the best!"

Sara's declaration of war continued. Late last night, she went back to her legislature and asked for more funding. She definitely received it, since she slept for around two hours last night.

Jake and I didn't dare attempt to put her anywhere near the travel swing, for fear the heavens would open up and acid rain would wash down upon us and melt our faces off. Kind of like what happened to the Nazis in *Raiders of the Lost Ark.*

After we bid farewell to my parents, Sam, and the Cottage of Which We Will Never Speak Again, we set off for another fun-filled three-hour drive. Sara was asleep when we left, so Jake and I thought we might luck out and enjoy a peaceful, quiet drive home, where we could nurse our hangovers properly.

After a half hour, she woke up and Baby Hitler appeared.

After two hours, Jake pulled the car over, silently got out, walked around to the trunk, opened it, and pulled out the travel swing. He smashed it a few times before throwing it as hard as he could into a field. He got back in the car.

Neither of us said a word.

Until forty-five minutes later when I wondered out loud if he thought we could sell Sara on eBay.

He didn't answer.

"IS THAT A NO?" I screamed over Sara's wails.

To recap:

Sara: cruel dictator.

Parents: dead.

Hangover: brutal.

Greg: probably well rested and tanned.

Travel swing: busted, lying in a field somewhere in northern Illinois.

Monday, May 26
. . . .

I feel like total crap again today. My head is killing me, my joints are achy, and I have hideous cotton mouth. After I dropped Sara off at day-care this morning, I actually contemplated calling in sick to work and going home and sleeping for eight hours. Until I realized I'd make it all the way back home and then feel horribly guilty and have to go pick Sara up at day-care. Not to mention, I have an enormous amount of work piled on my desk and I want to leave at a reasonable hour tonight.

"Clare, are you free around two?" Christina called from her office.

"Yes," I called back, and prayed she wouldn't ask me to do anything that required full brain capacity.

"Great, let's meet in my office at that time."

Crap.

Either she was going to give me a new project or I had dropped the ball with one of my events and I was going to get an ass-reaming. I quickly tore open my event files and scoured them for any detail I might have missed, but everything seemed in place and on time.

I figured she was going to give me a new project. One that would take her ten minutes to explain and about forty hours for me to complete.

Oh joy. As though I'm not in the office enough as it is. As though I didn't work late last week and have to race home just to see Sara before her bedtime. As though I didn't put her into her crib and cry because I only spent fifteen minutes with her before bedtime.

Mule Face, having heard the exchange, e-mailed me, *Ooohhh, someone's in trouble! What do you think she's going to say????*

I ignored her e-mail and pictured her in a bathing suit to make myself feel better.

At two, I walked into Christina's office and sat down on one of the plush brown leather chairs.

"So, what's up?" I said as I flipped open my leather binder.

"One second," she said as she finished typing on her computer.

I gazed around her office and stared at her perfectly pressed gray worsted wool suit. Bitch. She always has the best clothes.

"OK, sorry," she said, and took off her black Gucci frames. She swiveled in her chair to face me. "So, how's the golf outing going?"

"Great. Everything's going well. No snags. Should be a pretty straightforward event," I gave her my best I-Am-So-Capable-You-Don't-Want-to-Make-Me-Go-Crazy-by-Giving-Me-Another-Project-Do-You?

She stood up, and walked over to her office door, and closed it.

My stomach dropped a little.

"You know you're one of my best event consultants, right?" she said.

Oh no, I'm getting fired.

But I've worked my ass off in this job. All of my clients love me.

I think I made a little squeaking sound.

"And we always get outstanding feedback from your clients," she continued as she sat back down at her desk.

They're firing me because I'm too good. I'm a threat.

I'm going to have to become a cage dancer to pay our bills.

Maybe Sara can get a job. What is she qualified to do? Maybe she could hire herself out as a human tornado siren.

". . . an assistant," Christina said.

I only caught the last couple of words, since I was too busy mentally revising my résumé.

"I'm sorry, what?" I said.

"You've taken on so many new clients and brought this company so much business that we're offering you the opportunity to hire an assistant to help with your back-office responsibilities. To free up your time for more client interaction," Christina finished.

"Wow, whoa, I mean thank you," I said, dumbfounded.

"No, thank *you*. I think you do a phenomenal job and you really deserve this." Christina leaned back in her chair and tapped a pencil against the table.

I composed myself quickly and said, "Thank you, I won't let you down."

I walked out of Christina's office in a daze. In the span of ten minutes, I went from preparing myself to become a stripper to having an assistant at the most prestigious event-planning firm in the city. I nearly plowed over Mule Face, who was hovering outside the door, holding a Snickers bar. She gave me this huge fakey smile and congratulated me, having heard the entire conversation with her ear pressed to the door. I smiled sweetly at her, knowing she was *dying* inside that I'm getting an assistant and she's not. My smile didn't even break when she asked if it was due to some affirmative action initiative for mothers in the workplace.

As I sat back down at my desk, I thought, *This. This is what I've worked so hard for—recognition, accomplishment, accolades. This is why I work until it's dark out and have to speed home to see my daughter. I kick ass at my job.*

Yet even in my moment of triumph, my minute of victory, it was still hard to feel 100 percent happy. I know that with this assistant will come with greater responsibilities, longer hours, and increased expectations. No gifts come for free, and I will pay for this one with a pound of guilt.

Wednesday, May 28

· ·

The glow of my meeting with Christina still surrounds me. For as many times as I fantasize about running away, turning off my cell phone, and checking into a nice hotel, or for all the times lately that I've lamented about my mom's health, her lumpectomy next month, Sara's sleeping schedule, and my coworkers, my life really isn't that bad.

Sure, I'm exhausted pretty much all of the time, and working full-time and having a baby means that I really have a hard time doing anything 100 percent, but I really can't complain. And I have the option of working, not the necessity anymore. I have my own choices, my own direction—even if I'm not sure if the road I'm traveling is the right one.

Not to mention, Sara's a pretty good baby except for blips on the radar like the Great Tooth That Almost Killed Us All. And Jake's always willing to help out with the baby and household stuff.

So, my life really isn't so bad. Reese's life, on the other hand, isn't one that I envy.

Of course, she made a certain choice by marrying Matt right out of college, but I think the idea of getting married and having a family, at the time, was more important than *who* she actually created that life with. While Grace was planned, Brendan certainly wasn't, and Reese's paying for it in spades.

I arrived at her house during my lunch break to drop off a gift I bought for Brendan. Before I could even knock on the door, I heard the unmistakable sound of a newborn cry.

Reese answered the door in sweatpants and a baby puke–stained T-shirt. I think it was the first time since college that I've seen her in her pajamas.

"Hi, oh no! Is it noon already?" She leaned her head against the door and closed her eyes.

"Tough day?" I said, and walked inside.

"You have no idea," she said, and closed the door behind me.

I followed her into the enormous family room, decorated straight out of a Pottery Barn catalog, with white candles everywhere, huge plush couches, and tons of comfy throw pillows. Next to the television, Brendan was lying in his swing, squirming and crying.

"He just won't stop," she said as she picked him up. "What's wrong, honey?" she said to him. He screamed louder and stiffened his body. "He cries anytime he's not sleeping or eating," she said to me as she sat down on the couch next to me.

I didn't dare say the C word.

The C word used to mean a part of a woman's anatomy. A word that I can't stand.

Now, the C word is much, much more offensive.

C-O-L-I-C.

Thankfully, God didn't curse me with a colicky child. I guess he thought getting knocked up while on the pill was funny enough.

"Do you want me to take him and give you a break?" I offered.

"No, that's—," she said distractedly as she yanked up her shirt and stuck her boob in his mouth. "Ah, there." Her body relaxed and she closed her eyes for a minute.

"Where's Grace?" I asked as I snapped my head around the room. I hoped she wasn't playing in the kitchen with knives thanks to Reese's sleep deprivation.

"Napping, thank the dear Lord. I had no idea having two would be this hard." She exhaled loudly.

"I know . . . ," I said, and trailed off. *It probably would be easier if you had some help from that husband,* I thought. "So, a boy, huh? That's so cool."

"I know, one of each." Reese's eyes were still closed as she lay very still.

"I'm already worrying about all the stuff that comes with having a girl, like the mean girl cliques and her telling me how uncool I dress and how much I embarrass her." I laughed.

"That's nothing. A few months ago, I saw a five-year-old wearing eye shadow and complaining she looked fat."

I shuddered. "I'd rather you didn't tell me those things. At least we'll have each other. We can raise our girls together."

"No kidding. We can drink a bottle of wine every time they tell us they hate us." Reese opened one eye and looked at me.

"Then we'll become alcoholics." I laughed.

"Before I forget, since I'd swear my IQ seeps out in my breast milk, I got you something. It's on the kitchen table," she said, and nodded toward the kitchen.

"Reese, what? No, are you crazy? Why did you buy me something?" I shook my head.

"For being there for me in the hospital. If you wouldn't have been there . . ." She trailed off, her eyes glistening.

"You would've been by yourself," I said before I could stop myself.

She looked at me and her mouth wavered for a minute, but she set it in a thin smile. "Go get it."

I walked into her gorgeous kitchen and looked around at the cherry cabinets, granite countertops, and stainless-steel appliances that I'd drooled over many times. I picked up a green and pink–wrapped box and brought it into the family room. I opened it and inside was a beautiful light pink cashmere wrap.

"Ohhh, Reese. It's beautiful!" I held up the soft material and rubbed it against my cheek. "You're insane—you shouldn't have!" I said lightly.

"Yes, I should," she said.

"Well, now my gift is going to look stupid," I said as I awkwardly pushed my present over to her on the couch.

"Open it for me. I don't want to move him and risk another meltdown." She nodded toward Baby Brendan.

I opened the present and handed it to her.

"It's just a shorts and T-shirt set with little baby flip-flops." I awkwardly held it up like a *Price Is Right* model.

"What do you mean, 'just'? It's great!" she said.

"I figured you didn't have any boy clothes, and I didn't want to get you another toy that made noise since, yeah, we already had that conversation." I shrugged.

"Good call. Thanks, I love it," she said.

We sat silent for a minute as I looked down at my pink wrap. I rubbed my index finger against the soft stitching. I looked at Matt and Reese's wedding photo on the end table next to me. "So, what's going on with Matt?" I said quietly, without looking up.

She took in a long breath and exhaled slowly. She looked down at Baby Brendan and rocked him back and forth for a second.

"I think I'm going to ask him to move out," she said quietly.

"Really?" I said evenly.

"It's not working. I mean, I don't want to take care of two kids on my own, but it's harder to have him around, you know?" She didn't look up from her newborn son, quietly sighing as though he could sense the sadness around him.

I nodded mutely. "Are you still going to start graduate school in the fall?"

"Planning on it." She looked at me quickly and nodded.

"That's great. You haven't done something just for yourself in forever." I briefly covered her hand with mine and patted it.

She smiled.

I wanted to ask her so many things, like would she be OK financially, how she was going to tell Grace, was she going to ask for a divorce.

But I just said, "Is there anything I can do?"

She smiled. "Just that helps."

I leaned over and put my arm around her, which was somewhat awkward considering her boob was exposed with her baby attached to it. Her sorrow was palpable as we sat there silently.

As I hugged Reese, I felt terrible for the words popping into my brain: *I never want to be like this. I never want to build my life only for someone else. I never want to lose myself like Reese did.*

I threw my arms around Jake the second he got home today. He started to pull away after a second, but I held him close, one arm wrapped around him, the other around Sara. I closed my eyes and listened to Jake's heart beat in his chest against my ear and Sara's coos in my other ear and my shell of sadness began to crack.

I felt comforted by the presence of my husband and daughter, a safety that exists only when all three of us are separated only by inches. But it wasn't just their presence, it was the knowledge that while I don't ever want to lose myself in my marriage or child—to forget about my own identity and dreams—it is here, with them, that I feel most like me.

Saturday, June 7

. . . .

"Piece of cake."

That's how my mom described her lumpectomy yesterday.

Of course, she wouldn't tell me if it had gone otherwise, but she did sound surprisingly OK when I talked to her last night. My dad took her home after the surgery and she has strict instructions to take it easy. Which, to her, normally means only working on her laptop for eight hours a day, only doing four loads of laundry, and cooking a "light" meal of braised lamb with mint aioli sauce. But my dad's given her instructions to do nothing but lie around, watch television, read magazines, and nap. We'll see how long that lasts, considering I think the last time my mother took a nap was 1976.

After I hung up with my dad, I called Mark to see how he was handling everything, and also to get the scoop on his new woman.

"-ello?" he screamed into the phone. It sounded like he was inside Mötley Crüe's tour bus.

"IT'S CLARE!" I shouted.

"CLARE?" he screamed back.

"CLARE!" I said again.

"HOLD ON, LET ME GO OUTSIDE." After a minute, the deafening music was silenced. "There. Can you hear me?"

"Much better. Where are you?" I asked.

"I'm at Duffy's. Happy hour drinks are only two dollars for beer and three dollars for well drinks. You should come." He said it so casually.

"You're at a bar when Mom just had surgery?" I asked, incredulous.

"I talked to Dad. He said she's fine," Mark said. "Besides, I stopped at—"

"Hey, Mark! Is Shitface inside?" some guy said on the other end.

"Yeah, he's sitting at the bar. Sorry, anyway," Mark said, talking to me, "I stopped at a church earlier and said a prayer."

"Who's Shitface? Never mind, forget it. I just wanted to make sure you were OK."

"I'm great. You know, still freaked out, but good." I could practically hear him shrugging.

"Good. How's Casey?" I asked.

"Fine," he said.

"So what's the flaw?" I asked quickly.

"Uh, nothing. She's a really cool girl." He sounded confused.

"I like her a lot. I'm just curious as to why someone so normal would date you," I said.

"Yeah, yeah, whatever. Listen, I gotta go, some of my friends just got here." I could hear raucous yelling in the background.

"Just don't screw it up!" I yelled into the phone before I hung up.

"SCREW WHAT UP?" Mule Face yelled from down the hall.

Wednesday, June 11

. . . .

I think I got about four hours of sleep last night. Between getting home sometime near midnight and waking up every half hour or so thanks to Sara's Night of No Sleeping Ever, stumbling through the haze that is my new normal. I think there was once a time in my life when I got eight hours of sleep, but I really can't be sure.

Thankfully, I can slack off a little today at work since the golf outing kickoff party went smoothly. I just wish that translated into a free day off.

I broke down and purchased a new outfit for the cocktail party, since my ego wouldn't allow me to wear the Miss Piggy pants.

So, armed with a cute new black wrap dress, still two sizes larger than pre-Sara, and a pair of killer heels, I arrived at the club about an hour before the party was supposed to begin. Since there really wasn't much to do, I sat out on the balcony overlooking the golf course and sipped a glass of lemon water.

"Can I bring you anything else, Ms. Finnegan?" A white-gloved waiter appeared next to me.

"No thanks, I'm good." I smiled at him and leaned back against the white wicker chair. A few golfers were still teeing off on the last hole and I could hear their booze-soaked conversation floating across the green.

I exhaled and sipped my water, thankful for a few moments of silence.

Wouldn't it be great if this were my life?

What if I had a life where people brought me hot towels and lemon water? Where I could play golf, after I learn how to play, all afternoon and end the day with a cocktail on this balcony?

But you can have more time each afternoon. With Sara.

I closed my eyes and felt the sun on my face as it started to move west.

"Sleeping?" a voice said, startling me.

"Oh, hi! No, just relaxed." I smiled at Greg. "What are you doing here so early?"

His freshly pressed khaki pants and crisp white polo shirt offset his deep caramel tan. "Just finished a round. Didn't make sense to go home and come all the way back."

I nodded. "Want anything to drink?"

He shook his head. "I'm OK." He sat down next to me and exhaled. He laced his fingers behind his head and stretched. "Beautiful day, huh?"

"Absolutely. Should only help our numbers tonight. Rain always tends to screw things up a little for these kinds of things."

He nodded and we sat silently, next to one another on the balcony. The irony of the situation slapped me across the face. Greg and I here, at the golf club, together on the balcony. Standing shoulder-to-shoulder, as I once thought we would always. In college, this was the life I thought I would have, the life I thought I wanted. A childless career woman, married to Greg.

I was so certain an engagement ring would be the next present I received from him, rather than a bucketful of tears and a public breakup.

"I think I should head inside. People will be here soon." I stood up, drink in hand.

"I'm right behind you," Greg said, and followed me inside the club.

I only had time for a quick check of the waitstaff, bar setup, and cocktail tables before people began to rush it. People arrived seemingly all at once, in a blue-blooded herd, racing to the bar like *The Biggest Loser* contestants to a dessert buffet.

I wandered around the party, making sure everything was running accordingly. Events like this one are my favorite—they basically run themselves and everyone usually has a good time. As I was walking through the crowd, I felt a tap on my arm. I turned around and it took a few moments to register whom I was standing next to.

Ethan and Nate—Greg's two best friends from college, whom I haven't seen in close to 8 million years and who, if memory serves, intimidated me in college.

"Hey! Oh, hi! How are you?" I said quickly.

Ethan and Nate, both dressed in waffle-weave polo shirts and khakis, nodded at me, their faces unsmiling.

"Hey, Clare." Ethan nodded, his spiky black hair radiating from his head like shooting stars.

"Hi," Nate said curtly. He brought his drink up to his lips and the huge silver watch on his wrist nearly blinded me.

"Nice to see you guys," I said briskly. I cleared my throat and stood up a little straighter.

"What are you doing here? Are you a member?" Ethan said, his eyes darting around the room.

I shook my head. "I'm the event coordinator. I worked with Greg and the committee to pull this off."

"Oh," Ethan said. He and Nate exchanged a quick glance.

I looked at both of them, appearing exactly the same as they did in college. And for a moment, I was brought right back. To standing in front of them, feeling inadequate. Feeling insecure. Feeling like they knew I didn't deserve to be Greg's girlfriend.

But then almost ten years of distance reminded me of something else: that they're assholes.

I cleared my throat. "It's a great job. Careerwise things are excellent."

"Huh. And I heard you have a kid now?" Nate said. I swear, he couldn't have seemed less interested in my answer. But the voice inflection that would've left me cowering many years ago today fueled my confidence for some strange reason.

"Jake and I have a daughter, Sara." I nodded and smiled at both of them, who looked startled.

Probably because that was the longest they'd ever heard me speak. Other than "Hey," "Hi," and "What's up?"

"Nice to see you both. Take care," I said to Ethan and Nate. I walked

away, feeling their gaze still on me. Feeling their slight bewilderment at
the quiet girl who suddenly had a voice.

As I said good-bye to Greg at the end of the night, he said, "Nate and
Ethan said to tell you it was a great party."

I smiled, looking straight ahead across the club's lawn, as we waited
outside for the valet to bring Greg's car.

"What?" he said.

I turned to look at him. "Nothing. It was great to see them and catch
up."

The valet pulled Greg's car up in front of us and got out.

"Well, thanks for everything, Clare. Great party," Greg said as the
valet outstretched his arm and handed him the keys.

"Thanks. No problem." I smiled at Greg through the dark night.

Friday, June 13

. . . .

The kickoff party behind me, I figured the rest of the week would be
pretty slow at work. And it has been, except for the fact that my e-mail
in-box is dinging every five seconds with another pointless e-mail.

Here's a sampling:

> From: Jennifer Theriod
> To: All
> Should we have the office lunch next week at P.F.
> Chang's or Kona Grill?

Then every idiot in the company hits Reply All to the message, so I've
gotten thirty e-mails alone with people voting on which place to have lunch.

Another:

> From: Zoe Smithe
> To: All
> Do you guys want to chip in to buy Kathy's daughter
> a christening gift?

Once again, thirty e-mails with people debating on how much to spend, what to get, who would go out and get the damn thing, and should we, in fact, even buy a gift?

I played Grinch and voted that we shouldn't buy a gift at all. Simply because I don't want to get caught up in a revolving door of office gifts where we have to shell out ten dollars each week because so-and-so's son is getting married or so-and-so's grandmother turned eighty. Julie told me once she had to chip in at work because one of the other nurses' cat died and she couldn't afford a proper burial. So Julie had to chip in fifteen dollars to help cremate this chick's cat.

I had to buy a gift for Mule Face's wedding to her husband, Big D (Short for Dwight. Hopefully not anything else) last year. I think buying a heart-shaped picture frame made out of crystal and tinsel was enough for a while.

The good news today is that my assistant position is finally posted on the Internet. Let the flooding in of awesome candidates begin!

3:30 P.M.
How about, let the flooding in of average candidates begin?

People who have sent in their résumés so far: a high-school student looking for twenty-five dollars an hour, a fry cook at McDonald's, and someone who wrote, *IverygoodatjobIIiketohavejobhereismyresume* and attached a résumé in some foreign language to the e-mail.

4:30 P.M.
I'll settle for a candidate who speaks English and who functions at a third-grade level.

6:00 P.M.
Wifey1025 *really really* wants to be considered for the position since her parole officer told her she needs to find a job. I'll have to look into Signature Events' corporate policy on hiring convicted and possibly dangerous and stalkerlike felons.

Saturday, June 21

. . . .

"You sound tired. Are you still in bed?" Julie asked me over the phone at noon today.

"In bed? Are you serious?" I snorted. "I've been up since six thirty."

"Jesus, why in God's name were you up at the ass crack of dawn on a Saturday?" I could hear what sounded like a pill bottle rattling around in the background.

"I have a kid, remember? Kids don't generally sleep in. Because they are evil and want to punish their parents. Hungover?" I said.

"Un-freaking-believably. Hold on." I could hear her gulping down water and some extra-strength ibuprofen, I assumed. "OK, there."

"What did you do last night?" I asked.

"Went out with this new coworker. She had like one-and-a-half beers and was completely hammered. You'd have thought she was high or something."

"Sounds like that girl from our dorm freshman year," I said.

"Who?" Julie's voice squeaked out.

"God, what was her name? You know, the chick that freaked out after she had three beers?" I tapped my finger against my cheek as I tried to pull her name from the air.

"Oh yeah! What the fuck was her name?" Julie shrieked.

"Laurel!" I said triumphantly, and pumped my fist in the air.

"Yeah, Laurel! We played drinking games in our room, and after like fifteen minutes that bitch ran out into the hallway, threw herself down, and started screaming her head off and wriggling around on the floor because she was so wasted and out of it." Julie sighed happily, thrilled that I had helped her rescue a nearly forgotten memory.

"Remember how people were asking her if she was on acid or 'shrooms or something? We were like, 'No acid. Three beers.'"

"That was awesome. I wish I had taken some pictures instead of helping her back to her room."

"Oh, Julie, you're such a Good Samaritan." I laughed.

"Good Samaritan, my ass. I just thought we were going to get caught for drinking in our room. I couldn't throw that bitch into her own room fast enough. I would've stapled her mouth shut if I had the means." I could hear her pouring what sounded like pop over ice.

"You got her back later in the year when you peed outside her room," I reminded.

"That wasn't my fault. The bathroom was locked and I really had to go." I heard her take a long drink and sigh.

"Locked or required the turning of the knob and you didn't have the motor skills at the time to do so?"

"Who can remember?" she sighed. "Hey, so I think I'm finally ready to go on another Internet date."

"Really?"

"Yep. Next weekend. Oh, but hey, do you want to go out tonight? I have an extra Second City ticket."

I sighed. "I wish. I have Ash Leigh's first birthday party tomorrow and I need to be at full strength to deal with the giant disease *that* party's going to be. Want to come and keep me company?"

"I'd rather give myself a Brazilian bikini wax while on a Tilt-A-Whirl," she practically shouted into the phone.

"Funny," I said. I paused for a moment.

Screw it. I have to talk to her about it. I've turned to Julie for advice about every major life decision I've made; the choice to keep working or stay at home definitely qualifies.

"So, I need to talk to you about something," I said quickly.

"Oh no. You're pregnant again, right? Keep your pants on!" Julie sputtered.

"No! Lord, no!" I waved my arms around as though she could see me. "Not even close. And hopefully this won't be even more terrifying for you, but I, um, am considering the idea of staying at home." I closed my eyes and winced slightly. It was still hard to say out loud with any conviction. "But just considering," I quickly added.

There was a long pause and I thought she'd dropped dead.

"No fucking way," Julie whispered into the phone.

"Tell me about it," I said as I leaned forward and put my head onto my kitchen countertop.

"Well," she said thoughtfully. "You'd never have to deal with Mule Face again, so that's a bonus."

"True," I said.

"I mean, I honestly can't picture you being a stay-at-home mom, but whatever. If you think you'd be happy. But what would you do all day?" Julie whispered.

I shrugged. "I don't know, but I'm sure I'd be busy. I'd be with Sara. I'd love to ask Reese, but I suspect that question is slightly loaded, like, asking a working mom how she 'does it.' There's judgment implied, even though I really wouldn't mean it like that. I'm just honestly curious."

"Yeah, definitely. She gets pissed off really easily," Julie said.

Pot, meet kettle, I thought.

"Anyway, whatever you decide, I'll be happy for you."

My shoulders slumped with relief that she chose not to remind me of my college diatribes on Why Women Should Work.

"Thank you," I said quietly.

"No prob, Donna Reed," Julie said with a laugh.

Sunday, June 22

. . . .

An open letter to the attendees of Ash Leigh's birthday party:

> *Dear All:*
>
> *I'm not like you. Get over it.*
>
> *That means I don't wear a fanny pack or Mom Jeans. I don't know how to make anything involving a slow cooker. I don't know how to make nut-free treats for afternoon play group (which I can't attend because—let's review: I work), but I'm very good at ordering takeout, does that count?*
>
> *One more thing: My daughter is not even a year old yet. Please do not ask when I'm having the next one. I'll have the next one just as soon as we figure out a way for Jake to get pregnant.*
>
> *Also? Dressing yourself and your child in matching*

Crocs does not a good fashion statement make. So please put on something else. Your shoes are burning my eyes.

While I acknowledge your child is cute, I did not want to see five hundred pictures of her at Halloween, her rolling over, her next to a farm animal or picking her nose. M'kay? Find something else to talk about other than The Time Little Jackie Caught Croup or your son's bowel movements. I have a kid and I have plenty to talk about. Try reading a newspaper or picking up a book once in a while.

And? Lady with the bowl haircut à la the little kid on Family Ties? *You blow. I don't care your kid started sleeping through the night, or STTN as you called it, at six weeks. You are not a better mother than I am because my kid wants to party all night long rather than sleeping in her crib for fifteen hours straight. I will not bow down to you like the other loser moms there who fawned all over you, fetched you cocktails, and exchanged onion soup mix recipes.*

And earth to the lady wearing overalls. First off, overalls are cute on kids. Adults, unless employed as carnival workers, should not wear them. By the way? It's not called baby weight when your kid is eighteen. You don't need to "lose a few pounds left over from the pregnancy." After two years, "baby weight" turns into "fat." News flash: you look like you should be on the Facts of Life *reunion special. Repeatedly grabbing your muffin top, stretching it, complaining about it, showing me the stretch marks on your boobs, and then crying about how your husband would rather watch* Monday Night Football *than have sex with you made me want to kill myself. Please also tell your husband I didn't enjoy him repeatedly grabbing my ass.*

While I know I'm still pretty soft around the middle, I choose not to draw literal attention to it and reveal my fat to strangers. There's these girdle things called Spanx and they work awesome.

I would also like to remind you all I did not, repeat: did not, *dress Sara that day. As you may recall, I met Jake and Sara at the party since I had to run some errands. My husband, not I, chose her outfit. If I dressed my daughter in a onesie and pants, I would at least know to snap the onesie at the crotch, under the pants, rather than allowing the front and back flaps to hang freely over her jeans and flap in the breeze. Had I been home I also would have asked Jake to seriously rethink his outfit of light-colored 1987-style jeans paired with a black waffle-weave Henley shirt and brown loafers. You all knew he was a technology geek before he even presented his debate on LCD versus Plasma.*

Oh, and thanks *for so sweetly comparing my job as an event planner to the time you planned your parents' anniversary party. Now that you mention it, pulling off a black-tie gala that raises over a million dollars is just like gluing old photos of your parents to a poster board and baking frozen puff pastry appetizers.*

And speaking of my job, thanks for telling me that you think that the ladies at day-care are "raising" Sara. I debated telling you about the current decision in front of me, but you all proved that you share but one brain cell and not a shred of compassion. You guys rule!

Clare

P.S. Sorry. I think my life decisions are slowly turning me into a stressed-out bitch. Much like the ring that turned that Gollum guy in those Lord of the Rings *movies that Jake forced me to watch under the guise of "Oscar-Nominated Movie Night."*

Wednesday, July 2

. . . .

I just read back over my last entry about the tragedy of attending Ash Leigh's birthday party. And I pretty much want to punch myself in the face.

Because complaining about attending an annoying birthday party?

Grow up. There are bigger things to worry about—like today. My mom is starting chemo today.

A huge part of me wants to ignore it, crawl under my huge fluffy down comforter, stare at the grainy pattern of my jersey-knit sheets, and pretend that I'm still a little kid, playing hide-and-seek with Mark, and my only worry is whether or not I'll get the newest My Little Pony for Christmas. (It wasn't even a true worry: I always did.)

It's hard to look at Sara sometimes since she turns me into a very un-Clare-like ball of mush anyway. And she reminds me so much of my mom. So well, yeah . . . open up the goddamn floodgates.

Is it wrong I desperately want to regress, pretend I don't have a kid and go out dancing?

Or do something. Anything other than be an adult right now.

Jake and I have had the "She'll be fine, everything is OK, blah blah blah" conversation about fifty gazillion times over the past twenty-four hours. He won't even let me express my fears. The second I start to say, "But what if . . ." he holds his hand up in the air, waves it around, and somewhat harshly tells me that I can't think like that.

I know I can't.

But it's all I think about.

I talked to her an hour ago. She said she's fine, just a little tired. She said the effects won't really kick in for a few days, so next week should be a doozy.

I finally broke down and wrote an entry about my mom on my blog yesterday. I made Jake read the comments and delete any that weren't totally *OMG! OF COURSE SHE'LL BE FINE!!!! YOUR MOM IS AWE-SOME!!! YAY!!! TEAM CLARE'S MOM!!!!!* He did show me one e-mail from a Chiquita75 who suggested I take my mom out to Hooters when she's feeling better. Now *that* is the best idea I've heard in a long time.

Jake did his part today by renting out every gross-out funny movie from Blockbuster and continuously fetching me Popsicles.

Friday, July 4
. . . .

The sadness is still almost a solid shell around me, but I'm not going to write about it, much like not believing in Tinkerbell will make fairies disappear.

I instead choose to focus on the wonderful distractions of America's Favorite Holiday.

Jake and I took Sara to see fireworks tonight. After our experience, I can't help but wonder: is Fourth of July the National Act Trashy Holiday?

Is there a blast e-mail that goes out on July 3 reminding these people to launder their best wifebeater T-shirts, dust off their beanbag sets, and ice down the Milwaukee's Best? Oh, and don't forget your Confederate flag blanket!

I guess it makes sense.

Fireworks can be cool, but Question: why can't people just be satisfied with like a sparkler or smoke bomb or something?

Answer: because a smoke bomb or sparkler doesn't involve risking one's extremities.

Why do people spend like a thousand bucks on fireworks that last for ten minutes? And they're usually the kind of people who probably don't have a thousand bucks to spend. I mean, it's *literally* like burning your money. I should just offer to take these people's money, light some newspaper on fire, and throw it on the ground and they'd be just as mesmerized.

Also, the Fourth of July allows people to bring blankets and lie on them in grassy areas in the dark. Which, to teenagers, translates to a public acceptance of lying on top of one another while barely dressed, blankets only slightly covering God-knows-what their hands are doing.

We had a group of sexually active teens on a blanket next to us. As Jake and I set our blanket down on the grass, I poked him in the ribs. "They're emptying out their pop cans and filling them with cheap gin."

Jake shrugged and said, "You probably did the same thing in high school."

"True," I said as I sat down and started getting Sara comfortable. I started to feed her a few spoonfuls of rice cereal when I poked Jake again as he was typing an e-mail on his BlackBerry. "They're smoking weed now!"

"This weed rocks!" said the girl with the lip ring and dragon tattoo on her lower back.

"I know!" said the pregnant teenager, alternating between smoking tobacco and dope.

"Just ignore them," Jake said as he turned Sara away from the live version of the *Jerry Springer Show*.

I looked down and Sara was craning her neck at them, her "Mr. Burns from *The Simpsons*" expression on her face. Her eyebrows were pulled way down in a sinister fashion and she drummed her fingers together underneath her chin.

I didn't think I'd have to talk to her about premarital sex so soon.

Thankfully, the fireworks display started quickly and Sara was mesmerized by the blue, white, and red hues exploding in the sky. I thought we had suffered the worst until one of the hillbillies loudly asked, "If they can make fireworks in the shape of stars and circles and stuff, why can't they make them in the shape of something cool? You know, like a dog or a naked chick or something?"

Very philosophical question, indeed.

"Do you think they're related to Julie?" Jake asked with a smirk. I gave him looks of Death and threw a glow stick at him.

"I'd rather be related to those people than your mother," I said with a laugh.

Slam dunk, Clare!

Then, I nearly had a heart attack when I saw Greg off in the distance with some friends. I guess I shouldn't have been surprised to see him, as this fireworks show was the most popular in the city. But still. It was a bit jarring.

Dressed in pressed khaki shorts and collared polo shirts, Greg, Nate, and Ethan stood around a picnic table covered in appetizers, bottles of wine, and champagne flutes. Tanned, fit, and well-rested, the crowd of friends around Greg raised their wineglasses and cheered.

Surrounded by Milwaukee's Best cans and wifebeater tank tops, I was very aware that my section so would not have been offered lifeboats on the *Titanic*. We were most definitely in steerage.

And that tiny longing came back. To be over there, sans child. Or to at least suck the eight hours of sleep right out of their heads.

As the fireworks ended, Sara (with her infinite sense of timing) had a massive diaper explosion.

"EW!" the hillbillies on the blanket next to us gagged.

Yes, ew. And I wasn't totally grossed out when the girl wearing a white wifebeater T-shirt with no bra underneath screeched, "LARRY! I TOLD YOU! YOU CAN ONLY STICK IT IN MY BUTT! I CAN'T HAVE NO MORE KIDS!"

Jake and I thought the excitement for the night was over when we got home, but some of our neighbors in the next building over decided that 2:00 A.M. was a reasonably appropriate time to set off an additional fireworks display, complete with drunken yelling.

After Sara woke up and started screaming, I made Jake go outside and talk to them.

According to him, it went something like this:

Jake: Hi, guys, sorry to be a drag, but could you guys please stop it? It's two A.M. and my six-month-old just woke up.

Drunk Guy with Two Missing Teeth: Almosht done, go-in to bed now.

Drunk Girl with Bad Spiral Perm: FUCK HIM! WE AIN'T DONE YET!

Jake: Great, thanks.

I wanted to call the police but concurred with Jake's reasoning that being toothless and having a bad perm is punishment enough.

Monday, July 7

My very savvy readers overwhelmingly agreed with my assessment of Fourth of July as National Blow Off Your Hillbilly Hand Day. A few even posted similar stories, like CKLady, whose white-trash neighbor blew his hand off with an M-80 last year and his wife drove him to the hospital only after she and her friends set off the rest of the fireworks. Since the fireworks were illegal and they had paid good money for them and didn't want them to go to waste, obviously.

Jen2485, not surprisingly, wrote: *U r so judgmental. there is nothing wrong with having an American flag decal on your car. R u not proud to be an American? Guess not since u don't like 4th of July. U shuld just join the Taliban. Operation Enduring Freedom Rulez!*

I almost wrote her and said, *U R an idiot. Love ya!*

But no amount of sarcasm can change my reality or extinguish the gloominess that's beginning to form around me again.

I just got off the phone with my mom.

She sounds awful. Weak, tired, dazed. Sick. She sounds sick.

Because she is.

Friday, July 18

Saving me from another evening of sobbing into a pint of Ben and Jerry's and throwing DVD cases at the wall, Jake offered an idea tonight that brightened my mood.

"Clare, come in here," he called from our bedroom earlier tonight.

"Wha?" I said, distracted.

"Just come here," he said, his voice raising.

"*Shhhhhh.* You'll wake up Sara," I hissed.

"Please come in here," he said again.

"Fine," I said, and sighed loudly. I shuffled into the bedroom and put my hands on my hips. "What is so important? I'll have you know that you just tore me away from *Deep Impact*."

He looked up from the laptop and squinted his eyes. "The asteroid movie?"

"Correction: comet movie. Elijah Wood was just about to outrun the fiery wall of destruction on his ten-speed."

"Oh jeez, *so-ory*. Didn't mean to make you miss *that*. What's next? *Showgirls?*"

I started to sit down on the bed but froze mid-squat. "*Showgirls* is a good movie."

"Seriously. Did you seriously just say that?" he said, and covered his eyes with his hand.

"Give Elizabeth Berkley a break. It must've been hard to peak theatrically as a teenager on *Saved by the Bell*." I flopped down next to him and hugged my pillow.

"Fine. Jessie Spano aside, I thought only drag queens like *Showgirls.*"

"OK, fine. You caught me. I'm secretly a gay man. Is that what you wanted to tell me?"

"No, I wanted to show you this." He swiveled our laptop around on his lap and pointed to the screen.

"Who's buying a house?" I said as I studied the cute English Tudor with amazing cherry cabinets in the kitchen.

"Well, I thought we might."

My adoration stopped. Cruel joke.

"Jake. We can't ever afford that house. You're hilarious," I said as I started to hoist myself up.

He grabbed my wrist. "You don't like it?"

"I love it. Why are you torturing me by showing me houses we will never be able to afford?"

"I think we might be able to afford something like this." His finger tapped the computer screen.

"Uh, OK," I said, and rolled my eyes.

"No, really. We might be able to do it, especially with my promotion. No matter—no matter what you end up deciding about work. Besides, we'll have another kid at some . . ." He trailed off.

My lips formed a thin smile. "Did you seriously just say another kid?

Um, hi. Our daughter is like six months old. You're thinking about another kid?"

"Not tomorrow." He shrugged.

"I'm going to pretend you didn't even bring up the issue of having other kids." The notion of another nine months of puking and then another three of zero sleep doesn't exactly appeal to me right now.

"OK, but what about the fact that we could have so much more space?"

"I don't know, it's such a huge step. I mean, we'd have to pack up all our stuff, we'd have to find the right place, we'd have to—"

"This one has a whirlpool tub," he interrupted.

"We should totally buy a house."

Monday, July 21
. . . .

Jake and I spent the weekend molesting our laptop while marveling over real estate. So, naturally, I planned on continuing the practice today.

I stopped in the bathroom before I walked into my office this morning. As I stood at the sink, washing my hands, Mule Face trounced in, wearing what I've dubbed the "couch jacket" since it closely resembles the upholstery of my grandparents' couch, and practically threw herself into a stall. Now, it's embarrassing and uncomfortable enough to share a bathroom with coworkers. I always feel somewhat awkward when I see Christina in the bathroom, like it's too personal or something. Of course, I had no problem regaling her with graphic details of Sara's birth, but to be within twenty feet of her when I'm peeing? Awkward.

Anyway, Mule Face is clearly sick today. Yes. It was not good. It was also not good when she started moaning and grunting. I mean, it's bad enough that I had to be witness to her, um, issues, let alone with vocalization.

I scurried out of the bathroom faster than Butterscotch to the gay pride parade.

I regained my composure by drooling over real estate online. I quickly became bored with the houses we could actually afford and moved on to the houses we would never be able to afford unless Jake and I decide to peddle Internet porn. Of course, it was so much harder to go back to the "regular" houses after I'd seen houses with media rooms, lake views, and wine cellars.

I didn't have much time to dream about what I could afford with my porno empire, as I interviewed candidates for my assistant position this afternoon. Three interviews were scheduled, back-to-back. At first, I felt slightly guilty, as I wasn't sure if I would choose to stay home with Sara in the near future and leave this assistant most likely working for Mule Face, but my cards are still firmly resting against my chest.

The first candidate was a woman in her mid-fifties, a former stay-at-home mom who was looking to get back into the workforce. She seemed qualified for the position until she told me she'd have to leave by three o'clock every day to pick up her kids at school. Now, I'm a mom myself, but I no way expect my employer to let me off the hook a couple of hours early every day yet still pay me for full-time.

The next was a recent college graduate, who continually interrupted me to ask ridiculous questions like, "Would I have to start right *at* eight thirty? Is that set in stone?" I took that to mean she would probably be hungover most days and not able to function until sometime after ten. Now, I was fresh out of college not too long ago, but I didn't announce to my prospective employer I planned on getting trashed every night. I did, of course. I just didn't tell them straight out. (I'm sure it was noted, though, since I spent a good part of Friday mornings chugging soda, wolfing down cheese and egg sandwiches, and running to the bathroom.)

The final interview was a woman who seemed normal enough. She had a good résumé and excellent references. During the interview, I mentally hired her and she immediately organized my office, politely screened my calls, and became my new lunch buddy. I opened my mouth to ask a question about her previous position when Mule Face appeared at my door, holding a stack of saltine crackers and clutching her stomach.

"Ooohhh, I still don't feel well," she said, and crammed three crackers into her mouth.

"Er, uh, sorry to hear that," I said, and shifted in my chair. "Annie, I'd like you to meet—"

"Annie! Hi!" candidate number three said.

"Oh my God! I had no idea you were interviewing for this position!" Mule Face turned to me. "We worked together about three years ago." She turned back to Number Three and whispered, "You don't want to work with Clare, she's a drag." Mule Face turned to me. "Kidding!"

Kidding or not, I knew there was no way I was going to hire a personal friend of Mule Face. I can just picture their daily lunch sessions where they'd draw mean pictures of me and try to tape KICK ME signs on my back.

"How's Big D?" Number Three asked.

"Oh, you know, the same. He's been out of work now for a few months after his company got bought out, so I've really had to make up the extra money with my mail-order cosmetics."

"You must love having a cosmetics consultant in your office!" Number Three said, turning to me.

"Clare? Not a chance! She's never bought anything from me. I don't know why, my cosmetics are amazing!"

Yes. The oozing, scabby rash on your face was truly amazing, I thought.

"You have to try our new sea kelp facial toner. It gets rid of all those fine lines!"

Mule Face and Number Three chatted for another ten minutes until interrupted by my cell phone.

I pulled my phone out of my bag and saw the number was Sara's daycare. "Excuse me, I have to take this," I said as I flipped my phone open. Mule Face and number three watched as my mouth dropped open and I hastily stood up after I closed my phone.

"I have to leave. There's an emergency at my daughter's day-care!" I said as I shoved my planner into my bag and shut down my computer.

"Is everything OK?" Mule Face asked.

"Yes! Yes! I just have to go pick her up because . . . er . . . because." I finished my sentence and ran out the door. I chose not to tell them that Sara's day care had requested I pick her up because some kid *bit her* and she was hysterical.

As I drove to pick up Sara, I kept calm about my assistant prospects by reasoning that I had another few weeks to find a candidate until I got an e-mail just now from Christina. She said I needed to hire someone as soon as possible thanks to our budget. And she didn't seem too thrilled that I had to leave in the middle of the day just because some obnoxious kid went all T. rex on my daughter.

So, great.

Thursday, July 31
. . . .

Sky?

Any candidates you'd like to drop upon me? Please?

Because, if God listens to my repeated prayers, I'm going to be busier than the prophylactic vending machine during a porn convention. Since I think I've found my next client.

Today, I met Julie at a wine bar in the city after work. Jake picked up Sara up from day-care and gave me a reprieve.

I got there first, as Julie got hung up at the hospital due to a packed ER. The place was filled with stereotypical businessmen in pinstripe suits, Lincoln Park Trixies looking to pick up one of the aforementioned businessmen, and groups of drunken coworkers loudly bashing their bosses. After I had been standing awhile with my wine, two blondes fell off their bar stools and I was able to snag them since the blondes were too drunk to notice they were on the floor.

I settled in and played with a cocktail napkin until I heard, "Sorry, I'm so late. Sorry!"

I whirled around on my bar stool. "I've been waiting forever. I wasn't sure if you were going to show."

Julie was still dressed in her hospital scrubs. Pale blue V-neck top with lavender and yellow swirls all over it, drawstring pants, and bright yellow Crocs. "Yeah, yeah, yeah. Next drink's on me." Julie waved at the bartender and pointed to my drink. "Same," she yelled across the bar. "So, what's going on?" she said.

"Nothing, but I think your outfit is attracting some attention," I said, and pointed to a group of perfectly coiffed, anorexic-thin, bitchy women now staring at us.

Julie looked down at her hospital scrubs and rolled her eyes. "Grow up! This isn't high school," she called over to the *Sex and the City* fembots. They quickly looked away, concentrating on catching the interest of the wasted businessmen at the next table.

"Nice," I said. "I think you look good. You could be the hot new nurse on *ER* who isn't afraid to keep everyone in line."

"Always. God, this wine is good," she said as she took a long sip.

"Work busy?"

"It's a full moon tonight, which translates to a packed ER and exhausted Julie."

"I thought that was always just a myth."

"Nope. We get packed and the psych ward goes crazy. Pun intended. Labor and Delivery always gets slammed, too."

"Yeah, well, thank God it's someone else in Labor and Delivery."

"You had the easiest delivery ever, get over it," she said. "So anything new with Gregory?"

I shook my head. "Nope. Haven't talked to him since the kickoff. But I'm meeting with him again soon."

Julie rolled her eyes. "Have fun." She paused and her expression changed. She narrowed her eyes at me. "You're not thinking of . . ." She trailed off.

I reached out and gave her a light tap on the shoulder. "Julie! No!"

"OK, OK! Relax! Just checking."

I shook my head. "Not at all."

"Good, because you were always so goddamn insecure around him. All 'Whatever you want, Greg. Your wish is my command' bullshit."

I rolled my eyes. "Thanks." I fiddled with my engagement ring. "But like I said, no way. We're just working together." I grabbed my drink and took a long swig.

"Ah, Greg. What a douche bag." She laughed and swirled the wine around in her glass. Her lips curled downward and her expression softened. "So how's Mama?" she asked quietly.

I shrugged as I felt the fear in my stomach begin to bubble up again. "Tired. Sick."

"Yeah, but she's just gotta get through this. She's still going to be fine." Julie nodded her head firmly, her eyes soft.

"I know, I know." I tucked my hair behind my ears and rubbed my forehead. "Let's talk about something else."

"Wanna hear about my last Internet date?" Julie offered.

"Yes! Please!" I clapped my hands together, grateful for the distraction.

"OK, so. This new guy that I went out with the other night. Again, seemed totally normal, right? Well, we go out for Mexican." She grabbed my forearm and leaned in. "His suggestion! So, anyway. Great dinner, fine conversation. Seems like it might go somewhere. Until we get back in his car and . . ." Julie paused and leaned in a bit closer. "He started totally farting."

"What? Ew!" I leaned back in horror.

"That's not even the worst part. He kept blaming his car. Said it was his catalytic converter or something." Julie wrinkled her nose and shook her head. "What a loser."

"No kidding! That'll be such a great recap for the bl—"

"Holy shit!" she interrupted me.

"What? You almost made me spill my wine," I said, and daintily took a sip.

"Look!" She pointed across the bar.

I followed her self-tanning-lotion-streaked finger over to a corner of the bar. My gaze rested on two women huddled together, one with gorgeous highlighted blond hair floating around her shoulders in cascading waves and a brunette with glossy chestnut hair and bangs cut severely across her forehead. Two pink cocktails sat in front of them, lipstick staining the glasses. I didn't recognize them at first, so I squinted and leaned forward. The blonde looked vaguely familiar, but I couldn't place her.

"OK, I give up, who are they?" I said to Julie, and shrugged.

"Seriously? You don't recognize the blonde?"

I looked again.

"Nope."

"How about if I say news anchor?"

"No!" My mouth dropped open. I looked one more time. "Elise Stansfield? The former news anchor?"

"Yep! Isn't she amazing?" Julie whispered.

"Julie, there were rumors she slept with sources for information!" I said as I, like everyone else in the place, tried not to stare at Elise.

"Completely unfounded rumors. Never proven true," Julie said as she waved her hand around dismissively.

"She was fired, her husband divorced her, no news station will hire her, there was that huge article about how she's lost everything in the newspaper last year, and you envy her?" I shook my head, incredulous.

Julie pursed her lips and rolled her eyes. "She's a legend now. Her story was on the front page of every newspaper. 'Beloved Anchorwoman Falls from Grace.' So cool," she sighed.

"Can you imagine, though? Her whole life was basically ripped to shreds and they never proved anything. She went from being one of the most famous, revered people in the city to being . . . nothing. Trash. Her name has been on the Do Not Invite list for every event I've done in the past year." I leaned forward and put my chin in my hands. "I bet she didn't even do anything wrong." I stole another glance at Elise. "She kind of fell victim to the Lloyd Dobler thing," I said, and shook my head.

"What?" Julie furrowed her penciled-in brow.

"The perception that people are in real life they way they are in movies or on TV. It's from John Cusack in the movie *Say Anything*. He played this really amazing, unbelievable boyfriend in that movie, and people loved him for it. So when they come up to him, they expect him to be as nice and sweet as Lloyd Dobler and if he isn't people are horrified. I think he talked about it in an interview once."

"How does this relate to Elise?"

"She was a loved newswoman. People projected their own expectations on her. And when she made a mistake, the shit hit the fan."

"Whatever you say, Freud," she said. "Was *Say Anything* that movie with the guy who stood outside his girlfriend's house with the boom box?"

"That's the one. Such a great scene," I sighed.

"Great scene, my ass. There's a mentally ill man who stands outside my building and blasts music all the time. I usually end up calling the cops on him."

"Calling the cops on Lloyd Dobler. Only you would do something like that."

"Yes, I would," she said, and gazed across the bar.

"Another round?" I said.

Nothing.

"Julie?"

She stared at Elise.

"Yo, freak!" I said, and waved my hand in front of her face.

"What? Oh, sorry. Sure, whatever. I'll take another glass of wine," she said, and held up her empty wineglass, her eyes across the bar.

"No way, this round's on you, remember?"

"What?"

"Forget it," I sighed, and called to the bartender.

I was finally able to get Julie's eyes back to me after I waved my new Dior lip gloss in front of her face and promised to let her try it. After that, I kept her focus by telling her a story about a good vibrator advertisement.

We managed to have an actual conversation until two seats opened up next to us at the bar and Elise Stansfield and her brunette friend moved and sat down. Julie's eyes became as round as my belly at nine months pregnant and she uncharacteristically became silent.

"Get over it." I rolled my eyes and swished my wine around in the glass.

We sat silently, Julie starstruck and me studying the gunk trapped in my engagement ring setting.

". . . no time. Between the guest list, band, favors, presents, and everything, I think I'm going to explode. It's ridiculous what these parties have become," I overheard Elise say to her friend.

Her friend nodded. "Don't feel like you have to put yourself out. It's just a party."

"No, it's not just a party. You can't throw 'just a party.' These have become such a big deal," Elise said, and fluffed her hair around her shoulders.

"Clare, are you ready—," Julie finally said.

"Shhhhh," I hissed at her, and poked her in the knee.

"You should just hire someone to take care of everything for you. Honey, you don't have the time," the friend said.

"I know. I should. Let's talk about something else. I'm getting stressed at even the notion. So how's Judy?" Elise said.

I reached into my purse and felt my leather business card holder. Despite my choices and decisions tearing me apart inside and still not being ready to choose black or white, I knew I had to do it. My indecision does not excuse me from moving my career forward and landing new clients.

"Sure, let's go," I said to Julie. "Get the check."

I took a deep breath and stood up. I straightened my tweed skirt and tucked my hair behind my ears. I took a step toward Elise.

"What are you doing?" Julie rasped.

I held my hand up and walked over to Elise and her friend.

"Hi. Excuse me, I couldn't help but overhear your conversation. I'm Clare Finnegan and I work for Signature Events, a premiere event-planning firm. If you're ever interested in hiring a professional for your event, please keep me in mind." I thrust my business card forward.

Elise stared at me for a moment with her flashing green eyes before she reached forward and took the card out of my hand.

"Thank you"—she looked down at my card—"Clare." She turned away from me and took a sip of her cocktail.

I knew I'd been dismissed.

"Let's go." I yanked Julie's arm and managed to walk outside without tripping over anything.

"I can't believe you had the balls to talk to her!" Julie panted.

"Please." I waved my hand around. "She doesn't scare me. She's just a canned news anchor."

"A canned news anchor who has a shitload of money, tons of famous friends, and who is known by probably eighty percent of the city."

"Exactly. Which means a huge budget for whatever party's in the works." I grinned at Julie and stuck my hand out to hail a cab.

"God, you're such a badass, finding clients at happy hour."

"I know," I said, and ran my fingers through my hair.

It was one of the rare moments in my life when I felt pretty cool and it wasn't tempered by me publicly embarrassing myself in some way. I'm surprised I didn't trip and spill red wine all over Elise's gorgeous cashmere twinset.

Later, as I got home and replayed the conversation in my head, a small thought began to drill itself into my head. I started to wonder if I approached Elise to prove something to myself. Not just about landing a client myself, but to prove that I could land a client like her.

I'm not going to analyze that to death. Instead, I'm just going to focus my energy on praying that Elise calls. Because Mule Face will die if I land a famous client, albeit a local client more infamous than famous, but still. She'll shit in her elastic-waist parachute pants.

Friday, August 1

. . . .

My ego was still sailing this morning on the way to Sara's day-care. I mentally planned the entire sure-to-be-elegant-but-understated-and-full-of-years'-worth-of-gossip soiree at each stoplight.

I'd sit all of the Hollywood types around the venue, so as not to isolate them. I wondered if the event would be at Elise's sprawling estate on the lake or some hip club in the city. Obviously, an enormous stocked bar with a signature cocktail and drink menus printed on custom-designed parchment paper. Just as I chose the table linens (eggshell, rather than standard white—too stark and traditional) and centerpieces (either an Asian twist with bamboo plants and hibiscus flowers or simple candelabras surrounded by floating gardenias), my cell phone rang.

Reese. I figured she'd been up for a few hours anyway with Brendan and wanted to lament about motherhood.

"Hey! What's up?" I said cheerfully, very uncharacteristic for eight thirty.

"Clare," she squeaked out.

"Reese, what's wrong?"

I heard a few sniffles, then silence.

"Reese! Reese! Are you OK? What's going on?"

"I did it," she whispered into the phone. I could hear Grace babbling in the background and Brendan making gurgling noises, like a miniature troll.

"Did what?"

"Matt. I asked him to move out." Her voice squeaked like a mouse.

I immediately pulled my car over, nearly sideswiping an old woman in a red Camry who was so busy shaking her fist at me that *she* nearly rear-ended the car in front of her.

"Oh my God! Are you OK? What happened?"

"We hadn't spoken in almost three days, and this morning, he turned to leave without saying good-bye to the kids. So I just snapped. I didn't raise my voice; I didn't yell. I just simply told him I didn't think it was working and I would like him to move out, but I was willing to still work on things."

"Oh, honey," I said, and rested my head on the steering wheel.

"I'm fine, I'll be OK." She cleared her throat and sniffled.

"What did he say?" I said.

"He didn't really say anything. He just stared at me for a while and then said, 'If that's what you want,' and walked out the door."

Such. An. Asshole.

If I married Reese, I'd swim across shark-infested waters during a hurricane to keep her.

"What can I do?" Sara began to cry in the backseat. I reached my hand back and grabbed her car seat and awkwardly tried to rock her without dislocating my shoulder.

"Nothing. I'm great. Don't worry about me. I know you need to get to work." Her voice cracked in between words, as though worrying about her was a lost cause.

"No, Reese, this is more important than—," I started to say.

"Just call me after work," she said.

"Reese—"

"Clare. Please," she said.

"OK, I'll call you later." I hung up, my fingers shaking.

I started to pull back onto the road, toward Sara's day-care and work. I went about ten feet before I pulled my car over again. I snapped open my phone and dialed Christina's extension and left a message letting her know I was taking a personal day off. She didn't sound thrilled, especially after the whole Leaving Early Due to Hitting incident, but Reese was more important. I next called day-care and said she wouldn't be in today. I got back on the highway and drove over to Reese's house.

She answered the door in full makeup and wedge heels.

"You look better than I do." I laughed.

"I knew you'd show up, so I figured I should look halfway decent," she said as she leaned forward to hug me.

"Reese, your 'halfway decent' is my 'oh-my-God-I've-never-looked-better-in-my-life,'" I said as I held her bony shoulders tightly to me.

She thinly smiled as I released her. She turned to Sara. "She's getting so big," Reese said as she kissed Sara on the cheek.

We walked into Reese's family room, which was uncharacteristically quiet.

"Where are the kids?" I asked as I craned my neck.

"Down for their naps, thankfully," she said. She sat down on her leather couch and leaned her head back and closed her eyes.

"Are you sure there's nothing I can do?" I said as I sat Sara down on the couch next to Reese.

Reese opened her beautiful blue eyes and looked down at Sara for a long time. Sara stared back at her, transfixed by the petite woman next to her. Reese looked up at me, her eyes red and rimmed with tears. She twisted her hands in her lap and two perfect tears dropped across her cheeks.

"Oh, Reese," I said, and grabbed her hand. "You're going to be just fine."

She nodded and brushed two manicured fingers across her cheeks. "I still have most of my trust money, so I'm going to be OK."

I nodded. "Have you told your parents?"

She laughed ruefully. "Not exactly."

I figured she hadn't. I'm sure they're not going to be exactly thrilled to hear their daughter and their perfect son-in-law are separated, let alone heading for divorce. In her family, "looking the other way" is an art form.

"I'm starting DePaul in a few weeks," she said, changing the subject.

"That's so great. I think it's definitely a smart move. How long will it take to get your master's?" I asked.

"Two years. I can't wait to go back to teaching." She smiled.

"You're the perfect teacher. You're blessed with the patience of a saint," I said.

I looked around her house and I saw beautiful Pottery Barn end tables, sparkling Tiffany vases, and elaborate flower arrangements, but all that registered was gray. Reese had spent her life drawing lines between black and white, and now, despite her best efforts, the barrier had been removed and everything was awash with gray. Beautiful, perfect house and wonderful children, but no husband.

Reese had everything she ever wanted in a family but the missing piece of a husband.

I had everything I ever wanted in a career but the missing piece of feeling truly happy.

I put my arm around her and we silently sat together as I tried to will all of the mismatched puzzle pieces of our lives to transform into one beautiful picture.

I stayed for another hour until she started going into her typical Reese hostess mode of setting food out, offering me drinks, and fretting about the cleanliness of the house. I didn't want to stress her out anymore, so I hugged her for as long as she would let me and drove home with Sara.

I spent the rest of the day looking at my college photo albums, of old pictures of Jake and me and Matt and Reese. I showed Sara the pictures of her dad doing beer bongs and me after I gained all that weight freshman year. I laughed as I paged through the album.

Until a photo fluttered out of a page and down to the floor like an autumn leaf. It fell picture side down, the backing staring up at me. I gingerly picked it up and turned it over.

I squinted and looked at the girl in the picture. A girl who, by seemingly a different twist of the wind, would be a completely different person right now. Childless and focused on her career.

But would I be happier? jumped into my mind.

No, I certainly wouldn't be. I wouldn't have Sara.

Are you sure? Wouldn't it be easier? the devil on my shoulder whispered again.

No. I'm sure.

You wouldn't be miserable, right? At least admit to that. You never wanted this life. You never wanted your mother's life—trying to balance the impossible of work and home.

I looked at it for a long time before the spell broke. I crumpled it up in my hand and let it drop to the floor.

Yet as I stared at the folded picture on the ground, I wondered if I was supposed to pretend that my past goals and aspirations didn't exist. Like they weren't important or didn't mean anything.

You can't keep this up for much longer.

I picked the photo up off the ground, folded it in half, and stuck it in the back of the album. I kissed the top of Sara's blond head and rubbed my cheek against her soft hair. I held her tightly to me and rocked her gently until my arms felt weak. She remained silent and still and let me hold her, almost as if she was aware of my uncontrollable need to hold her close.

When I did let her go, she looked into my eyes, scrunched her brow, and blew a huge wet raspberry in my face, covering it with spit.

I laughed and my heart lightened about fifty degrees.

Saturday, August 2
. . . .

I didn't sleep much last night. I tossed and turned and yanked the covers away from Jake approximately every ten minutes. Possessed by the crazy-wife demon, I became irrationally angry when he had the *nerve* to breathe heavily, so I huffed and puffed as loudly as possible, hoping he would wake up. But thankfully, he stayed asleep.

I just about drifted off sometime after four o'clock when a high-pitched yelp jolted me awake.

"Jake!" I said, and poked him in the leg.

"Hsmissss," he mumbled, and turned over.

"Jake! Get up!"

Nothing.

"JAKE!" I gave him another ninja poke.

"WHAT?" he said, and sat straight up in bed.

"I heard something in the hallway outside. Go check it out," I said.

"It's fine," he said, and lay back down.

"Fine. I'll go check it out. It's probably an axe murderer awaiting his next victim and I'm going to get hacked into little pieces, but that's OK because you don't—"

"Jesus, I'm going, I'm going," he said as he swung his legs out of bed. He stumbled around in the darkness for a few seconds and tried to put a pair of jeans on. He threw a T-shirt over his head and shuffled out of the bedroom.

I didn't hear anything for a few minutes and I wondered if I should go and check on him, but I was scared the escaped mental patient outside had killed him and I didn't want Sara to be an orphan.

He walked into the bedroom chuckling.

"Did the serial killer tell you a joke or something before he decapitated someone?" I said.

"Not exactly." He laughed as he unbuttoned his jeans.

I stared at him as he lay back down in bed and closed his eyes.

"So what's so funny?"

"It was Champagne Wayne."

"Oh God. What was he doing?"

"More like *who* was he doing?"

"What?"

"Yep."

"Are you seriously telling me our neighbor is having sex right now outside in the hallway?"

"I'm pretty sure that's what it was, unless he bent that girl over to do a body cavity search. With his body parts."

"EW! We are so moving. I'm calling the Realtor tomorrow."

"Fine," he mumbled.

"Jake?" I said after five minutes.

"What?" he said, half-asleep.

"Do you think STDs can become airborne?"

Sunday, August 3

After I heard our skanky neighbor bone some hooker in the hallway last night, the search for suitable housing has become priority number one. I mean, I enjoy the low, low cost of rent, but I don't think Sara should have to live next to Mr. Walking Venereal Disease so Mommy and Daddy can save a few bucks.

So, I called a Realtor this morning, Rory Moonschmidt, my parents' friend. I was standing in the kitchen, holding Sara, whom I entertained by pointing to pictures in my new *US Weekly*. Just as Rory described how many bathrooms and bedrooms Jake and I could afford as I gestured toward a picture of Britney Spears eating a cheeseburger, Sara farted. She didn't just make a cute little baby fart. It was a reverberating, frat boy after eating White Castle and drinking beer fart. It was more like a boat's foghorn or a locomotive chugging to a stop.

Rory stopped talking in mid-sentence.

"Oh, that was, no, that wasn't, um, that. Uh, my baby. That was my baby," I sputtered as I felt my face turn crimson.

"Oh. OK," Rory said.

I looked at Sara and quickly tried to tickle her while making funny faces, trying to will her to make another noise, any noise so Rory would know she was there. I even tried to push on her stomach a little so she would fart again. But nothing. Abso-freaking-lutely nothing. That kid was silent for the first time in her life.

In fact, she remained silent the entire time I was on the phone, not even making one gurgle.

I'm sure Rory thinks I have some kind of intestinal problem. Great. She's probably going to start showing Jake and me houses with five bathrooms and soundproof walls.

Saturday, August 9

. . . .

There's nothing like coming home and seeing a drunk husband with his loser friend, equally drunk and somewhat stoned, sitting on the couch with two cans of Miller High Life to burst one's faux imaginary real estate bubble.

Today, I came home with an armful of groceries and spotted Bill-Until-Two-Months-Ago-I-Still-Lived-with-My-Parents. He came over to watch some college football game with Jake and the two of them wound up completely tanked by the end of it. Sara, thankfully, was asleep the whole time. I interrupted a debate over whether Tiffani-Amber Thiessen was hotter during her *Saved by the Bell* or *90210* days. It was a Valerie versus Kelly argument. I'm so glad they found something academic to discuss. (Although I can't really give Jake shit about it. Three years ago, Julie and I got into a "heated debate" over who was the hotter Corey: Haim or Feldman? A couple thousand drinks may or may not have been involved also.)

I wrestled the Boppy away from Jake, who had it around his waist as a place to rest his tall boy, and gave him an evil look.

"You know what you need, Clare?" Bill asked me.

"What?" I said.

"More cowbell!" He dissolved into hysterical, high-pitched laughter.

"Is he stoned again?" I asked Jake.

Jake shrugged but quickly kicked Bill out.

"Clare, I'm sor—," Jake started to say as he closed the front door after Bill left.

"Don't." I held up my hand. "I just—," I started to say as I felt the well of frustration beginning to surge inside. But I knew laying into Jake wouldn't help anything. So I dropped my hand back down to my side and exhaled. "I know." I sat down on the couch and kicked my shoes off. "I'm just tired."

Jake sat down next to me. "I'm sorry. I know my idiot friends are the last thing you want to deal with right now," he said quietly.

I shook my head. "It's OK. Like I said, I'm just tired. Work's been crazy lately." I silently wished that I were the slightly inebriated one on the couch, not stressing about the golf outing, worrying about my mom, or wondering if I missed Sara doing anything new at day care this week.

"Anything I can do?" Jake asked as he leaned back against the couch.

I shook my head again slightly. "No. I'll be fine. I just need a good night's sleep."

"I'm on it," he said as he leaned forward, grabbed my arm, and pulled me against his chest. "Tomorrow morning, I've got Sara. Before we go to any open houses. You sleep in."

"Deal," I said as I buried my face into his T-shirt. I closed my eyes for a moment and whispered, "Oh, and Jake?"

"Yeah?" he said.

"I'm still telling the Internet about this."

Sunday, August 10

. . . .

10:00 A.M.

I just got off the phone with Rory. She e-mailed over a list of three houses for Jake and me to check out today. According to her, they're "nice," "roomy," and, most important, aren't so far from the city that they might as well be in Iowa.

Judging from the pictures and the description, I just *know* one of these houses is the One.

4:00 P.M.

The One? Not exactly.

We pulled up to the first house, which looked even cuter than the picture online. It had white wood siding and navy blue shutters with beautiful pink impatiens in flower boxes resting on the windowsills.

I grabbed Jake's arm. "Oh my God! I *love* it. Let's get it!"

"Are you sure?" he said, and pointed to the house next door. The lawn looked like a rummage sale for plastic lawn ornaments and lawn jockeys. Pink flamingos, a family of deer, and a Santa statue encircled a giant wood cutout of a sleigh.

"Um, ya. Let's go in," I said. I figured it would be easy to give the pizza guy directions: *The house next to the one with all the shit in the yard.*

The interior was beautiful. It was perfect. The only problem was that we needed to breathe, oh, occasionally.

Not only did the owners appear to be very heavy smokers, as evidenced by the yellow ceilings, ashtrays in every room, and general odor of a dive bar, but they also had a cat. More than one, probably. Who all must be on strike from their litter box, as the entire place reeked of cat urine. I only stayed inside with Sara for about five minutes, as I wasn't sure what excessive exposure to cat piss would do to her still-developing wee brain. Now, I'm not one to complain about animals, seeing as how our cat is as well behaved as Stewie from *Family Guy,* but I don't think Jake and I have the funds to purchase enough gas masks to hand out to visitors before they even set foot through the door.

House Number One? Not the One.

We journeyed on to House Number Two.

This house was another equally gorgeous, redbrick colonial with white windows. It even had a garden tub in the master bathroom. Of course, it was decorated hideously, since a seven-foot-tall mural of a naked Indian carrying a dead white woman isn't exactly my taste, but it wasn't anything several gallons of paint couldn't fix. The shrine in the basement to Tupac Shakur didn't even deter me.

The ten thousand dollars a year in taxes did.

Apparently, when they built this subdivision, a onetime assessment was levied on each house to do general infrastructure work like road paving. People had the choice of either paying it upfront or rolling it into their yearly taxes. Guess which one these owners chose?

Moving on.

House Number Three was an old farmhouse from the 1800s. It was in an amazing location, one Jake and I thought we'd never be able to get near. It would be a huge investment opportunity and our property value would surely shoot up year after year.

The problem with House Number Three was location and nostalgic charm were about the only pluses. Now, I love old houses and their quirks, but living in this house would *literally* be like living in the 1800s.

No air-conditioning, one bathroom—on the *first floor*—narrow staircases, and no closets. Apparently, back in the good ole days, taxes were calculated per the number of rooms in a house. Closets were considered rooms. So, to save money, nobody built closets. Their gain? Our loss.

Also, the dirt floor cellar really creeped me out. And that's where the washer and dryer were located. I figured it would be a good excuse to never do laundry again, but the fuses (yes, fuses, not circuit breakers) were down there, too, and if the power ever went out and Jake wasn't home, Sara and I would be stuck in the darkness with no electricity (again, like the 1800s) until he came home.

And the no AC thing really wouldn't jive during the summer, when my hair expands to three times its normal size when it comes into contact with so much as a drop of humidity.

So, sadly, Jake and I aren't going to buy the Money Pit. My dad reminded us that we'd only seen three houses, it's a buyer's market, we have tons of time, blah, blah, blah. The problem is I'm already starting to panic. See, we can afford like 1 percent of what's on the market right now, buyer's advantage or not.

It didn't help when Marianne said, "Of *course* you're going to put at least thirty percent down, right?" and when I told her no, we didn't have extra tens of thousands of dollars saved up but that we were planning on making a modest down payment, she said: "Then you'd be at risk for foreclosure and default. You don't want to lose your house, do you?"

I started to freak out when Jake reminded me we hadn't even bought a house yet and I should probably wait until we find one and move before I start Googling what house foreclosure does to one's credit. But, looking at the spec sheets in front of me, I'm starting to worry if we even want to live anywhere we can afford. Not to mention, I'm afraid to look at more expensive houses, since I don't want to hamstring my decisions at this point.

So, today was pretty much a bust. Except I did discover Realtors give out free things, like juice and cookies at open houses. I think I'm going to go drown my sorrows in one of the oatmeal-raisins stuffed into my purse.

Monday, August 18

· ·

As if my working mom guilt needed another kick in the teeth, I was, once again, the last person to arrive in the office. I still arrived by 8:30 A.M., but it was clear that everyone else had already been working for at least an hour.

I collected a few things at my desk and left to go to Greg's office to drop off some golf shirt samples for the outing. Every golfer receives a collared shirt as part of the giveaway, and I needed Greg to choose between the lovely white waffle-weave cotton and the light blue nylon version.

Thrilling, I know.

I planned on dropping the shirts off with his secretary and sending him a follow-up e-mail, which was why I purposely stopped in around lunchtime. But, true to my luck, he had just gotten back from his lunch meeting.

"Clare! Come on in!" Greg said as he waved in from the reception area of the Thompson & Thompson, LLC, law firm.

I stood up and grabbed my bag. Except, out of nowhere, my ankle wobbled in my slingback shoe. My hands went toward the heavens and about a thousand pieces of paper, two golf shirt samples, and some miniature golf tees all scattered through the air like caps on graduation day.

"Oh!" I shrieked as my hands flailed through the air like a *Dancing with the Stars* contestant.

"Are you OK?" Greg said as he rushed to steady my elbow.

"I'm fine, I'm fine," I said as I fixed my errant shoe strap and surveyed the contents of my bag, which now littered the reception area. "Er, lemme just—" I kind of awkwardly half-crouched, half leaned over, and tried to pick up the hundreds of golf tees one by one.

"Here, let me help you." Greg bent down in his expensive suit and helped me corral all of the materials. He chuckled as he handed me the golf shirts.

"Thanks," I muttered under my breath. I looked over at him and laughed.

Golf outing paraphernalia shoved back into my bag, we stood up.

"My office is this way. Try not to break anything," Greg said, and pointed me down the hallway. "You sure your ankle is all right?" he asked as we walked down the oak-paneled corridor, past expansive offices with panoramic views of Lake Michigan.

"It's fine." I smiled at him despite the humiliation burning through me.

"Right here." Greg pointed to an office dripping with dark cherry bookcases, an enormous empty desk, and a pretty kick-ass computer monitor. It looked like a NASA command station.

So this was how he could afford that condo. Although I'll never admit it to anyone, I Googled Greg's name and found the property record for a condo he bought a year ago.

The sale price was more money than Jake and I will make in about five years. Either litigation was going well or Greg had a cocaine empire I was unaware of. (And if the latter is true, I'd be open to reading the business plan, as I'd like to live in a house that has indoor plumbing and is not located in a neighborhood consistently featured on *America's Most Wanted*. Just a request.)

"So here's the samples," I said, and slid the shirts across the desk.

"Oh, right," Greg said as he sat down across from me in his leather chair. He picked them up and studied them.

I looked around his office, his success evident in the fixtures. My office is littered with newspaper clippings of event coverage, the lamp on my desk is from IKEA rather than Tiffany, and I was excited to get a computer that had Microsoft 2003 on it earlier this year. Looking at Greg's computer, I'm sure he has Microsoft Armageddon on it, or whatever the upgrade is called.

"This one looks good," Greg finally said. He pointed to the blue nylon shirt.

"Great! I'll place the order," I said as I shoved both shirts back into my Bag of Death.

"Sounds good. Anything else I can do at this point?" Greg leaned back in his chair.

I shook my head. "Nope. Everything's under control and running smoothly." I stood up and glanced down at his desk while I rose. A photo caught my eye. "Hey! Is this from New Year's?" Before I could stop myself, my arm darted out and landed on the black-framed photo. I lifted it and brought it closer.

A photo of about twenty people, mostly his friends, from his fraternity house's annual New Year's party, freshman year. My eyes zeroed in on one person in the center. Looking happy. Like she was having fun. Like she got more than an average of four hours of sleep at night.

Me.

All of us smiling into the camera, cheering in the new year. Cheering to what we knew would be an amazing future. Or, at least, an amazing night until the beer ran out.

I remembered how nervous I was to go to the party. How I looked forever for a dress. How I didn't really know anyone there. How I awkwardly went to the bathroom every time Greg did, so I wouldn't be stuck standing there by myself.

How, when Jake and I started dating, I'd arrive at parties before he even got there and feel completely comfortable and welcome.

"Oh, sorry! Ignore that—I normally don't have old photos on my desk, but it got mixed in with a box from my home office," Greg said quickly. He looked embarrassed. "Not very professional."

I set the picture back down on his desk and smiled. "It's OK. I won't tell. Fun night, though."

Greg nodded as he quickly put the photo into a desk drawer. We stood silently for a moment until his cell phone began to chirp.

"Well! Thanks for everything and I'll be in touch!" I said quickly, and started toward the door.

"Thanks again, Clare," Greg called from his office as I walked down the hallway.

I drove back to my office in a fog.

I've come so far beyond that girl with too much eye makeup, too-high heels, and a mere shred of confidence. But despite all of that, I still felt spooked. Spooked because, despite my emotional growth, I felt something else as I stared at that picture.

Envy.

Envy for that girl's life. For her naïve view of the world. For her carefree attitude. For her self-allowances to make mistakes because, man, she had her whole life ahead of her. And she could be whatever she wanted.

Greg became exactly what he said he was going to in college—I've moved so far from that line that it's disappeared. If my goals have changed so drastically, does it just mean that they're adapting or that I've just given up? How much can my former dreams change before all of the good stuff gets edited out, like what my high school English teacher used to do to my creative writing assignments?

I have no answers, only questions. Like how was I supposed to prepare for Sara? She changed everything. How was I supposed to know that being apart from her would feel like a body part was missing? How was I supposed to know that having a child would make everything else in my life more muted?

Tuesday, August 19
. . . .

No rest for the weary.

Or it is no rest for the wicked?

Regardless, Sara's decided to adopt both as her motto.

Sara woke up every two hours last night, something she hasn't done in forever. Finally, around 3:00 A.M. or so, I closed her door, turned off the monitor, and decided to let her cry. Of course, I'll bet she fell asleep at 3:08 A.M. I'm sure her day-care teachers are going be thrilled with her today. Actually, she'll probably be a total angel for her teachers and have a meltdown the second I get her home.

As I sipped my coffee and blearily stared at my computer monitor this morning, my phone rang shrilly, jolting me out of my walking dead state. I sluggishly picked up my phone. "Clare Finnegan," I croaked.

"Yes, I'm looking for Clare Finnegan?" a woman's voice said.

"This is she," I said.

"Clare, my name is Elise Stansfield. You gave me your card a while back, if you recall."

I stiffened my spine, grabbed a pen, and crossed my legs. "Oh yes. Elise, thank you so much for calling. How can I help you?"

"Well, I'm planning, or should I say trying to plan, my daughter's sixteenth birthday party. I figured it would be a small party, one I could manage myself, but it's become completely out-of-control."

"They usually are," I said. "Sixteenth birthday parties are a pretty big deal. We do a lot of them at our firm."

"So I'm learning. Anyway, I checked your firm out and you came very highly recommended by Carolyn Wittenberg."

Carolyn Wittenberg? That coldhearted bitch actually recommended me? I worked on an event for her last year, and she reminded me of Cruella De Vil. If she were Satan's mistress.

"Oh yes. I truly enjoyed working with Carolyn last year."

"Well, I want to come in this afternoon to discuss what you can do for this event."

I closed my eyes and pumped my fist in the air, catching Mule Face's attention as she walked past my office. She stopped and stood in the doorjamb, blatantly listening.

"Of course, I can make myself available for whenever you are free."

"Good. Two thirty OK?" she said.

"Perfect. See you then, Elise," I said, and hung up the phone. I smugly smiled and pretended to brush some imaginary dust off my cherry desk.

"Who was that?" Mule Face finally asked.

"What? Oh, hi, Annie," I said with my best I-didn't-even-know-you-were-standing-there-as-I-am-so-busy-and-important-and-aren't-you-just-dying-to-know-who-I-was-talking-to?

"How's it going?" she said casually as she opened a bag of potato chips.

"Great. You?" I knew I was driving her insane.

"Who was that?" She finally caved.

"Oh, just a prospective client. I really can't say anything yet. Hopefully I'll have some good news," I said, and tapped my pen against my computer keyboard.

"Mmmm," she said. She turned and wiped her greasy fingers on my doorjamb as she left.

I checked my makeup and hair every five minutes from 1:30 P.M. on and lint-rolled my black suit until it was basically threadbare.

At three o'clock, there was still no sign and I gave up.

I threw my hair in a ponytail, rolled up the sleeves of my white blouse, and discreetly unbuttoned my still-too-tight-due-to-leftover-pregnancy-weight pants. Just as I'd settled in, Abby appeared at my door.

"Clare, Elise Stansfield is here for you," she said, looking somewhat bewildered.

"Really? Oh! OK, put her in the conference room and tell her I'll be just a minute." I quickly brushed my hair, smoothed my shirt, and sucked in my stomach to re-button my pants. I walked down the hallway, past an openmouthed Mule Face, and breezed into the conference room.

"Elise, hi. How are you? So nice to see you again," I said smoothly, and walked over to shake her hand.

"Clare, I'm well," she said. She stood next to the window in the conference room. She looked straight off the pages of *Town & Country* magazine. Her red cashmere twinset and stone-khaki pants were perfectly pressed and her brown suede Tod's driving moccasins probably cost more than my entire outfit. Her signature blond hair was pulled back tightly in a knot at the nape of her neck.

She walked over and sat down in one of the high-backed leather chairs.

"Did you find the office OK?" I asked her.

"Fine, fine," she said, and deposited an enormous Burberry plaid bag on the conference table. She put on a pair of Coach tortoise frames and rifled through her bag. She pulled out a pen and paper and looked expectantly at me.

Go time.

"Sixteenth birthday party. Here's what I've come up with: We hold it at a private home, either yours or one that we rent, it's more personal that way. The entire event will take place in a heated tent. The theme will be 'An Evening in Paris.' Various Cirque du Soleil performers will enact different routines throughout the evening, some suspended from the ceiling of the tent. In the center of the tent will be twenty-foot-tall ice sculptures of the Eiffel Tower and Arc de Triomphe. Tables arranged in a circular pattern, with a lounge area off to the side, draped in white with red lights. A water bar stocked with flavored water for guests as they arrive.

A candy sculptor during the cocktail hour designing custom sculptures made of candy. A backdrop of old video and photos of your daughter, all reshot in eight-millimeter for nostalgic appeal. Sixteen thousand balloons released at midnight and gift bags with a custom lip gloss and perfume named after your daughter."

I took a deep breath and sat back in my chair and waited for her reaction.

She put her pen down on her still-blank pad of paper and took her frames off.

I thought I totally blew it.

She looked back behind her out the window and slowly turned back to me.

"Sounds good. Let's get started," she said, and stood up.

"Oh! Great! OK! Um, let's set up a time to meet with your daughter so we can run this past her." I was slightly thrown, as I thought this was a pitch-session meeting rather than a "let's do it" meeting.

Elise waved her hand around. "She says she doesn't care. You plan it all," she said, and slung her bag around her shoulder.

"Er, Elise, in my experience, they *always* care. Believe me, my sister is around the same age and there's very little she *doesn't* have an opinion about." I knew I might've been overstepping my bounds, but the last thing I need right now is to spend eighty hours conceptualizing this party to have it all thrown out by a teenaged "no effing way."

Elise stopped and laughed. "Good point. We'll come in next week. Call me in a few days to set it up."

Before I could respond, she was gone and all that was left was a faint odor of Dior perfume and my still-shaking fingers.

Christina popped her head into the conference room.

"Was that Elise Stansfield?" she asked, and crossed her arms over her beautiful Chanel knit jacket.

"The one and only," I said nonchalantly as I stood up.

"Are you working with her?"

"I'm helping her plan her daughter's birthday."

"That's great!" Christina said, and raised her eyebrows. "How did you land her as a client?"

I shrugged casually. "I met her while out in the city one night."

"That's fantastic." Christina paused for a moment and clucked a little before she walked back into her office.

As soon as I sat down in my office, an e-mail from Mule Face popped up. It read: *That's fantastic!!!!!!!!!! Don't mess this one up or you'll be screwed!!!!*

Ha. Mess this one up? This event is going to be the crown jewel of my portfolio. I'm just hoping I can pull it off and not miss any more of Sara's bedtime. It's time to find the balance, time to give my career and being a working mom a good run. Because I love my job; when I'm running an event, I'm in control.

I can do this. I can pull off this event without affecting my time with Sara—but not without some help. I need to hire an assistant immediately to carry some of the load.

Wednesday, August 20
. . . .

Despite my professional coup in landing Elise Stansfield as a client, and re-posting the assistant position on the Internet, it's hard to be anything other than depressed today. Reese called me last night and said Matt is moving out today. He's renting an apartment in the city, and while there's still no official drawing up of divorce papers, it's not looking like they're going to be living happily ever after any time soon.

I never thought it would come to this. Yeah, she's so much better off and I think Matt is a total scumbag, but I always foolishly thought he'd come to his senses and wake the hell up or something and turn into the husband Reese deserves. But she's going to be so much better off.

Yet it still feels like we're all getting old enough to turn yet another of life's corners: divorce. There was a time a few years ago when everyone was getting married and rah-rah. Then, it was time for kids. But then what?

Now I know. Silly me. I thought it would be getting eight hours of sleep. But no.

It's Divorce.

Friday, August 22

· · · · · · · · · · · · · · · · · · · ·

Sara's scooting around on her belly. The first signs of crawling, according to Dr. Spock, she does this little army crawl where she propels herself forward by kicking her feet and swimming with her arms. She did it for the first time last night. I know because Jake told me.

I was detained in another late staff meeting. Christina sent an e-mail out around 4:00 P.M., asking everyone to meet in a half hour. Knowing that our meetings usually last at least an hour, I asked Jake to pick Sara up at day-care. We were supposed to meet our Realtor to look at a house, so we canceled that, too.

As I drove home sometime around 6:00 P.M., Jake called me and screeched into the phone that Sara had propelled herself across the carpet and tried to hit the cat. I didn't get to see it.

I arrived home an hour later, thanks to rush-hour traffic, and she was already in bed. All that movement had knocked her out.

I missed everything: another milestone, her shrieks as she excitedly pulled herself across the room, rocking her to sleep at night, kissing her good night.

When she's not with me, I feel like I'm an amputee—like this significant part of me is missing. And tonight makes me feel like I just got punched in my sawed-off arm.

Thursday, August 28

· · · · · · · · · · · · · · · · · · · ·

Mornings have become a routine. Get Sara up at 7:00 A.M. Spend fifteen minutes playing with her. Jake showers and gets ready. He takes Sara. I shower and get ready. Jake leaves for work. I pack Sara in the car and drop her off at day care. I kiss her good-bye and hug her close and drive the five minutes to work.

It's become such a routine now, emotion doesn't always register. It's simply lather, rinse, repeat. I still think about her a million times during the day and wonder what she's doing, who's entertaining her, when she ate last, and if she misses me. But for the most part, it's gotten a helluva lot easier.

Then there are the days when I take fifty steps backward and want to drive to day-care, snatch her up, and drive off into the sunset.

Like today.

I decided to celebrate landing the Stansfield party and take myself out to lunch. Alone. I never do anything like that, but I decided to take advantage of being a working mom and enjoy my lunch hour in a restaurant, reading the newspaper, rather than trying to wrangle my daughter while choking down a chicken salad sandwich.

Just as I'd ordered a drink and settled in with the latest movie reviews, a well-dressed mother walked in and pushed her gorgeous pram to the table next to mine. I smiled at her and went back to reading about the latest Cate Blanchett movie. Or, at least, I tried to. My mind kept wandering and I found myself repeatedly staring at her. A few times, she caught my eye, so I had to pretend I was signaling the waiter so she wouldn't fear I was a kidnapper waiting for the right moment to snatch her child.

I was so drawn to her because of how happy and relaxed she seemed. Just her and her baby out for lunch. I envisioned she would leisurely shop later, strolling through the stores, biding her time until she found the perfect pair of jeans or heels. After that, she'd head home and start a fantastic dinner and read some of her new book while the baby napped. And my face started to flush with envy.

I glanced at my watch. Ten more minutes until I had to be back at the office. No leisurely lunch, no shopping, no reading, no time with Sara, no anything. In fact, if I calculated it, I'd probably see Mule Face more than Sara today.

Yet I still love my job, my clients, my work. It gives me a satisfaction and sense of accomplishment that I can't find anywhere else.

I wish I could call my mom and talk to her about this, but she's still feeling really crappy. Besides, every time I talk to her about this, if I question my decision at all, she seems to get defensive and we enter into a whole "What My Generation Did for Your Generation" lecture.

Growing up, I was proud to tell my class on Career Day that my mom was a Vice President. But there are the opposite memories, the ones that exist in the black spaces, of not understanding when she said she couldn't be a chaperone on class trips or make me a snack after school each day. I wanted to understand, I tried to understand, but it didn't register in my young mind why my mom wouldn't rather be home making me cookies than flying around the country.

And as much as I hate to acknowledge those memories, I have to. If I choose to keep working, I will inevitably pass those down to Sara in some form. It's not fair to her to pretend those emotions don't exist.

It's like there's no way to win. Some days, I'll wish I could stay home with her. Then the wind changes and I'm so happy to go work, I look forward to dropping her off at day care. And I can't even feel either one of those things without feeling shame.

And pretty much every mom I've ever met has said the same thing. No matter what the choice, there's always something nagging and whispering, making choices malleable and questionable.

If this is what's considered "having it all," I'm jumping ship. Because I feel like it's impossible to do everything 50 percent, let alone a figure any higher.

And? Right now? The only thing I'm truly good at is beating myself up.

Friday, August 29

. . . .

At least I can always count on Julie to lighten things up.

I called her last night in the wake of my Irrational Working Mother Guilt and Anger Carnival, and she managed to say all the right things: I'm a good mom, I'm great at my job, Jake is awesome, et cetera.

But then I stumped her: "Yeah, but Jules, sometimes I feel like I've chosen the path of most resistance, you know?"

Silence.

"Like I've made all these choices, and they were good ones, and ones I don't regret, but I put myself in this position. I'm the one who stretched myself so thin."

Silence again.

"Everything seems so . . . hard all the time."

"That's because it is," Julie said shortly.

"I know, but with working and not sleeping and finding time for Sara and Jake."

"But who doesn't live like that? Who has an easy life? Nobody I know. So stop feeling so goddamned sorry for yourself and just live your life." Julie's voice came out evenly, despite her words.

"I know, it's just like sometimes I wonder what it would be like if— Never mind. Just tell me something funny and change the subject," I said.

So, she told me about her latest Internet date. Apparently, she was supposed to go to a blues festival with a new guy, Johnny. I interrupted her to ask her who goes by "Johnny" when they're thirty, but she threw out a profanity, so I shut up.

Julie and Johnny needed to stop at a bank to take out money for the festival. The ATM is broken, so Johnny pulls up to a bank teller portal. He puts his ATM card into the pneumatic tube and leans out the window to send it back to the bank but misjudges the distance and drops it.

Julie rolls her eyes and laughs but is starting to think Johnny is sort of cute. Johnny gets out of the car and tries to reach the tube, which has now rolled under his car. Except it has rolled just out of his reach. So, with cars beginning to honk behind them, he goes around to the other side of the car.

Still couldn't reach it.

By now Julie's beginning to wonder what the hell was going on.

He ran around to the other side, still no dice. Just out of reach.

Then, the bank teller came over the loudspeaker and said, "Sir, this isn't an amusement park. What are you doing?"

Well, apparently, "amusement" and "park" were the secret buzzwords that turned Johnny from a normal human being into Crazy Internet Blind Date Man.

Johnny jumped up and down, shook his fist at the bank teller, screamed at all of the cars honking behind them, and ordered Julie to "army crawl" under the car to get the tube.

She calmly told him to go fuck himself, gave him the finger, and hailed a cab.

She may think my life is difficult, but at least my chaos exists internally rather than including all of the customers at my local bank's branch.

Saturday, August 30

Jake saved me from my shroud of Working Motherhood Depression when he told me this morning that our friend Joel called him and invited us to go to the Cubs game today with him and his wife, Megan. We haven't seen them in forever, probably thanks to the fact that they're childless. Jake did force me to attend a Fourth of July barbeque at their house last year while pregnant. I went to bed sometime after Joel and Jake decided to sing karaoke to the Blues Brothers' greatest hits.

But, thankfully, I'm not pregnant anymore, so I think an afternoon of hot dogs, beer, blazin' hot sunshine, and about forty thousand screaming, jovial baseball fans sounds like the perfect distraction from Clare versus Superwoman Myth.

The only problem is it was too late to find a sitter for Sara, so she's going to be tagging along. The good news is she's gotten too heavy for me to carry in the Baby Bjorn anymore, so Jake gets to wear it. Score.

I went out last night and bought her the cutest little Cubs T-shirt and hat, which I'm sure will last on her head for like forty-five seconds before she rips it off and uses it as a pacifier or Frisbee.

Whatever. Jake and I are going to be the coolest parents at the game.

Sunday, August 31

Jake and I met Joel and Megan outside Wrigley Field at the Harry Caray statue. Which, by the way, is probably the dumbest place to meet anyone before a game. Seeing as how it's like the only discernible landmark by the field, *everyone in the free world* decides to meet people there. So, it was pretty much like trying to find our friends inside the ballpark, only the equivalent amount of people were stuffed like sausages into a one-square-mile radius.

I spotted them first.

"There they are!" I smacked Jake on the arm.

"Jesus, did you have to do that?" he asked, and dredged his arm across his profusely sweating face.

"Are you hot?" I asked brilliantly.

"Clare, I have close to twenty extra baby pounds strapped to my chest. It's ninety-five degrees out with no wind. Yes, I'm a little warm." He wiped his forehead again.

"Oh. Sorry," I said as I pranced over to Megan.

"Hi!" I said, and hugged her.

"Oh, she's getting so big!" Megan said as she leaned toward Sara.

Sara grabbed the blue beaded necklace Megan wore around her neck and held it tight.

"Sorry, hold on," I said as I tried to pry the beads out of Sara's viselike grip.

"There!" I said. Megan leaned back and her necklace broke into a million pieces and nearly caused several broken necks as people around us slipped on the scattering beads.

"Don't worry about it!" Megan said as I tried to bend down and collect all of the pieces.

"Nice shirt," Joel said to Jake, gesturing toward Sara strapped to his chest.

We walked in and followed Joel to our seats. My eyes rounded as we traipsed down closer and closer to the field. Jake turned around and looked at me, wide-eyed. Finally, we stopped three rows behind home plate.

"Seriously?" I said to Megan.

She just grinned at me.

I sat down in the seat, soaking in the wide views of Wrigley Field.

"Beer! Cold beer here!" a vendor called from the aisle.

"Four please!" Megan yelled. After the beers were passed down through the row, she handed me two.

"Two? I only need one," I said, and tried to hand one back to her.

She shook her head. "This is your first post-baby Cubs game. We're right behind home plate. Double-fisting is in order."

She had a point.

I, being the very cool and not at all dorky person that I am, whipped out my cell phone and proceeded to call everyone I'd ever met, tell them to turn on the Cubs game and to watch me wave to them. After fifteen minutes, my phone rang. Mark.

I snapped it open and before I could say hello, he yelled, "STOP WAVING. YOU LOOK LIKE A DOUCHE BAG."

"Hi to you, too. Jealous?"

"Yes, but stop embarrassing yourself. You're one of those people I hate. One of those people who get great seats and then spend the entire game calling people to tell them what great seats they have instead of watching the game."

"I'm watching the game, I just had to call people to brag."

"OK, what's the score?" he said.

"Um . . ." I squinted and tried to read the scoreboard, but the sun was out and there was a huge glare across the board. "Um . . ."

"Busted. Stop waving. Don't embarrass the family name," he said before he hung up.

I officially stopped paying attention to the game around the fifth inning, after I nearly got taken out by some fat girl trying to catch a foul ball.

Seriously.

She leapt straight up in the air like seven feet, before arching and shooting over about five feet, just enough to land within inches of my feet. And my child.

All I saw was a mass of flesh hurling toward me. My first instinct was to turn my body to protect my child. And then to grab my beer.

Of course, the ball was nowhere near us, so Fatty's spill was all for naught.

I felt kind of bad for her, since all of section 17 started laughing, including my husband, who nearly turned purple and high-fived me for remembering to grab my drink.

Clare: The Woman Who Can Have Fun Even When Fat People Are Flying at Her.

Sometime during the seventh inning, Jake unbuckled the Baby Bjorn and handed Sara to me. I was engrossed in a conversation with Joel when Megan silently pointed to my lap.

"What? Oh, whoops!" I'd rested my beer in front of me and Sara was leaning forward, straining to suck on the rim of the cup. Wanting to drink beer at a Cubs game. She's so my daughter.

After the game was over, we spilled out onto Addison Street.

"Cubby Bear?" Joel asked drunkenly.

"Hell yeah," I said, and started toward the bar.

I felt a poke in my ribs.

"What?" I said. Jake pointed to Sara, once again strapped to his chest, napping peacefully. "Oh, right. No bars for us."

We managed to convince Joel and Megan to take the train out to the suburbs with us and spend the night at our house. On the train, Jake and Joel decided the four of us should go to Barbados together. Joel suggested we all go next month and Jake thought that was a great idea until I pointed to our daughter.

It's really hard to hang out with childless couples who have very few responsibilities and lots of disposable income.

After we arrived at our house and I put Sara to bed, we opened up a couple bottles of wine. Joel and Megan gushed over our wine collection, and just as I was feeling very sophisticated Megan started laughing and pointing to Butterscotch. He decided to entertain our company by dragging his butt across our carpet, directly in front of Megan. He should've just gone all the way and put on a rhinestone thong and starting lip-synching to "It's Raining Men."

It was the perfect distraction.

Wednesday, September 3

· · · · · · · · · · · · · · · · · ·

I let Sara play hooky from day-care today. Well, it wasn't really hooky per se, because she does have a horrible cold and cough. Since I wasn't about to send her sick (like that bitch Jeannine did last week when she brought her chicken poxed kid in. Thanks for the early heart attack!), Sara and I spent much of today on the couch. She's been pretty lethargic all day and it breaks my heart to see her coughing and sniffling, so I've held her almost the whole day. I even let her fall asleep in my arms and held her the entire time she napped. I said a few prayers for her cold to migrate to me and spare her, but no dice.

Her nose is like a faucet and she keeps rubbing her face on my chest, so I slightly resemble the Creature from the Snot Lagoon, but I don't care.

She and I did get to watch a particularly good episode of *The People's Court*. She watched it so intently, I decided she's bringing me on as a participant.

Da Duh Duh.

This is the plaintiff, Sara Grandalski. She's suing for mental distress due to the expectation of good behavior.

Da Duh Duh.

This is the defendant, Clare Finnegan. She admits to forcing her daughter to go out to public places like restaurants and shopping malls with the expectation of no screaming.

It's all here on *The People's Court*!

Of course, everyone in the entire galaxy (including some aliens from Planet I Know Best) has given me advice on how to help her through the cold.

Marianne: Feed a cold, starve a fever.

Um, OK. I guess I should nix my plan to withhold food from Sara since she doesn't have a fever, right?

Jake: CALL THE DOCTOR, OH MY GOD, IS SHE OK? DOES SHE HAVE PNEUMONIA?

Drink a cocktail or something.

My dad: There's nothing you can do.

Thanks. Very helpful Doctor.

Doctor: There's nothing you can do.

Are you guys all in this together or something?

Reese: You should've stocked up on baby cold remedies before they took them off the shelf. I have a whole arsenal here.

I'll just get in my time machine and do that.

Natalie: Ash Leigh never gets sick because she's not in day-care.

Not. Going. To. Respond.

Me = down.

Natalie = kicking me.

Thanks.

The postman: Did you take her outside? Babies catch colds when they go outside.

Oh, right! I did take her outside once, in fact. Thanks for reminding me! Won't happen again.

Despite her being sick, I loved being home with her today. Just spending the day with her recharged my motherhood batteries a little bit.

Thursday, September 4

If nothing else, Sara's cold provided me with my next topic for my column in *The Daily Tribune*. I wrote about the difficulty of sorting through all of the information thrown at new parents and some litmus tests for Bullshit versus Very Good Advice. Guess which category most of Marianne's advice falls under?

After I had Sara, I ran out and bought every baby book my swollen fingers could grab at Borders. I went home, skimmed them, and took notes like a college student cramming for a final. I'm sorry to say, none of it really helped. The biggest issue was consistency. One book would say to swaddle at night, the next not to swaddle under any circumstances. One book said to give rice cereal at three months, the next not until they're at least six months old.

I mean, c'mon, people.

Can we all just get together and come up with some kind of parenting protocol? Babies don't come with an instruction manual. And this is a really big problem. There needs to be a book called *This Is the Only Book You Will Ever Need. It Will Teach You How to Feed, Potty Train, and Not Accidentally Injure Your Child*. Hospitals would give the book out to new parents as they leave with their newborn. Now it's just like, *We're going to pretend we still care about you by wheeling you to your car, but the second you are beyond these doors you are Not Our Problem. Try not to kill your child or let the door hit your still-fat ass on the way out. P.S. Don't forget to pay your bill.*

I swore I wouldn't ride in the backseat of the car on the way home from the hospital. I mean, only crazy, overbearing, nervous parents do stuff like that. And Jake and I were going to be hip, cool, flexible, and relaxed parents.

Um, right.

Jake asked me if I was going to sit in the front seat and I looked at him like he suggested duct-taping the car seat to the roof of the car. I wedged myself into the four inches of space next to Sara in the back and reacted to her every sigh.

It was just the first instance of a very important parenting lesson: you will go back on everything you said you wouldn't do. That's what parenting is about: making decisions and firmly digging your heels in, followed quickly by instituting the exact opposite.

When Jake and I finally got Sara home the first night, we freaked out. Even though I'd been around babies all my life, I was still *sure* her head was going to roll off if I didn't support it properly. I fretted about giving her brain damage if I accidentally touched one of the soft spots on her still-developing skull. I was terrified her umbilical cord stump would fall off too early and she'd be stuck with an ugly outie belly button and have to wear one-piece bathing suits her whole life because her mom wasn't paying attention when she changed her diaper and accidentally ripped off the scab too soon.

I'm ashamed to admit, I was also sort of wondering when her parents were going to come and take her back. It was mostly the narcotic drugs, but part of me couldn't comprehend the idea that she was our daughter, rather than some cute baby we were watching for a few days.

And then, miraculously, after a week, everything clicked. We had a daughter! We were parents! She was cute!

Then, another week passed and we surrendered like prom dates after four Busch Lights. She still wasn't sleeping for more than an hour at a time. I was still stuck sleeping on the couch since she'd only nap in her swing. I lived in fear of hearing her cries on the monitor, knowing it meant I'd have to get up and feed her, change her, rock her, something. I started to panic, not knowing when was the next time I'd get a full night's sleep. Not knowing when my body would somewhat resemble its old shape. (Still waiting on that one. Damn Heidi Klum for setting the bar so high.) Not knowing when, or should I say *if*, Jake and I would ever get to be alone again.

I knew having a baby would be a huge stressor. I knew our lives would change. I knew things would be hard. But I had no idea Just How Hard or Just How Bad It Would Get.

It was a complete mental breakdown, similar to what must go on at terrorist detention camps. My suggestion would be to bring in a posse of newborns when interrogating prisoners of the state. Chinese water torture? Nothing. Electroshock techniques? A joke. Withholding of food and water? *Ha.*

Spending time with a newborn? The key to unlocking a spy's mind.

A few more weeks passed and the fog lifted a little. And each week, it got a little easier. Because we cared about the little stuff a lot less. I didn't stress if she had to cry for a few minutes so I could take a shower. We didn't worry if her diaper was wet and it leaked through her pajamas. No big deal if she projectile-vomited all over the cat.

But it sure would've been nice to know.

Saturday, September 6

. . . .

Sara's cough still sounds like an eighty-year-old man with emphysema, so I left her home with Jake while I went shopping with my mom and Sam. My mom called me a few days ago and asked if I could help find Sam's Homecoming dance dress.

"Ha," I snorted. "I'm sure that's exactly what Sam wants—her uncool sister helping pick out a dress."

"Actually, she told me that I don't know what's in style and you are the only one who can help her."

"Funny, Mom." I laughed

"No, really," she insisted.

"Seriously?" My eyebrows knit together in confusion.

"I'm not kidding."

"Wow, OK. I'd love to come."

I hung up the phone and immediately dialed Sam's cell phone.

"He-ey," she sang into the phone.

"Hi! So, we're going shopping for dresses this weekend! Mom told me you want me to come along!"

"What? Oh, I just said you probably have nothing else to do." I could hear what sounded like an emery board being scratched across a fingernail in the background.

"Oh, well, um, OK. Do you have any idea of what kind of dress you'd like?"

"I don't know." She made a little *pffft* sound. "Listen, Jessica's on the other line. I have to go," she said, and hung up.

I hung up the phone, shaking my head. I fell into the trap again. She was never going to show her cards and be rah-rah sisterly with me.

I met my mom and Sam around noon at Nordstrom. Sam paced back and forth on her cell phone while my mom sat in an armchair. As I walked closer the lines on my mother's face became deeper and deeper, and by the time I stood next to her dark circles encased her eyes and her cheekbones looked drawn.

"Hi, Mom!" I said as cheerfully as I could muster.

"Hi, hon," my mom said as she stood up. She wobbled a little and I grabbed her elbow to steady her.

"Are you OK?"

"I'm great," she said, and smiled ruefully.

"Hi, Sam," I said pointedly.

"What? Hold on, hey," she said, and turned back to her cell phone.

"Where are we going first?" I asked my mom.

"BCBG. Duh!" Sam called over her shoulder as she bounced toward the door.

My mom and I trailed after her like an entourage.

"How's everything?" I asked my mom as we pushed the heavy glass doors of BCBG open.

"Just a little tired. I'm going stir-crazy, though. I'm not used to not working," she said as she pulled her cable-knit sweater closer to her.

"Mom, this is the first time in forever that you've had some time off," I reminded her.

"I know, I just feel like I should be doing something." My mom shrugged.

"You are doing something. You're working on getting better," I said, and put my arm around her shoulder. "On second thought, if you really want a project to work on, Marianne called me last week and invited me to join her knitting group."

"Oh, I can't."

"Why not?" I teased her.

"I'm very busy. I have cancer," she said, and smiled.

"Yeah, yeah. Go ahead and play the cancer card again," I teased her.

"THIS IS, LIKE, THE CUTEST DRESS EVER IN MY WHOLE LIFE. I WANT TO KILL MYSELF IT IS SO AMAZING," Sam shouted from across the store.

"Try it on. We wouldn't want you to commit suicide or anything," my mom said as we walked over to Sam.

"We wouldn't?" I said, and my mom elbowed me. "Oh, right. No, we wouldn't."

Thankfully, the dress fit Sam, so we decided to stop for lunch before looking for shoes to match.

"So how's the house hunt coming?" my mom asked me as we sat down at a café next to the shoe department.

"OK." I shrugged and sipped my water. "Haven't found anything spectacular yet."

"You're not going to get that one house, are you?" Sam asked as the corners of her mouth turned down in a frown.

"What house?" I said cautiously. I started to mentally build my armor.

"You know, that one you showed Mom. That one with the garage that faces the street. I just hate those kinds of houses. It looks like a trailer." Sam shuddered, as though the thought of someone buying a non-custom-made house terrified her.

I shot a pointed look at my mom but chose to remain silent for the well-being of all the restaurant patrons around us. We ate our lunch in silence, my mom afraid to spark a confrontation and Sam and I glaring at each other.

"I totally have to stop in the bathroom. I think I just got my P," Sam said as we walked out of the café.

"P?" I parroted.

"Um, hi. Period?" Sam said as she rifled through her bag. "Damn! I don't have a tampon."

"Oh, I think I might have one," I said as we walked into the bathroom. "Here you go," I said, and outstretched my arm.

She stared at me and slowly took the tampon from me.

"What?" I said.

She looked confused, but her face suddenly changed, as though the lightbulb went off. "Oh, you probably have so many left over."

"What?" I said again.

"Left over. Since you can't use them anymore," she said.

"What are you talking about, Sam?" my mom said.

"You can't use tampons anymore after you have a baby," she said very matter-of-factly.

My mom and I looked at each other. "You can't?" she said.

"No, because it'll totally fall out," Sam whispered.

My mom and I threw our heads back and roared.

"What?" Sam said.

I waved my arms around and tried to catch my breath and explain to her that yes, in fact, women can use tampons after they have babies. Everything kind of . . . goes back.

But she didn't let me explain.

"WHAT? YOU GUYS SUCK," she said, and stormed into a bathroom stall.

After my mom wiped the tears from her eyes, she tried to explain basic physiology to Sam, who was having none of it.

"OK. Jeez. Whatever. It's so not a big deal. Effing drop it, OK?" she spit through the door.

"So, hired an assistant yet?" my mom asked as we walked through the shoe department.

I shook my head. "Not yet."

"I'm so proud of you, hon. Moving up the ladder and advancing your career." My mom's voice swelled with pride.

I nodded, suddenly uncomfortable. "Yeah."

"You're going to be just like Diane Keaton in *Baby Boom*. Successful, professional mom." She stopped and considered a black leather flat.

I took a step toward her. "Mom, that movie terrifies me. It's like why would I enjoy a movie about a woman who is overworked, torn, and feels guilty all of the time? I'm already familiar with those feelings." I picked up a tan boot, turning it over to glance at the price. I still wasn't ready to buy all new clothes yet, since the "baby weight" was clinging on for dear life, but I reasoned that I could buy shoes, as my feet weren't hefty anymore. I'd quickly discovered that my body hangs on to fat when I'm stressed. Thus, I'm looking forward to being skinny, oh, *never*.

She set the flat back on the display. "But I thought you loved working."

I pretended to study the heel of the boot. "I—" I stopped as Sam shoved herself in between us and thrust a sparkly belt into my mom's hands, presumably for purchase.

"Why would she love working? Ew. I'm never working. I'm going to be a stay-at-home mom and change my name when I get married." Sam shook her head back and forth.

"You say that now, but—" my mom started to say when Sam interrupted.

"No way. I don't want to," Sam said firmly.

My mom's head moved back a little, reeling from shock. "Well, you can choose whatever you like, but I guess I'm just a little surprised that you are so willing to make different choices. I just thought you were proud of the way you were raised."

I stepped forward and put a hand on my mom's arm. "We are. But that's what it's all about, right? Making choices. And maybe"—I shifted uncomfortably from left to right—"maybe we might choose to make different ones at some point."

My mom sighed and nodded. "Of course, I just want you girls to be happy, whatever that might entail."

I leaned forward and hugged her. We quickly broke apart as we heard

Sam shriek, "MOM! Tory Burch is on sale! I'll die if I don't get new san-
dals!"

I laughed and walked behind my mom.

I just want to be happy, too—if only I knew how to get there.

Thursday, September 11

. . . .

"IT'S ALIVE!"
—Dr. Henry Frankenstein

Within the past twenty-four hours, life changed dramatically.

No longer can Jake and I lazily drop our laptop bags on the ground,
safe in the knowledge that they will remain untouched until morning.
No longer can I wait to sweep up any stray food that falls onto the floor. No
longer can Butterscotch lounge comfortably in Sara's old bouncy seat.

It happened. She's mobile.

Last week, Sara started her creeping. It looked like a half-drunk army
crawl but backward, like a crab. Jake and I laughed at the novelty, not
truly comprehending the slippery slope we were about to go down. We
also figured she'd creep around for a few months or something before she
got the strength or motivation to do anything else. But last night we put
her down on the ground to show Frank and Marianne her fabulous shim-
mying skills and she rocked a few times, then quickly went into a full-
blown crawl.

We sat in stunned silence, watching her head straight for the sleeping
cat. She shrieked louder and louder in excitement with every inch covered
between her and Butterscotch. He froze, unsure of how to react to the tiny
drooling person heading full-steam toward him. She stopped suddenly in
front of him, looked back at us, sitting on the couch with our mouths
open, smiled, and then reached forward and yanked on his tail with all of
her might.

I think villagers in Bangladesh heard the screech.

Butterscotch scrambled away, but not before looking over his left shoulder and giving her one good *HSSSSS* (translation: *"I hate you"*) before running into the bedroom, stomach swinging back and forth and skimming the floor.

We hoped it was a onetime thing, like the time I tried peppermint schnapps.

Right.

She moved her little butt all over the apartment and managed to get near every electrical socket. We spent the rest of the evening chasing after her, trying to contain her like a new puppy.

It was hard to get frustrated, though, since she was so excited about her newfound mobility. She shrieked and yelped with excitement at everything she fondled. Unfortunately, most of those things were Not Child Appropriate, like some cigars left over from a bachelor party, a bottle of Sirah, and kitty litter.

As I watched her groove around the room, I suddenly felt like crying. It was so neat to watch her learn a new skill, grow up just a little more, but it also means she really isn't an infant anymore. She's become a baby. She's become a little person. She's become a little girl. I'm excited about this and the other things to come, like talking, but it also means letting go of the wrinkly newborn I took home from the hospital just a few short months ago. She's growing up so fast, and I feel like a cup that will never be filled—like I'll never spend *enough* time with her, never walk out the door without missing her immediately. And I guess I just have to come to terms with that. Because I doubt it's ever going away.

It's like to move forward as parents, we have to keep letting go, like a lead rope we're following along blind into the woods; to move to the next tree, we have to let go of the rope and take a step forward.

But for now, at least for now, I'm going to stand still, close my eyes, and hold her to me before I take another step forward. (Or she does. Please let walking be at least six months away.)

Friday, September 12

· · · · · · · · · · · · · · · · · · ·

Thanks to Sara's newfound wacked-out baybee skillz, Jake and I stayed up until the wee hours of the night (OK, more like midnight) baby-proofing everything new we could possibly imagine to be harmful. We had figured we still had a while to do so, but clearly it was Do or Sara Might Die time.

Jake put a hand on my arm and stopped me just as I attempted to pad the corners of the kitchen cabinets with Saran wrap. I realize it was going a touch too far, but suddenly everything in our apartment has become the Boogeyman. Pens, drink coasters, a stray pebble of cat food, an errant thread from the carpet are not simply things anymore. They're Things That Might Injure My Child, which makes them the enemy. I've declared war on anything within Sara's reach, and now our home looks as comfortable as a mental hospital. No shoelaces, no sharp objects, every surface padded so as not to scrape her soft little knees.

I plied myself with copious amounts of caffeine this morning in an attempt to appear somewhat human, since my new assistant is starting today and I don't think my spending most of the day yawning and slumped over at my desk will provide the best first impression.

Not to mention she's starting at the perfect time. I'm starting to feel really overwhelmed and worried that the ball's going to get dropped for the golf outing.

I decided to hire Miss Teen USA, mainly because Betty Crocker had already accepted another position. I immediately questioned my decision to hire her when she appeared at my office door wearing a skirt a good three inches above her kneecaps, knee-high black boots, and a tight white long-sleeved T-shirt. It was like Hookers Gone Professional.

"Good morning!" Keri chirped as she took a big swig of the fountain drink in her hand.

"How are you?" I said, and stood up from my desk. I extended my right hand and she shook it limply.

"I'm good. Little tired. Late night last night. Le Passage," she said, and nodded at me.

"Oh. OK," I said.

"You've been, right?" she said.

"I don't think so, is it a restaurant?" I knew I sounded like a Huge Dork.

"Uh, no," she said. "It's a club."

"Hey there! Welcome to our fantastic office!" Mule Face appeared at my door. She was wearing a leopard-print metallic jacket with black Capri pants that had little beads dangling from the bottom. Let's just say animal prints should not be worn by individuals weighing a couple hundred bills.

Keri looked startled. "Hi. Hey." She shot me a bewildered look.

"Keri, this is Annie. She's another event planner. Keri's my new assistant," I said to Mule Face.

"Wow! You and Clare are going to have so much fun! Thank God you're here! She's been really forgetful lately!" Mule Face reached into the pocket of her jacket and pulled out a piece of saltwater taffy. She popped it into her mouth and rolled it around.

I smiled sweetly at her and hoped the candy would pull out all of her dental work.

"Thanks. Glad to be here," Keri said, shooting me another *who the hell is this person?* look.

"So, Keri. Listen. Do you like scented body lotions?" Mule Face asked.

"I should really show Keri her desk. Thanks for stopping in." I took a step forward and practically shoved Mule Face into the hallway.

"Word of warning, don't buy the face cream," I whispered to Keri as we walked over to the cubicle outside my office. "Information Services should be here shortly to configure your e-mail and phone and everything. Today, I just figure you can answer the phone and get your bearings. We'll discuss current projects and events tomorrow. Sound good?" I said.

She looked from me to the desk quickly and sat down. "Sure," she said. "So what's going on?"

"It's been crazy around here. I just started a new project, so there's been a few late nights already," I said, and crossed my arms over my chest.

"I hear ya. So—hey! Are you married?" she said, and grabbed my left hand.

"Yep, few years now," I said, and jiggled my ring finger.

"Wow, I wouldn't have guessed," she said, and released my hand and sat back in her chair. She took a long sip from her drink and said, "So what part of the city do you live in?"

I laughed. "Haven't lived in the city for a while now. I did right out of college, though. Loved it. Just got ready to move to a bigger place."

"So you live in the . . ." She paused and whispered, "Suburbs?"

"Unfortunately," I said, and smiled. "But it is nice with my daughter to have the extra room. She just started crawling."

Keri's mouth dropped open and she looked like her head was going to explode. "*You* have a *kid?*"

OK, now I really felt ancient.

"She's eight months old," I said proudly.

"Whoa," Keri said, and sipped on her drink. She paused, narrowed her eyes at me, and said, "So how old are you?"

"I'm twenty-nine," I said.

"Really? I thought you were much younger," she said.

I wasn't sure if that was a compliment or an insult, so I just said, "Most people do."

"That must be weird, I mean, for people to think you're younger when you have a baby," Keri mused.

"Sometimes people ask me if I'm my daughter's babysitter," I said, and leaned against Keri's desk.

"I bet," she said thoughtfully.

"And the dishwasher repairman the other day said not to forget to tell my parents what's wrong with the rinse cycle," I added.

We sat in silence for a moment while Keri pondered my evidently well-hidden adulthood and I pondered the great divide between us before I quickly straightened.

"So, let's plan on having lunch together in a few hours, OK?" I said, and she nodded.

I walked back to my office and sat down at my desk. According to her résumé, Keri graduated from college a year ago. That would make her about twenty-two or twenty-three. Only about six years younger than me.

Six years ago, I wasn't even married yet.

Six years ago, my choices were vast, the waters of my path unchartered.

Six years ago, I knew what the hippest clubs were, I knew when the hottest restaurants opened, I lived in the city, wore designer clothes, and went out every night.

Six years later, I prefer restaurants like Applebee's, since Sara can have a meltdown without anyone really caring; most of my clothes are crusted with either baby food, drool, or spit-up; and last night I fell asleep at 9:00 P.M.

I'm not even a cool working mom, with a fantastically awesome phone and teeny-tiny laptop. Nope, I probably have more in common with Mule Face these days than Keri.

I used to be Hip Clare. Now, thanks to a few extra Sara pounds still lingering, I'm Hippy Clare.

It's official. The transformation is complete.

Wednesday, September 17

Jake, sensing my growing frustration, decided we needed a night out together, as people rather than parents, so he took me out to dinner last night. A chance to go out together without worrying about who was going to have to change the diaper explosion halfway through the first drink. A chance to stop and catch my breath—especially timely since Elise is bringing her daughter Logan in tomorrow and I'd like to be somewhat presentable.

Marianne babysat, which Jake and I paid for with a tiny corner of our sanity, of course. The important thing is we got to spend a night out together, as adults.

Marianne arrived at our apartment, and before I could even take her coat she started waltzing around our place, pointing out uncovered sharp surfaces and kicking invisible bits of dust with her toe. She also admonished me for dressing Sara in a blue creeper, since it made her look like a boy, apparently. And girls should always "look like the little princesses that they are." Whatever. It was a free babysitter.

Jake and I went to one of those supercliché fondue restaurants. I always kind of laughed at the people who go to those, but seeing as how our favorite restaurants are of the chainlike variety and usually give out free balloons at the front door, a fondue restaurant seemed right up our alley.

Ah, how the mighty have fallen.

Thanks to the wobbly flesh still sitting around my midsection, low-rise jeans and tight-fitting tops don't exactly fit the same way, so I dressed up by wearing my favorite pair of heels. I still have hope that the muffin top will go away, but Reese insists it's permanent, regardless of weight. She said it's a well-kept secret of motherhood. I look at her tiny body, perfect once again after having Brendan just a short while ago, and secretly want to feed her a few doughnuts.

I figured Jake and I would spend the evening chatting about the latest non-fiction bestsellers, current world events, our ideas for an exit strategy in Iraq, the upcoming presidential elections, and our predictions for the Oscars next year.

Right.

We talked about Sara. We talked about how cute she is. We talked about how big she is. We talked about who she looks like more. We talked about how long her naps are. We talked about winning the lottery and buying her a pony and a life-sized Barbie dream house. And we lamented about how much we missed her.

And then I started talking about how difficult everything has become. How I feel like I'm sucking at everything—my job, motherhood, marriage.

Everything.

How the weight of all of the expectations that surround me is surely going to bring me down.

And Jake said: "I love you and I think you're doing amazing."

As I looked at him and nodded, I realized he truly meant it. That he believed it.

"It's so hard, because I feel like I have to choose a team. Whatever I do. And whatever team you're on, that's your allegiance, that's who you root for. It's like you can't root for the White Sox and the Cubs at the same time. If I stay home with Sara, I feel like I will still identify with working moms more," I said.

Jake looked at me critically. "Really?"

I nodded as I twirled my water glass on the table. "It's like to convince yourself you've made the right decision, you have to inherently believe that the other choice is the wrong one."

Jake shook his head and reached across the table, covering my hand with his. "Whatever you choose will be right."

I smiled ruefully at him. "I hope so. I just don't want to feel like I'm letting myself down—in my career or as a mom. I want to give myself fully to Sara, but I can't let myself disappear."

Jake and I drove home from the restaurant and I ripped open the door, ready to kick Marianne out and resume my rightful place as Sara's caretaker. She was already asleep when we got home, and even though Jake told me not to, I crept into her room and gave her a soft pat as she slept. I froze and held my breath as she stirred, but she only sighed softly and went back to her dreamland. I stayed in Sara's room while Jake escorted Marianne out. I watched Sara breathe in and out and wanted so badly to touch her soft curls.

Jake appeared behind me, whispered "We love you" to Sara, and pulled me out of the room. We fell asleep like ten minutes later.

Although our date night wasn't what I expected, and admittedly the best part was coming home to Sara, I've reasoned since she's part Jake, part me, my constant longing to be with her is the most romantic thing ever.

Thursday, September 18

· · · · · · · · · · · · · · · · · · · ·

"Clare, this is my daughter Logan," Elise said proudly as she put her arm around a short, chubby girl standing next to her.

"Nice to meet you, Logan," I said, and smiled at her.

Logan smiled back and fidgeted with the hem of her private school uniform.

"Let's all sit down in here," I said, and gestured toward my office. "Can I get you guys anything to drink?"

Logan shook her head and Elise said, "Pellegrino, if you have it." Thankfully, I had remembered an article on Elise mentioning her favorite drink being Pellegrino, so I stocked the fridge accordingly. I know how important it is to always keep a client happy.

"Of course, just one moment." I poked my head out of the office and nodded at Keri, who appeared with a bottle of the sparkling water and a glass. Thankfully, so far, she took direction well. At least she remembered that a head nod during this meeting translated to: "Pellegrino and a drinking apparatus."

"Great," Elise said, and raised her eyebrows, obviously impressed.

"So, Logan, since this is your party, don't hesitate to interrupt me and give me your opinion on something. Everything I've mocked up can be changed or altered if you want something different. So please speak up," I said to her, and she smiled.

I went into the pitch I gave Elise. I covered everything from the theme, linens, and sculptures to the food, drinks, and music. I brought up the video montage and Logan interrupted me.

"I want my friend Tim to do the video," she said.

"Oh, OK. Does he have experience?" I said.

"Yes. He's the greatest," she said firmly.

I didn't look at Elise. I didn't want Logan to sense I was undermining her, so I looked down and wrote down a note until Elise spoke up.

"We'll have to talk about that," Elise said as her mouth set into a thin line.

"Mo-om, I—," Logan started to say as her cheeks flushed.

"Later," Elise repeated, and Logan fell silent.

"So how does everything else sound, Logan?" I asked her as I leaned back in my chair.

"Good, yeah, I like it," she said, and nodded.

"Great! I'll get started then. If you both could work on the invitation list, that would really help," I said.

"Sounds good," Elise said, and stood up. I started to walk them to the door when Elise stopped and turned around. "I've been meaning to ask you, any relation to Michael Finnegan?"

I smiled at her. "He's my father."

"Really? He's my doctor," she said. "We've been going to him for years. He's such a great doctor," she gushed.

I wasn't surprised my dad had never mentioned Elise was a patient. He usually takes patient confidentiality to the utmost degree. He could be treating Osama bin Laden, for all we know.

"He is, he is," I said to her.

"Please tell him I said—," Elise started to say.

"Elise! Do you know Jim Kantore? The dentist? He's my uncle!" Mule Face called from her office. She appeared in the hallway in front of Elise.

"No, I'm afraid I don't," Elise said, bewildered.

"So, anyway, I'll work on those figures and e-mail them over," I said to Elise, putting my hand on her shoulder and stepping between her and Mule Face. Just as Elise and Logan reached the front door, Logan dropped her backpack and her school books tumbled out in a flash of paper and hardcovers.

"Oh!" Logan said. Elise and I kneeled down to pick up the books.

I held a well-worn paperback in my hand. "*To the Lighthouse* by Virginia Woolf." I looked at Logan and smiled. "I loved this book in high school."

"It's my favorite book," Logan whispered, and took the book from my hands.

"It was mine, too," I whispered back. I turned to Elise. "I'll send that e-mail today."

"I'll look for it," she said.

Logan beamed at me and waved before she and Elise walked out. I straightened my suit a little and squared my shoulders a tiny bit before I walked back to my desk. A renewed feeling of energy began to zap through me, reminding me a tiny bit of why I like my job and restocking the well of motivation.

Within seconds, Mule Face appeared at my office door, holding a large sleeve of French fries.

"What book was it?" she said as she pushed three fries into her mouth.

"*To the Lighthouse,*" I said as I reapplied lipstick with my compact.

"Huh. Never heard of it. Sounds boring," she said, and walked back to her office.

I smiled at my reflection in the mirror, mentally adding another book for Sara's collection.

Friday, September 19
. . . .

Today was a pretty good day, all around. First, this morning Keri showed me how to get around Signature Events' firewall so we could surf on You-Tube. It's quite simple, actually. Then, I got an e-mail saying our company's annual retreat had been postponed. Yes! No lame icebreaker activities this weekend. Then, Jake called to tell me he thinks he's finally overcome his nasal spray addiction since he went to the drugstore and didn't have an urge *at all* to buy any.

My mom e-mailed me and said she's feeling a bit better.

Finally, after work, I stopped at Trader Joe's.

Trader Joe's and I have a codependent relationship, much like Bobby Brown and Whitney Houston did. I'm willing to overlook its flaws since it usually treats me so, so good. I don't mind patiently standing behind people who must read every ingredient in a product *before* standing still for five minutes and pondering the purchase. I can ignore the onset of claustrophobia the minute I set food in the store.

I do all of this for the frozen enchiladas, veggie meatballs, and butternut squash soup. And besides, it's not like it's frustrating every time I go to Trader Joe's. And Trader Joe's is almost *always* a good partner, as long as I don't make it mad and mouth off, and then I deserve my punishment.

And even after it kicks my ass, I usually forget within a day or two. ("Trader Joe's didn't mean to hurt me. It's not Trader Joe's fault. It's just all the stress at work.")

"You've so joined the cult," Julie said to me when I phoned her tonight.

"Cult?" I said to her as I changed Sara's diaper.

"You're one of those suburban people. You are obsessed with Target and Trader Joe's and you go to bed early every night," she said proudly, as though she'd just discovered the key to unlocking cold fusion.

"That's called having a child," I said impatiently. "And don't talk shit about Target or Trader Joe's. They rule." I put Sara on the floor and she headed straight for an errant dry-erase board marker on the ground.

"OK, sorry. Next are you going to ask me to join your Coupon Club?" Julie said.

"Very funny, smart-ass."

"You've so drank the Kool-Aid!" Julie said.

"Whatever, listen. I wanted to talk to you about something." I bent down and pulled the marker out of Sara's chubby fingers and handed her a pacifier instead.

"OK?" Julie sounded suspicious.

"It's no big deal, and you can say no if you want, but a blog reader just e-mailed me the other day. She's been a reader forever and she and I have e-mailed a few times before. Anyway, she's been reading all of your Internet dating recaps. She said her brother just moved into town and doesn't really know anyone and was wondering if you'd be interested in another blind date?" Sara, clearly over the pacifier, started to wail. I bent down and picked her up and let her suck on the cordless phone antenna next to my ear.

"Wait, so one of your readers, who could be an AXE MURDERER, wants to set me up with her possibly molester brother?"

"Basically." I shrugged as I felt Sara's drool running down my cheek. "Just think of it this way: can't be worse than the others, right?"

There was a pause before she said, "Guess so. I'm in."

Sunday, September 21

· · · · · · · · · · · · · · · · · ·

I've read there are eighteen levels of hell, according to some Chinese legends. Helping Julie out with her romantic life probably falls somewhere in one of the outer, not-so-bad, reserved-for-kleptos-and-petty-thieves levels.

Helping Reese out these days?

Climbing-trees-with-razor-blade-branches, being-forced-to-watch-that-Spice-Girls-movie level of hell.

This morning, I had one foot in my apartment, one foot in the hallway, and Sara balanced delicately on my hip when an overwhelming sense of guilt washed over my body. I was ready to drop Sara off at my in-laws' and head to the salon for a much-needed massage. I stared down at her cherubic face and she smiled at me, drool running down her chin.

I knew what I should do.

Instead of dropping Sara off at the Grandalskis', I drove over to Reese's house. She answered the door, dressed in a velour tracksuit, looking totally confused.

"Clare, hi. Did I forget a lunch date or something?"

"WAAAAAAAAAAA!" Grace screamed behind her. Reese turned around and picked her up.

"Nope, just wanted to drop by and tell you not to be late for your massage." I pushed open her door and stood in her foyer.

"What?" she said.

"Your massage. You'd better hurry. Can't be late," I said, and gave her a nudge toward the door. "Give me the kid." I motioned toward Grace.

"I have to study for an exam!" Reese said.

"You can study later."

"I can't, who'll, I'm busy, I—"

"Yeah, yeah. I've heard it before. Bye-bye," I said, and gave her another shove.

"God, Clare, you don't know how much this means—" She started to walk out the door.

"Reese," I said.

"Yes?" She turned back.

I pointed to Grace, still on her hip.

"Oh, right." She put Grace down and crouched down next to her. "Mommy has to leave for a little bit. I'll be back soon."

"NOOOOOO!" Grace screamed, and clutched Reese's leg.

"I can't leave her like this," she said.

"Sure you can. I'm a mom now, too, remember? We'll be great," I said.

After ten more minutes of haggling, Reese finally left. Immediately, Grace started screaming, but I was prepared.

"Grace, do you want to watch a video?" I waved the tape in front of her.

She stopped wailing and stared at me, transfixed. She nodded.

"That's what I thought. Your mommy usually doesn't let you watch videos, does she?" Grace shook her head.

I popped the tape in the VCR and Grace settled in front of it.

There. That was easy, I thought. The only challenge was I had to listen to *Baby Tunes* for the next two hours, complete with songs like "Going Potty Is Fun" and "I Can Put My Clothes On by Myself." I wondered if there was a *Husband Songs* tape I could pick up for Jake. Like "I Always Put My Dishes in the Dishwasher and Not the Sink" or "Replacing the Toilet Paper Roll Is Easy!"

With Grace entertained, Brendan upstairs in his crib for his morning nap, and Sara bouncing in the Jumperoo, I settled down on Reese's huge couch with a gardening magazine. Just as I was engrossed in an article about bonsai gardens, Brendan woke up from his nap.

"Grace, I'm going to go get your brother, OK? I'll be right back." Grace didn't even look away from "Sharing Is Good."

I walked into Brendan's room and scooped him up from his gorgeous antique crib. His nursery has to be the most amazing baby's room I've ever seen. Reese commissioned an artist to do a replica of the drawings from the book *Guess How Much I Love You.* I started to walk out of the room when I caught sight of a plaque on the wall. It read, "First We Found Each Other . . . Then There Was You." Adorable. Perfect for a baby's room. Not so perfect for a couple who are separated.

Even though I felt slightly guilty for doing so, I held Brendan in my arms and crept into Reese's bedroom. Everything looked perfect, right out of the Pottery Barn catalog. I opened the closet and stared at the empty shelves, open, gaping wounds of Reese's former life.

Why are all of our choices black or white?

Why can't we have it all?

Brendan began to fuss, as though he sensed the overwhelming sadness in the room, and I closed the closet door and headed downstairs.

Halfway down the stairs, I realized everything was too quiet. I raced down the stairs with Brendan in my arms and walked into the family room. I found Grace, standing in front of Sara, coloring my daughter's face with a blue permanent marker.

"GRACE!" I screamed.

She froze, hand poised midair.

"What are you doing? Oh no! Shit!" I said. Grace started to cry. I put Brendan down in his swing and rushed over to Sara. "Oh God, you look like a blueberry," I said to her.

She grinned at me, straightened her legs, banged her hands down on the Jumperoo tray, and said, "GAH!"

"Grace, I know you didn't mean to do anything bad, but you can't draw on people," I said calmly to Grace. She looked me in the eye and continued to wail. Brendan decided to join in.

I looked at the clock. Only a half hour had gone by.

My blue-faced child took note of other kids wailing and her bottom lip started to curl. Recognizing the signs of a Sara scream-a-thon, I picked her up. "No, it's OK! Everyone's happy!" I turned to Grace. "Let's tell Sara how happy we are! Yay!"

That only made Grace scream "I WANT MY MOMMY!" as loud as her little lungs could muster.

And so it went on. For another hour and a half.

I finally got all of them quiet. Sara finally passed out from exhaustion, Grace became engrossed in an episode of *The Sopranos* (that is one secret that will die with me), and Brendan fell asleep after I fed him.

All was well in kidland when Reese came home, a renewed glow to her face.

"Clare, you have no idea how amazing the massage was." She closed her eyes and smiled. "It felt so good. I feel like I'm ready for a nap."

"I'm glad. You deserve it," I said lightly, trying to appear as though the past two hours had been the easiest of my life.

"The kids didn't act like beasts, did they?"

"No, not at all. Piece of cake," I lied.

"Why is Sara's face blue?" Reese said, looking alarmed.

"Oh, just, um . . . part of a game we played," I said.

Reese stared at me, not buying a word of it.

"Mommy," Grace whispered, tugging at Reese's jacket.

"Just a second, honey. Is she OK?" Reese said.

"She's fine. I told you, just a fun game."

"Mommy," Grace said again, slightly more insistent.

"Hold on, darling," Reese said. "Clare, tell me what happened."

"It's no big deal. It was nothing—"

"MOMMY!" Grace yelled.

"WHAT?" Reese said to her.

"That lady said a bad word," Grace said as she pointed to me.

"Time to go!" I said, and ran out the door.

Tuesday, September 23

I took a break this morning from proofing Logan's party invitation to surf the Internet. I logged onto Facebook, which Keri showed me how to access. (She's coming in so handy these days.) I pulled up Mark's profile, as I've been wont to do these days, as it seems to be the only way to keep tabs on his relationship with Casey. In the past week, I've learned that they've gone to numerous baseball games together and eaten Chinese food at some point and both love the movie *Wedding Crashers*. His status is still listed as "In A Relationship" and photos of her are still in his album, so I'm guessing they're still together.

Of course, it would seem to be much easier to simply say, "Hey, Mark, are you and Casey still dating?"

But I did that and his answer was, "Stop being such a freak."

So, Facebook is my only method of sleuthing. I also snuck over to Sam's profile and laughed a little at all of the pictures of her and her friends holding red cups. She has 871 friends. Facebook is pretty much the only way we all stay in touch with each other's lives. They read my blog, I read their profiles. It screams, *Dysfunctional*, but hey, at least I'm interested.

Wednesday, September 24

. . . .

4:00 P.M.

During my Internet trolling yesterday, I found a listing for a house I think Jake and I are going to check out tonight. It seems perfect on paper: three bedrooms, two bathrooms, updated kitchen, even a tiny half basement. Of course, I remain skeptical since I know any house that we can afford is usually not a house we'd want.

6:30 P.M.

Wow. It really wasn't that bad. It was like, a normal house. In a normal neighborhood. The house needed some updating, of course, and we'd have to paint it immediately, and it had Pergo instead of hardwood floors, but overall, it was really pretty good. And it's definitely in our price range. I don't want to jinx anything, so I'll just say we liked it. We liked it a lot. We're going to talk about it after Sara goes to bed.

12:37 A.M.

My head is pounding. I got into bed an hour ago and tried to fall asleep. Jake, of course, is soundly asleep next to me, snoring lightly. Sara is peacefully floating on her dream cloud. I, on the other hand, have been spinning and spinning for the last hour with no end in sight.

The conversation started as soon as Jake laid Sara in her crib and closed her bedroom door.

"So, so, so! What do you think? Should we get it? I think we should get it! Let's put a bid in tonight! I love it, love it, love it!" Jake practically hopped around in front of me.

"Let's sit down and talk," I said.

We walked into the living room, well, more like I walked and he threw himself joyfully down on the couch.

"Didn't you like it?" he asked me.

"Of course I did," I said slowly as I tucked my feet underneath me like a cat.

"But?"

"But." I stopped, then shook my head. "Nothing."

"What?"

"It's nothing," I said again. I couldn't bring myself to vocalize my innermost thoughts.

"Clare, you have to tell me what you're thinking," he said lightly.

"OK," I said, and stared out the window for a minute. "It's just—just that . . . OK, don't get mad," I said.

He raised his eyebrows at me.

"It's just . . . if we buy this house . . . I'm afraid if I decide to stay home . . . you lose your job . . ." I trailed off.

He leaned forward a little. "I'm not going to lose my job."

"I know. It's just this is such a huge step. I'm scared." I pulled my hoodie tightly around my body.

"I know," Jake said as he pulled me toward him.

"Can we just sleep on it?" I said into his T-shirt.

"Of course." He kissed the top of my head and squeezed me.

As I lay down to bed, I knew. I knew it was time to move forward, to keep pushing toward the next steps. Because that's what being a parent means.

Thursday, September 25

. . . .

This morning, Jake rolled over in bed and put his arm around my waist.

"Let's get the house," I whispered in his ear.

"But what about all that stuff last night?" he mumbled into my pillow.

"Just a conversation. That house is our future. Let's do it," I said.

"I'm in," he said.

So, we leapt out of bed as Jake dialed our Realtor and let her know we'd like to put a bid in on the house.

I ran to Sara's crib and announced, "Sara, you're going to have a big, beautiful new room in a huge, amazing new house!"

She stood up in her crib and extended her chubby arms toward me. I picked her up and held her close to my chest. I whispered in her ear that even though I go to work every day, she's still the most important thing in the world to me and there's nothing I won't do for her. She's my life. She's my heart, and now she was going to get an awesome new house to explore.

I released her and held her face close to mine. She shrieked and laid her head against my chest. And I knew she understood.

Friday, September 26
· ·

Holy shit.

Our offer was accepted.

We close on November 7.

Part of me didn't think they'd really accept it. Or at least, we'd go back and forth and have a battle of wills and I'd get to display my amazing negotiating powers and get them to throw in their plasma television or something.

But no.

No plasma television.

Just a contract on an amazing, larger-than-I'd-ever-thought-we'd-be-able-to-afford *house.*

House.

We have a house.

I must go obsessively stare at the pictures we took at the showing.

Saturday, September 27
· ·

Jake and I basked in the glow of the soon-to-be-our house for hours last night. We threw our hands up and wondered just what we're going to do with all that darn space. And the bathrooms. There are two and a half bathrooms! I've already claimed which one is "mine," and therefore Jake is not allowed to do anything but occasionally wash his hands in it.

We wondered if the fridge was so big, I could fit inside of it. I excitedly discussed what flowers to plant in the backyard. Jake planned about eight parties we could hold in our basement. I dreamed about the sure-to-be-our-new-best-friends neighbors.

We drank two bottles of wine, so by the end of the night it became, "It hasshs a front doorsh! Aweshome!"

My headache this morning did not dull my excitement. Realizing that we now have to pack up everything in our apartment did. Although we did a massive clean-and-pitch before Sara was born, several drawers, cabinets, and closets are still stuffed with random things, like strands of broken Christmas lights all knotted together. I don't want to even consider what to do with the wire hanger collection Jake's amassed in the back of the closet. On second thought, maybe we can hang it as a chandelier in our new living room and call it our art deco creation or something.

The minute I got home from work, I started pulling papers out of drawers and dishes out of the cabinets while Sara sat on a blanket in front of a Baby Einstein video. When Jake got home, all he could see was our daughter, looking totally confused while sitting on the floor, surrounded by stacks of dishes and bowls.

"Maybe we shouldn't pack up all of our kitchenware just yet," he said, and bent down over the ring of dishes and picked Sara up.

"Jake, you have no idea how much crap we have. We need to start *now*," I said, and dramatically flung my arm around.

"Yes, but we probably need things like forks between now and our close date," he said evenly.

"I have no problem eating with my hands," I said from behind our entertainment center.

"What are you doing?" he called to me.

"I'm packing up all of our DVDs. Do you think I should just throw out our videotapes, considering you refuse to watch them due to poor picture quality?" I held up a copy of *Dirty Dancing* in my hand.

"That one, you can throw out," he said, and pointed toward the trash.

"Very funny. You're not helping," I said, and set *Dirty Dancing* down atop the television.

"Clare, please. We have six weeks. Let's try and keep it together." He smiled. "That's why you're so lucky to have me. I'm so good under pressure." He looked at Sara, "Aren't I?" he said to her.

"Right. Like last week when we were stuck in traffic and I thought your head was going to pop off because we were five minutes late to a movie." I waved my hands around.

"Yeah, but I keep calm about the important stuff." He raised his eyebrows and chuckled.

Ignoring him, I walked over to the coffee table. I bent down and started pulling out the magazines stacked underneath it.

"What are you doing now?" he asked.

"I'm throwing all these magazines out." I said, and huffed as I picked up like fifty magazines.

"Wait—you're throwing all your old magazines away? The ones I've begged you to pitch for the past year?" He held his arms out like he was waiting for a huge announcement.

"Yes," I said tersely as I shot him a dirty look.

"I take it back. You're on the right track. Let me get you a garbage bag." He raced into the kitchen.

"Your *Sports Illustrated*s are next," I called to him.

Tuesday, September 30
. . . .

Reveling in the new house has halted.

Golf outing day.

Gah.

Wednesday, October 1
. . . .

I took today off. I tried to get out of bed and I couldn't do it. Literally, I couldn't do it. Not just because I'm exhausted and every muscle in my body aches, but also because I sprained my ankle yesterday. Badly sprained. So bad I was sure it was broken and went into the emergency room for an

X-ray. It's a lovely shade of midnight blue and inky black and my toes look like overstuffed blood sausages.

The event, by all measures, was a success. We raised $150,000 to benefit the foundation, all of the players seemed satisfied with their golf games, all of the volunteers showed up, and no one drowned in the torrential downpours that occurred an hour after the shotgun start.

Yes, downpours.

I met Keri at the club at 7:00 A.M. and we went straight to the golf pro's office. This time Len was forced to look me in the eye and actually speak to me, since there was no male present. Poor Len. It seemed difficult for him to have to deal with a professional, opinionated woman. I'm sure most of the women he deals with at the club have problems like, "My cart is dirty. Find a caddy to clean it off."

We did a run-through of the day and made sure we had every golfer's handicap listed for scoring purposes.

At 8:00 A.M. sharp, Keri and I sat down at the registration table with the foundation staff. I was thrilled to see my blog reader from the first meeting there. Although it was a little early to be answering questions like, "Are you going out and getting drunk again with Julie this weekend?" She even asked about my mom and said she's been praying for her.

Love my readers.

By 9:00 A.M., mayhem. Registration was filled with impatient golfers, not used to waiting for anything, standing in line to check in. It wasn't just checking their names off on a spreadsheet. It was checking their name off, giving them a golf shirt, giving them their golf balls, asking them if they wanted to buy mulligans. (Still not sure what those are, but whatever. I thought it was a kind of beer.) They also seemed to get really annoyed when we asked them the question, "Name?" Apparently, we were all supposed to know who all two hundred of them were. Like, "Hey! You must be Bob Rosenacker! I recognized you by your receding hairline, pointy nose, liver spots on your hands, and general bad attitude! Welcome! What size golf shirt do you wear?"

It got to the point where we tried to move everyone along as quickly as possible, so we'd ask their name, shove a golf shirt and golf balls into their hands, and point them to the locker room all at the same time.

"Name?" I said without looking up.

"I think you know it," a familiar voice said.

My head snapped up. "Oh, sorry. Things are a little nuts."

"That's OK," Greg said. He gestured to three men behind him. "I think you know these guys, too."

Tim Thompson, Greg's father, and Greg's two best friends, Ethan and Nate.

"Hey, Clare, you look great!" Mr. Thompson said, and shook my hand.

"Er, thanks," I said as I self-consciously smoothed my hair behind my ears.

They all stared at me.

"Oh! Right! You probably want to be checked in, huh? I think the weather is going to be great today. . . ." I babbled on for like four minutes straight while they all continued to stare at me. The foundation staff stopped what they were doing and stared at me, too, which meant the entire line was stopped, 98 percent of whom were staring at me, blabbing away like Robin Williams on speed.

A ray of sensibility entered into my brain sometime around ". . . haven't seen you guys since the kickoff party" and I somehow managed to give them their shirts and balls and allow them a brief opportunity to escape The Crazy Girl Who Is Trying to Make Flustered Conversation.

"Was that him?" Keri hissed to me after they left.

"Him who?" I said.

"Ex-boyfriend him!"

"Oh yeah." I tried to sound casual.

"He's so cute!" She looked surprised.

"Er, let's double-check the handicaps." I shoved a stack of paper at her and pretended to look through my purse.

Once everyone was checked in, lunch was served. Next, Len took over and did the shotgun start and the cranky men drove their golf carts to various holes to begin play.

I breathed a sigh of relief and began to clean up from registration until I saw Andrea, one of the foundation staff members, racing toward me with a panicked look in her eyes.

"No one is watching the BMW!" she gasped out.

"What?" I said.

"The BMW! For the hole-in-one contest!"

Crap. Someone has to be out there at all times to verify if anyone gets a hole-in-one for insurance purposes.

"I thought one of your staff was going to do that!"

"There was a miscommunication in the office and she's not coming. So . . ." Andrea trailed off and stared at me.

"We'll do it," I sighed, and signaled to Keri. Sitting in a BMW all afternoon watching crusty old men play golf was not my idea of a good time, but I really didn't have a choice.

We drove a golf cart out to the fourteenth hole. I only got lost twice and almost drove into the field of play like seven times, so it was a success. I parked next to the gleaming white car, opened it up, and sat inside. I ran my fingers over the smooth leather and breathed in the smell of a car I'll never be able to afford unless I sell my ovaries. Or Sara. It took me a while to figure out how to work the radio, since every gadget in those expensive cars has to be as difficult to operate as the oxygen regulator on a NASA spaceship. Apparently, rich people prefer to use things that are twice as difficult to figure out. It must be due to their superior intelligence.

"So, do you think the weather's going to hold out?" Keri asked as she took her sunglasses off.

"Definitely. I have a good feeling," I said confidently as I fiddled with the radio.

The golfers had played about three holes or so when the sky started to look threatening. It was sunny one minute, then *bam*! Inky black clouds everywhere. Within seconds, lightning started to flash on the horizon as I buried my face in the padded steering wheel. I didn't pick my head up when I heard the unmistakable sound of a bullhorn, signaling the pause of play. I kept my head down as the golf carts whizzed past me toward the clubhouse. I was afraid one of the players would throw a Rolex at my head or something.

"What are we going to do?" Keri shrieked.

"Nothing," I replied calmly.

So, we sat in the BMW, amidst a monsoonlike downpour, complete with excessive thunder and lightning. I was content to stay in my extravagant environment until my cell phone beeped with a text message. It was from Andrea and it said they needed me back at the clubhouse to talk to Len about the dinner menu.

I had two options: drive the BMW across the golf course, laughing maniacally while tearing up thousands of dollars' worth of greens, or suck it up and drive the golf cart back and pray I wouldn't get swept away in the winds, like the Wicked Witch of the West. (Or was it East? Whatever. Whichever one rode the bicycle in the air.)

I chose the second option since the BMW was a stick shift anyway.

We did not get swept away, but I did drive through sideways rain and some hail. Of course, the rain was all on my side of the golf cart, so Keri remained dry while I arrived at the clubhouse looking like a wet T-shirt contest contestant, due to my nude bra and white polo shirt.

Since my clothes were soaked (and see-through and porn star–like), I was forced to change into one of the leftover golf shirts, which (of course) was a size XXL. If I had a cute belt I could have worn it as a dress, but alas, I did not. So, I spent the rest of the day in a man's shirt large enough to house one of the people profiled on MTV's *True Life: I'm Obese* and soaking-wet Capris.

After an hour, the rain stopped and the greens dried out a little, so Len let everyone resume play. A few hours later, the golfers all stumbled back, and I do mean *stumbled* back, seeing as how every one of them was stinking drunk due to a very generous beverage cart attendant.

As I was coming around a corner in the clubhouse, trying to get everything set up for the winning foursome prizes, I literally ran right into Greg.

"Hey! Clare! How's it goin'?" He reeked of gin.

"Great! Just trying to get everything together!" I said, and stepped around him.

"Your hair's all wet," Greg said seriously, as though I wasn't aware of that detail.

"Er, thanks for telling me," I said quickly.

Man, I forgot how dense he is when he drinks. I chuckled to myself as I prepared the room for the dinner and prize ceremony. I probably should've also made sure the floor was completely dry, because during the handing out of prizes at dinner I slipped on a puddle on the marble floor. I skidded across it with arms flailing and wound up on the floor, my ankle badly twisted underneath me.

Although spirits were considerably lifted when one of the players, a very handsome doctor, had to wrap my ankle up for me. At least I had just gotten a pedicure.

The club also deeply discounted the bill for the outing, after I casually mentioned an ad on television I saw for a personal injury lawyer.

OK, so let's recap once again:

Lots of money raised? Check.

Event pulled off without a hitch? Check.

Clare publicly embarrassed, yet it turned out to be beneficial? Check.

Thursday, October 2

. . . .

The week's insanity continued today.

First, a water pipe from the office above broke, sending toilet water dripping down from the ceiling in my office. Within seconds, everything on my desk was wet and smelled like sewage.

Mule Face screamed and threw her extra-thick chocolate shake down onto the carpet of my office right when it happened, since she was standing next to my desk, recounting a story about the exact shade of purple she and Big D had painted their bathroom. So now, not only does my carpet reek of raw sewage, despite the eight hundred times my carpet's been cleaned, but I also have a huge brown stain in the center of my office. I'm sure, with the stain coupled with the smell, clients who come in are drawing some pretty interesting conclusions.

Then, the stationer for Logan's party sent over an invitation proof for the event. It was, once again, incorrect. The first time, the date was wrong. The second time, Logan's name was spelled "Legon," like a folkloric dragon.

The third time, the font was too small to read. And this time, they left off the RSVP line. So, I trekked over to the shop itself, sat down in front of the owner, and meticulously went through every change. I insisted the proof be corrected while I waited, to ensure they wouldn't send me another proof with the invitation written in Chinese or something. It's even become a running joke in the office, but unfortunately, Elise insisted on using this stationer since she knows the owner of the shop. You'd think it would mean we'd get even just a sliver of customer service. But no, the designer told me I'm too picky and I'm really holding up production with all of my changes.

I did laugh, though, when she accidentally said, "Our motto is: 'We're not satisfied until you're not satisfied.' Oh, wait . . . I meant . . . What did I say?"

And finally, Greg left a comment on my blog. I'd typed an entry about a trip to Home Depot with Jake to buy a new screwdriver and Greg left this: *Glad to have just found your blog, Clare. I'm already a fan.*

Friday, October 3

"You just missed your sister," Keri said to me today as I returned to the office from another meeting with the stationer.

"Sam?" I stopped and stood in front of Keri's desk, sipping my Diet Coke.

"She picked up the earrings you left on your desk," Keri said as she examined her manicure. "She said she wasn't going to stop by until later today but was in the area on the way to a pedicure."

"Oh, that's too bad I missed her," I said breezily as I started toward my office.

"She's really cute," Keri called to me.

I stopped and turned around in the door of my office. "I know and believe me, she knows, too."

"She's supernice, too." Keri smiled.

"Sam? You must be mistaken." I laughed and started back toward my desk.

"Nope, she was great. She gushed about your office and she told me how cool you are since you always let her borrow your stuff," Keri finished, and I slowly turned around.

I walked back over to her desk and set my drink down on it with a thud. "Now I know you're lying."

Keri laughed. "What is it about sisters? My sister and I are the same way. I brag about her to my friends and people I meet, but we can barely be civil to each other in person."

"No kidding. Every time Sam and I attempt to have a conversation, I sound like a senior citizen and she sounds like a seventh grader. It's like Elizabeth Taylor talking to Dakota Fanning."

"So it doesn't get better, huh?" Keri said.

"At least not from where I'm standing. Hopefully someday she and I can sit down and have lunch together or something like normal people, but right now it doesn't look good," I said ruefully.

"It sucks. Sisterhood is never the way it is in the movies." She said it simply, but it sounded like genius.

"No shit," I said. I glanced down and caught sight of Keri's shoes—a cute pair of red flats with a gold brooch on the toe. "Cute shoes, by the way!"

"Tory Burch." She beamed. "Your sister loved them, too!"

Inspired, I walked back to my office. I had an idea I'd been toying around with for a while, so I decided to bite the bullet. I dialed Sam's cell phone.

"Yeah?" she answered.

"Hey, Sam, sorry I missed you. I heard you got the earrings."

"Yup. Thanks. Did you want something?" she said.

"Can't I call you just to talk?" I sighed.

"Ummm, I'm kinda busy and stuff."

"Fine," I sighed. "I did actually have something to ask you."

"What?" she said impatiently.

"I was wondering if you'd be interested in walking with me in this breast cancer fundraiser walk on the twenty-sixth. I saw it advertised and thought it could be a cool thing to do. We would walk in honor of Mom," I finished.

There was a long pause.

"Sam?" I said.

"Ummm . . . yeah, yeah. OK," she said quickly.

"Don't you want to do it? I thought it would be something we could do together."

"I said yes, didn't I?" she snapped.

"I know, you just sounded . . . weird about it." My shoulders slumped forward as I realized this phone call would not end the way I hoped.

"No, I didn't. I said I want to do it." The ice in her voice could've chilled a pregnant lady.

"OK, OK. So, we'll do it. Great. I'll sign us up," I said, my voice still light.

" 'K. Bye," she said, and hung up.

I let out a breath as I hung up the phone. Well, I reasoned, at least she didn't say no. We're going to spend a day together, doing something for my mom. Or at least in her honor. I think if Sam and I can get through several hours alone together, gravity will cease to exist and several of the natural laws of the universe will reverse. Rain will fall from the ground up, weather patterns will move from east to west, Butterscotch will stop howling at our door for food every morning at five o'clock.

It might cause a global panic, but it's worth a shot.

Saturday, October 4

. . . .

Sara fell asleep in my arms this afternoon. It was time for her nap and she refused to go down in her crib. I'd rock her and jiggle her and her eyes would slowly flutter and close. Yet as soon as I'd place her in her crib, her eyes would snap open and she'd wail.

Part of me was secretly happy, as she'd developed some separation anxiety with her day-care workers this week. Meaning, she'd cry when I came to pick her up. Her tiny screams were like daggers of ice into my heart.

When I was on maternity leave, it was much easier to leave her in her crib for a few minutes and let her cry to see if she'd fall back asleep. I think part of it was because I was so exhausted all of the time, so beat-down mentally, I'd try anything for an opportunity to take a hot shower. Since I've gone back to work, I've become much softer. It must be my guilt monster, rearing its ugly head again. It's harder to let her cry, even if I know she desperately needs to go to sleep. Part of me feels like every moment I have with her, if she needs me in any way, even just for some company, I'll gladly give myself to her.

All of my baby books say I'm spoiling her and teaching her to cry whenever she wants attention. I'm sure I'll deal with the ramifications of it when she's two years old and wants to sleep in my bed every night, so Jake and I haven't had sex in months, because today I gave in.

This afternoon, I snuggled into the armchair and ottoman in her room and rocked her in my arms and let her sleep against my chest. I listened to her breath and marveled over her chubby cheeks, long eyelashes, and silky hair. Like I always do, I whispered promises to give her everything under the sun.

"Women's jobs are just as important as men's," I said to her. Because they are. Yet a tiny nagging thought swirled around in my brain: *Why are you doing this? You could have her every day.*

Am I just working to make a point? To support a nameless/faceless sisterhood of women and to show my own daughter that women should be independent? Are there other ways to teach her those things? Most days, I'm so tired I can't remember my ATM card's PIN number—is that the kind of example I want to set?

But I love my job. . . .

And so the carousel spun around me, not stopping to let me off at any decision, just the centrifugal force tugging me in different directions until I was nearly sick.

Tuesday, October 7

This morning, as I was working on my third cup of coffee, a notification popped up on my computer, telling me I had an e-mail on my AOL account. I maximized the window and saw an e-mail from david.castillo@ hipparentmagazine. I almost moved it into my spam folder but realized the subject line read "Clare Finnegan," not the usual spam subject line of "Cheap Viagra" or "Nekkid Babes."

The e-mail read:

> Clare,
> I was given your e-mail address by Kyle Tiesdale, your editor at *The Daily Tribune.* I'm a big fan of your blog and your columns. I'm the editor-in-chief of *Hip Parent,* a national magazine publication with a very devoted readership. We're in the process of trying to extend our reach, and I'd like to discuss the possibility of your doing some freelance work for the magazine.
>
> Please feel free to e-mail me back or give me a call at your convenience.
>
> Sincerely,
> David Castillo

I nearly fainted at my desk. I stared at the e-mail, slack jawed, for a few moments until Mule Face walked past, stopped in front of my office.

"What's wrong? Did you mess up something for Elise's event?" she asked while licking the spoon of her yogurt.

"No, no. Just received a surprising e-mail, that's all," I said, and quickly closed my browser.

"You'd better not screw anything up for that event, you know," she said, and slurped at her yogurt.

"Thanks, I've got it under control," I said, and bent down to open my desk drawer.

"No problem. I've got your back," she said, and swished down the hallway.

I opened my browser back up. I wiggled around in my chair, silently doing a victory dance before I called David Castillo.

David was great on the phone, albeit slightly brisk. He said they're interested in having me do a monthly piece on my recommendations on the newest baby stuff. In short, a buy it or skip it piece each month. I think it's hilarious anyone would value my opinion on baby products, seeing as how I found most of the stuff we Just Had to Buy for Sara before she was born completely useless. The most helpful baby product to date? An old sheet I cut up and made into a swaddling blanket. I doubt the readers of *Hip Parent* want me to write an article titled "Why Bouncy Seats Are Crap and Old Ripped-Up Sheets Rule," so I'm going to have to start becoming more open to trying new things.

The pay is nothing special; I'll be able to get one more pedicure each month and that's about it. But I think writing for a magazine read by people from Oregon to Texas is pretty darn special.

It's no wonder they want me to write for the magazine—they probably figure if someone like me can figure out my head from my ass while working and being a mom, I must have some kind of secret potion stored away.

I ran out of my office to Keri's desk and blurted, "A huge magazine wants me to write for them!"

She turned away from her computer screen and said, "Holy crap! That's amazing! What magazine is it? Like *Cosmo* or *Glamour*? You're totally writing for *Vogue,* aren't you?"

"Uh, no. It's *Hip Parent* magazine."

Her face fell a little. "Oh, that's still cool, I guess."

"At least it's Hip *Parent* and not *Dorky Parent* or something."

"How can a parent be hip?" she wondered out loud. She quickly caught herself and said, "I mean, you're totally hip, so *of course* they'd pick you. You're like the coolest person I know."

I smiled at her and patted her shoulder.

I know I'm not hip anymore, at least not in her world. And that's fine. But when thrown into the pool with other suburban parents? I think I measure up OK.

Thursday, October 9

. . . .

Everyone congratulated me on my newest writing gig. Even Marianne seemed impressed, although she asked me over the phone, "Are you going to use the F word in your articles?"

"What?" I said, and rested my head against the kitchen wall.

"The F word, dear. My friend Betty found your writings on the Internet and she was quite disturbed at how much you use the F word. I myself have never read your Internet book, so I told her I didn't know why and would ask you." Her voice was light, but I could tell she'd been waiting forever to say this.

"First of all, it's called a blog, not an Internet book." I kept my voice equally light, despite everything.

"So it's not a story?" She sounded bewildered.

"A story?" Now I was confused.

"I always assumed it was a book, a story." The alarm began to grow in her voice.

"It's more like a diary," I said.

"Oh, dear," she said. She fell silent.

"Marianne?" I said quickly.

"*Mom,* honey."

"Sorry. Are you OK?" I said.

"Does your Internet book talk about us? I mean, I wouldn't want anyone reading about our personal lives." She sounded like she was clutching a strand of pearls.

"No, I never really talk about family," I said. It's the truth. There's no way I'd ever mention Marianne on my blog. If I did, it would be: *Marianne is my mother-in-law. She's Jake's mom. She has brown hair.* Those would be pretty much the only things I could say.

"Oh, good. But you haven't answered my question," she insisted.

"What's that?" I said, and stared at all of the half-packed boxes on the countertops.

"Why do you use the F word so much? It's so embarrassing, let alone improper and vulgar."

"It's just kind of a joke. It's just to be funny." I gave a quick laugh.

"Oh, I see. And people on the Internet think it's humorous?" I pictured her eyes narrowing, preparing to shoot daggers.

"I guess," I said, and grabbed some packing tape and started sealing one of the boxes.

"Don't they have censors on the Internet? Like on television?"

Incredulous as to how she can function in today's society without having any clue as to modern technology and unwilling to explain it to her, I feigned hearing Sara cry and hung up the phone.

Monday, October 13

Despite my New Fabulous Writing Gig, I am officially in the Worst Mood Ever.

Christina made all of the office staff attend an afternoon company-wide retreat. She originally told me I could get out of it, since Logan's party is coming up, but then insisted everyone attend. Half of the staff work at an office across town, so she wanted everyone to get together and do "team-building" exercises. Which is such bullshit, since the only thing that "builds teams" during these retreats is a shared hatred and embarrassment for the activities.

Keri, with her sixth sense, took the day off.

Skinny bitch.

I knew it wasn't a good sign when I walked into the conference room and a short woman bopped in front of me and handed me an agenda. "Hi! Hi! Hi! Welcome! I'm Amy! I'll be your moderator!"

I stared at her and waited for her to stop vibrating before I took the paper and wearily sat down next to Mule Face, who was eating a sleeve of onion rings.

"OK, everyone! We're going to start by giving ourselves nicknames. I'm Awesome Amy. Go around the room," she barked. I glanced around, trying to figure out if Amy was our moderator or some crazed lunatic who escaped from the psych ward. When no one said anything, she pointed to Christina. "You go first."

"Er, Classy Christina," she said, and hung her head a little like a defeated dog.

I panicked and tried to think of a nickname for myself. Cute Clare? Cantankerous Clare? Colorful Clare? Shit, shit shit . . . um . . . Crappy Clare? It felt like high school gym class as I prayed for it to be over quickly, painlessly, and without serious bodily harm.

Mercifully, I thought of a name and said, "Cool Clare," when it was my turn. We then had to make name tags with our new names and had to call each other by those names all day.

"We're going to start with a game of one-eyed tag! Everyone, get up!" Amy shouted after we put our name tags on.

We all stared at her.

"Up! Up! Up!" she said.

We all slowly obliged and stood up, exchanging looks of dismay and terror.

"Now, everyone cover your right eye!" she said brightly.

"Um, excuse me, Amy," Mary, a staff member from the other office, said.

"Yes?" Amy did not look pleased.

"Why are we doing this?"

"Just do it!" Amy barked.

We were all scared into submission, so we obliged and covered our right eyes.

"OK, good. Now, I'm It and I'm going to chase you! Ready, set, go!" she said.

We all stood in place, staring at her from our left eyes.

"You don't want to be tagged by me. Let's try this again. When I say go, you run, got it? GO!"

We all made an attempt to shuffle around the room, but we were so confused by the assignment, we were all tagged out immediately.

"OK, great! Wasn't that fun?" Amy said when we finished.

We all mumbled and sat back down in our chairs. I figured she'd go into the psychological reason for making us play one-eyed tag, but she just went into the next exercise. Maybe it was to humiliate us into submission? Like the prisoners in Abu Ghraib?

Next, we had to form a human box around Amy. We had to keep her trapped in the box and move around so she couldn't escape. Which was a great metaphor for how we all felt. But once again, no explanation.

Finally, she broke us into two teams and we had to write and perform a cheer about how much we love our coworkers. I had to dig my nail into my thigh to stop myself from saying, *I love how I don't have to see most of you since you work fifteen minutes away! Rah! Rah! Rah! Yay, team!*

Just as we all were at our breaking points, Awesome Amy released us. Beat-down, we slunk into our offices or out the door, determined to forget the afternoon.

Wednesday, October 15
. . . .

> Dear Ass:
>
> Why do you have to be so big? Your enormity is simply uncalled for. Why can't you be more like the other asses? The round and perky ones.
>
> Yes, yes, I know. The whole having a baby thing really screwed you up. You used to be cute, small even. Now you're just one big white blob covered in stretch marks. I hate to say it, but you're ugly, Ass.
>
> I realize my part in all of this. I realize that eating Taco Bell and steak isn't exactly helping you regain your once-glorious form. I get it. I'll try to cut back. But I would really appreciate if you could at least make an effort to stop looking so heinous.
>
> Sincerely,
> The Person Who Owns You

Gah.

It's been long enough. I've been walking around with an extra ten pounds for several months now. And it's time to bite the bullet, admit I'm chunky, and do something about it.

For the first few months after Sara was born, I remained in total denial about my weight. When I showered, I pretended like I was washing a car or something. And forget about looking in dressing room mirrors or exposing my thighs to direct sunlight. It was easy to deny my chubbiness on maternity leave, since I wore my Miss Piggy pants every day anyway. But then it was time to go back to work and I was still wearing them.

Yeah, well, I'm still wearing them.

It also doesn't help I have to see Keri's teeny-tiny thighs every day.

Or, as I played one-eyed tag at the company retreat, I felt my butt flopping up and down like two jackals fighting over a bone in my pants.

So, I'm going on a diet.

But that's only part of the solution. I need to start working out, too, since losing weight will only solve the "mass" issue and not the "jiggle" issue. I'm going to ask my blog readers for their suggestions.

I considered not posting about my jiggly ass, due to the thought of Greg reading about my struggle of Clare versus Love Handles, but I'm not about to start censoring what I say. After all, if he read through the archives, he's probably read way more embarrassing material.

9:30 P.M.

My readers suggested everything from kick-boxing to Tae Bo to Pilates to yoga. I even had a few offers for running buddies.

I still haven't decided what technique I'm going to use to make my body look more like Jennifer Aniston's and less like Jabba the Hut's. The problem is, I've never really had to work out. Correction: I've never really wanted to work out. My body's never been perfect, but it never necessitated serious athletic commitment to make it look decent. Of course, inevitably, a few times a year, I would watch some great infomercial about the latest workout and spend two hundred dollars and order the damn thing, only to have it collect dust under my bed. The slide thing with the booties, the Firm workout tapes, the Pilates ring, and the yoga band are all hanging out together and laughing at me as I sleep. *Fat ass!* they heckle.

Periodically, I take all of them out, dust the videotapes, and then slide them right back under my bed.

And that used to be the only workout I needed.

But, unfortunately, since having Sara, my body decided to kind of give up a little, so I think it's going to take more than some light cleaning to whip this blubber into shape.

Love handles: Beware. Your days are numbered.

Tuesday, October 21

My diet is going well. If you don't count all of the beer I drank yesterday.

Last night, I dragged Reese out of the house and made her come on a Haunted Pub Crawl with me. Keri told me about it, since she seems to know everything in the city that involves drinking, so I called and made a reservation. At first, she protested, claiming everything from not being able to find a babysitter to not having anything to wear to not feeling like drinking. I told her Jake offered to babysit all the kids, she had a closet full of amazing clothes, and she could drink water for all I cared. It was just about getting her out of the house and into the outside world. Of course, I felt a little guilty after I imagined all of the liquid calories I would consume, none of which would help me say *arrivederci* to Miss Piggy pants, but I figured I could sacrifice in the name of friendship. Yeah, that was it.

We met our transportation for the evening, a school bus painted black, in the city. There was a group of about thirty of us. The bus drove us from one bar to another, all supposedly haunted with the ghosts of everyone from old mobsters to jilted bartenders.

We didn't see anything even slightly resembling a ghost, although Reese claimed ghosts were stealing her drinks because they kept going missing. The fact she was stumbling around after the first bar indicated no ghosts were involved. It was great to see her out, having a great time, having seemingly forgotten about Matt for the evening.

"Thanks so much for taking me out, Clare," she slurred to me at the third bar.

"Of course. It's been forever since we've been out together. I needed to get you out of that house before you turned into a pasty white albino."

"You were right. I am having a good time," she said, and patted me on the back. "I love you." She leaned forward and hugged me.

"I love you, too." I laughed.

"Hey, can I buy you a drink?" a cute guy behind her said.

"No, I'm—" She stopped and looked stricken.

"We're OK," I said quickly. I grabbed Reese's hand and pulled her over to a corner of the bar. "So, how's little baby Brendan?" I asked brightly.

"I didn't know what to say," she said. Tears formed in her eyes. "I almost said, 'I'm married.' But I'm not. I am, but I'm not. Oh, Clare, what am I going to do?" She buried her face in her hands.

"Reese, you're going to be great," I said, and put my hands on her cheeks and kissed the top of her head.

"But the kids. He hasn't even come over to see the kids. It's like he doesn't care." Her voice came out muffled.

"I'm so sorry, Reese. You're such a great mom, though. Those kids are the luckiest kids in the world. Shit, will you adopt me?" I said, and tried to laugh.

"I just feel so guilty. I feel like—" She stopped and put her head down on the bar again.

"Is she passed out already?" Julie appeared by our sides.

Reese picked her head up off the bar and wiped her cheeks. "Julie, what are you doing here?"

"My shift ended early, so I thought I'd play domestic and meet the two moms out for some drinks. You guys drink your second beers yet?" She leaned over the bar, massive boobs resting inches from the bartender's face. "Something strong, surprise me," she said, and winked at the bartender.

"Very funny. Yes, we've had more than two beers," I said.

"Great. I'm here now, so that means no more tears. No crying, only lots and lots of drinking, some dancing, and possibly some male heckling. Either of you two have a problem with that?" Reese and I smiled and shook our heads. At least Julie's attitude distracted Reese from thinking about Matt.

"Good." The bartender brought over a shocking green drink. "What the hell is this?" Julie demanded.

"It's a Tree Frog," the bartender said.

"Do I look like the kind of girl who drinks fluorescent-colored drinks?" She looked him squarely in the eye.

"Um, no, I, you said, um . . . ," he fumbled.

"Exactly. Now bring me something normal," she said. She turned to us. "Can you believe that idiot?"

"I'll drink the green thing," Reese said.

Julie pushed the drink over to Reese.

"Want an umbrella with that?" I teased her.

"Any further along on your big life decision?" Julie asked me as the bartender placed a beer in front of her. "Better," she said to him.

I shook my head. "Not really. It's a game of tug-of-war and I'm that ribbon in the middle."

"Wait, what are you talking about?" Reese said.

I reached into my purse to pull out my ChapStick. "It's . . . nothing. I just can't decide whether or not to continue working." I took a quick swig of my drink.

"You're kidding! But I thought you loved your job," Reese said, eyes wide.

"I do, so that's why it's not an easy decision," I said simply. I averted my eyes as all of the questions I wanted to ask Reese fought to leave my mouth.

Would you have chosen differently? Are you happy at home? Do you feel like in devoting your life to your kids you lost yourself?

Thankfully, she intuitively knew to change the subject. "I almost forgot! I have new pictures of the kids!" Reese said just as I set my beer down. She reached into her purse and pulled out an album. She handed it to Julie, who leafed through it.

"I'll be right back," Reese said, and walked toward the bathroom.

As soon as she was ten paces away, Julie handed me the album. "Why do all parents take their kids to a pumpkin patch and then force you to look at the pictures?" she asked.

I laughed and took the album from her. "I don't know. We feel compelled or something." I mentally shoved my own pumpkin patch picture album a little farther down into my purse.

"She's got cute kids and all, but damn," Julie said, and shook her head. "Cut her a break, Jules," I said.

"I am. Doesn't mean I want to see a thousand pictures of children, though." Julie wrinkled her nose.

Seeing an opportunity to change the subject, I wanted to ask her about her date with my blog reader's brother, Trevor. My reader said he seemed to really like Julie. "Have you gone out with Trevor yet?" I asked her as casually as I could.

"Yep." She shrugged as she played with her pack of cigarettes. "He was nice. No drama. Dinner and drinks."

"That's good, right?" I said, and twisted my engagement ring around.

"I guess." She took another swig of her drink

"Well, give it a chance. This is the first blind date that didn't turn out weird, like in a strip club or—," I started to say.

"Strip club. That would've been awesome!" Julie interrupted.

"No, I'm not going to a strip club, so don't even think about it." Reese reappeared. She looked down at her watch. "God, it's still so early." She reached forward and grabbed the green drink and downed it as Julie and I watched, mouths open.

"All right! Nice job! Let's get you another, Mama!" Julie cheered.

Approximately a half hour later, Reese puked all over the black bus. Not her finest moment. Julie forgot Reese hadn't really drank in several years and bought her a couple of shots before we left the third bar. We just pulled out into traffic, on our way to the fourth bar, when Reese's hands flew up to her mouth and she tried to stick her head out the window. Except the window was up, so she puked all down the side of it. We were kicked off the bus .5 seconds later.

We knew Reese was too wasted to try to get back to the suburbs, so I called Jake and asked him not to kill me, but Reese and I were going to crash at Julie's overnight and I would head to work in the morning. Thankfully, he didn't ask for a divorce on the spot. He even told me to have fun with the girls.

So, the three of us headed back to Julie's tiny apartment. Reese seemed to sober up after we plied her with lots of ice water and crackers. The three of us lounged around on a million pillows and blankets in front of the television, reminisced about our college days, and cried a little about my mom.

I don't remember who fell asleep first or what time it was. I do remember waking up, looking over at my two best friends, smiling, and then snuggling back down in between the two of them.

And life was good.

Sunday, October 26
. . . .

"Is she up yet?" I asked my mom as she answered the door this morning at seven.

"Still in the shower, but awake." My mom smiled.

I looked at her. Her laugh lines seemed more deeply etched, her hair just a touch thinner, and her cheeks just a bit looser in the morning light, as she stood in front of me, not wearing any makeup.

"Are you sure you don't want to come?" I asked my mom even though I knew the answer.

"I'd love to, I'm just not up to it these days. But it means so much to me that you girls are . . ." Her voice cracked and became hoarse. She cleared her throat. ". . . that you girls are doing this," she finished.

I put my arm around my mom's shoulders. "Of course," I choked out.

"Clare! What are you doing up so early?" My dad appeared with a cup of coffee.

"Dad, you know the walk is today," I said.

"Oh, really?" He smiled at me.

"Dad!"

"He's kidding. He's just trying to get a rise out of you," my mom said.

"I'm joking. I think it's great you girls are doing this." He paused. "Just try not to harm each other. The hospital ER is always slammed on Sundays."

"Dad, you know Sam and I never fight." I grinned back at him.

"I recall a few years ago, when you still lived at home, and your mother was out of town and you and your sister wound up pulling each other's hair and fist-fighting."

"Oh yeah. That was for a good reason," I said.

"What was the reason?" my mom said.

"She took my flatiron," I said.

"Ah, yes. Good reason," my dad said.

I heard the shower shut off upstairs.

"I guess she's out," I said to my mom as I flopped down on the couch.

"How are you girls going to do this?" she asked, sitting down next to me.

"I have no idea. Maybe we'll just walk in silence for four hours. Or maybe we'll call a truce. Or maybe we'll discuss the recent political turmoil in the Sudan. Anything's possible," I said to my mom.

She smiled at me. "Good luck."

"Good luck with what?" Sam appeared, hair still dripping wet.

"The walk today. You two. Together," my mom said.

Sam rolled her eyes. "Whatever. It'll be fine. I'm bringing my iPod anyway."

We drove into the city, parked the car, and walked over to Grant Park, where the walk was to begin. We checked in and walked over to a patch of grass to wait for the event to begin. I sat silently next to Sam as she listened to her iPod.

I let her listen to her music for the first half hour of the walk, until I yanked one of the earphones out of her ear.

"Sam, that's enough," I said.

"What? Jeez? Rip my ear off, why don't you. What's your prob?" she said, and took the earphone out of her other ear.

"I thought we could talk. That was kind of the point of doing this together."

"Oh." She paused and watched a very fit woman speed-walk past us. "What do you want to talk about?"

"Um, I don't know. I just thought we could catch up." She didn't say anything, so I continued. "So, how are you doing with all of this?"

Her head snapped like a rubber band in my direction. "With what?"

"With Mom."

"I'm fine," she said quickly.

"No, you're not—," I started to say, and stopped myself. I switched tactics. "That's great you're doing so well. I'm having a hard time with it. I mean, she's our mom. She's always been like Supermom, so it's hard to think of her as sick. I don't know, what do you think?"

"I know," she said slowly, and nodded.

We turned the corner onto Michigan Avenue, a swarm of pink T-shirts and pink visors. I was already sweating, thanks to being 100 percent out-of-shape. At least I could get exercise *and* feel philanthropic at the same time.

"Has it been hard to be at home?"

"Yeah, kinda. It's hard to see her sick, you know?" she said.

"I can imagine. It's hard for me to come over and see her, let alone see it every day. Must make it hard to think about anything else."

"Sometimes," she said quietly. Then, she caught herself and shrugged. "It's fine. It's whatever."

"I know. Just don't feel like you can't talk about it. I know we're not the best of friends, but I'm here if you want to talk," I said.

We walked silently for five minutes, our feet pounding the pavement. As the crowd turned onto Canon Drive, Sam stopped suddenly.

I stopped next to her. "What's wrong?" I said.

She twisted her hands in front of her and gazed out onto Lake Michigan, as though contemplating something. She met my eyes briefly. "Thanks," she mumbled, and leaned forward and hugged me quickly.

"You're welcome," I said, my voice cracking a bit. "Sam, it means so—"

"Hurry up, we're totally going to be the last effing people to finish this race. I have major plans tonight," she cut me off, and started briskly walking in front of me.

It was a start. A good start.

I'll take it.

Friday, October 31

. . . .

Happy Halloween!

This has to be my third-favorite holiday. The first being Thanksgiving, for obvious gastronomic reasons, and the second Christmas, for obvious gift-receiving reasons

I mean, what other time can you shove pounds of chocolate into your mouth and claim you're just "celebrating"? Plus, calories don't count today, right?

Right?

I realized this year would be extra-special since Jake and I had an excuse to go trick-or-treating: Sara. I went to every kid store I could think of in search of a costume for her, but I didn't find anything I really liked. I lamented to Julie, who ignored my questions about Trevor but sent me a link to an online store with some of the weirdest infant costumes I've ever seen. Costumes like a whoopee cushion, a taxicab tree air freshener, and a roll of toilet paper. I'm fairly certain the owners of the company did a serious amount of weed during their creative design sessions. Anyway, I voted for the whoopee cushion, but Jake didn't seem to find it as funny as I did, so she's going trick-or-treating as a pumpkin.

I say she's going trick-or-treating, but really, it's Jake and me pushing her around in a stroller. We're going to knock on doors, say, "Trick or Treat!" and point to Sara while sticking our hands out for candy. It's like, *We made an effort to dress our kid up. Now you are socially obligated to give us candy. Fork it over, lady!* I will allow myself to have but two pieces of chocolate this year, as my goal is to decrease the size of my ass rather than tack on a few more rolls.

I posted a photo of Sara in her pumpkin costume on my blog, and wifey immediately left the first comment of: *OMG! I WANT TO EAT HER!* And I honestly took it literally. I quickly scanned through the other comments, including one from Greg wishing me a Happy Halloween, before I closed my laptop and shoved it under the bed.

I'm even going to dress Butterscotch up tonight. I found a hysterical ballerina costume for him, complete with sparkly tutu. I had no idea they make costumes for cats, apart from the weird freaks who dress their cats up in sweaters and stuff. I pulled the costume out last night for him and he rubbed his face all over the pink satin and purred as if to say, *Thank you so much for the beautiful sparkly pink costume. I'm going to look so fabulous dressed as a prima donna ballerina. Can we watch* Showgirls *again?*

Monday, November 3

. . . .

Elise came into the office today to approve the final expenses for Logan's event. She was supposed to come in around 3:00 P.M. but didn't arrive until almost 4:00 P.M. She rushed in, clutching a red alligator messenger bag and her Prada purse. I quickly closed my Internet browser, as I was salivating over our new house, closing on Friday, for the seventh hour this month.

"Sorry! Sorry! Sorry! I got caught up at Logan's school. Have I totally thrown your schedule off?" Elise panted as she sat down in my office.

I turned away from my computer and smiled at her. "Not totally."

"Traffic was a nightmare trying to get here. Do you think this city plans construction projects for when it will be least convenient for commuters?" She sat back and ran her fingers through her silky hair.

"Most likely. Don't get me started. My husband rages about this on a daily basis."

"So," she said, and flipped open her messenger bag, "lay it on me." She pulled out a pen and paper, snapped on a pair of reading glasses, and looked at me.

"OK, well, I worked up what I believe is going to be a very accurate estimate for everything. I also built in ten percent for error, as is wise to do with any event, especially ones taking place at someone's home, since you never know what might arise on the day of the event." I slid a spreadsheet across my desk to her. "The various components are itemized in the budget, so it should read somewhat easy."

She fell silent for a moment as she scanned the paper. She stopped when she came to the total amount. She looked up at me. "Remember when birthday parties were a bunch of crepe paper and balloons?"

I smiled back at her. "No kidding. A few gift bags, a homemade cake, and some pin-the-tail-on-the-donkey and I was happy."

"No shit. Well, I guess it is what it is," she said, and took her glasses off. She paused for a moment and then stood up.

"Anything else you need to me to do right now?" I said and stood up to walk her out.

"No, I don't think—" She stopped as she saw the picture of Sara on my desk. She picked the black frame up. "Is this your daughter?"

"Sara," I said. "She's ten months old. I can't believe how big she is."

"She's beautiful," Elise said, and set the frame down on my desk. "Who takes care of her during the day?"

"She goes to a wonderful day care."

"That's great. God, I remember the first time I brought Logan to day care. It was like *Sophie's Choice*. You get one foot out the door and the guilt just sucker punches you."

"No kidding. It was nearly paralyzing in the beginning, but I'm at least managing to function these days. It helps to have exciting events to work on." I smiled at her. "But I'm still hoping to leave the house one day without a smidge of guilt."

"I wish I could tell you it happens, but it doesn't. It never will." She smiled ruefully at me.

"A girl can dream, right?" I said.

She turned to leave and then stopped. "I almost forgot, Logan wanted me to give you this," she said, and held out a manila folder.

"What is it?" I asked, and took the folder from her.

"I think it's pictures of the flowers she wants for the table centerpiece," Elise said as she fished around in her enormous bag for her car keys.

I opened the envelope and pulled out pictures of pink peonies and roses. "Beautiful!" I said. "I remember she said she wanted pink."

"She wants to do pink in honor of my mom." Elise smiled wanly.

I looked up at her and smiled. "How so?"

"My mom passed away three years ago from breast cancer," she said.

"Oh, wow. I'm so sorry," I said. I bit my tongue hard as I heard Mule Face coming down the hallway, so I just said, "These are great. I'll let the florist know."

Friday, November 7

· · · · · · · · · · · · · · · · · · · ·

6:30 A.M.

Closing day.

In approximately four hours, Jake and I will be home owners. We will also own a mortgage, which requires us to pay a Scary Amount of money every month.

But it's time to move on. Time to take another step forward. Time to keep moving firmly through Responsible Adulthood.

Must not freak out. Must meditate myself into a Zen-like state.

Ommmmmm. . . .

WAAAAAAAA!

So much for meditating. Sara's up.

4:46 P.M.

Closed.

The closing was totally overwhelming. It was basically Jake and me signing documents reading, "We really, *really* promise to pay the bank." By the end, I didn't even pay attention to what our lawyer said about each paper, I just heard, "Blah, blah, blah, you owe a lot of money, blah, blah, blah, sign, blah, blah, foreclosure, blah, blah, blah, here is the key."

The entire time, one thought ran through my head: *Why the hell are they giving us this much money?* I mean, I was impressed when the bank lent me money to buy my car. This had a few more zeros on the end. It was like I thought we were getting away with something.

Until they asked us to fork over a few thousand bucks for escrow.

Really pulled the wool over their eyes, huh?

But we did it. We closed.

Sara was at Marianne and Frank's house, so Jake and I swooped over and picked her up before heading straight over to the new pad. Walking around, I realized the shiteousness of our apartment and the fabulosity of the new house.

Apartment: old and busted.

House: the new hotness.

We walked around and let Sara crawl on the rug in the living room for a while until we had to head back to the Old and Busted to finish packing.

Tonight, we are spending the last night in our apartment. While I'm very excited to move into the new place, some twinges of sadness are creeping into my brain. My nostalgia is getting the better of me. But it's hard to not feel a little sad. I mean, this was the place Jake and I returned home from our honeymoon. This is the apartment where I announced to Jake that I took a pregnancy test and, um, it wasn't negative. This is where we lived when we brought Sara home from the hospital.

This is where we lived when I cried about having to go back to work. When I actually went back to work. When I hated it. And this is where we lived when I started to accept, and finally like, being a working mom.

In short, a lot of amazing things happened in this place and while we lived here.

I've already taken a million pictures of Sara's nursery and shed just a few more million tears, thinking about how we painted and decorated it just a few short months ago. She has a new room, with a beautiful view of an old oak tree, as opposed to her current view of a parking lot. And I can't wait to bring her into the backyard and look at the birds and the leaves and watch her pudgy toes wiggle in the grass. Not to mention the joy Butterscotch will feel when he realizes there are, like, twenty new rooms for him to piss on the carpet.

But this is the place where Jake and I started our marriage, where we started our family. Our family will continue in the new place, but this one will always be the first. This is the apartment we'll talk about when we tell Sara stories about after she was first born.

So, it's hard not to feel a little wistful.

I must go post more photos of our new abode online so the drooling and manic jealousy can begin.

Sunday, November 9

· · · · · · · · · · · · · · · · · · ·

All that flowery shit about missing our old apartment and sniffling about Sara's first home?

So over it.

I've spent the past forty-eight hours up to my elbows in corrugated cardboard boxes and packing tape, and I still can't find my toothbrush.

The movers came yesterday morning at the crack of dawn. Sara and I hung back and watched Jake direct the movers. I was somewhat wary when they showed up, since two of the three of them were smaller than me, but before I could even offer them a cup of coffee, those guys had our china cabinet tucked into the moving van and were shrink-wrapping our couches.

Sara looked totally confused and started whining. She wanted me to put her down on the carpet and let her suck on the rolls of packing tape on the floor. Since I never let her do that in front of strangers, I held her tight as she fussed.

Within an hour, the entire contents of our apartment was loaded onto the moving van and Jake and I were following the van in our car, also packed to the gills.

I waved one last time to our apartment, one last time to our neighbor Champagne Wayne's apartment, site of many, many swinger parties and sexually transmitted diseases.

As the movers unpacked the van at the house, I spread a blanket out on the living room floor and tried to entertain Sara. She had zero interest in any of the toys I brought her and wanted to suck on the carpet instead. So, I walked around and jiggled her. *For three hours.* Three hours until she finally fell asleep in my arms, exhausted from all the overstimulation. It took so long to get her asleep, I was terrified to put her down, so I sat on the still-shrink-wrapped couch, feeling like I was at my grandmother's house, frozen until Jake carefully took Sara from my arms and I collapsed on the floor.

I lay there for a moment until I read the box next to me: KITCHEN.

(Of course the box was in the living room, shows how smart our movers were, huh?) I remembered this box had V.I.C.—Very Important Contents: *wine*. I ripped open the box, located the wine, a corkscrew, and some plastic cups, and self-medicated while Jake put Sara to bed.

After two glasses of wine, I offered to order a pizza and did well until asked my address. I froze. I couldn't remember our new address. And Jake was outside, so I ran outside and tracked him down so he could tell me where we live. Might be a good idea to figure it out myself sometime soon.

We unpacked only the essentials last night, like the inflatable air mattress and toothpaste. We set up shop in the master bedroom and let Sara sleep in her stroller bassinet on the floor. I just wasn't ready to put her in an empty room. I was worried it would scare her.

As Jake and I lay on the inflatable air mattress, I snuggled against his back.

"Feel like home yet?" he mumbled into his pillow.

I shook my head against his T-shirt.

"It will," he said, and sighed.

I nodded into his back and knew he was right.

Sunday, all three of us woke up the minute the sun rose, since the previous owners took all the window treatments. Our bedroom faces east, so at 6:23 A.M. we all woke up to a blinding sunlight beating down on our heads. Pre-baby, Jake and I would've grabbed pillows, covered our faces, and fallen back asleep. But post-baby, we were up for the day. Sara woke up ready to party in her new house. I let her crawl around in a few of the rooms and she shrieked and cooed at all the open, empty space. She stopped in the center of the dining room, looked me square in the eye, and made the loudest-sounding poop I'd ever heard. Complete with beet-red facial grunting. Then she was off again. I took it to be her stamp of approval.

She didn't sleep much at all today, so the only thing I really got accomplished was to unpack my makeup. Of course, I didn't have time to actually put any of it on, but it's unpacked. Butterscotch doesn't seem to like the new digs. He slunk around, stomach dragging the floor, all through the house before finally hiding under the couch and hissing at anything daring to come near. After a few hours, he moved to under the dining room table, which he has claimed as his room and thus refuses to let Jake enter. Sara and I are cool. Jake? Hell no. Every time Jake attempts to so much as enter the room, Butterscotch comes out from the table, guns blazing, claws out, teeth snarling, mouth hissing. He chases Jake out of the room each time.

I think it's pretty funny. Jake does not.

Unpacking is so overwhelming, I don't know where to start. I should probably start by organizing my clothes, but I don't have the strength to fold the frillion pairs of pants I own. Or I could unpack all the kitchenware, but I really don't feel like washing everything.

I'm tempted to just start throwing everything out so we don't have to unpack it. I mean, we don't actually need more than like two plates and three forks, right? And Lord, all those horrid wedding gifts we felt too bad to throw out, couldn't sell on eBay, and were forced to pack and thus now unpack.

Screw it. I'm going to take a bath in my tub. Yes! I have a tub now! Many of my readers told me my master bathroom resembles a "spa" and looks very "warm and cozy." Wifey1025 offered to send me some of her homemade bath salts. Which I'm sure contain just a smidge of rohypnol.

Tuesday, November 11
. . . .

We might have to move.

Seriously.

Everything's still packed. It wouldn't be too difficult.

Still riding our new real estate high yesterday, I was delighted when our new neighbor came over to introduce herself. Well, I was delighted until she started screaming at the top of her lungs that our dog woke her up this morning and left shit in her yard.

Did I mention it was 7:15 A.M.?

Yes, I opened the door this morning, still in my pajamas, Sara crawling around at my feet.

"Hi," I said, and smiled at the large, boxy woman with the pageboy haircut in front of me.

"I hate dogs." She scowled at me.

"Um, what?" I said, and rubbed my eyes, unable to process what she said.

"Dogs. I hate them," she said again.

"Uh, can I help you?" I said, totally confused. Part of me still thought I was dreaming.

"Your dog woke me up this morning. I work nights and I need my sleep. But your dog started howling and made me get out of bed. What do you have to say?" Large portly woman placed her hands on her hips.

I prayed for Jake to get out of the shower and come downstairs and help me figure out what the hell was going on. I instinctively stepped in front of Sara.

"Excuse me, I think you're mistaken. We don't have a dog," I said firmly, still smiling, hoping the crazy lady would leave and I could have a cup of coffee before work.

"Oh yes, you do. You pet owners are all the same. You never respect anyone's property," she spit at me.

"I'm sorry, like I said, we don't have a dog." I started to close the door.

She put her hand on the door and pushed it so I couldn't close it. "You gonna clean up that dog shit in my yard?" she said.

"Please leave," I said. She let go of the door and I closed it. I scooped Sara up and watched Psycho Bitch waddle back over to her house next door. *Great, she lives next door,* I thought.

Today, when Jake got home from work, he found a pile of dog crap on our front porch. Psycho Bitch fully admitted to putting it on our doorstep, to teach us a lesson about cleaning up after our pets. Jake told her to stay away from our property or else he would call the police, but Psycho Bitch told him she was going to send our dog to the pound. Yes, very good. Send our imaginary dog to the shelter. Also, please let me know when my imaginary dog asks you to shoot the President. I'd like a heads-up.

I suggested we send Butterscotch over to her house and let him hump all of her underwear, but Jake didn't think it was a good idea. Regardless, if I disappear and the police are reading this diary, Psycho Bitch strangled me and I'm buried in her backyard. Look there.

Wednesday, November 12
. . . .

"Want me to sunbathe topless in your backyard?" Julie offered.

"Um, no. That's OK," I said as I switched the phone receiver to my right ear.

"Just let me know. I have no problem using the girls as a weapon."

"I'm fully aware," I said as I examined a hangnail.

"So I went out with Trevor again last night," Julie offered.

She had my attention. "Really? How was it?"

"Fine. We went to a sports bar and split some wings and a pitcher of beer." Her tone gave absolutely no indication of how the night went.

"And?"

"And nothing. We just had some wings and a few beers and watched some football game."

"That's it? That's all you're going to tell me?" My voice started to raise an octave. She was entitled to privacy, but *please*. Give a girl some details.

"Yep," Julie said cheerfully.

"Huh," I said, stunned.

I think it was the only time Julie's ever described a date without minutiae, including her predictions of sexual tendencies and anatomy. Either this guy is a secret agent in the witness protection program and has blackmail materials on her, forcing her to remain silent about the details of his life . . . or she actually likes him.

Both are equally probable.

"Hey, listen, what about those concert tickets I mentioned last week?" I changed the subject.

Her pause told me her face was blank.

"You know, the tickets I got through work to some showcase at the House of Blues. Free drinks, free backstage passes, free VIP admission." I nodded my head, thinking she was definitely having a premature senior moment.

"Oh, right," she said slowly. "Um, I don't kno—"

"What?" I shrieked. "How could you not know? Do you have other plan—" I stopped myself as the lightbulb went off. "Oh my God! You DO like this guy! You're not committing to plans to leave your weekends free to be with your BOYFRIEND!" I shrieked again.

Julie's face turned pink. "Not even close! I just don't know what my work schedule is," she started to say. "Screw it. Yeah. You're right. Now you know what I've had to deal with between you and Reese." She shrugged.

"Wow." I exhaled loudly and sat for a moment. I leaned forward and smiled. "I think it's awesome."

And it is. But . . . Holy Crap.

Sunday, November 16

. . . .

This morning, I opened my front door to walk to my car and drive to Elise's house but immediately stopped. Psycho Bitch stood in her driveway, talking to an equally portly older couple. I froze, unsure of whether I should walk to my car and pretend I didn't see them or wait it out. After a vision of Psycho Bitch throwing canine excrement at my car, I decided to wait it out.

I crouched on my front porch, hidden behind a bush, and waited for them to finish their conversation. Those jerks stood around for fifteen minutes shooting the shit. I learned the portly older couple were her parents. And they were all on diets. They compared weight loss recipes, their exercise habits, and inches lost.

Finally, I could wait no longer, so I stood up, brushed evergreen needles off my pants, and hustled to my car, head down. Their conversation halted and I could feel three sets of eyes follow me as I jumped into my car and pulled out of the driveway.

I arrived at Elise's at the same time as the party rental company. I pulled up to her estate, the enormity startling me even though I'd been here before to do the event walk-through. A beautiful redbrick Georgian with black shutters, it whispered, rather than shouted, money, in opposition to most of the other houses on the block, with huge white pillars and fountains in the driveway.

I hopped out of my car, waved my arms around, and started directing the tables, chairs, and tent setup. Within five minutes, Elise walked out to the backyard, a cashmere sweater thrown around her shoulders.

"Good morning," she said, and rubbed her forehead.

"Morning! How's it going?" I said as I approved the chair design.

"Dreadful. I was tossing and turning all night, worrying about this party. It means so much to Logan, I just want everything to go according to plan," she said.

"Don't worry, it will. That's why I'm here. Logan will be thrilled," I said, and smiled at Elise. "She still in bed?"

"Of course. She's a teenager. She'll be up in a few hours. She's so excited," Elise said, and sipped a mug of coffee. "Can I get you some?" she asked, and raised the mug.

"Love it, thanks!"

"Be right back," she said, and turned to walk back into her palatial estate.

Within an hour, the tent was erected, the flooring installed, and the electrical wiring started. I sat back and sipped on coffee and barked orders at everyone. Everything was going according to schedule when Logan appeared at my side, curly hair frizzed back into a ponytail.

"Looks good," she said, and hiked her glasses up with one finger.

"Good morning! I thought you might like it." I gave her a pat on the shoulder. "Excited for tonight?"

"I totally can't wait!" she squealed.

"Do you have your dress laid out and everything?"

"Yep! It's designed after the one in *The Princess Diaries*. My mom's even having someone come and do my hair and makeup. I'm going to look so good!" she said, and clapped her hands together.

"You're going to look amazing." I nodded in agreement.

"I'm cold, so I'm going to go inside. See you soon!" Logan waved and turned to run back in the house, pajamas pants decorated with chili peppers billowing behind her.

"Hey there!" Keri's voice called out as she walked across the lawn.

"It's starting to come together." I nodded and pointed toward the workers smoothing out the white fabric for the dinner tent.

"This is so cool. You must be so proud. You've done such a great job," Keri said as she lifted her paper coffee cup toward me.

"Thanks, I am. Now we just need to pull it off," I said, and smiled at her.

By 4:00 P.M., the tent was set up and the last-minute prep began. The caterers scurried around like mice underfoot to prepare the appetizers and signature cocktails at the bar. The candy sculptor warmed up his candy wheel and tools to whittle the sugary red candies, and the giant ice sculptures were in place.

After Keri changed into her dress, I grabbed my bag out of my car and walked inside Elise's house to change. I walked through her amazing kitchen, complete with dual Sub-Zero fridges and miles and miles of granite countertops. I found a bathroom and was just about to close the door when I heard a scream.

A scream not of terror but of despair. A sound I recognized: the scream of a teenager.

I paused and stuck my head out the door, craned my neck, and tried to hear the conversation.

". . . awful . . . make fun of me . . . look ridiculous!" Logan.

I debated whether or not to intervene, so I slowly crept toward the bottom of the stairs to see if I was needed. A loud thud sounded and a bedroom door ripped open and Logan walked out, round face flushed red and streaming with tears, hair pulled severely on top of her head in a matronly bun.

"Clare! Tell me! Doesn't my hair look wretched?" Logan screeched. "I'm going to look so ugly for my party," she sobbed.

"You look beautiful, sweetheart! It just needs an adjustment—let Maxie try to fix it for you," Elise said from inside the bedroom.

"MOM! I told you I'm NOT letting her touch my hair! She already messed it up once!" Logan shouted into the bedroom. "Clare, you have to help me!" she said, and turned to me.

"Um, OK," I said, and slowly crept up the stairs.

Logan and I walked into her bedroom, where Elise was perched on a massive antique four-poster bed, dressed in a silk robe, hair in Velcro curlers. A terrified hairdresser cowered in the corner. Logan led me into her bathroom

"Fix it," she commanded.

"Uh, er . . ." I gingerly touched the lacquered bun on top of her hair. "I'm not sure what to do. What did you want?"

"I wanted my hair half-up with curly tendrils coming down the sides. Didn't I?" Logan said, and glowered at the hairdresser.

"I'm not sure, uh—" I pulled a bobby pin out of the bun and half of it collapsed. "Sorry," I said.

Logan's thick hair hung out of the bun like a deranged rooster tail. "I don't care, just fix it," she said.

I thought about asking Keri to frantically call around to salons, but a better idea struck me.

"Hold on," I said to Logan. I grabbed my purse and dug around for my cell phone. I snapped it open and dialed a number.

"Ya?" Sam trilled into the phone.

"Sam! I need your help! I'm in the middle of a serious hair emergency and I need some advice."

"Cut it off," she said quickly.

"What?"

"Cut your hair off. It looks scraggly."

"No, it's not for me. It's for my friend, Logan." I smiled at Logan. "The hairdresser goofed when doing her hair and she wants it half-up, half-down with curly tendrils." I looked at Logan and she nodded.

"OK, easy. Send me a phone pic."

I snapped a picture and my phone beeped thirty seconds later. I put Sam on speakerphone as she directed me where to place each tendril and curl. I wove Logan's hair together and pulled soft curls out around her cheeks. I spritzed the ends with hair gel and scrunched her curls with my fingers and then finger-combed the curls out.

Logan kept her eyes closed the whole time. When I was done, I gave her a pat on the shoulder, "Look," I said.

She opened her eyes and her face grew into a grin. "Looks awesome!" she said.

"Thanks, Sam. You rule," I said, and snapped my phone shut. "So, what do you think?" I said to Elise, who had been watching silently from the bed the entire time.

"I think she looks wonderful. Like a princess," Elise said.

"Great! Now I need to throw my dress on so I can direct the caterers!" I got one foot out the door before a hand hooked in the crook of my elbow.

"You're a lifesaver," Elise whispered in my ear.

"Anytime," I whispered back.

An hour later and the guests arrived. They oohed and ahhed as they walked into the heated tent, which was transformed into a modern-day Paris, complete with twinkling white lights hung from the ceiling. After the cocktail hour, it was time for Logan to make her entrance. She walked into the tent on the arms of two gorgeous teen models we hired for the event.

"No way! Her hair is like totally tight!" a girl behind me squealed.

I flashed Logan a thumbs-up sign and winked at her as she walked past.

The rest of the event went smoothly—cake cut on time, teenagers boogying for hours, and the food psychotically delicious, not that I tried any of it. My mouth watered as I walked past the mushroom and mashed potato bars, but I refrained by remembering the trauma caused the other day thanks to an accidental glimpse of my bare ass in the mirror.

After the last guest had left, I had sent Keri home with all of my gratitude, and Logan was out in the driveway squealing over her new car, Elise handed me glass of champagne.

"Sit," she said, and pointed to an empty cocktail table. I wordlessly followed her command.

"Nice job," she said, and raised her glass. We clicked our champagne flutes together and I took a tiny sip.

"I'm just glad Logan had a great time," I said as I played with a stray rose petal on the table.

"She did." Elise looked at the flower petal in my hand. "The flowers were beautiful."

"They were, weren't they?" I said. I took another sip of champagne, trying to will up some liquid courage. There was something I wanted to ask Elise, something I wanted to run by her, but I'd been too chicken.

"They were a lovely tribute to your mom," I said carefully.

"Thanks." Elise smiled at me.

"I know what it's like," I said, and looked down at the flower. "My mom has breast cancer."

"Oh! I'm so sorry, Clare," Elise said, and leaned forward and patted me on the arm. Her flowing curls still bounced around her shoulders after three hours of dancing.

"Thanks. I've had this idea and . . . kind of . . . wanted your opinion," I said.

"What is it?"

"I want to throw a fundraiser, something not too big, fairly intimate, in my mom's name to raise money for breast cancer research. I'm not really sure what I'd want it to be, or where, or who would come, but I . . ." I trailed off and looked up at her.

She slowly took a long sip of champagne and set her glass down on the table. "You organize it, I'll chair it," she said, and smiled.

"Really? I mean, I don't know really anything yet, but I just know I want to do it."

"Really. I think . . ." She paused. "I think it would be good for me to start getting out there more. You know . . ." She stopped. "You know what I mean," she finished.

I nodded. "Deal?" I said, and stuck out my hand.

"Deal," she said, and shook it.

We clinked glasses once more and drained the rest of our champagne. As I sipped the fizzy liquid, a thought ran through my head:

This is why I do it. This is why I love my job. This is why I stay on the emotional roller coaster.

Because I suspect it's completely and utterly Worth It.

Tuesday, November 18

. . . .

"Splish Splash, Sara's takin' a bath, on about a Tuesday niiiight!" I sang off-key as I rinsed the soap off Sara's arms. "Rub-a-dub, she's chillin' in her tub . . . something, something, something, something!"

Sara grinned at me and kicked her legs out, splashing water all down the front of my T-shirt.

"What are you doin'? Huh? You trying to soak Mommy?" I said to her.

"AHHAH!" she shrieked.

"Jake, your daughter is a little water baby!" I called to him in the next room.

"Sara, are you playin' in the tub?" he said in a high-pitched voice.

She looked very serious as she stared at him, then looked at me, then back to him. Her face broke out into one of her awesome smiles—the kind where her nose crinkles up and her entire gum line shows.

"Isn't she such a supermodel?" I asked Jake. "She's prolly the cutest baby ever," I said as I stood up, plucked her out of the tub, and wrapped a hooded towel shaped like a dragon around her.

"Prolly," he said, and bent down and nuzzled his face against her fluffy towel.

After I put Sara to bed, I sat down in front of the television with my laptop to write my next column for *The Daily Tribune*.

This column, I wrote about the not-so-warm-and-fuzzy moments. Here's my favorite part:

> *"People always ask me if I can remember what life was like before I had my daughter. They always seem shocked when I quickly respond that yes, I can. Not only do I remember what it was like, but I often miss it. I longingly remember sleeping in, disposable income, free time, movie theaters and books. I sometimes miss being just a person, rather than a mom. Once earned, the title of mother is one that permeates throughout your entire existence."*

What I didn't say was that I miss being sure of my choices, of knowing I'm on the right path. When I was in college and didn't want children, I was so certain it was the right decision. Now, ever since Sara was born, from the second she came out, the straight lines of my life have become watery and wavy. And figuring out my life feels like grasping sand—each time I feel as though I have it in my hold, it slips through my fingers and I'm back to the beginning.

Wednesday, November 19
· · · · · · · · · · · · · · · · · · · ·

Today, I started pulling together some ideas for my event with Elise. I think we should do a simple holiday luncheon, possibly with a fashion show. The models could be breast cancer survivors, and we could hold the event at a country club. The event will raise money for breast cancer research at a local hospital. I think we should be able to get most of the components, like the invitations and the favors, donated from local stores, thanks to some of my connections.

I haven't told my mom about it yet. I think I'm going to wait until Thanksgiving to tell her.

Thursday, November 7
· · · · · · · · · · · · · · · · · · · ·

"Is it wrong that I'm thankful your parents won't be here for Thanksgiving?" I said to Jake this morning as I poured him a cup of coffee.

"Not at all. Thanksgiving is the time of gift giving, and they've given us a conflict-free holiday," he said as he took the cup from my hand.

"I think that's Christmas, but all the same," I said as I raised my mug to him and then lowered it to my mouth and took a sip. "What time is their flight?"

"In a couple hours. What time is it?" he said, and craned his neck to look at the clock. "Shit! I have to leave." He leaned forward to kiss me.

"Tell them I hope they have a great trip," I said.

As Jake walked out to the garage, the monitor crackled and I heard

Sara start to stir in her bedroom. I walked upstairs, tiptoed in, and peered over the side of her crib.

"Happy Thanksgiving!" I said brightly.

She looked up at me, recognized my face, and grinned brightly.

". . . something in my car?" I heard Jake's voice yell from downstairs.

I picked Sara up and walked to the top of the stairs.

"What?" I called.

"Did you spill something in my car?" he said.

I froze. I didn't think he'd notice. I broke his "no cups without lids" rule the other day and brought a cup of diet pop in his car. Well, I hit a freaking pothole and the pop went everywhere. I thought I cleaned it up.

"Nope," I called back.

After Jake left for the second time, I turned on the parade for Sara and me and started pulling out all the ingredients to make the stuffing. In a momentary lapse of judgment, I heard myself offer to host Thanksgiving this year. I thought it would mean just buying some cute fall leaf centerpieces and decorating with some apples and stuff. I kinda forgot that also meant I'd have to cook turkey and stuffing and all that other crap. Must've been why my mom agreed so quickly.

I don't really mind, though. I know my mom's too exhausted these days to spend all day cooking, and besides, how hard can it be to cook a turkey? If I get into trouble, there's a 1-800 help number practically tattooed on the turkey itself. I'm sure they get some great questions like, *Um, hi. I was wondering if it would be possible to cook my turkey in my fireplace using only crumpled newspaper and some matches?*

Ha!

I'm going to be like the Emeril of Thanksgiving. Jake does not believe this, seeing as how last year I tried to cook dinner for my family and we wound up ordering pizza. But that was in our old apartment and I'm confident that in my new, fabulous house I will be a cooking genius.

2:00 P.M.

Does Emeril's house smell like B.O.?

The entire house smells since I cooked the celery and onions for the stuffing without turning on the fan or opening a window. Not a smart move. Jake walked in from dropping his parents off at the airport and asked why the place smelled like feet. He wasn't in a very good mood since the airport was a total zoo and he practically had to ask his parents to do a tuck and roll out of the car since the airport cops wouldn't let anyone stop for more than two seconds.

He plucked Sara out of her ExerSaucer and flopped down on the couch and said, "Ah, yes. This is what Thanksgiving is about. Watching football and taking a nap."

I walked out of the kitchen and stood in front of him. "You wish. You have to go out and buy beer and wine for tonight."

He didn't look up at me. "I thought your parents were bringing the alcohol."

"They are. But I thought we could get some extra, in case we run out."

"Seriously?" He looked up at me, trying to look as pathetic as possible.

"Won't work this time. Take Sara with you. I have to finish the sweet potato casserole and put it in the oven."

He made some fake whining noises but scooped Sara up, bundled her in a jacket and hat, and left, grumbling about how holidays are supposed to be relaxing. (I have no idea where he got that idea. He must not live in My Universe.)

I finished the sweet potato casserole and put it in the top tier of my oven (I have two ovens! How cool is that?) and pulled out everything for the mashed potatoes. I started peeling the potatoes when I realized it was time to baste the turkey again. So, I opened up the bottom oven, grabbed the baster, peeled back the cheesecloth on the turkey, and squirted some juice all over it. Then, in an act of pure genius, I grabbed the turkey pan with my bare hand.

So, by the time Jake got home, I was whimpering, my right hand in the freezer, moaning about finishing the mashed potatoes. He's the best husband in the world, because he made me an ice pack, and offered to finish the potatoes. I sat on the floor with Sara and watched a video with her while he peeled the potatoes. He whittled most of them down to the size of golf balls, but that's OK. He tried.

The mashed potatoes are on the stove, so Jake and I have a few minutes before we have to start getting ready for people to arrive. I'm going to run and write an entry on my blog. I think I'm going to write about my confusion over the lack of quality movies revolving around the Thanksgiving holiday. There are a few standouts, but I can count them on one hand. There's tons of great Christmas movies, why no love for Thanksgiving?

9:00 P.M.

The tryptophan is seeping into my brain, but I'm going to try to recap Thanksgiving.

My parents and Sam arrived on time, clutching a case of beer and two bottles of wine.

"Happy Thanksgiving!" I said as I opened the door.

"The place smells amazing!" my mom said as she walked in the door. "Clare"—she leaned forward to hug me—"thank you so much for doing this."

"Piece of cake," I said, and hid my burned hand behind my back.

"Happy Thanksgiving," my dad said. "Where's the squirt?"

"She's napping. I wanted her to go down before dinner or else she'd be a beast," I said, and took my parents' coats. I turned to Sam, who still hadn't said anything. "Sam?"

She stared off into space.

"Sam?" I said again.

"Oh, sorry. What?" she said. Her eyes looked glazed over and her hair was haphazardly thrown into a ponytail.

"Are you OK?" I asked her, and put my hand on her arm.

"I'm fine. Stop acting like a freak," she said, and walked over to the couch and threw herself down on it.

"She doesn't feel well today," my mom whispered in my ear.

Right. Got it. The night before Thanksgiving is usually one of the biggest nights of the year to go out, thanks to all the college students being home from school. She's totally hungover, I thought. *Again.*

"Hey, guys! Happy Thanksgiving!" Jake said as he walked into the living room. My parents stood up to hug him as Sam grunted from the couch.

I walked into the kitchen, poured a glass of pop with lots of ice, walked over to Sam, and wordlessly handed it to her. She looked surprised but accepted my offering like a dying man in the desert.

The doorbell rang and I walked to the front door and opened the door.

"Hey!" I said to Mark and Casey. "How's it going, guys?" I said, and gestured for them to come inside. "Casey, you look beautiful!" I said to her.

"Thanks, Clare, your house is amazing. God, I hope I can afford a house like this someday." She beamed at me.

"Mark, if you guys break up, we're keeping her. You can find a new family," I said to him.

"That doesn't surprise me," he said.

"You guys hungover, too?" I said to them as we walked into the living room.

"Dying," Casey whispered to me.

I pointed to Sam's soft drink and nodded at her. "You're not the only one."

"What can I do?" my mom said.

"Help me baste the turkey again," I said, and we walked into the kitchen.

My mom opened the oven door and checked the turkey.

"Hey, Mom, there's something I want to tell you," I said.

She stopped, turkey baster in hand. "Are you pregnant again?"

"WHAT? NO! Are you kidding me?" I said to her.

"Just checking." She smiled at me.

"I wanted to tell you that I'm planning this fundraiser thing. With Elise. For breast cancer. It's a holiday luncheon and fashion show. We're still figuring everything out, but I wanted to tell you since you're kind of the reason I'm doing it."

She closed the oven door and walked over to me. She set the turkey baster down on the kitchen island, put her hands on my shoulders, and drew me tightly to her.

"I love you," she whispered to me.

"I love you, too," I whispered back. After a few seconds I said, "OK, Mom, um, I have to warm up the sweet potatoes."

She released me and put her hands on my cheeks. I could see how sunken in her cheeks were and the wiry hairs sticking out from her thinning hairline. "I'm so proud of you," she said, and kissed me on the forehead.

"Thanks," I said quickly. Not wanting to blubber all over the corn pudding, I quickly switched gears. "So, Casey and Mark, huh?"

"I know. I think this is the longest he's ever dated someone. It's the only one he's ever brought to a holiday, anyway. I think this one might be the One," she said.

"I know! Scary, right? And she still appears to be somewhat normal," I said, and shook my head.

As I folded the sweet potatoes over in the dish, my mom said, "So, still wondering if you can have it all as a working mom?"

I smiled, not looking up from the orange glob of sweet potatoes in front of me. "Mom, I don't think anyone can have it all." I turned back to her and raised my eyebrows. "You taught us that we could, but I don't think it's possible. At least until our definition of 'all' changes to accommodate reality."

My mom sighed and walked over. She put her arm around my shoulders. "I just want you to be happy. Whatever your 'all' includes. My choices don't have to be yours."

I set the dish down on a trivet. "I know. I'm just starting to figure that out."

The turkey basted and the sweet potatoes ready, I went upstairs and woke up Sara and brought her downstairs. Casey fawned all over her and insisted on holding her, but Sara wanted to crawl and romp around the room. My mom and I set the dinner table while Casey and Jake watched Sara. Mark and my dad brought the food from the kitchen to the dining room. And Sam lay on the couch and nursed her hangover.

We all sat down at the table, Sara in her high chair next to me, happily squishing mashed potatoes with her fingers.

"So, you guys still happy with Sara's day care?" my dad asked.

Jake and I nodded. "They're great," I said. It's true. No matter what decision I make, Sara's day-care had been one of my best choices.

"That reminds me!" Mark clapped his hands and rubbed them together. "Hey, Mom, what was the name of the babysitter we had who smoked in her car all the time?" he called down the table. "I was telling Casey the story and couldn't remember her name."

"Sylvana! It was Sylvana!" I gleefully exclaimed. "Are we telling old babysitter stories?" I clapped my hands.

"No, no. Please don't," my mom said, and put her head down on the table.

"Yes! Yes! How about the woman who drove on the sidewalk one time and almost killed our neighbor's dog?" I chimed in.

"Or the one who used to take naps in Mom and Dad's bed?" Mark called out.

"Guys, stop. You know this drives me nuts. Not in front of Casey," my mom moaned.

"Don't worry, Mrs. Finnegan. I had a babysitter once who locked me in my room while she had a keg party in my parents' backyard." Casey laughed.

"All right, guys, enough," my dad said, his eyes twinkling.

"Or how about that lady who thought you were epileptic because you threw such a horrible tantrum she thought you were having a seizure?" I said to Mark.

"Do I have to play the cancer card again?" my mom said. "Drop it. Sam, pass the stuffing."

We all fell silent.

"Sam?" she said.

Sam was still staring into space.

"SAM!" Jake said.

"What? Jeez, I'm not deaf, OK?" she said as she slid the stuffing over to my mom.

"I don't even want to know what you did last night, Sam, to produce a hangover this epic," Jake said, and poked her in the ribs.

"Sam, are you hungover?" my mom said to her.

"Nice job. Make it more fawkward, why don't you?" Sam spit out to Jake, who laughed in response.

"What the hell—," my dad said and peeked under the table.

"What?" Jake said.

"Clare, your cat is smashing his face against Sam's purse," he said.

"Oh, is it pink?" I said, and took a sip of wine.

"EW! YES!" Sam shrieked. She reached under the table and ripped her pink Juicy Couture purse away from Butterscotch, who looked stunned. "Your cat is disgusting. Why does he have to lick my purse?"

"Because it's pink," I said. "And it has rhinestones. He's like the Liberace of cats."

"Liber-who?" Sam said.

"You guys have a lot in common—you both like pink purses, *Sex and the City* reruns, and sparkly jewelry." I pointed to Butterscotch's suede collar, with "Princess" spelled out in sparkly beads. I happily shoveled mashed potatoes into my mouth, proud that I'd practically starved myself all week just so I could partake in the gastronomic celebration of the holiday.

"Effing dorks," she muttered.

After dinner, my mom tried to help clean up. I could see she was exhausted, so I insisted she go home and get in bed. Besides, Sam was snoring away on the couch, having fallen asleep watching a recorded episode of *The Hills*. Casey helped me clean up a little while Jake put Sara to bed after my parents and Sam left.

"So, things seem to be going well with you guys, huh?" I said to her when we were alone in the kitchen.

"They really are. He's so great," she said to me as she scraped a serving dish into the garbage disposal.

I smiled at her. "Well, we're happy to have you. Mark actually acts like a somewhat normal person around you. It's nice. We didn't think he had it in him."

She laughed. "Not when he's around his friends."

"That," I said to her as I waved around a dirty spoon for emphasis, "will never change."

"What will never change?" Mark said as he walked into the kitchen.

"You. Being a freak."

"And to think, I was actually thankful for my family this Thanksgiving," he said.

"Oh, whatever, go back to the city and drink beer or whatever it is you kids do these days," I teased.

After I pried dirty plates out of Casey's hands and sent her and Mark on their way, Jake and I snuggled up on the couch under a wool blanket, lit some candles, heated up some pumpkin pie, and watched the news. Jake started snoring almost immediately, so I poked him and we went upstairs to bed.

My feet are killing me, my stomach feels like it's going to explode and has bloated to the size of Argentina. The turkey hangover is starting to fog my brain, but I did it.

I pulled it off. I am the Queen of Thanksgiving.

Monday, December 1
. . . .

Time for the turkey haze to dissipate.

I need to work on my review for *Hip Parent* magazine. My first product is the Diaper King. The Diaper King is one of those trash can doodads that holds dirty diapers in a closed environment, apparently reducing the smell.

I own one—I've just never used it. Because a regular garbage can works awesome, too. And it doesn't take instructions to figure out.

The Diaper King, along with several "Tummy Time" play mats, sits in Sara's room, unused. The funny part is these were our "must have" items when we registered. I actually researched the different brands of diaper disposal systems, trawled message boards for advice, and scoped out the products in-store before committing to the Diaper King and putting it on my registry.

And when we received it at our shower, I unwrapped it and set it down in Sara's room next to her changing table. Where it still sits. Never having been opened.

I fully intended to use it, until a huge ten-page booklet of instructions plummeted out of the box. They weren't the easiest things to understand; they read like stereo instructions, so I threw the book in a drawer, figuring I'd learn how to use it later.

Well, then Sara was born and exhaustion prevented me from reading any words longer than five letters. And when we moved, Jake and I pitched most of the stuff from our drawers, so . . . yeah. Then one day, I sat down and read the instructions on the can and discovered you need to place a garbage bag in it and that seemed really hard. . . .

I'm going to call Reese and ask her what to do. She always knows this stuff.

8:35 P.M.

Reese: Wait. You've never used it? So you've never emptied it? Clare, I put one of Brendan's diapers in there like two months ago.

Me: Aha! *That's* where the smell has been coming from.

12:35 A.M.

Finally managed to throw together a review. After calling around to everyone I know who has kids and finding not a single person who used theirs and/or figured out how it works, can't say I can recommend it.

My first review is done.

Golf claps for Clare.

Wednesday, December 3

· · · · · · · · · · · · · · · · · · · ·

My review high lasted two days.

Today was officially The Day When I Almost Had a Nervous Breakdown. And to be honest, I kind of wish I did have a nervous breakdown, because I would be in some nice mental institution right now instead of sitting behind my desk, listening to Mule Face eat Parmesan-crusted kettle chips at ten in the morning.

Sara didn't sleep well at all last night. She probably sensed that it would be a great time to wake up every hour, since Jake is out of town until tonight at a tech conference. She woke up at 12:00 A.M., 1:30 A.M., 2:45 A.M., 3:15 A.M., and 4:46 A.M., at which point I just brought her into bed with me and prayed she'd lie down on Jake's side of the bed and sleep.

Right.

She crawled all over my bed, under the covers, and pulled my hair a few times until I gave up, got up, and made some coffee around 5:15 A.M. As I gave her a bottle, I vaguely recalled the days when 5:15 A.M. was more of a bedtime than anything. I think it was like twenty years ago or something. I've almost completely forgotten what it was like to stay up past midnight, so it must've been decades ago.

Sara passed out for an hour after she ate, allowing me the fleeting luxury to take a shower, blow-dry my hair, and put on makeup. It was like I was on vacation. Except right after I put the last coat of mascara on and bent down to wash my hands, I felt my back wrench. Not just wrench but spasm. It convulsed so hard, I collapsed on my bathroom floor, sweating. I knew exactly what I'd done—right after I had Sara, I stood up too quickly while holding her and I pulled my back. Dr. Clarke said it was due to all the pregnancy hormones, which make joints loose, still hanging around in my body. I said it was due to God hating me.

Thankfully, I saved some of the fabulous drugs from after Sara's delivery, so I managed to crawl over to my vanity drawer and pop a couple of narcotic painkillers. I laid on my bathroom floor and waited for them to kick in as I heard Sara babbling in her crib, giving the State of the Cradle address to her teddy bear. After fifteen minutes, my pain was more bearable, so I gingerly picked up my purse and hobbled into Sara's room to get her ready for day-care.

Getting her out of the crib provided somewhat of a challenge, since I couldn't fully lift her. So, I kind of slid her up the side of the crib, pressed her against the outside of it, and slid her down. It would've been much easier had she not been kicking, screaming, and flailing the entire time like a skydiver whose parachute never opened. After that, I tried to entice her to crawl her way to the front door by waving toys in front of her (yes, I realize I was treating her like a dog), but she sat on the floor in front of her crib and stared at me, openmouthed. So, I was forced to half-carry, half-drag her across the carpet to the front door. Cue the flailing and screaming again.

After about a half hour of sweating, cursing, and negotiating, I got her outside and into her car seat. I buckled her in, shut the door, and wobbled over to the driver's side. I pulled the handle. It released, but the door didn't open. Fear shot through me as I tried it again. My hands started shaking and I peered into the car. Where I saw my keys. In the ignition. Which would explain why the car was running. I also saw my purse, cell phone, and house keys. Not to mention my daughter. Brilliant move!

Panicking, I froze. My options were: walk over to Psycho Bitch's house to use the phone and call a locksmith or walk over to my other neighbor's house, the one whom I've never met and could be a serial killer. Since I'm pretty sure that Psycho Bitch stole my *US Weekly* last week, I figured I'd roll the dice and lumbered over to Serial Killer's house.

I rang the doorbell, still half hunched over, near tears.

A young woman in her thirties with a baby on her hip answered the door.

"Yes?" She smiled at me.

"OhmyGodIlockedmykeysinmycarandmybabyisinitandmypurseand-cellphoneandmyhusbandisgoneandI'mClareandIlivenextdoor," I blurted out.

"What?" she said.

I burst into tears and tried to tell her what happened. It didn't help I started manically laughing in the middle of the story. Finally, I got the story out, and the very nice woman with the baby, whose name is Gina, let me use her phone to call a locksmith. I stood outside in the subzero temperatures next to the car so I could make sure Sara was OK. I also formed a plan of what I could use to break the car window should Sara start choking or something.

Fifteen minutes later, the locksmith showed up and unlocked the car. I flung open the door, at least tried to fling open the door in my near-crippled state, and scooped up a sleeping Sara. She opened her eyes, looked at me like, *What?* and then laid her head back down on my shoulder and fell asleep again.

I dropped her off at day-care an hour late and lumbered into work, crouched over like a cripple. Just as I was about to click on the PDF of the breast cancer fundraiser the graphic designer sent, Mule Face walked by and called me Quasimodo. I debated calling the local police department with an anonymous tip that a very large woman wearing a velour pant-suit in my office might possibly be aiding terrorists.

I'm wondering if this is Karma's way of saying, *Checkmate, Clare!*

Thursday, December 4

Although my back is healing, this week is not getting any better.

I just got off the phone with Reese. She's filing for divorce after Christmas. Apparently, Matt didn't show up at her parents' house for Thanksgiving. He told her he was working, but she suspects he already has a new girlfriend. She's going to wait until after the holiday to file, since she says she just wants to enjoy Christmas, without worrying about lawyers and legal proceedings

I told her to go for the throat and try to get everything, but she said, "Not my style, Clare." I know she's not like that, but in this case I think it's totally OK to go all crazy ex on him and demand he pay her legal fees and not be allowed to drive with the kids in the car. Or maybe I've just been reading too much about celebrity divorces.

Either way it's sliced, Reese and Matt's marriage is over. Which I'm thrilled about. Which we're *all* thrilled about. Julie offered to throw her a "divorce shower" complete with male strippers, but I think looking at gross, greasy naked men and their penises is the last thing she needs right now. It's just their marriage represented an idealism we all held, right out of college. We knew, just *knew*, we'd all have amazing marriages, wildly successful careers, huge mansions, and beach houses in Maui by the time we were thirty. Reese and Matt are the first casualty, the first reminder that nothing has gone the way anyone planned. My life certainly hasn't.

But I really can't complain about any of the curveballs I've handled. Although I would still like to put in a request to sleep past 7:00 A.M.

The hardest part is all of this is happening to the kindest person I know. Probably the sweetest person I've ever met. Anytime I've needed her, Reese has been there, encouraging me with supportive words or even just helping me to see the gentle humor in a tragedy. If anyone deserves to have the white picket fence fantasy, it's her. I know people say life isn't fair, but this is really unfair.

I know she'll be great. I know the kids will be fantastic. I know she'll be enough of a mother to them, they won't depend on their father. I know all that. But the hole in my heart still aches for her and the kids.

And a small part of me wonders when the hell I went down the rabbit hole. I mean, Reese is getting a divorce and Julie's dating someone who, from all available information, appears to be normal. There must be a portal to this alternate universe in Sara's diaper bag or something.

Friday, December 5

. . . .

1:20 P.M.

Can this week get any worse?

I'm sitting here in my office, trying to go over the floral design concepts of pink peonies and white roses for the breast cancer fundraiser, but I cannot concentrate because Mule Face decided everyone in the office needs to get into the Christmas spirit and is blasting holiday music. We're going on hour number five. Christina's on vacation, so she isn't here to yell at Mule Face and make her turn it off.

She's turned on a radio station that has already started playing Christmas music round the clock. Normally, I enjoy me some Bing Crosby and Tony Bennett singing carols, but after about an hour and a half the station ran out of song titles. It started recycling the old ones, playing them on a loop, so I've gotten the extreme pleasure of hearing each song three or four times.

I've also been trying to brainstorm Jake's gift for Christmas, but my computer keeps eating my Internet Explorer. Every time I try to open the Internet, to research my Super Seekrit Christmas Gift, my hard drive decides it hates technology and shuts down.

Not to mention Mule Face has busted out her horrid Christmas sweater collection, complete with knit images of Rudolph, decorated with sequins and velvet buttons. She has also been pushing gingerbread cookies on everyone and reminding us her makeup line is a great stocking stuffer.

I think I'm—wait.

My ears are officially bleeding. It's Paul McCartney's "Wonderful Christmastime." *Again.*

I'm so going over there and smashing her radio against the wall.

1:38 P.M.

Stephan in Accounting beat me to it. He told her, "If you don't turn off that godforsaken music, I'm going to strangle myself with a strand of twinkle lights."

She laughed and tried to flirt with him, until he made fun of her cat poster. And if there's a deal breaker for Mule Face, it's someone who doesn't adore photos of Mr. Kitten Star, her cat.

4:30 P.M.

Mule Face has driven the entire office to drink. We're all going out across the street to O'Callaghan's for a drink. Or fifty.

11:30 P.M.
Bad.

Saturday, December 6
. . . .

I'm lying in bed right now, seriously praying for my own death.

A bunch of coworkers and I left the office just before five, showing fake disappointment to Mule Face since she couldn't come. We walked across the street to O'Callaghan's, a tiny Irish bar with a "cash only" policy. Commandeering the corner table, I signaled to the waitress and had her bring pitchers of whatever beer was on special.

I sat down next to Keri, who was texting on her phone.

"Big plans tonight?" I said to her.

She shut her phone and dropped it into her purse. "Not really. I think I'm doing a holiday pub crawl with some friends if you want to come."

I smiled. "I wish I could."

"Oh, right. We'll have to go out another time, then." She twirled her gold bangle bracelet around on her wrist.

"Sound—" I was interrupted by the jukebox suddenly blaring "Jingle Bell Rock." Our table threw our hands in the air.

"Jesus!" Stephan from Accounting yelled. "It never stops!"

Thankfully, the waitress appeared with three pitchers of beer.

"How much?" I yelled to her across the table as I reached for my wallet.

She shook her head. "It's been taken care of."

"What?" I leaned in.

She turned and pointed to a guy sitting at the bar.

"Hey!" I pasted a smile on my face and waved.

I poured myself a beer and walked over to Greg.

"What are you doing here?" I shouted over "Rudolph the Red-Nosed Reindeer."

He was wearing a suit, but his tie was askew and his jacket was off. "Had a client meeting out this way. Just stopped in to have a beer before I head home."

"Thanks for the beers, you really didn't have to do that," I said, and shifted in my boots. I glanced down at my black pants and noticed a faint guacamole stain still visible from where my burrito had exploded everywhere during lunch.

"No problem. It's good to see you again," Greg said. He pointed to the empty stool next to him. "Wanna sit down and have a drink?"

I stood, my head darting back and forth between my empty seat at my work table, my coworkers all laughing and high-fiving, and the seat next to Greg.

"I should really get back—," I started to say when he waved his hand.

"Stay. One beer. I'm about to leave anyway."

"Um, OK." I awkwardly perched on the stool next to him, but not before I saw Keri's look of surprise.

"Everything going well with you?" Greg said as he took a long swig of his beer.

"Yep." I nodded my head and fidgeted with my drink. "Jake and I just moved into a new place and Sara's doing awesome."

"Congrats. That sounds great." Greg looked up and stared at the television above the bar.

"Thanks." We sat silently and I wished I could morph myself back to my table, back to the safety of a conversation about leggings or something with Keri. To endure the silence, I brought my glass up to my lips and drained it. The liquid courage relaxed me a little.

"No, I'm—," I started to say, but the bartender placed another beer in front of me.

Oh, well. I'm almost at my goal weight anyway. Besides, 'tis the season to grow a beer belly, right?

"Hey, you know what I was thinking about the other day?" Greg said as I eyed the full beer in front of me.

"What?" I said as I gave another fleeting glance at my coworkers.

"That time in college when a bunch of us rented those cabins up in Lake Winnebago."

"You mean the time when you and a bunch of your friends almost got arrested for trying to buy beer with fake IDs you bought off the Internet?" I laughed and took a sip of the beer.

"Yeah, well"—he looked at me—"it almost worked." He leaned in closer and laughed. "Anything for beer when you're a college student, right?" He held up his beer bottle.

I raised mine and we clinked in agreement.

The crowd started to change from after-work coworker groups to hard-core Friday night drinkers as Greg and I swapped college stories. Stories I hadn't thought about for years. Stories I hadn't allowed myself to remember.

"And then, remember Ethan said—" Greg was talking animatedly, hands outstretched, cheeks flushed.

"Clare, um, we're all leaving," Keri said as Greg's arm nearly brushed against her.

"Oh! Right!" Embarrassed that I'd stayed this long, I started to stand up when I felt Greg's hand on my arm.

"At least finish your beer," he said.

I looked at my half-finished beer and back at Keri. "I'm leaving in a minute, too."

"OK," she said, and shot me a questioning look. I smiled to let her know it was fine. I waved to my coworkers and turned back to my beer.

Neither of us spoke for a long time as I fiddled with my beer glass.

"Clare?" Greg said, and cleared his throat.

"Hmm?" I grunted, not looking at him.

"I've gotta say, I'm still amazed that you . . . suburbs . . . baby . . ." He trailed off and gestured around with his hand.

I smiled and crossed my legs on the bar stool. I nodded. "I know. Best-laid plans, right?"

Greg nudged me on the arm a little and fiddled with his watch. "Definitely. That's great. I guess people change." He laughed and drained his beer.

I opened my mouth and then quickly closed it. I reached forward and took another sip of my beer. I set the empty beer glass down and looked at him. "They do."

Sitting at the bar, in that shred of a seemingly insignificant conversation, I saw.

I saw my life. My old life—the Before Jake and Before Sara Clare. The plans that I made; the goals that I so firmly believed in. I saw myself with a high-powered career, living in the city, being irritated by all of the children out in public. All of my choices easy, black and white. I knew I could've been happy in that life; that life would've been enough.

But only because I wouldn't have known this one was possible.

That it was possible to laugh every day of my life, to make someone else laugh every day, to be unafraid to act goofy or insane, to love more deeply than I knew I was capable of, and to receive without asking. To have Jake and Sara and our messy, sometimes confusing, beautiful life together.

Life with the color brightness dial turned way up.

I shrugged. "I guess my goals have kind of been moving targets. Things aren't always black or white anymore; sometimes they're just gray." I stood up and pushed my empty glass forward. "I've gotta get home. It was great to see you."

I left the bar, left my old boyfriend and the goals he used to represent inside. All of my old dreams and choices were worthy, admirable. But like the pair of stone-washed jeans from college hidden in the back of my closet, they don't make sense in the present. It's OK to keep them and look at them occasionally, but they don't work anymore; I've got a new, much more comfortable pair.

Sunday, December 7

. . . .

I'm living in a Hallmark movie!

Like, a really, really awesome one! Because today I put on my . . . drum-roll please!

Skinny jeans!

Well, OK, so they're just my pre-pregnancy jeans and not my true skinny jeans, which are like a size 2 from ten years ago. But it's something! I thought for sure they would combust due to the beer I drank the other night, but no! God himself has rewarded my introspection with lost inches and the Miss Piggy pants have officially been banished. Not to mention, I paid my dues eating those boring salads when everyone else was ordering from Chipotle or buttery paninis from the deli downstairs. I was starting to wonder if being skinny is worth being depressed all the time.

My answer: it is!

It's like my wardrobe has suddenly quadrupled in size since I can fit into all of my old clothes. I can also officially burn my maternity pants and control-top panty hose! Not to mention, I'm going to go to Nordstrom and buy that beautiful pale pink silk wrap dress for the breast cancer fundraiser.

I still haven't started the whole working-out thing, but I probably should since even though I've lost weight, my thighs still bounce around like Jell-O whenever I move. And I still have a little bit of a muffin top and spare tire, but the rest of me is skinny, so who cares? The spare tire is still decorated with the faintest silvery stretch marks, forever reminders of how huge my stomach was. But the only time people will see my bare stomach is at the beach, and that happens like once a year.

Besides, most of the people I usually see on the beach shouldn't even be allowed to wear shorts, let alone a bathing suit. I'll just find the fattest person on the sand and park my towel next to theirs. Problem solved.

Monday, December 8

Today, I picked Sara up and looked at her. I mean, really looked at her. I hoisted her up out of her crib and put her down on the floor of her nursery and studied her.

She's changed so much.

What happened to my baby? When she was born, she was so chubby, with soft blond hair ringing the top of her head. Sometimes I forget what she looked like when she was born. Every day it's like *Hasn't she always looked like this?* And then I look at pictures and am taken aback.

As I watched her crawl around on her bedroom floor, I tried to sear into my brain every detail about her—everything from the way her toes look when she crawls, the way her right eyebrow moves when she smiles, and the hilarious way she sticks out her lower lip when she's tired, whiny, or hungry. I wondered if, in twenty years, when she's all grown up, her blond hair streaked with highlights and thrown up into a ponytail, I'll try to remember her that way. Or if I'll always want her to be this—this little person crawling around on my floor. I can't imagine wanting her to be anything other than the chubby baby at my feet.

Sometimes, I look at her and see the woman she's going to become—the proud, headstrong, confident woman I hope she'll be. I look at her and hold her close and pray that my love will be enough, that we'll always be best friends and she'll never tell me she wants to run away and move to her friend Sally's house. But I know she will. And I'm trying to be OK with it.

I'm OK with it because I know someday I'll have to let her go, to hope I've taught her the best and to let her make her own mistakes and fall and pick herself back up again. But now, as I react to her every physical move, as I lurch forward every time she pulls herself up and wobbles a bit, I can't imagine letting her fall.

I watch Jake as he holds her, talks to her, and contorts his body in every possible shape just to make her giggle. I watch as he gazes at her with such pride and love. I watch as he scoops her up in his arms the minute I walk in the door with her. I don't have to watch when I turn my back to leave in the morning with her, I know a piece of his heart is in my arms.

Sometimes I look at the three of us, when we're all snuggled in bed together on a Saturday morning, Jake sipping coffee and making faces at Sara while I hold her in my lap, and I can't believe our little family. I can't believe I ever doubted it would be "enough." I'm astounded sometimes when I realize I don't need anything else, anyone else or any other time. I just want the two of them, next to me, laughing.

Sometimes I think about how scared Jake and I were when we first found out about Sara and how quickly we fell in love with her once she was here, once we realized she was meant for us. Like pieces of a puzzle, we all fit together.

For almost a year now, we've been three. As I sat down to start planning her first birthday party, I was struck by how it seems like it's been so much longer than a year.

Tuesday, December 9

My fundraiser with Elise is in less than two weeks. I still have eight thousand details to figure out. Send out the invitations, which are cream linen with pink embossing, arrange the seating, finalize the centerpieces—gorgeous white hydrangeas, pink peonies, and sprigs of mint and stephanotis—take last-minute RSVPs (*why* do people forget to RSVP until the day before?), and help Elise figure out her speech, which I'm assuming she wants to be more than just, *Thanks for coming. Give us more money.*

We went back and forth about the location and finally decided to have it at the golf club.

Keri's been working her ass off to help me with the event, despite continuing hangovers. I've learned not to ask for too much before 10:00 A.M., after she's had her breakfast croissant and at least two large cups of coffee.

I took a break from working this afternoon to pump Julie for any information about Trevor, but she's still as locked as a chastity belt.

All I got off her was: "Movie. Drinks in Old Town. Maybe. I said maybe. Shut the hell up about meeting him, OK?"

Wednesday, December 10

So stressed. So, so stressed.

I'm freaking out about this fundraiser. I usually panic a little before any event, but this one is different. It's so much more important. It's for my mom and I don't want to let Elise down.

It doesn't help that Mule Face has instituted the return of All Things Christmas today. She, once again, blasted Christmas carols from her office all day long. I think I heard "Grandma Got Run Over by a Reindeer" seventeen times.

It did provide a good distraction for me, though. After I heard "We Wish You a Merry Christmas" four times, I began to wonder—just who are these obnoxious carolers wishing me a happy holiday? They're pretending like they're being all nice by wishing me a Merry Christmas, but in reality, they're just in it for the "figgy pudding." They inasmuch say so. Not to mention they become outright demanding by insisting they won't leave until they get said pudding.

I would be all: *What is figgy pudding anyway? I promise, you don't want any. Seriously. Just leave. Your singing is annoying me. No? You won't leave? OK, then. How 'bout we discuss this downtown? Yeah, yeah. Tell it to the judge.*

And then the judge will assess them to be flight risks and remand them without bail.

Also? I may have watched too many *Law & Order* reruns lately.

Nonetheless, this song now very much disturbs me.

Or maybe the stress has just eaten into my brain and rotted away the portion for understanding creative expression.

Friday, December 12

. . . .

When I got home yesterday after work, Jake listened to me vent about Mule Face's Christmas music, the traffic on the way home, the stupid blue holiday lights Psycho Bitch put around her evergreen, the guest list for my fundraiser, and the jewelry store commercial I keep seeing.

He nodded the entire time, rubbing my back and holding my hand as I ranted and raved about the McDonald's workers only putting two Splendas into my coffee instead of three. When I finished, I looked expectantly at him, sure he would offer some great philosophical view on *why* everything sucked today.

He looked thoughtfully at me and said, "Guess what I bought today?"

I wanted to immediately freak out and ask if he'd heard anything I'd just said, but I took a deep breath and asked, "What?"

"This new, really awesome ice scraper for my car."

I stared at him for ten long seconds.

"What?" he said, confused.

"Seriously?" I said slowly.

"What?" he said again.

I opened my mouth to fillet him about his lack of interest in my superimportant topics but quickly realized I didn't have the strength and said instead, "That's great. It's supposed to snow tonight."

Sunday, December 14

. . . .

Jake and I aren't generally the gambling sort of people. We don't obsessively play the lottery, we stick to video poker while in Vegas, and I never let more than two days go by without cleaning the litter box.

So that's why it was completely out of character for us to entrust our child to the care of Sam today.

Jake and I still needed to buy about 99 percent of our Christmas gifts, since I haven't had any time lately thanks to work-Reese-Julie-work-work-Elise-blah-blah-blah. Which led Jake and me to be just desperate enough for a sitter that we decided to use my sister. Of course, we were only a half mile away the entire time and called about every fifteen minutes.

But it was OK.

Sara's alive. And not visibly injured in any way.

And get this—Sam actually told Sara that she missed her.

Of course, this was before we left and the Gatorade incident happened. Sam brought a bottle of red Gatorade with her. She set it down on an end table while she took Sara's sippy cup in the kitchen to fill with juice.

Just as Sam returned, sippy cup in hand, she saw Sara pull herself up on the end table, eye the Gatorade bottle, pick it up, hold it in the air as though to take a sip, and dump the entire contents of the bottle all over herself.

Deep red liquid ran down all over Sara's head, her clothes, and our carpet.

I'm sure the scream of, "NOOOOOOOOOO!" was heard by some Alaskans.

Although there's a faint pink stain still lingering on our carpet, the comedic value of the story outweighs the bottle of carpet cleaner it will cost me.

Not to mention, apparently Psycho Bitch / Dog Poop Neighbor Woman came over and accosted Sam about borrowing some sugar. Apparently, she thought we stole her baking supplies while she was at work.

Tuesday, December 16
· · · · · · · · · · · · · · · · · · · ·

My mom made me chicken noodle soup every time I stayed home sick from school when I was little. It was the kind without any real chicken, just some broth and a few shoestring noodles and some parsley. She served it to me on a tray in bed and sat on the edge while I happily slurped away at the hot liquid. She'd ask, "Is it too hot?" and I'd shake my head no and hug Bugle Bear, my favorite worn stuffed animal, to my chest.

She used to let me stay home from school even on days when she doubted that I was really sick. My favorite part was when I got to go back to sleep for a few hours in the morning. Then, I'd wake up and watch television and my mom would make me some soup. The worst part was when the clock inched closer to 3:00 P.M., the time I would've gotten out of school, the time when I'd turn into just every other kid, not a kid lying in her pajamas while everyone else was sitting behind a desk, wearing a school uniform.

When I had the stomach flu, my mom would put a garbage can or an old stove pot next to my bed on my desk chair. She'd bring in a cool washcloth and run it over my head. She'd stay in my room until I fell asleep.

She stayed home from work and took care of me every time I was sick from birth until age eighteen, when I went off to college and the days I felt sick were for an entirely different reason.

And then she became sick herself.

And there were days when I wanted to sit by her bed and make her wheat toast and tell her to eat it slowly, she didn't know what her stomach could handle; to take tiny sips of ginger ale; not to push it. But she waved me off and told me to go back to work; she told me she was fine.

So, I did. And now, she really is going to be fine. This is her last round of treatments. She's almost done.

And she's going to be more than fine. I don't need to make her chicken noodle soup, because she's not going to be sick anymore. I don't need to feel guilty about not being there every day to help her, because she's going to be strong again. I don't need to cry every time I look at Sara, since she's going to know, love, and bond with her grandmother for years to come.

I don't need to ask why, since it doesn't really matter anyway. All I need to do is say thanks.

With all of this gratitude, I'm reminded that when I die my résumé isn't going to be listed in my obituary. It will be my daughter's name, her existence, that will be worthy enough to include in those few, short lines.

Friday, December 19

· ·

I know I've asked for a lot of favors lately and my mom's health is the best Christmas gift ever, but could I eke out just one more favor?

Please?

Because today is the day.

Today is my fundraiser with Elise.

I couldn't sleep much at all last night. I kept having weird dreams about forgetting to turn in my assignments for high school gym class because I was on maternity leave. I'd wake up in a panic because I missed my tennis exam, only to realize (a) I graduated from high school well over ten years ago and (b) Olivia Newton-John wasn't my gym teacher.

I'm excited but 100 percent freaking out.

Part of me wants to fast-forward to tonight, when I'm snuggled up next to Jake in my red plaid pajama pants, sitting on the couch, wiped but totally proud of myself.

8:13 P.M.

Red plaid pants are in action.

Wiped? Yes.

Proud? Yes.

Still shocked? Yes.

I stood in front of my closet for ten minutes this morning, staring at my entire wardrobe. I'd already bought my outfit for today, but it was like my brain couldn't yet process putting anything on, so I stared at my bridesmaid dress from Reese's wedding for a few minutes before I forced myself to slowly start getting dressed.

Jake took Sara to day-care this morning, to give me a few extra minutes to languish in the shower and perfect my makeup. The house was silent and cold as I pulled on my black leather boots and wrapped my comforter around my shoulders, trying to calm my nerves. I took a deep breath, stood up, shrugged off the comforter, grabbed my bag, slipped on my coat and gloves, and walked out the door.

I stopped and grabbed a gingerbread latte on my way over to the country club. I hoped the caffeine and sugar would somehow numb part of my brain and allow me to coast through the day without too much stress.

No such luck.

I walked into the club, and as I waited in the reception area for the event manager to appear and do a quick run-through of the event I felt a tap on my shoulder.

"Ready?" Julie said behind me.

"What are you doing here so early? The event doesn't start for hours!"

"Thought you might need some help. Or at least a drinking buddy if you need some liquid courage."

"I might take you up on that," I said.

"Clare, ready to do the walk-through?" Olivia, the club manager, appeared next to me.

"Let's do it," I said.

An hour later, Elise arrived. I didn't recognize her until she was almost right in front of me. She wore a gorgeous buttery leather skirt and cashmere cowl-neck sweater. But on her head she had a huge hat, society lady at the Kentucky Derby style.

"Elise! I almost didn't see you! You look great," I said as I leaned forward to hug her. I turned to Julie, who was salivating to my right, "This is my friend Julie."

"Nice to meet you." Elise shook Julie's hand.

Julie shook her hand, eyes wide. "Beautiful hat," Julie croaked out.

"Thanks," Elise said.

"Is your speech ready?" I asked her.

"Think so. I have a surprise at the end," she said.

"What is it?"

"A surprise." She winked at me.

Soon, nearly every local celebrity packed the garden room of the country club, sipping glasses of wine and munching on the passed hors d'oeuvres. Reese and my mom arrived and I rushed over to hug them while Julie flirted with the bar staff.

"You guys look amazing," I said.

"Let's talk about amazing," Reese said, and gestured around the room with her hand. "I think everyone here has been in *Chicago* magazine at least twice."

"Except for us," my mom said, and smiled. "Clare, I'm so proud of you. You've done such a great job. I can't believe how many reporters are here," she said as she surveyed the room.

"Thanks. Sometimes it helps to have a blog," I said, and smiled. I'd posted information on my blog about the fundraiser, including a link for readers to donate. I stressed about it for a long time, not wanting my readers to think I was pandering for money, but it's not like I was pocketing the cash for a new laptop or something.

Apparently, the URL got passed around to a few local press members, and with that coupled with my connections at *The Daily Tribune,* I had myself a nice little fundraiser.

"Hey, Mama." Julie appeared and hugged my mom. "Reese, dear, no kids equals a glass of wine. Shall we?"

"We totally shall," Reese said, and followed Julie over to the bar.

"Oh God," my mom said.

"What?"

She pointed over my right shoulder. I turned around and saw Marianne. "I told you she was coming," I whispered. "And there's Natalie behind her with—" I stopped.

"Ash Leigh," my mom finished.

Christ.

"Hello," I said tightly as they walked over. I told Natalie like seven thousand times this wasn't an event to which she could bring her kid.

"I know you said no kids, Clare, but I just couldn't leave her today." Natalie smiled sweetly at me.

I started to have flashbacks to my wedding reception when my cousin Yvonne brought her bratty three-year-old.

"Lovely to see you, Marianne!" my mom said. "And Natalie, you look beautiful as always."

"Clare, your directions were very vague," Marianne said, and frowned at me.

"Are we having any normal food at this lunch?" Natalie asked, and wrinkled her nose.

"You should probably go check on everything," my mom said, and gave me a little push. "And I need to run to the bathroom. Please excuse me."

We both made clean getaways while Marianne, Natalie, and Ash Leigh sequestered themselves to a couch and glared at everyone.

After a few drinks, everyone took their places at the tables, which looked incredible. Pink linens and pink and white rose centerpieces glimmered with the flickering of tea candles. I sat down in between Julie and my mom.

I overheard Julie ask Natalie, "So, my coworker, who just had a baby, said you can't really understand child abuse until you have one of your own. Is that true?"

Natalie glowered at her.

"I mean, does having a kid yourself kinda make you understand those whole baby microwaving incidents?" Julie continued, and pointed to Ash Leigh. I caught Julie's eye and she smirked at me.

"I have no idea what you're talking about," Natalie said, and adjusted Ash Leigh on her lap.

Elise and I made eye contact across the room and she nodded at me. She stood up and walked over to the podium. She put on her reading glasses, cleared her throat, and adjusted the microphone.

"First of all, I'd like to welcome you all to our luncheon and thank each and every one of you for coming to support this worthy cause. We've all been touched by breast cancer in some way, maybe through a friend, a relative, a neighbor, or maybe even ourselves." My mom smiled at me. "As we know, advances are happening each day, and the hope for a cure increases with every treatment we uncover. But new advances and exceptional medicine requires exceptional resources, which is why your generosity is so important and makes such a difference. So, thank you for truly making an impact and raising money for this important issue." She paused as people lightly applauded.

"But raising money is only one part of the impact we can have. We need to put ourselves, as leaders in this community, out in society and show how important this issue is to us as women. As some of you know, my mother passed away from breast cancer a few years ago. So, this issue is near and dear to my heart. I thought long and hard about how I could outwardly show my support for breast cancer survivors and remind people to support this cause. And I came up with this." Elise paused and looked around the room for effect. She reached up and lifted her enormous hat off her head. A collective gasp went around the room as everyone saw Elise's blond hair cropped short to her head, Mia Farrow style. Gone were the signature highlighted blond locks.

"I cut my hair and donated it to an organization which makes wigs for cancer patients. I encourage each and every one of you to do the same. With your hair, your resources, or your time. My point is not to shock anyone. My point is we each have something to give." She paused again and ran her left hand through her short hair. "In closing, I think it's appropriate to paraphrase the message from my favorite holiday movie, *It's a Wonderful Life*. In the movie, the angel Clarence remarks how each person's life touches so many others. I think we can all learn a little from Clarence, and remember the importance of making a difference in the lives of others. Thank you." Elise took her glasses off and set them down on the podium. She stood, her hat in hand, note cards in the other, and smiled at the crowd.

Chairs wobbled as people stood up. The press ran up and snapped pictures, their flashes going off like Christmas lights exploding. I looked over and saw tears streaming down Reese's flushed face.

My mom put her hand on my shoulder and whispered, "She's really something, isn't she?" I nodded.

"She fucking rules," Julie said to Marianne, who looked startled by her cursing.

After Elise sat down, the room was still buzzing. During the fashion show, throughout lunch, all anyone spoke about was Elise and her hair.

After people started to leave, I raced over to Elise and grabbed her arm.

"Amazing surprise!" I said.

"Thanks, thought you might like it," she said, and picked up her wine and sipped it.

"I can just see it now. The headline will read: 'Elise Stansfield: Breast Cancer Hero.'"

She rolled her eyes. "Don't get carried away."

"Seriously, you were amazing," I said.

"Elise, can I get a moment for a few quotes for my article?" a reporter from *The Daily Tribune* asked her.

"Your public awaits," I whispered to Elise as I walked back to my table.

As I sat down and watched the reporters fawn all over Elise, snapping pictures and shouting out questions, I realized something:

It doesn't have to be black or white.

Work or stay home. Give up one or the other.

Because as I looked down at the luncheon program with coffee cup stains in front of me, I realized it was all a shade of gray. One part personal and one part professional.

Dovetailing together.

In an amazing way.

Rumor has it *The Tribune* is doing a huge spread on our event, with multiple pictures and quotes from Elise. There's already a link on the Web site to a few of their pictures. I'm betting it's only a matter of time before Elise is crowned the new queen of the city.

And with my fabulous day, a newly planted little seed began to grow in my brain. An idea watered by the knowledge that I can make things happen, not just let things happen to me. And that my professional and personal lives can play in the sandbox together.

I'm going to find my own path; I'm just not sure what that will be yet.

Monday, December 22

· ·

Still on a high from the fundraiser, I didn't mind it snowed overnight and my car was covered in an inch-thick layer of ice and snow. As I opened the front door to leave, Jake called, "Betcha wish you had my ice scraper now, huh?"

I rolled my eyes and closed the door behind me while balancing Sara on my hip. "Your dad's insane," I told her. She grinned at me underneath her woolen hat, tied around her chin.

I placed Sara in her car seat in the back and got into the driver's side. I turned the car on to let it warm up before I started scraping the ice. I saw Jake walk outside to his car and I rolled down my window a little.

"I want to see if this thing is actually as awesome as you say," I said to him.

"Trust me, it is," he said confidently. He reached for the door handle and gave it a good swift yank.

Nothing. It was frozen.

"Goddamn it," he muttered.

He tried again. Nothing.

"Motherfucker," he said under his breath. He reached for the handle again and violently jerked it.

In one swift, clean move, the handle ripped off the side of the car into his hand. He stood there, stunned, holding his car door handle. I sat silently and watched him walk around the other side of the car, open the passenger door, and throw the handle into the backseat. He leaned over and grabbed the Ice Scraper to Which All Others Cannot Compare. He shrugged at me as he walked up to the windshield. He smiled and pointed to the ice scraper.

I flashed him a thumbs-up sign.

He tugged at one of the windshield wipers, trying to lift it up to scrape underneath it. But it was frozen, too. He wiggled it a little, trying to dislodge it from the glass, and guess what? Yep. It came off in his hand.

He threw it down on the driveway and roared.

So, let's recap:

Driver's side handle: in the backseat.

Windshield wiper: on the driveway.

The climax of the entire incident was when he put the scraper to the car window and the entire scraper immediately dissolved and disintegrated into about twelve pieces.

His back was to me when the scraper met its demise. He didn't even turn around as he walked back into the house, defeated and humiliated.

By this time, my car was fully warmed up, so I turned my windshield wipers on and the ice and snow fell right off my car.

I called him from my cell phone and told him about my great ice-scraping technique, which involved starting my vehicle.

He hung up on me.

Sara and I laughed as I drove her to day-care.

Tuesday, December 23
. . . .

Jake did not find it funny when I read him several of the comments on my blog regarding the Great Ice Scraper Calamity.

He also did not find it funny when the return Nazis at Target interrogated him and asked him to provide a full reenactment of the incident before they would refund his $4.99. They also told him he's only allowed to return like three things per calendar year, so the scraper coupled with the T-shirt and socks he returned three months ago put him at his limit. And with the holiday season coming up, did he really want to use his last chance on a $4.99 ice scraper?

Apparently, he got kind of mad and yelled something about the clerks being in the Gestapo. Whatever.

He may not think any of it is funny, but I still can't stop laughing. It makes all of the stress of Christmas completely manageable.

Not to mention, as I drove home from work amidst the pre-Christmas flurries, an idea struck me. One that might allow me to intermix my professional strengths with my personal goals. An idea that's a beautiful shade of gray.

I'm not ready to completely explore it yet, as I still need to allow it percolate for a while, so I'll just call it my Fabulous New Idea That Shall Not Be Named for Fear of Jinxing It.

Thursday, December 25

· · · · · · · · · · · · · · · · · · · ·

The holiday hangover has officially begun.

The past two days, Sara received enough crap to fill Paris Hilton's closet. Including a toy that is, once again, possessed. It randomly plays music, lights up, and buzzes without anyone pressing a button. Jake yelled, "The power of Christ compels you!" at it a few times and it seemed to stop. Marianne gave her one of those dolls who shit their pants, despite Sara being way too young for dolls and still shitting her own pants. The best part is the doll also laughs and farts. I'm not kidding. While the doll laughs, she also makes fart noises. So Jake and I, being very mature and not at all childish, made the stupid thing fart until the motor wore out.

Not that a trip to my parents' house was much better. When we walked into my parents' house on Christmas Eve, my nasal passages were immediately attacked with the stench of glögg. Glögg is some kind of horrible spiced wine my parents' neighbors from Sweden give them every year for Christmas. Since my dad is the only one who drinks it and the neighbors give them like five gallons every year, my parents have a small arsenal of horrible-tasting holiday wine in their basement.

Anyway, glögg is meant to be served warm, so my dad pours some into a saucepan and lets it simmer on the stove. Which fills the entire house with the smell of brandy and rotting fruit. Not to mention I stole some when I was in high school (during the days when my friends and I would drink just about anything to get drunk) and my friends and I drank it at a sleepover. Well, not surprisingly, we all got sick and puked for hours straight. Mulled wine mixed with Domino's pizza does not a good combination make. One sniff of warm glögg and I'm brought right back to my friend's basement, throwing up in her sink and getting yelled at because I'm puking too loud.

After I finished gagging, my dad and I had our usual conversation about our preference for a tree made out of green pipe cleaners while my mom and Jake defended their need for a real tree.

Mark and Casey entertained us with stories about a road trip they took to her parents' house a few weeks back. Apparently, her parents live downstate. Which means she and Mark had to travel through some pretty hillbilly areas to get there. Mark begged to stop at the live-action Civil War reenactment, but they were running late. He said he really wanted to go since, at this show, the South wins. I think they also said they pulled off an exit and saw a very tall person in a clown costume, pushing a midget in a wheelchair.

Mark also whispered to me that he had picked out some jewelry and winked at me. My mouth dropped open and he quickly turned back into Mark, my brother, and punched me in the arm and said, "Don't be a loser."

The gift giving was also a success. Everyone loved their gifts. My parents gushed over our present of converting all our old home movies into DVDs, Sam said a quick "thanks" for the earrings, and Mark feigned surprise when he opened his rugby shirt.

"How did you know?" he said.

"Maybe because you e-mailed everyone your Christmas list, in Power-Point presentation form, complete with animation," I said.

Jake also loved his gift. I made him a montage video of Sara's first year set to music. It included pictures from right after she was born to video of her walking now. We both got a little misty-eyed as we watched it until I heard a crash, turned around, and saw Sara pulling a Pottery Barn vase off an end table.

There's very little time for sentiment when there's a toddler around.

And my own little ideas are still germinating, as a Christmas gift to myself.

Saturday, December 27

There's also very little time for sobriety when Julie's around. She finally relented and Jake and I met her and Trevor out for a drink last night.

Or it was supposed to be "a drink." It would up being about fifty.

It started off with some sushi and sake. And then more sake. And then some tequila.

And that's how we wound up at a karaoke bar.

Jake and Trevor did a duet to "Soul Man," complete with sunglasses. Jake may or may not have convinced me to join him onstage for a stirring rendition of "O.P.P." In the middle of which he realized his jackassery and left me onstage to rap all by myself.

I also may or may not have eaten a gyro sometime around midnight.

Jake, thankfully, had slightly more sense than I did. Because at one point, Julie actually convinced me that we should call up Matt and tell him how much we hate him. Jake apparently distracted us by showing us how to take pictures with his cell phone. For which I am so, so grateful. Because I have a slight suspicion that calling up Matt when drinking would fall into the Things That Make Clare Trashy category. Not to mention Reese would probably strangle us to death with one of her Frette hand towels.

Anyway, the bottom line: Trevor's fantastic.

Tuesday, December 30
. . . .

Today was a perfect day.

As I drove home from work yesterday, with Sara in the back snoozing away, a light dusting of snow began to fall. The meteorologists on just about every news channel predicted a snowstorm. I didn't hold my breath, since they usually say that at least four times each year and we wind up with an inch. I drove home, the radio muted, the only sound Sara's light snoring. I twisted my car through the already-slushy streets and took in the slowly forming Winter Wonderland. Kids, still on school break, began to run outside and throw themselves down into the snow, furiously forming snow angels. Evergreen bushes, decorated with strands of white lights, donned tufts of snow, looking like radioactive green cupcakes with glowing sprinkles.

And, sure enough, every driver in the Chicagoland area drove like either (a) They had never seen this white stuff: Apparently it's called snow? Whatever it is, I better not hit my accelerator *at all*, or (b) Snow!

Whee! Let's see if I can get my Toyota Camry to turn this corner on two wheels!

I wanted to attach a speaker atop my car and drive through the streets screaming, *Two inches! Two! I guarantee that's how much snow we'll actually get.*

But, by about eight o'clock, the snow started falling in sheets and Jake and I could barely see out the front door.

By the time Sara went to bed, snow was piled up against our back door.

By the time Jake and I went to bed, our cars had a good foot of snow atop them. We snuggled into bed, each not daring to ask if the other thought we could stay home from work the next day. Like kids in grade school, we didn't want to jinx it.

So, when I woke up at four this morning, I dared to peek out our bedroom window. I silently pumped my fist as I saw the snow still furiously coming down. I jumped back into bed and rubbed my feet together before drifting off.

Two feet of snow—that's how much fell by the time we woke up this morning.

The city restricted all travel to only emergency vehicles on the roads, to allow the snowplows to get through. Victory!

Jake and I curled up on the couch with Sara and watched Christmas movies, drank cider, and napped while Sara did. It was glorious. The three of us, a couch, and three fuzzy blankets made the best family day ever.

And I realized how amazing it was as it happened. Too many times in my life, I've been only able to appreciate moments like these after they're long gone. But this was one time, as I settled down in our worn couch, Sara in between Jake and me, plush blanket pulled around us, that I was able to see the picture as it was being painted. I peeked under the white cover before the masterpiece was finished. And as I munched on leftover Christmas cookies and sipped eggnog, I felt the comfort of enjoying the day as it happened, not from the distorted lens of the future or the long distance of the past.

The only problem was I hadn't been to the grocery store yet, so we were forced to eat ramen noodles like college students, but we didn't mind.

I caught up on all my daytime television—soap operas, horrible talk shows titled *Please Help Me Find My Baby Daddy,* and canceled sitcoms like *Step by Step.*

I also spent a gluttonous time watching the Food Network, swearing I would make the shitake mushroom and spinach ragout. One thing that bothered me was how every cook, at the end of their show, tastes their own food and is like "OH GOD! YUM! IT'S SO GOOD!"

Like they're going to say anything else.

I want to see a show sometime when one of the chefs takes a bite of their own food and quickly spits it out and says, *Ew! Gross! I really screwed this one up!*

The upside is that the day off really gave me a chance to think about my Non-Jinxed Idea. After a bit of mental marinating, it's starting to come into focus and I think I'll be ready soon to start making it a reality.

Thursday, January 1
· · · · · · · · · · · · · · · · · · · ·

Last night was New Year's Eve.

I was so depressed last year when I couldn't go out and party like everyone else on New Year's Eve. I swore I'd go out the following year and have a killer time, to make up for taking a year off. This year, I'm so over it.

New Year's Eve is so overrated. Either you spend it at a bar, with a jillion other people whom you don't know, overpay for drinks, and then get annoyed with everyone or you spend it at someone's house, watching Ryan Seacrest and falling asleep. I chose the second option.

I told Jake to go out with the boys and have a great time and invited Reese and her kids over to spend the night.

We went to dinner at 4:00 P.M., since Brendan goes to bed now around 7:00 P.M. We hung out with the senior citizens and ate mozzarella sticks before going home.

After the kids were in bed, Reese and I settled in to watch a fantastic double feature of *Teen Wolf* and *Teen Wolf Too.*

While I swapped out *Teen Wolf* for its sequel, I asked her, "So, how's everything?"

"Good. I mean, hard. But good." She fell silent as she studied the stitching on the arm of the couch. "I filed for divorce this week," she said quietly.

"Really? Oh, honey. I'm so sorry, I mean, it's the best thing, but I'm so sorry it didn't work out," I said, and placed my hand over hers.

She nodded and looked at me. Her chin quivered a little, but she cleared her throat and twisted her hair into a ponytail.

"How's Julie? I haven't talked to her in a while," she said.

"Er, great!" I said quickly as I concentrated really hard on zipping up my sweatshirt.

"Clare?" Reese said as she dropped her arms down and folded them across her chest.

"What?" I said as I played with my sweatshirt's zipper.

"Clare?" she said again.

I sighed and looked at her. "Julie's doing great. She's dating someone new. Trevor. She finally . . ." I paused and softened my eyes. "Found someone."

Reese nodded and smiled, despite a brief moment of furrowing her brows. "That's great. I'm so happy for her."

I nodded, thinking how it wasn't supposed to be like this at all.

We were all supposed to be happy. At the same time. Not piecemeal, not netting zero.

"Reese, I just want to make sure you know that I'm so proud of you and that you've given me the courage to find out what I want, even if it's different from according to plan. Things didn't go business as usual for me"—I pointed toward Sara's room, and Reese smiled—"but I think everything will turn out fantastic. And I know it will for you, too." I reached forward and grabbed her hand and squeezed it. "I know it." I raised our hands in a pseudo–victory pact. "To the scary-but-awesome future ahead!"

I thought she would well up thanks to my Oscar-worthy speech, but instead she appeared to be staring over my shoulder. "Clare?" she said.

"What?"

She pointed behind me. "I think a large woman is staring at us."

"Wha?" I whipped my head around and saw Psycho Bitch, wearing a Happy New Year's headband, glaring at us from the sidewalk as she walked down the street. "Oh." I waved my hand around. "Her. She's crazy. It's fine. I mean, she might throw dog poop on my door or threaten us for stealing her baked goods, but she's harmless. Now let's get back to some werewolf lovin'," I said.

Wednesday, January 7

· · · · · · · · · · · · · · · · · · · ·

I posted a video of Sara laughing on my blog today. It's footage of Jake holding her above his head, like an airplane, while she giggles hysterically. Everyone seemed to like it and proclaimed her the cutest laugher ever.

It was really just a ploy, since I can't post what I was supposed to post today. Which are professional pictures of Sara. Or should I say "professional" pictures.

A while back, one of my readers e-mailed me and said that she's trying to get her fledging freelance photography business off the ground. And she'd love to shoot Sara and blow up a bunch of the pictures for free, as long as I'd post a couple pictures on my blog.

Normally, I decline these requests, but she seemed really nice, and she's a mom, too, and she totally caught me during my "I Love the World Because It's Christmas" phase. So, I agreed.

And the photo shoot looked normal enough. Until she e-mailed me the pictures five minutes ago, with a reminder to post them. Which leads me to my conundrum.

She Photoshopped half of the pictures. She added a bunch of effects, several of which make it appear as though my child is wrapped in tulle or cellophane. Or possibly in a body bag of some sort.

A few more make it appear as though she's a constellation. I'm not kidding. It's my daughter, standing there, on a giant background of stars. Next to the Big Dipper.

It's like Baby's First Acid Trip. Now what the hell am I supposed to do?

I promised to recommend her, so I'll just have to post one of the normal photos. But I cringe thinking of the hate e-mails I'm going to get when one of my readers uses her and she Photoshops the kid's head into a collage of Easter eggs.

At least I can hope that, thanks to the distraction of toddler videos and photography, no one will ask about The Day Coming Up of Which I Am in Great Denial, a.k.a. tomorrow.

Sara's first birthday. I've planned the entire party for Saturday. I've cleaned my house, bought presents, gift bags, and a cake. But I've done it all while pretending it's someone else's child who's turning a year old.

Turning a year old means turning into a kid. Turning a year old means no more baby.

So, like a woman about to turn forty, Sara's just not going to age. I'm going to tell everyone she's eleven months old. For the next few years.

Thursday, January 8
. . . .

I have a one-year-old.

When people ask me how old my daughter is, I can no longer say a number followed by the word "months." I will have to say a number that is followed by the word "year."

She's practically a teenager already. She'll be swapping clothes with Sam and flatironing her hair tomorrow.

And as though all of the ups and downs, challenges and triumphs of this past year weren't stressful enough, I've made a decision. *The* decision.

I know what I'm going to do about my career.

Saturday, January 10

. . . .

And on Sara's first birthday party, the Lord said, "Let there be lots of primary-colored plastic crap."

I stayed up late last night to finish my review of Bumbo Baby Seats for *Hip Parent* magazine. (My verdict: I worship them even more than epidurals.) Of course, as is always the case with parenting, Sara somehow knew I needed a few minutes to sleep in and woke up at the crack of dawn. I tried to tell her it was her party day, to go back to sleep and rest up for the crazy day in front of us, but she just wanted to walk around her room and pick up blocks and put them in her trash can. So, I sat in the chenille glider and watched her, my eyes half-open, the room still pitch-black.

I woke up Jake an hour later and we switched off. I figured I'd sleep for an hour or two and then wake up and start getting everything ready for the party. Well, Jake apparently lost track of time, let me sleep in, and I woke up an hour before people were supposed to arrive.

The party was great. Sara got lots and lots more toys, adding to the already-embarrassing collection from Christmas. Natalie made Sara a hideous painting. "For her room," she explained. Apparently, she's been taking art classes and decided she's the next Picasso.

Which is true. If Picasso sucked at painting.

Not to mention she spelled my daughter's name out in sequins in the middle of the painting: SARAH.

Nice. She spelled my kid's name wrong.

Then, Sam told me I probably ruined Sara's life already by having her birthday so close to Christmas and every kid she knew whose birthday was in December or January got screwed out of birthday gifts. I pointed out her chipped nail polish and she left me alone after that. Although I did overhear her talking to one of her friends on the phone and couldn't resist a comment.

"Yeah, yeah. I know, I'm almost done here. . . . Of course I was going to go. . . . I know, it would've been fun . . . but you know how close my sister and I are, I couldn't not be here," Sam said into her phone very matter-of-factly. I stood around the corner in our dining room, unsure if my eardrums deceived me. "Yeah, talk later." I heard her snap her phone shut.

I took a deep breath and considered the options for a moment.

Screw it.

I walked around the corner and stood in front of Sam, still messing around on her phone. I smiled at her and she glanced up.

"What?" she said as she clicked on her pink phone keyboard.

"Nothing." I smiled at her and put my hand on her arm. "Thanks for coming," I said, and gave her forearm a little squeeze.

She looked startled and her eyes met mine. "What? Did you think I'd miss it?" Her eyes quickly narrowed and she squinted at me. "You guys always think the worst about me and—," she started to say when I shook my head.

"Nope, just happy you're here." I nodded my head briefly before walking into the kitchen. I clapped my hands together and said, "Time for cake, everyone!"

We sang "Happy Birthday" and watched Sara smash cake all over her face. I swear, my daughter is Pig Pen's long-lost sister. I think she got like two crumbs into her piehole. The rest wound up on the floor, on the cat, on the high chair, and thrown on Marianne. (I silently high-fived Sara for the last one since Marianne asked me if I'd iced the cake with store-bought icing. I said of course I did and she snorted a little and remarked that she used to make her own icing.)

Jake proposed a toast to my mom, in honor of her finishing chemo and treatments. As we all took a sip, I cleared my throat—this was as good a time as any.

"So, everyone," I started out in a voice a few octaves too high. "I have an announcement."

"You're pregnant!" Natalie screeched as she threw her plate in the air, embedding cake into our carpet.

"No!" Jake said quickly as he bent down to collect the mess on the floor. Everyone turned to peer at me.

I cleared my throat again. "As you all know, I've been going back and forth a bit in my decision to work or continue staying home. I love my job and I've worked hard for all of my accomplishments, but I also miss Sara constantly. I've wrestled with the decision over the past several months and, after my last event, had an idea. It doesn't have to be a black-or-white choice, and I found a way to find the gray area. Everyone," I said as my face broke out into a wide smile, "I'm going to start my own event company."

I looked around the room at silent faces, eyes bugging out and mouths slack jawed. I cleared my throat again. "See, I'll be able to work at home, so I'll see Sara more and run my own schedule, but I will still get to have the career I love. And I'll get to choose which events to take on." I stopped and looked around again.

Nothing.

"Hello?" Jake said as he nudged his mom next to him.

"I'm so happy for Sara! Now she doesn't have to live with a working mom anymore!" Marianne said as she clasped her hands in front of her chest. I'm surprised my mom didn't punch her out. But she was too busy making her own analogies.

"Like in *Baby Boom*!" my mom said triumphantly. She raised her glass in the air.

"What?" Natalie said as she screwed her lips into a scowl.

"*Baby Boom*. In the movie, Diane Keaton is torn between being a working woman and a mom and in the end decides to start her own business, to have the best of both worlds."

"Oh. The only movie I've seen in the past few years was *Twilight*. Isn't Edward dreamy?" Natalie said, and sighed.

Not wanting my big moment to get overshadowed by vampire romance, Jake stepped forward and lifted his glass again. "Er. OK, anyway, cheers to Clare and her new venture!"

"Did you get fired or something?" Sam said, her eyes narrowing.

I sighed. "Nope. More like I fired myself."

"Did you quit your job?" Marianne said, looking confused.

I shook my head. "Not yet. I'm still getting everything in place, but my goal is to quit within two to three months."

"Oh. I was going to invite you to join my quilting circle next week."

Marianne looked disappointed while I made a mental note to get caller ID on my new office phone.

After a few more toasts and pats on the back, Sara started to crash from her sugar buzz, and soon everyone left. With Jake in the dining room, desperately trying to find a way to make Sara's new talking caterpillar Leapfrog toy say dirty words, I started cleaning up.

Saying the ideas germinating in my head made them seem real—and much more scary. Up until now, it had just been a brief plan, one that I had yet to put into action.

But in the quiet places of my heart, I knew this was right. My dreams and goals flexed and found a new way to grow into the spaces of my life.

Wednesday, January 14
· · · · · · · · · · · · · · · · · ·

There's a possibility I might die thanks to wayward gang members before I can even get my event business off the ground. I should probably start carrying weapons around, like old wine bottles. Because I'm such a good mother that I totally would not hesitate to break off the neck of a Pinot bottle and cut a bitch up to protect my child.

These ponderings are necessary since Jake and I wound up in the ghetto tonight.

OK, scratch that. Jake and I wound up in what I call the ghetto. He called it "a shortcut to the restaurant."

Except there was no restaurant. There wasn't much of anything. Just a few liquor stores, gun stores, ammo stores, a few more liquor stores, a bar, and a pawnshop. And a few cars set on fire.

Yet he insisted we were perfectly fine, it was a totally normal way to go, and Judy wouldn't fail him.

Judy is what he's named his new navigation system in his car. His parents bought it for him for Christmas. I was eternally grateful when he opened it, since I thought it meant no more screaming at each other about which way to get on the highway. But it does not mean that. It means driving through an area peppered with drug dealers and waving off hookers as they approach the car.

It also meant I twisted around to face Sara in the backseat in a desperate attempt to distract her from staring at the loitering teenagers on every block.

Yet Jake insisted Judy wouldn't let him down and she'd guide us to our destination. After fifteen minutes, I told Judy to screw off and directed us back to the highway. She got really pissed and was like "PROCEED TO THE HIGHLIGHTED ROUTE. TURN AROUND. TURN AROUND WHEN POSSIBLE. YOU ARE GOING OFF INTO UNMAPPED TERRITORY. JAKE WILL NEVER LOVE YOU AS MUCH AS HE LOVES ME."

Judy's a bitch.

Sunday, January 18
. . . .

"Your latte, Ms. Event Planner Lady," Julie said as we sat down at Starbucks this afternoon.

"Whatever. It's still in the planning stage; it won't officially be launched until the spring. Besides, I haven't even quit my job yet," I said as I raised my cup to my lips.

"Yeah, well, you'll probably get to plan your brother's wedding, whenever he and that horrible bitch get engaged." Julie smiled.

"Oh yeah, she's terrible. Nice, sweet, pretty. Hate her!" I laughed as I raised my coffee. "He asked me to go ring shopping with him next week."

"Well, regardless, I'm really proud of you. I feel like you're going to be so much happier and finally feel a little more balanced." Julie pulled a tube of ChapStick out of her pocket and carefully applied it.

"Definitely. I always thought that it had to be one or the other—working or staying home—but the breast cancer fundraiser really opened my eyes; it made me realize that I can mix the black and white of my life together and make an awesome shade of gray. Not to mention that I'm so excited to make something happen. For me. You know?" I slowly rotated the paper cup in front of me.

"For sure." Julie nodded and took a sip of her drink. She leaned back. "OK, I have news. And you can't freak out. Deal?" she said.

"Can't promise. I never know what's going to come out of your mouth. But go ahead." I set my drink down on the table and laid my palms flat down.

"I'm taking Trevor to meet my dad."

"Whoa! Big step!" Freaking huge step, in fact. Julie's beer-bellied, NASCAR-watching, profanity-spewing father is the ultimate relationship litmus test. But he's also one of the most awesome people ever.

"No kidding!" Julie rolled her eyes.

"He's going to do great." I nodded my head and smiled at her. I have a great feeling about the two of them. Maybe my little Julie is finally growing up.

"Whatever, I'll let you know. So, I saw the article about Elise," she said, swiftly changing the subject.

"I know, isn't it great?" I said.

"Totally. She's so redeemed herself. Every news station is going to be fighting over her."

"They already are." I smiled.

"I've said it once and I'll say it again: she rules."

Monday, January 19
. . . .

Jake stayed home from work today with Sara. He claimed he had a head cold, but I think he's still just a little tired from going out with Bill-Until-Two-Months-Ago-I-Still-Lived-with-My-Parents on Saturday night.

I walked in the door and dropped my keys on the entryway table. I tiptoed through the foyer. Jake walked out of the kitchen and said, "Hey, I—"

I put a finger to my lips and whispered, "Where is she?"

He smiled and pointed to the family room.

I crept down the hallway. Sara was sitting on her play mat and playing with her Little People firehouse, sunlight streaming through the window and reflecting off her blond curls, forming a halo of light around her head.

"Sara," I said to her in a low tone.

Her head snapped and she shrieked when she saw me. "Erghhh!" she gurgled.

"Mama's home," I said to her as I walked over and picked her up.

We sat down on the couch and I held her close to me.

"Whatcha do today? Whatcha do? Did you play? Did you sing songs?" I murmured in her ear.

She leaned back a little, looked at me in the eyes, and smiled. She put her hands on either side of my face and laughed. I grabbed one of her hands, held it, and kissed it.

Jake walked in and sat down next to us on the couch. He put his arm around me as I rocked Sara until she started to get sleepy in my arms.

"I love you," I whispered to her.

She dreamily opened her eyes and looked up at me before letting herself lazily drift off. Jake and I stayed on the couch, watching her sleep. I held her in my lap as I rested my head on Jake's shoulder and we silently watched the snow begin to fall outside.

I assumed that when I had a child, when I acquired the title of mom, I'd have so many things in place already—financial success, personal achievement, confidence, wisdom. But maybe Sara had to come first. Maybe, instead of each achievement being a ladder rung to the next and arriving in an all-for-one package deal, they had to be catalyzed by her.

And this feels like just the beginning; I can't wait to see what happens next.

As the snow lightly pelted against the windowpane, Sara reached up, grabbed my hand, and held on tight.

Funny, smart, and sassy, this debut novel will have you laughing for a good nine months.

When twenty-seven-year-old event planner and blogger Clare Finnegan discovers she's pregnant, she begins her slow transition from beer bottles to baby bottles.

"Witty, wonderfully written...what a great new voice on the women's fiction scene."
—Susan Reinhardt, author of *Not Tonight, Honey: Wait 'Til I'm a Size 6*

🦊 **St. Martin's Griffin**   **www.stmartins.com**